**Garry Kilworth** was born in York in 1941 but has travelled widely around the globe ever since, being fascinated by the folklore, myths and legends of the places he has visited. He has been attracted by various forms of fantasy and supernatural writing but has more recently written a number of acclaimed and much-loved stories for children. Garry has twice been short-listed for the Carnegie medal. For more information visit www.garry-kilworth.com

You can find out more about Garry and other Atom authors at www.atombooks.co.uk

BY GARRY KILWORTH

*The Knights of Liöfwende Trilogy*

Spiggot's Quest

Mallmoc's Castle

Boggart and Fen


Attica

Jigsaw

The Hundred-Towered City

# ATTICA

Garry Kilworth

www.atombooks.co.uk

ATOM

First published in Great Britain in 2006 by Atom
This paperback edition published in 2007 by Atom
Reprinted 2009

A CIP catalogue record for this book
is available from the British Library.

ISBN 978-1-904233-56-5

Typeset in Bembo by M Rules
Printed and bound in Great Britain by
CPI Mackays, Chatham, ME5 8TD

Papers used by Atom are natural, renewable and recyclable
products sourced from well-managed forests and certified
in accordance with the rules of the Forest Stewardship Council.

**Mixed Sources**
Product group from well-managed
forests and other controlled sources
www.fsc.org  Cert no. SGS-COC-004081
© 1996 Forest Stewardship Council

Atom
An imprint of
Little, Brown Book Group
100 Victoria Embankment
London EC4Y 0DY

An Hachette UK Company
www.hachette.co.uk

www.atombooks.co.uk

*To the memory of Nelson,*

*a three-legged cat with a four-fold personality*

'In the attics of my life
Full of cloudy dreams unreal
Full of tastes no tongue can know
And lights no eye can see
When there was no ear to hear
You sang to me'

*Attics of My Life*
THE GRATEFUL DEAD

# CONTENTS

# ATTICA

# CHAPTER 1

# Encounters in a Garden

The attic smelled of dust and ages. Jordy peered through a shaft of sunlight speckled with motes to a dim network of beams and rafters. He reminded himself he was a boy who wasn't afraid of eerie places. But the silence and the gloom of the attic, along with that atmosphere of dead air, were enough to disturb the most resolute of boys. A sound came from the depths. Were there birds up here, inside the roofing? Or worse still, rats? Who could tell? There could be rotted bodies in trunks, old festering secrets from bygone years, evidence of horrible crimes. Anything.

'Jordy, come on, this box is heavy – my arms are falling off!'

He jumped at the sound, which seemed very loud to him.

'Sorry, Clo,' he said, reaching back down the steps for the box of oddments. 'I – I was just . . .'

'I scared you, didn't I?' cried his step-sister. 'You jumped a mile then.'

'Not scared, exactly,' he replied through gritted teeth. 'It's just a bit spooky up here. Come and look.'

'No, thanks. Too dirty. Just push the box in. You don't need to go all the way up. Those places get filthy. My mum and your dad' – none of the children had quite got used to the new arrangements yet, and were still awkward with what to call their parents – 'will have to bring the heavy stuff up themselves.'

'I'm quite strong.'

'Me too, but not when it comes to lifting furniture . . .'

She continued talking, but Jordy wasn't listening. He was staring into that half-lit world of the attic. You couldn't see the walls: they were hidden in darkness. The pillar of light coming from a single window tile seemed to be the only substantial thing up there, and of course that wasn't solid, it was just air, sunshine and swimming dust. He could see a pile of old clothes under a rafter, with what looked like a crumbling hymn book or Bible on top. The rags looked like the carcass of some grotesque animal, but he could see now that they were a soldier's uniform, by the black buttons and the battered cap perched on top. Probably a long-dead soldier from a forgotten war.

Jordy shuddered and retreated down the steps.

Then, to rid himself of his dark mood, he put on a mock hoarse voice and said to Chloe, 'Don't go up there. It's *horrible*.'

'Oh, you—' Chloe punched him on the shoulder.

They went downstairs together, to join the rest of the family.

They were in the front garden, staring at the furniture which was left over now that they had filled their new three-bedroomed flat. Not that it was much to look at, Dipa conceded. Most of it was junk. When two single parents set up home together, it resulted in the meeting of two great furniture tidal waves. The contents of two separate homes rushed together and formed a huge pile of tables, chairs, sideboards, dressers and other household goods.

It was Dipa who took charge as usual.

'From what's left we'll keep our sideboard and your desk,' she said. 'The rest can go to a charity shop.'

'What about my old piano stool?' said Ben, sounding a little peeved. 'I made that myself. Look, Nelson needs it.'

'Nelson would sleep on a bed of glass if it was warm enough,' snorted Dipa, 'and you know it.'

Nelson, their three-legged ginger cat, was stretched out on the satin-covered seat in feline bliss, his warm furry body soaking up the sun. Nelson had lost a front leg in an uneven battle with a pickup truck. He now used his disability to attract sympathy when he wanted something, limping more than usual and letting out a pathetic *yowl* which soon turned to a rumbling growl if he didn't get what he wanted. He could also move like lightning still, chasing the sparrows in the yard.

Smiling, Dipa placed a hand on her new husband's shoulder. 'Your woodwork skills are astonishing, darling, but we don't have a piano.'

Ben sighed in resignation. 'All right, one of each. That's fair, I suppose.'

The three children, fed up and bored with moving difficulties, stood by and watched. Jordy was Ben's only child: a tall lean boy with a languid air of superiority about him. Next came Chloe, very pretty, her pitch-black hair inherited from Asian ancestors. There was a defiant look which made you wary of upsetting her. Finally, two years younger, there was Alex, with a squarer build than the other two and a quieter disposition. Alex had dark eyes that looked out at you, but didn't let you look in. You rarely guessed what he was thinking.

'Can we go for a pizza now?' asked Jordy. 'You said we could have lunch out.'

'Well, I'm certainly not cooking anything,' Dipa said, 'so you'd better. I'll call the charity shop first, in case it rains and ruins all this lot. Ben, can you give the kids some money, then go and tip the removal men? They're sitting in the cab of their lorry, waiting.'

Dipa didn't stop for replies. She bounded through the front doorway and up to their first-floor flat. Their new home was in one of those big Victorian terraced houses which had been owned by a Mr Grantham before the conversion to two flats. Mr Grantham, a very elderly man, now lived on the ground floor, having sold the upstairs flat to the Wilsons.

Dipa telephoned a charity shop, told them where to find the furniture, then went to join Ben. The pair followed their children into the city and to a pizza place they had found earlier. Jordy, Chloe and Alex were in a much better mood now that they had fizzy drinks and food inside them.

'Hey, here they are,' cried Jordy, as Dipa and Ben entered, 'fresh from battles with sofa and sideboard.'

Right at that moment Ben's mobile phone rang: the theme tune from the TV programme *ER*. He answered it, then said, 'Sorry, folks, gotta go. Stuart's not turned up for his shift this afternoon. Sick or something.'

The children groaned, but they were used to this. Ben was a paramedic and Dipa was a doctor, so their parents were often called away. At least Dipa was not starting at the hospital until the day after tomorrow, so she was safe for forty-eight hours. She jammed a piece of Chloe's pizza in her husband's mouth and told him to get a takeaway later. Then once he'd gone she settled down with the kids to enjoy their company.

Mr Grantham was a solitary and distant person. In truth he was not a happy man, though his life had not been a terrible one. He had fought in the Second World War, had been married for fifty years, and had for most of that time been reasonably content. But now there was nothing to do but sit and think, and for some reason he could not dwell on happy times, but rather on those occasions when he was treated badly.

'Noisy bunch,' he muttered, as he heard his new neighbours going up the stairs. 'No consideration.'

Then the television went on upstairs. Loud at first, but then turned down lower.

He had his own television of course, but he rarely switched it on these days. Half of it he didn't understand: these 'reality' shows as they called them. Youths and girls draped over chairs, yelling at one another. The other half was full of very young, gaudy and loud presenters too full of their own self-importance. Every programme seemed to be crammed with confrontations. Mr Grantham didn't much like his own company but he cared even less for the ghostly company of spiky-haired young men and bouncy, grinning young women. They didn't even speak the Queen's English, most of them. No, he preferred the radio these days.

Mr Grantham was not looking forward to sharing his house with these strangers, but financial difficulties had forced him into it.

Two weeks after the move a hot, bright day came to bless the Wilsons in their new home. It was the summer holidays. Jordy was playing a computer game in his bedroom, Alex was making a huge and complex kite out of a kit, and Chloe had decided to take a book to read outside.

The back garden was communal. Mr Grantham had retained the right to use it, while at the same time conceding that the new occupants would also like to enjoy it. Not that there was much to it, in the way of flower beds and shrubs. There was a rough-looking lawn of sorts, and apple trees at the bottom, and what used to be a vegetable plot. Mr Grantham's back would no longer allow him to dig, though he still mowed the grass. He was out there sitting in a deckchair watching the butterflies and birds, when Chloe came with a canvas seat and plonked herself nearby.

'Hope I'm not disturbing you, Mr Grantham?' she said, flashing him one of her famous smiles. 'I won't make a sound, I promise.'

Nelson had followed Chloe out into the garden and sprawled himself on the grass next to Mr Grantham's deckchair.

'Suit yourself, young lady,' grunted Mr Grantham. 'It's your garden too.'

'Chloe,' she said. 'My name's Chloe.'

'And mine's Mr Grantham.'

They settled into silence, broken only by the sounds of nature and Chloe's pages being turned.

'What're you reading?' asked Mr Grantham at length. 'One of them Harry Potters?'

'Not this time,' said Chloe. She held it up. 'It's a book called *Holes*. It's about a boy in America . . .'

'Oh, don't tell me the plot,' said Mr Grantham quickly, waving skinny fingers at her. 'Nothing so boring as hearing the plot of a novel second-hand. Drives you potty.'

Chloe refused to be annoyed by this old man. She always considered herself good at charming reluctant people and this was a challenge.

'Harry Potty?' she said.

Mr Grantham, despite himself, chuckled.

'Very good, very good.'

'I always carry a list of my top twenty favourite books,' said Chloe, taking a folded sheet of paper from her jeans pocket. 'Do you want to hear it?'

'Not especially. Do you want to hear my life story?'

He was being sarcastic and was startled when Chloe replied, 'Yes. I expect it's very interesting.' She put the book down in a deliberate way. Nelson gave a great big yawn and rolled over onto his back, his remaining three legs sticking in the air. His eyes were looking up at Mr Grantham's face as if in expectation.

'Well,' said Mr Grantham, flustered. He waved away a wasp that came too near. 'I don't expect it's *that* interesting, to a young person like you.' He changed the subject. 'This your cat? What's her name?'

'Our cat, and *his* name's Nelson.'

'Likes water and sailing ships, does he?'

Chloe smiled. 'No, of course not, but he's lost a limb – in the same place as the admiral.'

'Oh, very good.' Mr Grantham made an attempt at tickling Nelson's tummy and received an indignant glare in return. 'Where are you from, Chloe? You from India? Were you born out there?'

'No, I'm from here. I was born in Portsmouth,' she replied, without any asperity. 'My dad was half-English – he wanted us to have first names which sounded British – but my mum's parents came from Bengal. My brother Alexander was born in Brighton. Jordy was born in the West Country, I think. Minehead. He's not my real brother, he's my step-brother, but we get on OK. Where were you born?'

'Funnily enough, India,' he said. 'My dad was in the army out there. So I first saw the world in the Far East and you're from England.' He turned awkwardly in his deckchair. 'That dark-haired one. The smaller boy. He passed me in the hall without a good-morning or a how-are-you.'

'That's Alex. He doesn't mean anything by it. He's just quiet. Lost in a world of his own. He wasn't being rude. Sometimes I get annoyed with him and yell at him to pay attention to me, and he simply looks startled – you know, like a rabbit with a fox or something. You can tell he's somewhere else, on another planet. Some boys are like that. Most girls are like me though, aren't they? Chatterboxes.'

She smiled, knowing by his amused look that she was charming the socks off Mr Grantham. He was a crusty old man, even Dipa and Ben had said that, but Chloe was good at getting under the armour of such people. When they had had their dog, the woman at the kennels had been regarded as a ferocious dragon, but Chloe had made her a friend.

Her new step-father had been an easy nut to crack at first, but she noted with some chagrin that now he was *family* he was not so swiftly charmed. Neither she nor Alex had liked him in the beginning, though that had not stopped her from being enchanting. Ben was not what they would have chosen for their mother as a second husband. He didn't seem ambitious enough. Ben seemed happy to remain just a paramedic, which was not much different from a nurse, while Dipa was way above him as a doctor.

Their own father had been a businessman, full of drive.

'Penny for 'em.' Mr Grantham interrupted her thoughts. ''Less they're private, of course.'

'I was thinking about my dad.'

'Oh yes?'

'Not the one you've seen, my *real* dad. He died of a heart attack two years ago.'

'Oh, I'm sorry.'

'That's all right.'

'You have a new dad now, then?'

'Ben's divorced. His wife ran off with a neighbour.'

Mr Grantham's eyebrows went up. 'That's a bit more information than I think I should have.'

'Yes, sorry,' said Chloe, biting her lip. 'Ben's all right, really. But he's not my dad.'

'Of course not. I expect he'd agree with that. At least you've got a family. All mine have gone.'

Things were getting a little gloomy.

'Can I get you a drink or something?' asked Chloe brightly. 'A cup of tea?'

The words 'cup of tea' seemed to stir the old man's energy levels and he perked up.

'You wouldn't mind? The back door to the kitchen's open. I could really do with a drink and I can't always get up once I'm sat down.'

'I don't mind.'

Chloe went into the kitchen, which was a mess. Nelson, limping badly and full of hope, followed at her heels making soft *meow*s. Chloe ignored Nelson and found the teabags and the kettle. The milk was in the fridge. She gave Nelson the cream from the top in a tin lid. He lapped it up quickly then, sensing that was it, went back to Mr Grantham's feet.

'Do you take sugar?' she called, and when he waved over the top of the deckchair, cried, 'How many?'

He held up one finger.

The sugar was harder to find, but she tracked it down eventually. She made two cups of tea in rather dubiously clean cups and took them out to Mr Grantham.

He said, 'Got yourself one, eh? Quite right and proper.'

He sipped the tea with thin lips, staring into the yards of the houses that backed their own. Chloe noticed that the backs of his hands were covered in dark nebulous islands like coffee stains. Blue veins stood out under the thin layer of skin. Mr Grantham was very, very old.

'Were you married?' asked Chloe, trying to spark off the conversation again. 'Did you have a wife?'

Mr Grantham put down the cup with a shaking hand, making it rattle in the saucer.

'I had a wife, a very nice lady,' he said, his translucent blue eyes beginning to moist over. 'She died several years ago. It's becoming harder to remember her face now.'

'You have photos though?'

'Oh yes, I have lots of photos of Florrie. Of her, and other people. But they're just ghosts now. It doesn't seem real any longer, that old life. It feels as if I've read about it, in a history book. Funny how the mind works.'

The pair of them spoke no more that day. Chloe read her book and Mr Grantham read his memories.

Jordy teased her a little when she told him about her conversation with Mr Grantham.

'I wouldn't know what to say to an old guy like that,' he said. 'What've you got in common?'

'Secrets,' she said. 'Girls just love secrets. To hear them and to tell them. Old men have got lots of secrets. Things we wouldn't even dream of. You don't know anything about girls, do you?'

'Don't want to,' he said haughtily. 'Especially if they support Manchester United.'

She said, puzzled, 'I don't support *any* football team.'
'That's even worse.'

A week after their first meeting, Chloe again found Mr Grantham in the garden, contemplating nature. This time it took quite a while for her to get him to open up, but once he did Mr Grantham was even less reluctant than before to share his thoughts with her. She asked him at one point if he had gone to university, as she was thinking of doing that one day.

'University? No, no, never went there.' He almost chuckled. 'We didn't do things like that in them days. I went to a village school. Left at fourteen. Never took exams or anything like that. Went to work in a grocer's, behind the counter. Just before I was twenty, the war came along, and I joined up.' His eyes narrowed at this point. 'I was engaged to a young woman called Susan then. She gave me a silver pocket-watch before I left for overseas, with her photo in the lid which covered the face. It was musical. Played *Frère Jacques* when you opened it.'

'Oh, were you very much in love?' Chloe recalled that his wife's name had been Florrie. 'You didn't marry in the end?'

His mouth formed a thin bitter line.

'No, no, we didn't marry. I came home after the war, from POW camp in Germany, and she'd run off. Married a much older man than me. They'd moved away, so I never saw her again.'

'Oh, how sad.'

Mr Grantham rallied. 'Probably for the best.' But he didn't sound as if he meant it. 'I met Florrie a little later. She was a good wife. We loved each other.'

'What about the watch? Have you still got it?'

'I think it's up in the attic somewhere. I chucked it there when I heard Susan was married to another man. This was my parents' house, you see. I've lived here almost all my life, except for India and Germany.'

'Don't you want the watch?'

He humphed. 'I'm too old to go climbing around in dusty attics. Much too old now. Pity though.' His eyes became distant. 'I wouldn't mind seeing that watch again. It would've hurt too much, earlier, but now – well, feelings get a bit dusty too, with time. I've not had a bad life, but I've been thinking more and more about how I cursed Susan for running away with that fellow Perkins. It sort of ruled my life for a few years and I got very bitter. Eventually I met Florrie and things came all right again, but it was a bit dark for a while. A bit dark. I'd like to make my peace with Susan's memory now. Getting the watch back would help. I feel bad about chucking it aside like that.' He gave Chloe a wry smile and nodded towards the heavens. 'You never know who you're going to meet up there, do you?'

'I'll ask the boys. They won't mind having a look up there for you. Me too. I wouldn't mind.'

'You're very kind.'

'Rooting around in an old attic might be fun,' said Chloe. 'You never know what you'll find.'

'That's very true. Treasure and trash, that's what you'll find in attics.' He turned and stared into her eyes. 'It would be nice to find treasure, wouldn't it?'

Once Chloe had gone, Mr Grantham had a sudden flash of guilt. He liked Chloe. She was a nice girl. Since they had begun their infrequent conversations sprigs of apple blossom had begun to spring from the flinty beds of his thoughts. Should he warn her? He wanted to. But he just didn't know.

What if harm should come to them? It hadn't to him, but maybe he'd been lucky. Then again, you couldn't live your life in perfect safety. That would be very dull and boring. You had to have some danger and excitement. That's why boys bought motorbikes and girls backpacked around the world.

No, he wouldn't warn them. Let them find out for themselves. They could always turn back, if they were too afraid to go on. It was that kind of place. It might make his old heart race and bang against his ribs to think about it, but theirs were stronger, stouter organs.

Later, while Dipa was preparing dinner in the kitchen, Chloe told Alex and Jordy about the 'secrets' she'd learned from Mr Grantham. Predictably, Jordy was a little scornful and said they weren't exactly headline revelations. Equally as predictable was Alex, who was more interested in the pocket-watch than in any ancient love story.

Yes, he said, he wouldn't mind helping Chloe look for the watch. 'Those old watches with real brass works,' he said reverently, 'are ten times more interesting than modern watches. Digital watches are the worst, but the ones which try to look like old watches are just as bad. All they've got inside 'em is a chip. Just that. A rotten old computer chip. But just think of all the engineering that went into making an old watch! All those cogs and wheels, the hair spring, levers and – and,' he said almost darkly, 'there's a thing called an *escapement*. If you didn't have that, the whole works would go out of balance and tell the wrong time.'

Jordy stared at his normally quiet step-brother and said wonderingly, 'Once you wind him up he just goes on and on, doesn't he?'

'Are you being unkind?' asked Dipa, entering the room with a steaming dish of potatoes. 'What's all that about? Nelson, *stop* threading through my ankles or I'll drop this dish.'

Nelson continued weaving awkwardly between her legs and then toppled over when he caught the edge of the carpet. He was a cat who refused to acknowledge that he had only three legs. Giving the carpet an aggrieved look, he jumped up into Dipa's chair.

'No, I'm not being unkind – at least I didn't mean to be,' said Jordy. 'We were just talking about . . .' he caught Chloe's warning look just in time 'about old-fashioned pocket-watches. Alex seems to think they're cool. He thinks wrist-watches are naff.'

Dipa placed the dish on a mat on the table and stepped back to look at her youngest child.

'Well, that's because he'd look so smart in a waistcoat, wouldn't you, Alex? With a shiny silver watch–chain dangling from the pocket.'

'Nobody in this house understands me,' Alex sighed. 'It's the *works* of a watch I like, not the watch itself. Wrist-watches are OK. But I know Jordy likes his because it looks snazzy on him and because it tells him the time to a hundredth of a second, even at ten fathoms under water. He likes it because of how it looks and what it does and what it's capable of doing at the bottom of the ocean, though what use that is to him I'll never know. I like watches because of how they're made and what's inside the case.'

Chloe said, 'And I couldn't care less about any of it. Can we eat now?'

Dipa returned to the kitchen to get the rest of the meal and Alex said, 'Shall we all look for it? The watch, I mean?'

'I'm going to,' said Chloe.

'Oh, all right,' Jordy agreed, not wanting to be left out. 'I'll come too, but I warn you,' he twisted his face into a mask, 'it's *horrible* up there!'

# CHAPTER 2

# Crossing the Threshold

The three of them didn't discuss why they didn't let Ben and Dipa know they wanted to search the attic. It wasn't that each of them didn't think about it. Chloe certainly did. Jordy did too. (And who knew what was in Alex's head?) But for some reason, unknown even to themselves, none of them mentioned it. Not that it was anything their parents would have objected to. They simply kept it secret. They deliberately waited for a Saturday morning when Dipa was working and Ben was going out to do the shopping. Chloe asked Jordy to go with her. Alex, however, was engrossed in making another kite and said he wouldn't join them after all.

'What's that?' Ben had asked, coming into the kitchen and catching the end of the conversation. 'You lot going to the cinema?'

'We might do later,' Jordy had said. 'Is it all right?'

'What about lunch?' Ben had asked. 'Are you going to eat thin air?'

'We'll grab a bite in town,' Jordy had said, and knowing Ben was disapproving of hamburgers added, 'from the Italian sandwich bar.'

Once Ben had gone Chloe and Jordy found themselves at the trapdoor of the attic, climbing through, armed with torches. Once more the dust and dead air assailed Jordy's nostrils, but this time he wasn't so worried by it. He had a means of light with him and he had Chloe. Still, once he was standing on boards inside, shining the torch into the recesses of the attic, a strange feeling came over him. It was as if they were trespassing on the sacred burial ground of another culture. There was the sense, not of being watched, but of being *felt* by something or someone. The first step he took he walked into a cobweb and covered his face with sticky threads.

'Urrgh!' he grunted.

'What's wrong?' Chloe was whispering for some reason. 'Step in a cow pat?'

'Very funny. There are spiders up here.'

Chloe said, 'Don't try to scare me. I'm not worried about spiders.'

'I am,' said a deep voice behind her, sending a shock wave through her. 'I don't like 'em.'

It was Alex, who had changed his mind after he'd accidentally snapped the spine of his home-made kite.

'Don't do that!' she hissed at him. 'You made me jump.'

'Nearly gave me a heart attack,' said Jordy, his voice coming out of the darkness.

Alex shone his torch around the rafters. The beam found some hanging flimsy cobwebs, grey as old bread. 'They're dead,' he muttered. 'I don't mind dead ones.'

The three of them split up, each searching separate corners of the attic, ducking and weaving under rafters and stepping over beams. Jordy's area contained the water tank and when he shone his torch in there he was disgusted by the dead insects floating on the surface. 'We *drink* this stuff,' he called to the others. 'It's filthy.'

'No we don't,' corrected Alex, 'unless you drink your own bathwater. That tank feeds the boiler.'

'All right, I wash in it. It's still filthy.'

They rooted around in the odds and ends that were up there, kicked aside old cardboard boxes, gingerly lifted clumps of dirty clothes with their torches. They were looking for that glint of old silver which would perhaps tell them they had found the treasure they were looking for. Now that they were up there, Jordy actually felt they were on a wild-goose chase. The watch could be anywhere, if it was there at all. Who could trust an old man's memory? Mr Grantham might have *thought* he'd thrown it up there, all those decades ago, but maybe he threw it somewhere else? Or maybe the watch didn't exist at all?

A beam of light came near him, as he turned over a cardboard box full of clothes with his toe. A woman's mouldy hat lay flattened beneath it, the ribbon around the crown a sort of pale yellow colour.

'Where's Alex?' asked Chloe, the person behind the light. 'I can't find him.'

Jordy shone his torch around the attic, finding different shapes, but none of them belonging to Alex.

'Alex?' called Jordy. 'Alex?'

No answer. Suddenly his torch caught some bright shining eyes that looked up at him balefully. Jordy jumped back, alarmed. Then a familiar sound came from the creature who owned the eyes.

'Nelson! What are you doing up here? How did you get up those steps?' He stroked the cat's back then said, 'Did Alex go down again, d'you think? Maybe he got bored?'

Chloe replied, 'No, he'd have said something. One minute he was just here, to my left, and the next moment he'd vanished.'

'Which way was he going?'

Jordy was suddenly afraid that his step-brother might have hit his head on a beam and was lying unconscious somewhere. Vivid tales of people with concussion had been his bedtime stories from his paramedic father. You needed to get someone with concussion to hospital as soon as possible. He didn't want to alarm Chloe though, so he said, 'Could be at the back there, in that patch of darkness. You go back down to the flat, I'll have a look.'

'No,' she replied sharply. 'I want to look too.'

Like seasoned aircraft pilots they did a square search of the attic to the edge of the floor boards. The unboarded part went out into the darkness. Jordy decided to go further, but had to tread on beams. One wrong step and his foot could go through the ceiling into the flat below. Chloe followed him. They had to concentrate on hopping from one rough beam to the next. Strangely enough, after a long spell of doing this athletic dance between beams, still having to crouch because of the rafters, they came to some more boarding.

Jordy stepped on to it with relief. His legs were beginning to ache.

'Our attic must continue into next door's attic,' he called back to Chloe. 'There can't be any wall between the two houses up here.' His torch light streaked into the darkness ahead.

Chloe came up alongside him. 'Perhaps that's how they built houses in those days.'

'What days?'

'When it was built – Victorian times.'

She shone her torch beam alongside Jordy's, then called out, 'Alex? Are you in there?'

A faint reply came to them, seemingly from a distant place, like a whisper on the still air.

'Was that him?' asked Jordy.

'I don't know. Let's go on a bit.'

'Could have been a bird or a bat or something.'

Chloe was scornful. 'A bat? Bats don't yell.'

'Well, sounds might get distorted up here. There are all sorts of things like roofing insulation, tanks and water pipes and things. You hear all kinds of noises in the plumbing, don't you? Anyway, aren't we trespassing? I mean, we must have other people's homes under our feet now. What if someone comes up and catches us? Won't we get into a row?'

Chloe considered this. They were one house in a terraced row of houses. Without a doubt they had crossed over from their own home into someone else's. Perhaps the whole row had just one attic between them, without any walls between. Did that make sense? She thought it did.

'We need to find Alex,' said Chloe logically. 'He might be hurt.'

They moved on, more easily now there were boards under their feet. The deeper they went into the attic, the more the darkness seemed to close around them. Then suddenly they came upon an area where there was a sky-light, but high above. When they took stock and stared at their surroundings, they found the edges of the attic had moved back and back, leaving a huge space between. Above them the roof itself went up to dizzying heights. In front and behind, there was no beginning and no end. They were still in that triangular shape of the inside of a roof, but the apex was somewhere high above their heads, while the lower angles on either side had moved beyond the range of their vision.

'Wha— where are we? It's grown a bit,' said Jordy. 'The attic. It's become – I don't know – maybe we're in a bigger house, at the end of the row? Is there a big house there? I can't remember.' He peered into the dimness. 'I can't see the corners. And where's the roof?'

Chloe sneezed violently, making him jump.

'Sorry,' she said croakily. 'Dust up my nose.'

She looked above at a forest of stout rafters, criss-crossing this way and that. A bewildering maze of angled roof timbers, with gloom filling the spaces between. Every so often there was a main support for the roof, a thick roughly hewn wooden pillar that shouldered the architecture above it.

A very big building, certainly. A manor house, perhaps? Or a vicarage? Or maybe even a church? She could see great beams curving overhead, like the flying buttresses of a cathedral. No, there was a skylight there, high above the beams, like a square sun above the network of lumber, its sharp shaft of light penetrating right down to the floor beneath. You wouldn't have a skylight in a cathedral roof. In the sunbeam it threw down danced those bright specks which her mother used to call 'angel dust'.

Chloe said in awed tones, 'Where are we?'

'It's *massive*, isn't it?' He looked back into the darkness from which they had come. 'We could get lost up here. You remember that story of the kid who climbed into the trunk during a game of hide-and-seek, and the lid locked shut behind him? They found him a hundred years later, just the dried-out bones covered in dusty rags . . .'

'Don't!' warned Chloe, knowing Jordy was trying to scare her. 'Stop it now.'

Jordy said gleefully, 'Nobody ever found him.'

Chloe ignored him. 'Where's *Alex*?' she said, in a tone which registered her frustration with her brother. 'He's always sliding off somewhere.'

'I'm here,' said a voice behind them, making both her and Jordy jump again.

'Why did you run off?' cried Chloe, rounding on her younger brother. 'How did you get there?'

Alex looked annoyed and surprised. 'It was you two who went off. I just followed your torch lights. You were a long way ahead of me. I had to run to keep up with you in places.'

Jordy said wearily, 'Oh, come on, Alex.'

'No, I'm telling the truth,' cut in Alex, sounding angry. 'It seemed like you were trying to get away from me.'

Chloe flushed. 'That's not true and you know it.'

Alex was sulky. 'Well, that's how it seemed to me.'

Jordy said, 'Let's all calm down. We've found each other now. No, we weren't trying to get away from you, Alex. We were looking for you. Chloe was worried about you. She thought you might have banged your head on a rafter or something. I don't understand how you got behind us, because we searched the attic – our attic, that is – before we set out. Now we're somewhere in this much bigger attic . . .' He looked up, to see two birds – or birdlike creatures – glide from one rafter to another.

'It is big, isn't it?' Alex murmured, looking up and around him. 'It's giant size. Maybe we've shrunk? That's what's happened.'

Chloe said, 'Don't be silly.'

'In that case, the attic's grown.'

'Now you're being even sillier.'

Chloe sounded angry but Jordy knew that Chloe, in her heart, was upset by their situation. Jordy himself didn't know what to think. It was all very extraordinary, very weird. Out there in front of them was a kind of thicket fashioned from scores of old fishing rods, with their lines going back and forth creating a tangle of cords. Dangling from the lines like loose wicked thorns were fishing hooks of all sizes. It really was like a dense bramble bush, which had obviously been there a long time: it was covered in spiders' webbing from top to bottom.

He muttered, 'Come on, we've got to find our way home. I hope I recognise which is our trapdoor.'

Jordy started to walk back the way he had come, but Alex cried, 'That's not the right direction.'

'It's this way.' Jordy pointed. 'Isn't it, Clo?'

'Well, I thought we came from that way.'

She pointed in a different direction still.

'Now we're stuck,' growled Jordy. He made a decision. 'I'm the eldest. It's my responsibility. I say we go my way.'

'You and your two months,' Chloe said. 'You think because you were born in July and me in September you're the boss.'

'Well, somebody's got to be.'

'Not necessarily. You've heard of democracy, haven't you? We'll vote on it.'

But a vote did nothing to get them any further, since they voted three ways. It was settled in the manner it always was when they were unsure which way to go. Jordy started out in the direction *he* wanted to go and the others felt they had to follow or lose him. Both Chloe and Alex still grumbled that it was the wrong way, but they felt they ought to stay together. Jordy felt no triumph on this occasion: he was simply praying he was right.

Chloe decided they were like explorers crossing uncharted regions as they walked the boards of this huge vault of wood and plaster. Deeper and deeper they went, failing to find their own trapdoor, and finally even Jordy was forced to admit they had probably gone wrong. He said he was sure he had the right direction, but the others said obviously not. So they turned round and began to retrace their steps. At least, they believed they had turned round, but after a while Chloe wasn't even certain about this.

'Look,' she said, peering up into the gloom above, 'you can just see the apex of the roof. It's running opposite to the lines on the floorboards. We're going level with them now. If we walk at right angles to the cracks, we should get back to where we started.'

It seemed Jordy was too worried to argue with her this time, so the three of them did what Chloe considered to be sensible, yet after an hour or two they still didn't know whether they were any nearer to their own part of the attic. They were all becoming quite tired, and thirsty too. Piles of junk containing the clutter that one finds in an attic were here and there on the landscape.

Chloe picked up an old bottle made of green glass, with a loose glass stopper rattling in its neck.

'Cod bottle,' she said, having once collected old bottles. 'These are quite rare.'

'Is there any cod juice left in it?' asked Alex, through parched lips. 'Anything to drink?'

'You don't get cod juice in a cod bottle. It's just called that. I think they used to have lemonade in them.'

Alex wandered off a bit while the other two sat down to rest on the floorboards. Alex was one of those people who usually have luck on their side, and this time was no different. He found a water tank hidden in the shadows. Using his hand as a cup he drank from it, ignoring the dead spiders and one or two down feathers floating on top. Then he called the others. They stood and stared at the water for a while, reluctant to drink.

'We don't know when we'll find another waterhole,' said Alex. 'You'd better drink. And Clo should fill that cod's bottle.'

'Why do you call it that? A waterhole?' said Chloe. 'You make it sound as if we're wild beasts, lost in the desert or something.'

'He's right,' Jordy said. 'It is a waterhole. There's nowhere else to drink, is there? And the light's going . . .'

The other two followed his gaze upwards, to see the square sun dimming in the rafter-crossed sky.

'We must conserve our torch batteries,' said Jordy. 'Don't use them unless you have to.'

'Who made you boss?' murmured Chloe, but the heart had gone out of her protests. She found herself gripping her torch as if it were a talisman, as if to let it go would be to abandon any chance of escape from this arid wooden place.

The smell of the water was tempting her now. Her throat was so dry she was rasping her words. She filled her bottle, pushing it right down under the scummy surface. She watched as the escaping air bubbles were replaced by water. Then she took the bottle out and drank from it, not caring that the glass container had probably lain in the attic for over a hundred years. She told herself if there had ever been any germs on the neck, they themselves would have died of thirst before now.

Jordy too succumbed and drank directly from the tank, skimming the surface free of dead insects with his hands first.

'If we all wake up with stomach ache,' he muttered, 'I won't be at all surprised. No one's brought their mobile, I suppose?'

'Not me,' Alex said. 'Why would I?'

True, thought Chloe, who did not even bother to answer. Why would they take a phone to search the attic? It wasn't as if they were even going out of the house.

Normally, if they were camping or sleeping somewhere strange on holiday, they would sit up and talk into the night. Yet here, in this great attic they could think of nothing to say. Chloe simply sat there, hugging her knees through her jeans, staring up at the roof. She half hoped that stars would appear up there, now that the sun had gone down. Only one single such twinkling light came to comfort her. It was a bright one, probably Venus, caught in the skylight window. It did cheer her somewhat, to know that there actually *was* a real world out there.

'See that?' she said, pointing it out to Jordy. 'The Evening Star.'

'But locked in here,' he muttered. 'Trapped inside a bloody great attic.' He reflected for a moment, before adding, 'No wonder they call them trapdoors.'

A silence fell between them again. A little later Jordy's torch went on for a few seconds. He inspected his wrist. Then it went out again.

He whispered to her, 'My watch is going backwards.'

They both lay down on the boards and tried to sleep. In the middle of the night Chloe heard noises in the darkness. Not loud sounds, more like people walking softly, or small creatures scratching around. They were not even particularly alarming noises. Simply sounds which told her she and her brothers were not alone.

Later Chloe felt something soft brushing her face. She pushed it away, too sleepy to do anything else. An animal curled in the hollow of her stomach and joined her in sleep.

They woke early. The light was grey and dingy for a while, then the sun came through the skylights. The first thing they did was drink from the tank without any fuss. Alex found half a bar of chocolate in his pocket, which he shared out. Had it been in Chloe's pocket, or Jordy's, they would have starved. Alex was the only one who didn't gobble down chocolate as soon as it was in his hands. He saved things for later. On this occasion his restraint did not irritate Chloe. Instead of saying in a sarcastic voice, 'Oh, you're so good, little brother' she said, 'Well done, Alex.'

'Could have told us last night,' muttered Jordy, chewing his three squares.

Alex replied with some logic, 'Then you'd have had nothing for breakfast.'

Chloe suddenly looked around her, remembering.

'Nelson came in the night,' she said. 'Isn't he here?'

The two boys stared around them. 'Can't see him. You sure?'

'Yes, positive. Oh well, he'll find his way back.'

When Chloe had filled her bottle again, the three explorers set out once more. They were assuming that they would find their way out, but Chloe wondered what Ben and Dipa were doing. She guessed her mother would be frantic. Neither Chloe nor Alex had ever stayed out all night before – not without their mother knowing exactly where they were.

Chloe wasn't sure about Jordy.

She had picked up inferences from her step-brother that things had not been too stable in his family, during and after the divorce. Chloe had the idea that Jordy had run away at least once, when the split in his family had come. Then Jordy's mother had declined custody of her son, a rejection which must have hurt him. Perhaps he might still have chosen to be with his father, but to have a mother who did not seem to want him must have been painful.

Maybe Ben was at this moment blaming Jordy, thinking that perhaps he'd run away again, taking the other two with him.

'What is this place?' muttered Jordy.

'Obviously it's a giant attic.'

'We guessed *that*,' Jordy snapped, 'but why is it so big?'

'How am I supposed to know?'

They looked at each other for a moment, then Chloe said, 'Can we stop arguing for a while? We're all in a fix and we need to pull together to get out of it. Can we just be friends?'

Jordy stared, then grinned. 'Yeah, sorry, Clo. I don't mean to be mean. I mean – well, you know what I mean. Just because we don't always agree, doesn't mean anything.'

She smiled too. 'There's about three million *means* in there.'

'You're no good at maths. There are only about half a dozen. OK, let's not worry, let's get walking.'

'Have you thought,' she asked, 'how Ben and Dipa are going to be worrying?'

Jordy shrugged. 'Not much we can do about it, except keep going. Got to find a way down, is all.'

Chloe knew that Jordy's pretence at a casual attitude was a front. She knew he felt responsible for what happened to them in any adverse predicament, such as this one. That was because he was male and because he was the eldest. It was stupid of him, of course, but his real mother had drummed some rubbish into him about men being stronger and having to take care of women, who were supposedly weaker.

Chloe felt well able to take care of herself and didn't need a guardian who was only two months older than she was, even if he was a male. But she couldn't tell him that, because he would take no notice and it would only make him all the more anxious. Jordy was a product of someone who believed in the old order, when men ruled the world and women did as they were told. Men were made of iron, women were fashioned of thin glass. It was a load of old rubbish, really.

'We don't break any more,' she muttered. 'We're made of tougher stuff these days.'

'What?' said Jordy, turning his head, a puzzled look on his face. 'What did you say?'

'Nothing.'

Suddenly Alex stopped dead in his tracks.

'Did you see that?' he asked, staring off to the right of where they were standing. 'Someone's out there.'

'Where?' asked Jordy, straining to see through the dimness into the far side of the attic. 'Out there?'

'Someone moved. I saw a shadow jump.'

Chloe said, 'Perhaps it's someone who's just come up from the house underneath us?'

'It didn't move like a person,' Alex said. 'It moved like – like some other creature. I don't know what. An animal or something.'

'Stop scaring me,' cried Chloe, her heart beating faster. 'Don't play games, Alex.'

'I wasn't – *look*, there it is again. In the shadows. Maybe it's Nelson?'

'I saw it. I saw it,' cried Jordy. 'It wasn't a cat, it was – I dunno – it *must* be a person.'

Alex shook his head. 'No, it wasn't. It didn't move right. Look, again! It's sort of jerky. Now it's gone. Gone into the blackness.'

'I think it's a person,' said Chloe quickly. 'I think we've got to look for him – or her. Whoever it is. They can tell us the way out.'

# CHAPTER 3

# Sky with a Thousand Windows

'Who?'

*Young people.*

'You can tell they're new to the attic. They keep twisting their heads round trying to catch the dust sprites. No chance.'

The youthful board-comber sees them through the holes in his Venetian carnival mask from afar off and he shivers in another person's shoes.

He wears several layers of ankle-length coats, all too big for him. He has on his head a great floppy hat, also several sizes too large. These clothes do not belong to him, but were some other's, for the board-comber himself owns nothing; no clothes at all. He takes them where he finds them and they become part of him, but never belong to him. The camouflage is perfect. When he feels the need to transform himself into a pile of rags he simply falls on the floor in a heap.

*I am afeared of people,* he tells the bat hanging from his left earlobe. *But they draw me to them.*

'That's because you was people once yourself,' says the bat. 'You think of them as family.'

The board-comber, like all his kind, was once an ordinary boy, but he has lived here too long. He does not like direct contact with his old race, for now he's different, he's not a person. He wears the mask – it is the mask known to Venetians as Cocalino the jolly friar, with red nose and cheeks and bright red lips – not because he wants to scare anyone, but because he's not what he used to be. He's something different now.

But he likes to see children, follow them, gather bits of conversation like dust on a draught.

'They're looking,' the bat cries. 'You should hide.'

The board-comber drops to the floor and is instantly a pile of rags. Those looking from afar cannot see his eyes, peering out between the folds. All they see are old coats, thrown in a heap, with a hat on top. Those who look more carefully might notice the frozen features of Cocalino, who beams at them with an expression of merry contentment.

*Have they gone yet?* he asks the bat. *Anyway, how can you see them? You're a blind creature.*

'I am at the moment. You're squashing me.'

The board-comber lifts his head slightly and finds he has indeed been crushing the bat.

*Sorry.*

'How many times?'

*I know. I'm sorry.*

'So long as you really are.'

*I really am.*

'They've gone now. You can get up. Are we going to comb the boards any more today? It's getting late.'

*Just a little longer. The light's still golden.*

The pair of them, horseshoe-bat and board-comber, exist in the attic for one purpose: to collect things. They comb the boards like shell-gatherers comb beaches, but not for shells of course. Not this board-comber at least. It is interested solely in soapstone carvings made by the Inuit Eskimos. That's his bag. That's what he seeks. Others might collect paintings, or toy cars, or books, or porcelain figurines. This one scours the tideless reaches of the attic for Inuit carvings. Head down, he walks the long wooden planks, inspecting flotsam, jetsam or any kind of drift-junk, turning over heaps in case a gem of a soapstone carving lies beneath. When he finds one, his heart fills to bursting with joy. He could shout his pleasure to the four high draughts but doesn't, for board-combers are shy creatures and do not like attention. They wear masks to hide their features and they wear their many layers of clothes not just as a disguise but to become shapeless things of no worth.

'Look,' says the bat, 'a recent chest of drawers. Is your heart going pitter-pat?'

*Oh, it is, it is. Do you think there's one in a drawer?*

'Who knows? You have to look.'

*They're so rare in this part of the attic. We should have emigrated over the boards.*

'If they weren't rare, you wouldn't be interested in them. Who wants to look for something common?'

*That's true.*

He searches the chest of drawers thoroughly, finding only a few bits and bobs of no interest at all. Cotton reels. Buttons. A few old postcards. A scarf.

*Those young people. They might have one in their pockets?*

'Fat chance, unless they've just been to Alaska or Northern Canada.'

*Maybe they're straight from Cape Dorset?*

'The eternal optimist. Is it likely? How many people go on holiday to Baffin Bay? I could count them on my claws. You just take those drawers out and look behind them.

Sometimes humans hide things behind drawers, so that others can't find them. Anything there?'

*Only a dead bat.*

'You liar.'

*Had you, there.*

'Not a chance. Can we rest up now? You need to go to sleep and I need to go out and hunt. I'm starving.'

*Shall we count our treasures first?*

'We know how many there are. We counted them last night.'

*I want to see them again.*

The board-comber takes a leather satchel out of the folds of his coats and lays it carefully on the attic floor. Having opened it, he begins to take out carvings and carefully unwrap the rags which protect them. First there is a beautiful jade-green dancing bear, which is so finely balanced it can stand on one leg without a prop. Next comes a seal-skin-coated Inuit drummer, complete with drum and drumstick. Then a dark-grey whale, so shiny it brings tears to the board-comber's eyes. After that a ruffled-coated wolf is revealed: white and savage-looking, but with tender eyes.

There are thirty-seven pieces in all. Five of them were found in the same box. They're heavy, but the board-comber never minds the weight. In fact, he likes it, because it reminds him of his success. There is nothing to match the finding of another Inuit carving: no feeling like it. It's what keeps the board-comber in the attic, what turned him from a person into what he is now. He strokes the bounty of the boards, finding great pleasure in the smooth stone which has been transformed from a simple chunk of rock into a work of art.

*Beautiful*, murmurs the board-comber. *Aren't they?*

'Oh yes,' replies the bat, 'quite beautiful.'

But being lost in his bonanza the board-comber has not

noticed that the bat flew away long before the question was even asked.

The sun had multiplied. There were skylight windows all along the heavens now, a hundred, maybe a thousand. They let in a grubby light. The boards had opened up into a wide plain, with hills on the periphery. These hills were fashioned from furniture – chests, chairs, side-tables, wardrobes – and junk such as umbrellas, books, walking sticks, rolls of carpet, workman's tools. At about one o'clock (an hour before noon on Jordy's watch) the trio came to a forest of hat stands. These were of the kind that had a central pole and curved prongs like horns at the top, of which some were leafed with hats, scarves, feather boas and the odd coat. In parts they formed thickets and in other areas they were spaced apart, to allow for clearings where the party might rest up and look about them.

'It gets weirder,' said Jordy. 'What's that?'

He indicated the piece of paper which Chloe had taken from her pocket.

'Oh, just my books list – you know, my favourite reads.'

'Oh, that.'

Jordy was not a great reader. He liked sport. It is possible to be good at both, and interested in both, but he was not. Alex was not interested in sport at all, nor especially read-ing and writing – in fact, all three bored him somewhat. Alex was destined to be an engineer.

'That *thing* is still following us,' said Alex matter-of-factly. 'I saw its shadow on the edge of the woodland.'

'Alex, we're talking about a *person*,' replied his sister. 'It's not right to call him or her a *thing*. It must be someone who's looking for something in their attic. We mustn't assume they mean to harm us.'

'Why?' asked Jordy. 'Maybe it's just waiting its chance?'

'I'd rather think good of people, than bad, wouldn't you?'

Alex said, 'Listen, stop arguing, you two, we came up here to look for Mr Grantham's watch.'

Chloe drew a breath, then nodded. 'I agree. Mr Grantham is an old man and this is very important to him. We have to stop being petty and put our minds to the task in hand.'

Jordy was looking around him at the vastness of the attic and shaking his head. They both expected him to disagree, but instead he said to them, 'You're right, both of you. But it's going to be a *huge* task, don't make any mistake about that! This place is massive – just look at it.' He slapped one of the large pillars that rose like a giant rainforest tree into the dark regions of the rafters above. 'We've got a search on here that would try the patience of a saint, as my gran would say. It's a big job. A *very* big job. I hope you two know what we're getting into.'

'A quest!' cried Chloe. '*Lord of the Rings.*'

'I hope not,' Jordy said to her. 'Those Hobbits had a hell of a time getting to where they wanted to go, didn't they? Oh, I know, I only saw the movie and didn't read the book, but I know the story.'

'I wasn't going to say anything,' Chloe said.

They all had a drink from Chloe's bottle.

Jordy then insisted they stand in a circle and grip right hands, repeating an oath after him.

'We the challenged,' he cried, 'do solemnly swear that we shall search this attic for the lost timepiece of Mr Grantham, who does not appear to have a first name. We shall not falter through lack of courage. We shall not hesitate to cross hazards, be they deep gorges, cataracts or high mountains. We shall keep each other's safety in mind, and if brother or sister fall, we shall go instantly to their assistance. We are the intrepid trio. We are the watch-finders. We shall prevail where others have failed.'

'That's a really cool oath,' said Alex, impressed. 'Don't you think so, sis?'

Chloe agreed, smiling. 'Good as any I've read.'

Alex stepped out of the forest of hat stands and was almost run over.

'What the heck—' He jumped aside.

A little man in a little vehicle swished by him.

'Hey,' cried Alex automatically. 'Look where you're going!'

Then he stared dumbly, into the distance, at an amazing sight.

Jordy came out of the hat stands now, brushing down his sweater.

'Cruddy dust is everywhere.' He looked at Alex. 'What's the matter with you?'

'I was nearly mown down. Look, a village.'

'A *what*?'

'Huts and what-not. Over there. Oh, there's another one of those car things.'

Jordy stared, equally amazed. Chloe came out of the woodland now, wearing one of the hats. They turned to look at her. 'Well,' she said, defensively, 'it doesn't really belong to anyone. Don't you think I look cute?' She fluttered her eyelashes. 'I can be cute, if I want to be. Just because I'm brainy doesn't mean I'm not pretty.'

'Never mind the hat,' Jordy said.

She glared at him. 'Never mind the— Oh, what's that?'

Alex said, 'We think they're cars.'

'Very small cars.'

'From that village over there.'

Chloe removed the hat and stared.

The machines, which looked hand-made, seemed to be powered by old-fashioned mechanical sewing machines. There were pedals that the drivers pumped, Alex noticed, which provided the motive energy to propel them around. The drivers had no cover of course, but were open to view. This would not matter, he decided, in a place where it never seemed to rain or snow.

'Wow!' he said. 'I'd like a go on one of those things.'

'I'll tell you what,' Jordy said, obviously not as impressed as his step-brother, 'you'll never pick up a speeding ticket.'

'Yeah, but the – the . . .'

'Ingenuity?' offered Chloe.

'Yeah, that,' Alex said.

'But where are these people from?' asked Chloe reasonably. 'What are they doing up here?'

'Travellers,' replied Jordy, nodding. 'Yes, that's what they are. Travellers, inhabiting someone's attic. I guess they must have permission, because to the people in the house below they're probably making a horrible racket, thundering around up here. I suppose they camped nearby and the people in the house took pity on them and said, "why not use our attic till the weather gets better: it's big and airy and we don't use it much, except to store junk in." Something like that.'

'The weather's been wonderful,' Chloe pointed out. 'Sunshine pouring through all those skylights.'

'Well, now they've got used to being up here, they're probably reluctant to leave, eh?'

Alex remarked, 'You don't think they look sort of . . . strange? I mean, they're kind of small and lumpy – there are bumps all over their heads – and they haven't got any hair!'

Chloe replied firmly, 'Alex, we do not pass judgement on people just because they look a little different from us.'

And they did look a *bit* like real people, with two arms,

two legs and a head and torso. But they were so pale they were as white as baking powder. A sickly-looking white. As Alex had said, they were kind of small and lumpy, with rounded shoulders and bald heads. And their skulls were covered in scabs and bumps where presumably they had banged them on low rafters or the angled ceiling. They must never have washed, because there was plaster dust and bits all over their heads and shoulders. Their eyes – Alex particularly noticed this – appeared so washed-out they seemed to have no colour at all.

Alex stood in front of one that was on foot and said to him, 'Hi, my name is Alex. I'm up here looking for a silver pocket-watch. You haven't seen one, I suppose?'

The creature, shedding plaster dust as he walked, looked a little frightened behind those pale eyes, but he made no reply. Instead he skirted Alex and continued walking to wherever he was going. Once, he did glance back, but not to any real purpose. It was almost as if he'd forgotten something: like switching off the iron, or a shopping list he'd meant to bring. Then he was gone, among the cardboard huts which served as houses to these unusual beings of the attic.

Jordy said, 'Zombies then.'

'They can't see us,' stated Alex. 'We're invisible to them.'

Chloe argued with this. 'No,' she said, 'they *can* see us, because they drive round us. They're just pretending they can't see us.'

'They're not exactly *friendly*, are they?' Jordy said. 'Grumpy lot. They never seem to smile. Maybe they can't? Like animals.'

Alex said, 'We had a cat once that smiled.'

'Cats can't smile,' Jordy said emphatically. 'They might look as if they are – showing their teeth or something – but they don't have the facial muscles for it. We did it in human biology.' Whenever Jordy stated that he had 'done it' in some subject at school, it was for him an irrefutable fact.

Alex was stubborn though. 'His name was Dylan and he smiled quite a lot.'

Chloe interrupted. 'You know, Dylan Thomas? Dylan *Tomcat*. I named him,' she said proudly.

'Do tell,' muttered Jordy.

They said no more on the subject, knowing that such a quarrel could go on for hours.

Instead they walked around the dwellings, unhindered by the occupants who treated them as if they did not exist.

It was a sort of shanty-town gathering of makeshift huts. It didn't appear that they slept in them. Instead they apparently slept in wardrobes, standing up. Alex got the fright of his life when he opened a wardrobe only to be confronted by a flour-white villager standing bolt upright, but with its eyes closed. He shut the door quietly and walked away, hoping he had not disturbed the creature at his or her rest.

That was another thing. You couldn't tell which were women and which were men. They seemed to wear anything they could lay their hands on. Men and boys had on dresses – sometimes – and women and girls wore business suits. But there seemed to be no set rules, for women also wore dresses and some men had on jackets and trousers. Or boiler suits. Or dressing gowns. Or jeans, sometimes with underpants worn on the outside. Or tights on their heads, the legs wrapped around their necks like scarves. Or long socks and shorts. Anything went.

It appeared they grabbed a handful of clothes from a pile and threw them on, back to front, the right way around, upside-down, whatever. Everything was fashionable.

'Don't open the wardrobes,' warned Alex. 'Unless you've got a hammer and stake in your hands.'

'Vampires?' cried Jordy. 'Really?'

'You'd think so, to look at 'em, wouldn't you? Weird. Really weird. I can't even sleep on my back, let alone standing up straight. That's how they do it, Jordy. They look as if they're standing in coffins, but they're just bedrooms – tall, thin bedrooms.'

'Well,' said Jordy, as they held a meeting with the sewing-machine cars whizzing round them, 'what do we do? Do we stay here for a while, or go on? There's water here. They've got these open upturned umbrellas which they fill from tanks and hang outside their houses. And they've got food. I don't know about you, but I'm starving.'

'We can't steal their food,' Chloe argued. 'That wouldn't be right.'

'Do you want to eat dead spiders?'

'No.'

'Then we have to take what we can find.'

Alex asked, 'Well, what is it, this food? Vindaloo? Shishkebabs? Liver and bacon? What?'

'I think it's that stuff you can grow without water – you know, it takes its moisture from the air? Doesn't need soil or anything? What d'you call it? Hyro-something?'

'I can't remember,' Chloe answered truthfully.

'Hydroponics,' murmured Alex, but no one was listening.

'Well, anyway, it's that. Looks a bit twiggy and spooky. They grow it in big trays behind the village. We could go and take some. There's plenty there. These people seem to just wander in and out of that area and take what they feel like.'

'Well, they can, because it's theirs.'

'We *need* it, Clo. We're going to starve to death, else. Look, they also eat dust and dead spiders, insects, beetles – anything they find. They won't starve on account of us.'

Alex said, 'Jordy's right. We're all hungry. We've got water. We need food.'

So they went and helped themselves to the crops, not knowing whether the plants were ripe or not. No one objected, even though they were watched. No one seemed to mind this blatant theft. They ate it, washing it down with water from the tanks. It was tasteless but it took the edge off their hunger. Of course, they still dreamed of cola and chips, and roast dinners, and curries.

'We could get into trouble for this,' said Chloe, feeling guilty once she was fed. 'It could be forbidden or something, among these people.'

Jordy sighed. 'We can't ask them. No one answers. Oh, come on, you two – look at them. They're docile. Even if they did get mad at us, what could they do to us? They're only little.'

'They look quite strong,' said Alex.

'Nah, we're all right. They're harmless creatures.'

'Have you heard them talk? Like doors creaking.'

'There are ghosts here.'

'I know, I've seen them.'

'They're stealing the crops. And they brought one of those mouse-killers with them. A three-cornered thing made of ginger. Savage. It's stealing our cattle.'

'What can you do? They're ghosts.'

Two villagers stand with their arms folded outside a hut, watching the three ghosts pick at their spindly plants. One is a stocky male wearing a blue shapeless frock and a top hat. The other is his sister who has on a boiler suit with a football fan's scarf for a belt. On her head she has a military officer's peaked cap with a feather stuck in the hatband. The male has on odd socks and old leather sandals with the stitching coming loose. His sister is wearing Wellington boots with the toes cut out for freedom of movement.

'We could try exorcising them. It's been done before.'

'Messy business though. All that blood.'

'Well, it's that or let them run wild.'

'They'll be gone in a day or two – they always are.'

'I wonder why they haunt us like this?'

The male villager with the lump over one eye shrugs his shoulders.

'They're lost between worlds. Poor wandering souls.'

'They're certainly ugly. D'you think it's something they did in life? Something bad?'

'Who knows? Perhaps.'

'I think we should exorcise them.'

'So you said, but are you going to clear up the gore?'

His sister is silent at this suggestion. She does not want the ceremony either. Most children in the village have never seen an exorcism but she remembers one from her young days. Above all, it had been a noisy affair. She remembers the noise. The ghost had screamed a lot. It had opened its mouth and horrible sounds issued from between its teeth. She remembers its teeth very vividly. And the red tongue quivering inside its mouth. That ghost had had a very large mouth which had contained a lot of noise. Then there was the struggling, the violent jerking, and at the very end of the ceremony, the twitching. A lot of mess though, as her brother had remarked.

'Do you think they want some of those books? With the pictures in them? We have some your cousin once found in the region from which these three emerged. Shall we give them to the ghosts?'

Her brother lifts his tall battered hat and wipes some plaster dust off his bald head with a dirty tea towel he carries in his pocket.

'With pictures of other ghosts?'

'That's what they often come looking for.'

'You could be right. We should put them out, where they can find them.'

'That's what we'll do then. I'll bring it up at the council meeting.'

'Good.'

'Yes, good. We probably won't need knives after all.'

# CHAPTER 4

# Board-combers into Bundles

It seemed the villagers had put a pile of photograph albums purposely where the three could find them. Chloe leafed through a couple of them, but of course they meant nothing to her. They were mostly black-and-white photos, many out of focus and misty. A lot of the people in them wore suits, or full dresses. Others were in uniform. A great many of the subjects had obviously posed for the photo. These were pictures from the beginning and middle of the last century. They were from old wars, one of which Mr Grantham had fought in. To Chloe they were ancient history.

Those pictures which had no human subjects were of totally unrecognisable landscapes. Foggy, dark mountains. Dense, dark forests. Bleak, cold-looking, dark oceans. Why anyone would want to take a picture of such uninteresting scenes was a mystery to Chloe.

Then suddenly she came across one which, when she opened it, had 'Property of Susan Atkins' written inside.

Susan? That was the name of Mr Grantham's fiancée. But there must have been a million Susans out there, past and present. It was unlikely to be Mr Grantham's Susan.

However, the album was small and would fit easily into the bag Chloe was now carrying. It was light too. She would take it back and – if they ever got out of here – show it to Mr Grantham.

Alex was in the process of stopping a villager in a sewing-machine car. The driver jumped out and ran away on being confronted by the boy. Alex then went down on his knees to inspect the vehicle. Chloe showed him the album and asked him what he thought.

'Those old photos were probably taken with Brownie box cameras,' he said to his sister as he wobbled a pedal made of cast iron, pushing it down to see how the gears worked which eventually turned the wheels. 'I saw one once in a backstreet shop. Those places are probably not as bad as they look. It's just that the cameras weren't that good.'

'How come you always think you know so much?' said Jordy, joining them. 'Smarty.'

Alex said, 'Only about things like this.' He spun the governor wheel of the sewing-machine car, so that an armature whirred rapidly. 'When this sewed dresses and things, that was the arm that made the needle go up and down. Now it gives this vehicle its forward motion.'

Jordy grunted. 'He talks like a robot. He *is* a robot.'

'You leave him alone,' Chloe defended her brother.

Jordy was about to protest that he didn't mean anything by it, when he noticed a movement coming from the wardrobe village. A lot of the stumpy, thick-chested inhabitants had gathered under a rafter and were muttering and pointing towards the trio. It seemed they had weapons in their hands: hockey sticks and cricket bats. Some even had long knives, the edges of which glinted wickedly. They began to move towards them and Jordy felt a sort of hard lump in his throat and a panicky feeling in his stomach.

'Uh-oh, trouble,' he said, trying to keep his tone even. 'We might have to make a run for it.'

'What's upset them?' asked Chloe, seeing the mob. 'Why are they doing this now?'

Jordy said, 'I dunno, but they're cutting off our retreat. Maybe it was you, messing around with their photo albums.'

Alex had moved away from the sewing-machine car now.

'Maybe it's because you stole some of their food and drank from their umbrellas without asking,' he said.

'Or because you nicked one of their cars,' riposted Jordy, 'and started taking it to bits.'

Chloe cried, 'Stop arguing. They're still coming.'

The villagers were indeed in an ugly mood. They were making low grating sounds in the back of their throats. It was an eerie noise which scared the three children, who began to back away into a corner, towards the edge of the attic. They were not used to violence, even though Jordy had done karate at one time, and had boxed a little. They were kids who came from neighbourhoods where things were settled with words rather than weapons. Alex and Chloe, especially, were beginning to get very frightened. Jordy put on a brave front, but he too felt the terror of the moment.

Just when it seemed the villagers were about to fall on them and start beating them, a bugle sounded from afar in the attic. There were startled looks on the faces of the advancing locals. They stopped dead in their tracks. One of them shouted something. They all began running back to their wardrobes where they took up stances of defence, as if they expected an attack.

Sure enough, out of the dusty columns of light came another set of villagers, all swishing golf clubs. They were also bearing makeshift shields: lids of cooking pots and dustbins. This group were generally thinner and less robust than the wardrobe people: they had a willowy appearance to them. They were just as bald, however, and carried just as much plaster dust on them, and had a similar number of lumps on their skulls.

The two groups stood about twenty metres apart and began to yell and wave their weapons at their adversaries, obviously each daring the other to come forward. Finally both sides rushed together and began striking their opponents with their various clubs. In the confusion the three children were forgotten. Chloe, Jordy and Alex made off as quickly as they could, running out into the wide open area of the attic, anxious to be gone once the combatants had finished their fight.

As well as Chloe's bag they took with them a backpack they had found, filled with edible plants they had taken from the hydroponics beds. The 'food' was quite light, even when crushed down, and the boys took turns in carrying the backpack. With Chloe's water bottle they were prepared for another trek across the attic. All of them had their particular cravings, of course: with Chloe it was chocolate; chicken tikka masala for Jordy; hamburger and chips with Alex. The vegetables they had to eat were nourishing and kept them alive, though they were hardly enjoyable.

But at least they wouldn't starve to death.

Jordy could hear the sound of hockey stick on dustbin lid for quite a while, before the noise of battle faded away behind them.

After half a morning's walk they came across another village, which Chloe called 'the wash-tub village' where the inhabitants obviously curled up in wooden tubs to go to sleep. They passed one or two tubs in which village children were resting, coiled neatly round like a length of rope on the deck of a sailing ship. It was possibly part of the reason why the wash-tub villagers were so lean.

Here there were no sewing-machine cars, but old golf trolleys propelled – or rather, yanked rapidly forward – by casting with a fishing rod, catching the fishing hook in a plank or rafter, and winding in the slack. This transport was not so efficient as the sewing-machine cars, but there was less to go wrong. The drivers sat astride the golf bag attached to the trolley, and balanced it on its two wheels with tremendous skill. When they reached the end of their lines they removed their hooks from the wood with sets of what looked like long-handled pliers.

The children watched enthralled as some of the villagers – obviously those who had chosen not to go to war with their fellows – were engaged in casting huge distances with heavy lead weights. They stared as the drivers then reeled in the line with astonishing speed, thus covering a great distance in a very short time.

'We should try that,' Jordy said. 'Better than walking.'

'The skill required,' Alex pointed out, 'must take years to acquire.'

The children passed by the village warily, encountering the same strange looks they had been used to with the wardrobe people. Not wanting to antagonise the wash-tubbers as well, they thought it best to get out of the area as quickly as possible. It seemed easy to upset these people, especially when you didn't know what was expected of you. As Chloe pointed out, this was an unknown culture. They might well have been Marco Polos, travelling through China in a bygone century.

'These people are probably from abroad,' said Chloe, warming to Jordy's theory that 'travellers' had been allowed to use the attic of the house below during inclement weather, 'with a culture quite different from ours. We must have done something that was insulting to them, in some way, without realising it. That's what's upsetting them.'

Jordy said, 'Never mind them, have you seen any trap-doors lately?'

'I haven't seen a trapdoor since we left the forest,' replied Alex. 'Not since you mentioned your watch was going backwards.'

It was true: the long and level boards stretched far away, both behind them and ahead, with not a trapdoor to be seen. The long lean boards were light-grey with age, like flattened days, and seemed endless. It was as if infinity had been pieced together and placed before them, to become eternity. Time and place were one, a single entity. The grey days were planks, the grey planks were days. A whole section of boards made a month. Several sections were a year. A region turned into a century. A cluster of regions became a millennium. Square supporting timbers embedded in the millennia, beams and rafters, angled buttresses held up a whole history and prehistory, time on the shoulders of place, until the millions of plank-days, plank-months, plank-years curved away into unknown futures and pasts.

'We must come to the end of the attic *soon*,' muttered Jordy. 'Even if we've got a furniture warehouse below us. I mean, I've seen them from the motorway, these big storage depots, and they're massive. How we managed to wander from our house into one of those I don't know, but that's what it's got to be. Maybe there was an industrial estate behind the trees of our back garden? I haven't looked properly, have you?'

The other two didn't answer him.

He had to admit to himself that the horizons stretched far and wide on all sides, vanishing into the gloom of recessed corners and niches. Above them there was a sky full of triangulated rafters, and high, high above the rafters the occasional dirty square sun which let in the light of the outside world. Bright golden light full of golden flecks of dust. Magical really. To Jordy they looked like teleportation shafts that could transport you to a golden world, but of course when he stood in one nothing happened. They were just sunlight and dancing dust motes piercing the gloom.

He had to admit his warehouse theory was unlikely too. Were the largest warehouse in Britain below them, it was improbable that it could support such a huge attic. Yet Jordy reminded himself that, when you were in a house without furniture, an open space such as one might find in the attic of a massive storage depot, it always *appeared* bigger than it was.

Yet wherever he looked, there appeared to be no end to this attic: it seemed to go on for ever.

Moving out on to the wooden-plank plain, beyond the villages, Jordy, Chloe and Alex left the edges of the attic for the central desert. Here previous wanderers had placed upside-down umbrellas and parasols, open to the heavens, their spikes in the cracks between planks. These seemed to be situated under leaks from the roof, which dripped into their 'bowls' whenever it rained in the real world outside. Thus the children had the benefit of these oases, as they crossed the flat, wooden, arid areas of the attic, where even the spiders were scarce. Occasionally, above them, a bat flew in the darker regions, flashing across one of the dirty skylight windows. On the floor were some beetles on their backs, having fallen from a great height somewhere up in the sloping lanes of the roof.

Jordy said, 'I wonder what this place is called?'

'Attica,' said Chloe. 'I call it Attica.'

When she received no reply, she added, 'The word "attic" comes from Attica, a region in Ancient Greece. Athens was the capital.'

'You're such a damn swot,' grumbled Jordy.

'No, I just like literature and language. I'm not as clever at science, maths and geography as you two. Well, maybe science, but not geography. At least, not the geography of the modern world. I'm better at the geography of the classical world.'

'All right, all right,' grumbled Jordy. 'You're better at everything. Who cares right now? We're lost. Can you make a compass with your bare hands? No. Can you draw me an accurate map of where we've been? Some things you're good at and some things I'm good at.'

Chloe did not want to quarrel so she let this go, even though she was sure Jordy could do neither of those things.

Once or twice they ran into impassable hedges, consisting of mangled wire coat hangers twisted together into an impossible mass. Some of these barriers were more than two metres high and almost two kilometres wide, with no gaps in their twisted entanglements, just a torn rag or two to attest to victims who had tried to get through. There was no way over these metal hedges, whose glinting wicked hooks clawed at their clothing much as the thorns of African bushes might do.

To Chloe this was indeed the crossing of a continent fraught with unnatural dangers and hazards. She still had the feeling they were being followed and she often spun round, hoping to catch the creature who pursued them, only to find perhaps a lump or two on the horizon, but nothing that moved. All was motionless. Even the dust lay unmolested like a fine covering of tawny flour upon the ancient planks. The scene before them, and behind them, was almost holy in its silence and stillness.

Now that she knew there were people here like the Atticans, who could do them harm, she was especially vigilant. Who knew what beings might come at them out of the far reaches of the gloom? Now they had met with life of a kind, anything might be possible. Expect the unexpected.

'What's that, in the distance?' said Jordy, pausing to take a drink from an oasis umbrella. 'Can you make it out?'

Alex and Chloe peered into the gloaming of their twilight world. There seemed to be hills ahead, gentle at first, but rising to a monstrous-looking mountain. Visible in the haze of sunlight which came through chinks and cracks in the roof, they saw that the hills were fashioned from heaps of chairs, and others of sports equipment, but the mountain itself appeared to consist entirely of rusty weapons of war.

On this formidable vastness of dark metal they could make out old corroded guns, their muzzles like thousands of small black mouths jutting from the upper crags; rusty bayonets and swords which stood out as vicious spikes on the lower ridges to impede any climber; slippery helmets forming slopes of dangerously loose scree. The whole mountain exuded menace, forbidding and hateful, dominating the scene ahead. It rose to impossible heights far up into the arrowhead shape of the roof, higher than the bats flew, higher than the light from lower windows. Up, up into the impenetrable darkness of unbreathable space. There its peak no doubt shaved the topmost rafter of the roof with its pointed blade.

'Have we got to climb *that*?' asked Alex, in hushed tones.

'Dunno,' said Jordy. 'We'll find out when we get there. Could be we've found our way into a government storage place, where the army keeps all its old weapons. I mean, government buildings are massive, aren't they? And you never get to see how big, because they won't let you on their sites.' His next question was almost a pathetic plea for support. 'Did anyone see one near our house, any-where?'

Neither Chloe nor Alex saw the point in answering.

Chloe had not felt so helpless since that time at school when she was on what her teacher Mrs Erland had called 'expedition training'. They had gone to Scotland, to the Highlands, to learn orienteering with maps and compasses. Chloe and her friend had set out, each with one of those items, and they had been separated by fog. Thus, though Chloe had the map, she had no compass, and the fog had prevented her from seeing the sun or stars, so she had absolutely no idea which way to go. Fortunately she had had her sleeping bag and its waterproof cover with her, and some provisions. She was eventually rescued by a search party.

All the feelings she had experienced during that incident in Scotland came flooding back to her now. Not just a sense of helplessness, but varying degrees of anger directed both at herself and others.

Jordy seemed to have rallied his own strength of spirit and asked, 'You OK, Clo? You look a bit down. Don't worry about that old mountain up ahead – we'll probably find a way round it.'

'Oh, I'm not worried, Jordy.'

'How about you, big buddy?' cried Jordy heartily, put-ting an arm round Alex's shoulders. 'You OK?'

'Couldn't be better,' murmured Alex, without convic-tion. 'Happy as a kookaburra. Hey!' His voice brightened and he pointed. 'There's Nelson, out there on the horizon.'

There indeed was the chubby princely shape of Nelson, rolling along on his three pins as if he were still at home. Nelson was a cheering sight to the three chil-dren. The familiar figure barrelled along seemingly unconcerned by the plight he was in. He had something in his mouth.

'Nelson! Nelson!' called Chloe.

The ginger tom saw the children and came to them. He dropped a dead mouse at their feet.

'Oh, Nelson,' said Chloe softly, in admonishment.

All his life Nelson had been bringing his human friends such gifts. But were they pleased? Not a bit. Never. Often, they were annoyed. There was no fathoming such ingratitude. But he still kept trying.

He allowed himself to be fussed and stroked with such affection as he had never known before then, seeing that his gift had been spurned, he picked it up again and wandered off into the gloom. It seemed so normal to the children, to see their cat rolling along without a care, that they too took heart.

Jordy especially felt that, as the eldest, he ought to show a bit of leadership. Leaders, according to the captain of the cadets he used to belong to when he and his dad were on their own, do not reveal any private concerns to their followers. Leaders show a granite jaw and talk tough. They share the problems, but not their worries. It was one thing having three heads to sort out an obstacle, but another to lay one's fears on the shoulders of the rest of the group. Things were not *desperate*, he kept telling himself, only *matters for concern*. If they all stuck together, and used their common sense, they would come out of their travels unscathed.

So far they hadn't found a single watch, which told Jordy something about their search. It seemed to him that the watches must all be gathered in one place, just like the war weapons ahead of them. There must be a hill of watches somewhere, which would make their search easier, he felt. After all, to look for one watch, which might be hidden anywhere, was daunting. Looking for a whole sparkling hill of watches, then sorting through them for the one they wanted, seemed a much easier task.

'What's that?' he cried, alarmed, as he saw something out of the corner of his eye. 'Over there!'

But when the other two followed his pointing finger, all they could see was a bundle of rags under a feather-boa tree. Chloe took her list of books from her pocket. It comforted her to see how many fantasy novels there were on it and to recall how many of them ended happily.

'If I find something to write with – and on,' she told herself, 'I'll transfer the list, maybe update it, on a better bit of paper.'

'What?' asks the bat. 'Come on, spit it out.'

*We ought to warn them*, says the masked board-comber. *We ought to tell them to beware of Katerfelto.*

'You need to protect the girl, is that it? You think she's got a map in her pocket, don't you?'

*She does keep looking at that piece of paper.*

'It might be a shopping list. A tin of boot polish. A dozen eggs. That sort of thing.'

*I think it's a map.*

'That still doesn't mean there's something in it for you. No one would have a map showing a cache of Eskimo ornaments, now, would they?'

*Inuit. You must call them Inuit. There could be lots of things*, mutters the board-comber, *which I could use to trade. Stage jewels. I know lots of board-combers who collect stage jewels. Porcelain figures. Stamps. Cigarette cards. If there's treasure on that map I want it.*

'You want? *You* want? That's a bit selfish, isn't it? What about those poor kids over there? They were nearly killed by those villagers, you know. Did you go and help them then? No. And why? Because you knew you could get the map afterwards, once they'd been murdered. If it's lost up the mountain, though, you'll never be able to get it, will you? You're terrified of Katerfelto.'

*So are you.*

'Yeah, well, I'm not after a map, so it doesn't count.'

The bat begins swinging back and forth on the board-comber's ear.

*Stop that.*

But the bat keeps on swinging.

When evening time comes round, the bat flies away on its usual jaunt to find food. The board-comber, in a heap by an ostrich-feather shrub, watches the children from beneath the brim of his hat. He watches and he watches. When he hears slumber, when he sees slumber, he crawls from his outer clothes as if they were a snail shell. They are left behind. Once or twice, perhaps it is practice, he darts back again, quick as a rat, into the clothes. However, the children really are asleep and besides now it's so dark only a wolf or a bat could see him. He slithers and slides until but a metre or two from the sleeping forms. There he writes in the dust. Then he shoots back again, flashing through the darkness, to enter his coats.

'Did you enjoy that? Your trip out?'

*Wha— you back, are you?*

'Yup, full of insects.'

*No burping to prove it.*

'Wouldn't dream of such bad manners.'

*Yes, well, I know you.*

'And I know you, mine host. Here, lend me your ear, I come to bury my claws, not to prise them. The evil that men do lives after them . . .'

*Quiet, I need to sleep.*

'Did you warn the children?'

*I left a message — messages.*

'Uh-oh, you couldn't resist, could you?'

*What?*

'Asking them about the map.'

*No, no – I never asked them about a map. I simply asked if they knew about any stamps or coins.*

'Same thing. Same thing, old host. Now you'll have them looking in every trunk, under every pile of books, for treasure – you realise that?'

*Why should they?*

'Because children are like combers: they collect things, especially if they think they're valuable. You should know. You were one once. Maybe you're still one, how would I know? I'm just a bat.'

*I'm going to sleep.*

'All right, you sleep, I'll keep watch.'

*What for?* asks the board-comber, looking round nervously into the pitch-black darkness.

'You know.'

The board-comber shudders involuntarily, as he remembers that the Removal Firm could be near. While he has no particular reason to worry, he fears he may have done something wrong without realising he has transgressed. The Removal Firm do not listen to reasoning or excuses: they act on their belief in a creature's guilt.

'Hey, have you seen this?' cried Alex, on his way back to the others from a drinking umbrella.

'What?' asked Chloe, not very interested, thinking it might be an old steam-engine toy or something of that nature.

'It's a word, written in the dust.'

'What does it say?'

'Something about Kate somebody.'

'It's probably spider tracks.'

'No,' said Alex firmly, 'it's a word all right. Here, I'll show you. Look.' He pointed.

'That says "Katerfelto". That's not a word, is it?'

'I dunno. Look, here's some more. "Any stamps? Any coins?"'

This made Jordy come over and look.

'Cool,' he said, 'Attican graffiti. Stamps and coins. Hey, that *would* be something, gang. Treasure indeed. I once heard a man found an envelope in his attic which had a stamp worth thousands. Mauritius stamp, I think. He was an East German and very poor, so it meant a lot to him.'

Chloe said, 'It would mean a lot to anyone, that amount.'

'And coins!' crowed Alex. 'There must be coins up here. Old war medals. This could turn out to be a treasure hunt. We could be rich.'

'Well,' Jordy said practically, 'first we have to find Mr Grantham's watch.'

'That's true,' agreed Chloe. 'But picking up treasure on the way can't do any harm.'

The two older children had forgotten completely about the first word etched in the dust: *Katerfelto*. It was overlooked in the excitement of realising they were in a potential Aladdin's Cave. Their minds were now tuned to seeking stamps and coins. They scoured the floor with their eyes, looking for the glint of bright gold, burnished silver. Or the dirty yellow of ancient paper envelopes, perhaps held together by a rotting rubber band. This was an adventure to lift the spirits!

On then, into the sunlit-shafted world of Attica, like three lost mice within the walls of an enormous castle. At noon a dust storm rose, seemingly from a single powerful draught coming from the direction of the mountain. The grey choking motes were blown from the boards and from the cracks between, into a thick blizzard. The children tied handkerchiefs around their mouths and noses, but still the dust got into their lungs. There were cobwebs flying about too, and the light airy bodies of dead spiders, along with threads of cotton. They stumbled forward, there being nowhere to take cover, into the blinding, choking storm that threatened to suffocate them.

When they were just about exhausted they came across a deserted Attican village, the huts of which were old cupboards. Each of the children found one and crawled inside, closing the doors. Outside, the storm continued to rage for quite a while, until it finally abated and they were able to come out of their dark holes and into the dim and gloomy light. Stillness reigned now. And they were unharmed. Perhaps not safe, for they wondered where the villagers were, who once lived in these abandoned homes.

Yet no one came, after the storm had gone, and they assumed they were in a ghost village, a ruined place, long since evacuated for some reason. It stood in the shadow of the great mountain and Chloe could feel the sadness there, in the woodwork of the cabinets and cupboards, in the piles of junk that littered the floor between the huts. Someone had once loved this village enough to decorate it with gardens of silver candelabras overhung with artificial waterfalls of crystal chandeliers. The cut-glass 'jewels' and 'gems' on the chandeliers shone like diamonds in the spears of sunlight. The candlesticks and candelabras glistened like silver flowers in their beds below these hanging wonders. Yet there were no owners to appreciate their beauty.

Where, thought Chloe, had the people gone?

'Deserted!' stated Jordy, as if his decision was based on a long scientific study. 'Not a soul around.'

'Well, *duh*,' Alex scoffed. 'Maybe they were massacred?'

'Who by?' snapped Chloe, who was already feeling

nervous, having sensed that a horrible deed had taken place here.

Alex did not like to upset his sister. He shrugged, 'Who knows? Some other tribe, maybe. I don't know.'

'Attican wolves,' Jordy said. 'I heard them last night.'

Chloe shook her head firmly. 'That was just the wind, howling round the eaves of the house. No, no – one thing we haven't seen is live animals up here. Not if you don't count the bats and insects. This is a strange world and getting stranger the deeper we go, but one thing you can count on, I reckon, is that it won't be like the outside world.'

'There are no wolves in Britain.'

'Yes, there are,' she replied firmly. 'In zoos and game parks. And the outside world isn't just Britain, it's everywhere. There are still wolves up in Alaska.'

'Well, we'll see,' said Jordy, still not willing to give ground. 'We'll just see. Something killed them off, that's for sure.'

'Or simply chased them away,' Alex said, sorry that he had raised this issue now that Jordy and Chloe were going at each other. 'Maybe it was disease or something.'

All three then looked at their hands in horror.

'Don't touch anything,' muttered Chloe, wiping her palms on her jeans. 'Don't lick your fingers.'

Alex said, 'Who licks their fingers?'

'You bite your nails,' remarked Jordy. 'I've seen you.'

They found the nearest water umbrella and washed their hands thoroughly. Chloe would have liked a bath, but she knew that wasn't possible unless they came across another water tank. She stared at the vacated village while the other two washed. If they had all been killed, or died of disease, there would be bodies. She could see no corpses. Then there was Jordy's theory of wolves. Perhaps not wolves, but something else, something like a monster made of old kitchen sinks with washtap teeth and plugholes for eyes? Something like that would surely swallow the villagers whole and leave no trace.

Alex had gone to sit on a pile of books to inspect his fingernails.

'Now you've gone and mentioned it,' he complained to Jordy, 'I really want to bite them. I didn't before.'

'Mental reaction,' said Jordy, joining him. 'Now if I said "Liquorice Allsorts" what do you want to do now?'

'Bite my fingernails.'

Chloe sat down next to her brother, then reached into her bag for the bottle of water she carried. On yanking it out she caught the photo album by a silken cord which hung from its spine. The album flew through the air and hit one of the cupboards, bursting open. The sepia-brown prints inside fell out, the glue of their photo corners long since having lost its stickiness. They floated to the floor like autumn leaves to gather at the feet of the children. Alex laughed and kicked them, to see them raised in a cloud again, and settle once more. Some of them fell face down, others on their backs. Suddenly Chloe darted forward and picked one up, reading the words written on the reverse of the photo.

'*Lance-Corporal John Grantham*,' she cried. 'Look!'

She turned the photograph over and there, not plain to see but since they knew who it was they could recognise him, was a very young unsmiling Mr Grantham. He was wearing a peaked cap and was in uniform, proudly displaying a single stripe on the sleeve. He was sort of half-sitting, looking slightly over one shoulder. The uniform looked unsullied and the photo, Chloe guessed, had been taken before he left England for the war in foreign places.

They picked up some of the other photos and began

poring over them. A great many of them were of people Chloe did not recognise: older people in very old-fashioned boots, suits and shapeless frocks. Some of them were of Mr Grantham. There were several of him standing with a pretty young woman in a polka-dot frock. They guessed this was Susan. She looked happy, being helped over a stile in a meadow by a grinning John Grantham in baggy trousers and sleeveless jumper with zig-zag stripes. There was a dog there too, a mongrel by the looks of the startled beast, caught playfully grabbing a trouser turnup.

Jordy was looking puzzled.

'What?' asked Chloe. 'Come on, tell.'

'Well,' he said, looking at the photo he was holding, 'it's all a bit of a coincidence, isn't it?'

Chloe shrugged.

They were interrupted by a yell from Alex, which sounded very much like a cry of triumph.

'What about this then, eh?' he said. He waved something whitish, a piece of paper. 'What about this!'

# CHAPTER 5

# Quest for the Golden Bureau

Alex had found a letter, still sealed in its envelope, tucked between the pages of the album. He looked at the date where it had been franked.

'The stamp must be rare. This letter's from the nineteen forties.'

Chloe said, 'That doesn't automatically make it valuable. Depends on how many were printed, doesn't it? Let me see.'

Chloe took the letter and studied the stamp, but she was no expert and had no more idea than her brother. However, one thing struck her as strange about the stamp. On it and around it were several different frank marks. It had been franked in three different countries. By the look of it the letter had never been opened. The address on the front was L/Cpl J. Grantham, Stalag 21, Scheinfeld, Germany. Turning it over she saw scrawled on the back: Addressee not found – returned to sender.

'This is a letter to Mr Grantham,' she said wonderingly. 'Look how yellow the paper is.'

'Never mind the paper, what about the stamp?' asked Alex impatiently. 'Is it valuable, sis?'

'Don't know,' she said. 'What's a Stalag?'

'Prisoner-of-war camp in Germany,' replied Jordy promptly. 'The trouble with you is you don't watch war films. *Stalag 17.* There's this officer in it, who escapes—'

'Please,' groaned Chloe. 'When you go on about war films or Westerns you never stop. The point is, this letter is in Susan's album. She must have written to Mr Grantham after he was captured by the Germans, but he never got the letter. Maybe he moved camps or something, but it was sent back, probably through the Red Cross in Switzerland. Maybe when she got this back unopened she thought he was dead.'

'I bet the stamp's worth a lot,' said Alex.

Jordy snatched the letter from Chloe and to her horror he tore it open and took out two sheets of writing paper.

'Jordy! You can't do that,' she cried, reaching for it.

'Why not?'

'You might have damaged the stamp,' said Alex, equally incensed with Jordy. 'Just ripping it open like that.'

Jordy ignored his step-brother. 'Clo,' he said, 'this letter is something like sixty years old and it would have stayed here for another sixty if we hadn't found it. We'll give it to Mr Grantham if and when we get out of here, but it may contain some clues to finding the watch. You never know. I'm willing to try everything and anything to find my way back, aren't you?'

Chloe saw the sense in Jordy's general argument.

'Leave no stone unturned,' stated Jordy, 'that's my motto.'

'Or rather no letter unopened,' muttered Alex. 'Well, go on, read it then. See what it says.'

Jordy started reading it silently, but after a few lines he handed it to Chloe.

'Here, you'd better read it. It's a bit too mushy for me. Girls read these things better than boys.'

Chloe took the letter and, despite her feelings about the invasion of Mr Grantham's privacy, read it out in a quiet, moving voice. The written words spoke of the writer's deep love for her fiancé John, saying she would rather die than hurt him. But the fact was her elderly mother was very ill and needed a lot of medical care which was expensive. Susan pleaded with John to forgive her, but circumstances had forced her to marry an older man, a wealthy grocer, and they would all three be moving to Scotland. She ended the letter with the words, 'you know me, John, Im not so romantic as some people. Not so's it would mean me losing my mum. Life is hard and I have to be pratical and see to her no matter how it hurts me and does things to me. Arthur has found her a nursing home in a place where the air is good for her lungs and away from the bombs. Hes going to pay for her keep and buy us a cotage near to it. Hes a good man, though you will probably not think it and hate him.' The letter ended with more protestations, with a short description of the true state of her heart, and with several calls for forgiveness. Then it bluntly asked him to forget her and find another more worthy of his love. 'It wont be the same with Arthur but he cares for me and I cant do nothing else really. You do see what Im saying John? Please dont hate me for ever.'

Many of the words in the letter were blotched, no doubt by tears. Susan had been weeping when she wrote it.

Chloe blinked away the moisture in her own eyes after reading the letter, though deep down she wondered how Mr Grantham could possibly fall in love with someone whose grammar and spelling were so atrocious. But that was just Chloe. The love of *her* life would have to be perfect, but that didn't mean others necessarily needed to have the same standards.

'Well,' said an obviously unimpressed Jordy, 'she certainly dumped him all right, didn't she?'

Alex asked in a solemn voice, 'Is there an *exact* date on the letter? It might help with the stamp, you see. The franking's a bit smudged.'

'You two have no souls,' complained Chloe, folding the letter and handing it back to Alex.

'Oh, come on, Clo,' cried Jordy. 'It was half a century ago.'

'Love is eternal.'

'Yuk!' said Alex, stuffing the letter in his jeans pocket. 'Anyway, why'd she marry this other bloke to pay for her mother's doctors? National Health's free.'

'There was no such thing then,' Chloe said. 'No National Health. You had to pay for medical treatment in those days.'

Chloe turned from her brothers and gathered up the photos, putting them in her bag. Then the three sat down to talk of their plans. There was a massive mountain of weapons in front of them, which was going to be difficult to cross. Jordy suggested that one of them – he meant himself – should do 'a reccy' first, before all three of them went any further.

'I'll go and see how hard it's going to be. You two stay here in the village and wait for me.' He scanned the distance. 'Shouldn't take too long. I'll be back before you know it.'

'I don't like us splitting up,' stated Chloe emphatically. 'Anything could happen.'

'We're not splitting up. I'm just going to scout ahead. Look, it makes sense for you to stay here, near to food and water. There's some old hydro-whatsit beds at the back of the village and their supply tank is nearby. You'll be fine until I get back.'

'We'll be fine,' said Alex, 'but what about you?'

Jordy let out a hollow laugh. 'Oh, don't you worry about me – I'll be all right.'

He took Chloe's water bottle and some food. Then he set out before there could be any more arguments. They watched him go, until he had climbed the mound of foot-stools. Once, an antique stool slid from under his heel and he almost went flying downwards. Another time he stepped on a satin-covered affair and his foot went right through it, making him scrape his knee. But eventually he reached the top of the hill where he turned and waved, to show them he was all right.

'We ought to pick up the next set of binoculars we find,' murmured Alex. 'They'd be useful.'

The two remaining children spent a desultory morning, mooching about, doing nothing in particular. Evening finally came, the light fading from the skylight windows above. The yellowed boards of the attic stretched out behind them: the mountain stood square and daunting before them. There was no sign of Jordy. They could see his tracks in the dust: clear footprints leading into the foothills.

'He said he'd be back quickly,' Chloe stated to her brother. 'Where is he?'

'Got held up, I suppose.'

'By what?'

Neither of them wanted to guess.

In the middle of the night, Chloe was wakened by a sound. She leapt to her feet and shone the torch. There, trapped in its beam was a bat, hanging from a nearby rafter. There was a pile of rags near it which Chloe did not recall having seen before. However, to her astonishment the bat seemed to speak to her in clear English.

'There's a map, you know.'

'What?' whispered Chloe, anxious not to wake Alex and scare him half to death with talking bats. 'What do you mean?'

'There's a map of this place. It'll have whatever it is you're looking for. If you give me *your* treasure map I'll tell you where it is.'

Chloe was puzzled.

'I haven't got a treasure map.'

'Yes you have, in your pocket. I seen you take it out. You're always looking at it.'

Chloe put her hand into her jeans pocket and found her list of favourite books. The sleepiness left her and her head began to clear. She realised that with a map there was a chance of discovering a place of watches. It was the best chance they had of finding Mr Grantham's watch. And here was a creature who knew where there was a map of Attica.

'Oh – oh, *this* map?'

'We could swop. I'm always – I mean, my master is always – trading things for things. It's how we get what we want. *You* want to find something. I can tell. And I want . . . well, never mind what I want. You haven't got any, I can see. But you might know where other things are which can be swopped for the things that I – no, that my master – wants.'

'I'm sure we could trade,' said Chloe, who had been taught by an elderly aunt how to drive a bargain. 'You tell me where the map is, and I'll give you *my* map.'

The bat hummed to itself for a while, then spoke again.

'I tell you what, lady. You give me *your* map and if it's treasure, then I'll tell you where my chart is.'

'Chart?'

'Chart, map, it doesn't matter what you call it. You need

charts to cross the seas. You need maps to cross the deserts. Chart-cum-map is what you want.'

'Seas and deserts? Is the attic really that big?' Chloe's heart sank for a moment.

'Really, really. Big and dreary!'

However, once she had absorbed the information – considered it was probably correct, for why would the bat lie? – Chloe remained firm. 'My list – my map – only when you tell me where to find yours.'

The bat hummed louder now, in an annoyed fashion, but Chloe was not afraid. When adversity calls, people either crumple or they find courage within themselves to rise above it. Chloe was definitely of the latter kind. Hope surged within her soul and filled her every vein and muscle. She told herself that to fall on the floor and cry was nothing short of pathetic. To stand up and look adversity in the eye, show it you were not made of clay, was the only way to survive.

'Listen, bat, or whatever you are, you have the choice. Tell me where to find the chart–map or get lost. And don't think of lying to me. I'll know whether you're telling the truth or not. My grandmother was a witch. She passed on some of her skills to me.'

'A witch?' chirped the bat in a higher tone. 'A proper witch?'

'As proper as you'll ever meet,' fibbed Chloe.

There followed a short period in which the bat seemed to have a conversation with itself in low inaudible tones. Alex flopped on to his back and started snoring. Chloe carefully turned him on to his side again so the air stopped whistling out of his nose and mouth. Finally the bat called to her again and told her it was a deal.

'The map,' it said, 'is to be found beyond the Jagged Mountain, in a writing bureau of lacquered gold of a most exquisite oriental design. However, the bureau is in the hands of ancient ink imps,' added the bat with a sinister note entering its voice. 'These imps, who live in the ink wells stored in the writing bureaux, are naturally very antagonistic towards humans. They have made weapons of pens with sharp brass nibs. The inks the imps come from were made in China a thousand years ago by sorcerers who dealt in magical texts. They are inks of many colours. The clerks of those old enchanters used them to draw maps of secret regions such as Xanadu, to sketch pictures of individual demons and devils, and to record their recipes of spells in characters unknown outside the books of the damned.'

'You're kidding me,' laughed Chloe softly. 'Ink imps?'

'Ink imps, talking bats, scoff all you want, lady – just remember I told you they're there. In this place—'

'I call it Attica.'

'Good name, lady. Well, let me warn you that in deepest Attica effigies have come to life. Those who were abused in the other world, where you come from, are naturally very mean and aggressive towards humans. Dolls, Guy Fawkes effigies, shop dummies, tatterdemalions, they'll attack you if they get the chance. If you don't want to believe me, I don't care.'

'Are you the one who wrote "Katerfelto" in the dust?'

'Might have been,' said the bat. 'Could have been.'

'What does it mean?'

The bat said, 'It's a name.'

'Whose name?'

'Katerfelto's, of course. Ah, you want to know who he is? Katerfelto is the monster who lives on the Jagged Mountain. He's made of bundles of shadows, tangled together like thick coarse hair. He can be as big and menacing as a thundercloud, or as small as a scuttling spider. If you face him he can do nothing but slink around and make menacing shapes, but if you run from him he'll chase you down and overcome you with a darkness as thick as the suffocating quicksand of a swamp. If he catches you and enfolds you with his darkness, you will never again see the light.'

Chloe shuddered. 'He sounds terrible.'

'He *is* terrible. Katerfelto is the King of Gloom, the Prince of Terror. If you fail to meet his eye you will choke on your own fright. You will run until you fall gasping on to the boards and there you will shake yourself to death. But since he is made of nothing but darkness and fear, he is therefore hollow. Those who stand in his path and refuse to be intimidated will not be daunted. However, it's not an easy thing to do, to look terror in the face, so don't think it is. No matter how empty his form really is, he appears grotesque and formidable, ready to swallow all those who oppose him. Such a cold and evil presence you have never experienced before in your life. Not at all easy to ignore or face up to with courage.'

'How did he come to be?'

'He was formed from the basest materials of the human emotions known as *hate* and *arrogance*, mixed with *love* – a love of power, those dregs of feelings from which wars spring. This ugly concoction, drawn from the weapons soaked in such emotions, emerged and became Katerfelto.

'Now,' said the bat sounding weary, 'where is my map?'

Chloe said, 'A deal is a deal.'

'Just put the map on the boards.'

She did as she was asked and the bat then gave her instructions on how to get to the place of the golden bureau.

'. . . and now go back to sleep.'

Chloe closed her eyes and after a while feigned sleep. A

little later she was alarmed to see a pile of clothes, topped by a wide-brimmed hat, sliding towards her. It stopped when it reached the piece of paper. A thin, white, bony arm shot out of the heap of rags and snatched the list, drawing it into the pile. Then the heap slid back again into the deep dark shadows at the edge of the village, under some low rafters. There was a muttering and a mumbling, as if the bat were talking to itself again, then finally a shriek which woke up her brother Alex, who sat bolt upright.

'What is it?' cried Alex. 'Is that a ghost?'

'It's all right,' replied Chloe, patting his back. 'It's only that pile of rags over there. The one with that funny mask on top.'

'Pile of rags?' Alex's eyes were wide and round. 'What pile of rags?'

The bat fluttered in the rafters.

'You – lady – you – cheated.'

'No,' replied Chloe calmly.

'Yes, you cheated. This is no map.'

'Oh yes it is. It's a map to knowledge. It's a map to other worlds, the worlds of fiction. It's a map to great literature.'

'Great literature?' scoffed the bat. '*Flat Stanley*?'

'*Flat Stanley* is highly original. It's for younger readers than me, of course, but I loved it when I was little. I couldn't have written it – could you?'

'I couldn't write a shopping list, but that doesn't make this a map.'

'It's all I have.'

'You'll regret this, lady.'

The heap slid away into the darkness and the bat followed shortly afterwards.

'Lady?' repeated Alex. 'What lady?'

'It meant me,' said Chloe. She hugged her knees. 'And

I've got some good news. I know where there's a map of Attica.'

Alex yawned and shook his head. 'Where?'

'Over there,' she replied vaguely, unwilling to tell her younger brother that there might be live and hostile ink imps waiting for them. Alex had an engineer's brain and engineers were not the most imaginative of people. At least, they were good inventors, but not good at believing in fantastical creatures. 'I'll show you in the morning.'

'Oh, all right, sis.' He yawned again and lay down. 'Did – did that bat really talk?'

But Chloe found she was too tired to answer and fell asleep.

The following morning a shaft of golden light struck Chloe in the face and she woke feeling dreadfully thirsty. Alex was already up and eating some of their stores. He offered her the bottle of water. She drank from it gratefully and then joined her brother at breakfast. They munched away, staring into the distance. There were slanted pillars of light all around them today, marching off like pylons into unknown regions. Obviously it was a very bright day in the outside world. Chinks and cracks in the roof also sent down smaller blade-like beams of light. It was as if Attica were a stage and the lighting manager had just arrived and turned on all the switches.

Chloe's eyes searched the area for signs of the bat and the heap of clothes, but they were both gone. After the encounter last night she was now ready to accept that they were in some strange world, rather than in the rogue attic of an ordinary warehouse or palace. She didn't know whether Alex would accept what she believed to be true, but she knew that it was best to let him come to his own conclusions in his own good time.

'Makes you feel a bit better,' she said, 'when it's sunny.'

'Yup,' agreed her brother. 'It do.'

However, the Jagged Mountain (as the bat had called it) remained very much shrouded in darkness. Jordy was still nowhere to be seen. Chloe was worried about him but she knew him to be a resourceful person – annoying when it came to books, but quite resolute and tough – and she knew he was no wimp. However, she and Alex could not wait around for ever and if Jordy didn't return before noon, she thought perhaps they ought to follow him.

Jordy did not return, despite anxious prayers from Chloe.

'Well,' she said, 'I suppose we'd better go and look for him.'

'What about Katerfelto?' asked Alex, looking nervously at the distant mountain. 'What shall we do about him?'

'If we run into him, we'll have to face up to him.'

Alex's Indian cousins, some being Hindus, had spoken to him about Shiva, the Moon-god of the mountains. There was some thought in Alex's head that perhaps this great god would protect them.

'All right,' he said to his sister. 'If you can face him, so can I.'

The pair prepared for the journey. Chloe found another bag, a backpack through the straps of which she slipped her arms. It was much easier to carry that way and it held both the torches as well as food and water. Thus by noon they were ready to leave. One more quick glance around the floor to see that they had all the photos which had fallen out of the album, then they were off towards the first of the foothills.

Instead of heading towards a hill of footstools, as Jordy had done, Alex and Chloe decided to try a different route.

# CHAPTER 6

# Pursued by Mad Mannequins

A strange light was coming from the valley ahead of them. There was one thick sunbeam bearing down from a skylight in the roof which struck the centre of the Vale of Mirrors. But this was reflected back and forth over a thousand thousand times. It went from dazzling brilliance in the first mirror, to a silvery-dull echo of a gleam in the last. All the shades of light between these two extremes were to be found in the valley.

'It's a very bright scene,' mused Alex. 'I wonder how much candle-power is in there?'

Chloe said, 'What candles?'

'Candle-power is a measure of luminosity,' replied Alex in a haughty tone, 'whatever the light source is. Didn't you know that?'

'No, and you knew I didn't, which was why you mentioned it.'

Alex smiled. 'Oh no, I wouldn't do that, sis. You know me . . .'

They entered the Vale of Mirrors, walking between two giant antique looking-glasses with ornate gilt frames. Even as they stepped into the gap that separated these two guardians of the valley Chloe realised this was no ordinary clutter of mirrors, which were there in a hundred varieties. Someone had collected these and brought them all to this place.

She said wondrously, 'Look how many . . .'

There were mirrors from dressing-tables with wooden frames; from wardrobes; from retail clothes shops. There were bevelled mirrors with silver chains; spherical mirrors from ballrooms; hand mirrors, bathroom mirrors; fairground mirrors. There were huge mirrors from stately homes; tiny mirrors from musical boxes; long, lean mirrors, short, fat mirrors, mirrors with the quicksilver peeling away. There were mirrors from Turkey, from Samarkand, from Chad, from Fiji, from New England, Venice and Shanghai. There was every mirror, every looking-glass, from all the kingdoms and republics that the world has ever known. They stood, lay, were stacked, were scattered, were shattered, were placed in every position thinkable. There were mirror pools and mirror doors and mirror portholes. You could drown in mirrors, you could float in mirrors, you could lose your soul in their reflective surfaces, you could go stark – staring – mad.

The two giant mirrors which were the pillars of the valley entrance seemed to lock Chloe in a dual embrace. The trouble was, she hesitated and stared into the one on the right, and saw Chloes curving away into infinity. It made her dizzy to see millions of herself on both sides, sweeping off into a netherland of space, growing imperceptibly smaller until she disappeared. She turned away but the one on the left was even worse, for she was upside-down and arcing away on her head into a distant greyish otherworld.

She tore her eyes away, saying to Alex behind her, 'Don't look!'

But of course, he did.

Once they had entered the vale it was even worse. She was everywhere. Alex was everywhere. When they moved, a hundred other Chloes and Alexes moved, all in different directions. Some of these copies were fairground-mirror images and they warped and distorted the originals. They mocked the children with their willowy forms, or their fat, toadish, lumpy shapes.

Once out of the fairground cluster it was even worse, for at least she knew the right from the wrong Chloe in those undulating surfaces. In the clear mirrors she lost count of the times she bumped into herself, walking straight into a reflective surface and striking her face. It was utterly confusing to have so many altered images all moving at the same time, so she began to wonder which was the real Chloe and which were the fakes.

'This is horrible,' she said to Alex. 'We have to get out of here.'

She turned to find Alex staring into a mirror which was not reflecting his form, but that of their living-room, back at the house. In this large mirror Dipa and Ben could be seen walking about, mouthing the names of the children, as if seeking them. When Alex let out a cry of anguish his parents looked out of the mirror at him, clearly not seeing him, but as if they had heard his yell and wondered where it came from.

'Don't stare at it,' ordered Chloe. 'It's lying. Don't let it fool you, Alex. There's no one behind it.'

Alex tore himself away, just as Chloe confronted a looking-glass in which there was a scene of herself as a little girl picking daisies on a hillside. She remembered the picnic, which had been several years ago. Then coming up behind her was her father – her real father, not Ben – who was laughing and waving from a patch of bright-red poppies.

There was her father, in the full flush of life, before he had died of his heart attack. His eyes were smiling, his skin was glowing in the sun and the wind, his hair flicking back and forth. His arms were stretched out to scoop her up, to cuddle her close to him.

'Daddy?' she yelled. 'Daddy, Daddy, Daddy.'

Chloe became hysterical with a mixture of misery and joy. She ran towards the mirror, clawed to get inside its duplicitous surface, to touch its deceptive reflections. She felt if she tried hard enough she could enter the silver pool and join her father. Then she felt Alex pulling her jersey, yanking her back. He was in tears, calling for her to stop.

'You told me not to look,' he accused her, shaking her roughly. 'Don't you look either.'

And so they did their best, even though aircraft zoomed at them firing cannons and shooting rockets. Even though ships lurched out of fog banks and bore down on them with wicked-looking bows. Knights charged out of misty marshlands, lances pointing at their breasts. Eagles flew, talons hooked and beaks glinting, straight at their faces. Monsters stalked them on every side: monsters bearing shapes of which they had never dreamed, with open slavering jaws and hands with finger-claws as long and spindly as the legs of a crayfish. There were hideous mouths full of needle teeth. Spooks and ghouls came, rising from cruddy graveyard earth. Frightening corpses with the rotten flesh dripping from their bones. The mirrors tried every trick they knew to bend the children's minds to their will.

'Don't worry, Alex,' said Chloe, gripping her younger brother's hand and pulling him along with her, 'we'll get out safe.'

'Someone's watching us,' he replied, looking round. 'I know they are. Someone's here.'

'No, you're imagining it – it's just us – and reflections of us.'

Alex was convinced there was someone there. Someone hiding at the backs of the mirrors, following them.

The way through was bewildering, being a path of mirror tiles on the ground and walls of mirrors for their avenues. They did not know whether they were going out or coming in, or walking in circles, or running mad. Several times they came across Atticans who looked as if they had been in the Vale of Mirrors for years. The faces of these distressed souls were locked in madness. Clearly their reason had flown long ago, for they simply wandered in and out of mirrored lanes and alleys, stumbling over their feet, seemingly hardly aware of where they were or what they did.

And of course these corridors of mirrors on either side of them continued to produce a multitude of images that sent both children spinning away in their minds, into a swirling whirlpool of Chloes and Alexes on a descent into the same kind of insanity which bedevilled other unwilling lost occupants of the Vale of Mirrors.

'My head's spinning,' said Alex. 'I feel sick.'

'So do I. You have to fight it.'

Finally Chloe looked up and found salvation.

'Alex,' she said. 'Look up there!'

Alex followed her gaze but could only see, high above them, a single rafter running the length of the heavens.

'What of it?' he said.

'Keep your eyes on that rafter, Alex, and just follow it. Don't worry if you bump into a mirror, don't look at it, just feel your way round it. So long as we stare at that rafter we won't be looking at reflections of ourselves. Walk carefully and slowly, so you don't hurt yourself. When you're aware of an obstacle in front of you, slide round it, but keep going in the direction of the rafter. Eventually it must lead us to the edge of the valley.'

This they did and blessedly found themselves out of the Vale of Mirrors and at the foot of Typewriter Hill.

Chloe felt immense relief wash through her.

'We're out. That was horrible, wasn't it?'

'It wasn't the best time I've had. Where are we now?' Alex looked around him. 'Oh, this should make you happy. Word machines.'

A great jumble of typewriters faced them. They were mostly old, heavy-looking instruments, but a few were portables. The latter were in light cases and had smarter-looking keys than the standard desk typewriters. Some machines had pages stuck under the platen roller, with their typewritten words still legible. Chloe read one or two of them.

Dear Mr Glubb,
You will note by the enclosed that your bank statement shows a deficit of seventeen pounds. We would greatly appreciate

Boring!

Hi Roger,
Bet you didn't expect to hear from me again! Well, here I am. Are you still going out with Jill, because I have no commitments at the moment. I know we had some bad

Intriguing, but the letter stopped after the word *bad*.

The next sheet Chloe read was the most fascinating of all. Like the two letter writers, the typist had simply stopped typing. The page remained in the machine and, like the others, the machine must have been put up in the loft without anyone having the interest to bother to remove the piece of typing paper. It seemed to be the start of a story.

### Chapter One

The night sky was full of stars. Suddenly one dropped, then another, and then two, three, five more, until stars were showering on the Earth, falling, falling like glittering hail (rain?). Walter Smelton (Smileton? Smuggleton?) looked up and a falling star struck him blind in his right (left?) eye

'Now that might have been a best seller,' murmured Chloe. 'I wonder what happened to the writer? Maybe she was attacked by a rival, just as she was about to astound the literary world.'

'How'd you know it was a *she*?' grumbled Alex. 'Could've been a bloke.'

'Blokes aren't sensitive enough to write about falling stars,' replied Chloe. 'You have to be a woman to appreciate beauty.'

'Load of tosh if you ask me.'

'I rest my case,' she said.

The pair of them began to climb the typewriters. It was not as easy as it had looked from the base of the hill. There were footholds and handgrips, sure, but there were also hollows which grabbed at their feet, clinging on to them with keys like fingers. Their bare hands were scratched and cut by the rough edges of the metal frames. Their clothes snagged on hooks. While the typewriters were locked fairly tightly together there was the odd landslip and when it did occur it was quite dangerous. If one of those heavy instruments had struck either Chloe or her brother it would have bowled them off their feet and sent them hurtling down to the ground below.

'Are we getting there?' gasped Alex, clawing at the typewriters, heaving himself upwards. 'It's getting steeper.'

Chloe turned her attention back to the hill. They were almost at the top now. She looked up, expecting to see the roof closer to them, but it was still miles above their heads.

Chloe offered Alex a drink of water, which he took gratefully.

She then had a drink herself.

Alex grinned.

'What?' she said.

'You don't wipe the bottle any more. Whenever Jordy or me took a drink before, you used to make a face and wipe the bottle before you drank from it yourself.'

'Well,' she said, sighing, 'that was when I was civilised.'

'What are you now? A savage?'

'Wild, like the animals,' she said.

'Wild and trapped, that's what we are. Animals in a zoo.'

Chloe agreed. 'Yes, and now we've got to get out.'

She began to descend the far side of Typewriter Hill, with Alex following her. It was more difficult going down than it had been going up. Any climber could have told her that would happen. It was all in the knees. The knees suffered on a descent. And that was usually when the climber was most fatigued, the muscles giving out, the legs wobbling.

However, they made it to the bottom and rested again.

Studying the great mountain ahead of them, Chloe was aware that there was still no sign of Jordy. Jordy had been gone now for quite a while. She knew that, while he was not the most sensitive boy in the world, he would not deliberately cause her anxiety. Wherever he was she was certain he would be trying to get back to her and Alex, knowing they would be getting frantic.

'I think I need a bit of a sleep now,' said her younger brother.

'Good idea,' replied Chloe, intending to stay wide awake. 'We need to get our strength back.'

Alex curled up on the bare boards and was soon asleep.

Chloe remained sitting upright, but soon her eyelids began to feel very heavy. Alex's steady breathing did nothing to help her stay awake. Soon she too was slumbering peacefully at the foot of Typewriter Hill.

Alex woke to find Chloe slumped over and snoring lightly. He smiled grimly, intending to tell her when she woke that she too made noises while she was asleep. But he realised his sister must have been quite tired to sleep so soundly, so he tip-toed away from her, intending to explore the surrounding area.

He soon found some cardboard boxes which looked worth investigating. Alex went to them and studied them for a while. He was not foolhardy enough to open them immediately. He had been in Attica long enough now to know that some unpleasant surprises were to be had for those who did not approach unopened boxes cautiously. However, after going around them he found the words Camping Equipment scrawled in permanent ink on the side of one of the boxes.

What a find! he thought to himself excitedly. They could use camping equipment all right.

Still he opened the first box with the thought in mind that a monster might leap out at him. He was ready to run at the first sign of danger. But he was pleased when nothing of the kind occurred. In fact, to his great delight the box was full of maps with a few compasses. Compasses! He took three. Now they could navigate their direction. No more looking up for rafters to guide them through rotten vales of mirrors. Now they would know north, south, east and west, and all the little points between.

The maps weren't much good. They were of places like the Lake District, the Yorkshire Dales, Scotland and Wales.

The next box, a much larger one, had in it three sleeping bags and a grubby tent. He didn't see a lot of use for tents. Sure, when it rained outside it dripped through the roof in places, but not badly enough to warrant the fag of erecting tents everywhere they went. The sleeping bags might be useful but they would have to carry them. There was a hiker's backpack in the same box, which Alex was happy to find and claim for his own.

The third and last one contained odds and ends. There was a pair of binoculars, brass ones, probably once belonging to a naval man. He kept those. There was a Swiss Army knife with lots of gadgets, such as a bottle opener, a pair of scissors and a tiny saw. He kept that also, hooking it to an old Boy Scout's belt which he looped around his waist. Finally, there was a small cooking stove with a solid fuel canister attached and a box of long-stemmed matches, the sort which go with such a stove.

'Wow!' he said. 'One cup of tea, coming up.' He paused before adding ruefully, 'If only we had some teabags.'

When he straightened up, with all his new equipment packed away in his new backpack, he found himself curiously surrounded.

'Where did they come from?' he said aloud. 'I didn't see them.'

Alex was referring to a group of mannequins – shop dummies – which were standing in different poses around him.

'Did you do that, Clo?' he called, laughing. 'Did you put these here while I was packing?'

No answer.

'Clo?'

One of the mannequins moved in a jerky fashion towards Alex. Startled, Alex ran forward and pushed it over. It fell to the floor, kicking and jerking its arms. It made no sound, for indeed it had no mouth. It was probably also blind, for it had no eyes either. It was a blank dummy without clothes: a nasty pale pink colour. (There were others of darker hue and some of pure white alabaster.) This one's joints were on swivels and when it fell to the boards it bounced and knocked its head the wrong way round.

Before he could gather his senses the other mannequins grabbed at Alex and held him fast in their stiff hands.

'Hey!' he cried, frightened out of his wits. 'Let me go.'

They ignored him. Their grim countenances stared blankly at him as if they could sense rather than see him. Their heads moved from side to side in a jerky fashion. Their arms and legs worked in the same way. But they held on to him with surprising strength. One of them helped the fallen comrade to its feet, then the mannequins marched their prisoner away, into the shadows beyond the place where Alex had found the boxes.

When Alex recovered his composure he found himself tied to one of those sturdy pillars which held up the roof. Around him were shoe boxes stacked neatly into walls and racks of clothes that acted as screens between what appeared to be private areas where the mannequins lived.

They came out of their dwellings to see the captured castaway: most were whole but there were some with missing limbs or, even more bizarre, missing heads. All of them, without exception, were as bald as billiard balls. They kept fingering Alex's mop of thick black hair, running their cold hard fingers through the curls.

'You leave me alone,' he cried. 'You'll be sorry.'

They stared at him silently. Here was one of those who had kept them as slaves when they had been shop dummies. In those far-off days they had been forced to wear clothes they detested and made to stand in windows while they were ogled and gawped at by humans. Now when they caught one of those mortals they made them suffer the same kind of humiliation. They dressed them in hideous fashion garments, designed by people with flyaway minds, and made of uncomfortable fabrics. The colours were flamboyant, the buttons, zips, hooks and eyes, next to bare flesh. They put on them shoes that were either too big, or too small. They arranged them in unlikely groups, so they looked like a bunch of badly dressed fools on an outing.

Alex struggled wildly as they forced him into such clothes.

'You – rotten – beggars!' he yelled. 'You wait until my sister gets here. She'll kick your backsides for you, you – dummies.'

He grabbed an arm and, without meaning to, wrenched it from its socket. Everyone stopped, seemingly shocked by his action. Alex stood there in a floppy hat with a ribbon and wearing a loose ankle-length frock with a price tag dangling from the collar. He was holding the lone detached arm. After a few minutes of stunned silence he offered it to the owner, who snatched it back with their other limb. There were a few awkward moments while mannequins crowded round and assisted in getting the arm back into its owner's socket, then they started on Alex once more.

Once he was dressed, Alex was again strapped to the support pillar in the middle of the village. The mannequins paraded round him, pointing and jeering silently. He could tell by their gestures that they were making fun of him, even though their expressions never changed and no sound came from them. There was something about their blank faces which was rather horrifying. They were in human form but did they have *feelings*? Alex decided that a creature without emotions was more dangerous than a creature full of hate and malice. Yet, he finally decided, if they wanted to humiliate him it was because they felt they had been mistreated themselves. Therefore they did *feel*.

'You can laugh all you want,' he said to them, as they walked around him, pointing at the price tags on his clothes and shaking their heads vigorously. 'Well – actually you can't laugh out loud, because you don't have the equipment. But you're laughing inside, I can tell. And I don't care. I'll stand here all you want for now. But you can't keep me for ever.'

He said the last sentence with a conviction that he did not really feel inside. They continued to mock him with their presence, though Alex noticed that every so often the mannequins froze, as a group. Quite without warning they simply stopped in their tracks, remained motionless for about five seconds, then came to life again. It was as if they could not quite throw off their previous occupation when they had stood as still as statues. Locked within them was a remnant of their old existence: in those days the only time they altered their pose was when a human did it for them.

'Must be in their genes,' muttered Alex to himself, dismissing the laws of science and reason in this otherworld. 'Next time they do it, I'll undo this strap and make a dash for it.'

But it wasn't long enough, five seconds, for him to get a head start. Especially all togged up in the clobber they'd dressed him in. They always managed to run him down. And when they did they poked him around, making his eyes water. Then they showed him a pair of barber's scissors and pointed to his hair. They snipped the air in a taunting way with the scissors, making Alex quite aware what they intended to do.

'You'll be sorry if you do,' he snarled at them after the third time. 'I'll knock your blocks off when I get help.'

But help, it seemed, was a long way away.

# CHAPTER 7

# On the Mountain of Shadows

Now Chloe was all alone. Alex was nowhere to be seen and her calls for him had gone unanswered. Jordy was somewhere out on or beyond the Jagged Mountain. It was as if the attic had a plan from the start, to divide the three children, to separate them, and then to deal with them in its own manner.

'Alex?' Chloe yelled, desperate for an answer. 'Alex, where are you?'

A mocking draught blew down from Jagged Mountain.

Alex and Jordy: both lost somewhere. Chloe wondered whether this was retribution for her tricking the bat. The bat had thought it was getting a map and all it got was a list of books.

'Those *stupid* boys,' growled Chloe, clenching her fists in frustration. 'How do they manage to get lost?'

Yet, even as she said the words, Chloe realised that in fact neither of them might be lost. They could have been abducted by someone. Or some thing. Still, at least *she* hadn't been kidnapped. It was now up to her to find her brothers. If they were lost, she would find them. If they had been taken, she would free them.

She decided to start from where she last saw Alex and roam outwards in ever increasing circles until she came upon a clue. That seemed the most sensible plan, though she realised it might take some time.

'What is it?' asks the bat.

*Looks like they've captured one of the visitors.*

'Which one?'

*Who knows, you've seen one young person, you've seen them all.*

'Well, what are you going to do about it?'

*Why should I do anything? They tricked me with that piece of paper they gave you. All it had on it was words. I know what a map looks like. It's got squiggly lines and arrows and things. It shows you where to go. This isn't a map at all.*

The board-comber waves Chloe's book list under the nose of the bat hanging from his ear.

'So, you don't like people, but you don't like mannequins either. They always chase you away with brooms and mops. You could help the boy escape. You know you could.'

*I'm still angry with the visitors.*

'It wasn't that one who gave you the list.'

*I suppose not. It was the one with long hair.*

The board-comber crawls closer to the mannequins' village, the chin of his ceramic Venetian carnival mask scraping on the floorboards. Alex is wilting like a flower without water. Flowers, like humans, are remembered things which the board-comber has not seen for decades. The board-comber wonders if he should feel sorry for the boy. One thing is certain, young people were good at rooting out treasure, and where there's treasure there's trade. The board-comber is ever desperate to increase his collection of Inuit carvings: his heart beats faster at the thought of a new one.

'You've been seen!'

*How would you know – you're blind . . .*

But the bat is right. A lone mannequin suddenly appears from the side of the attic. It bears down on the bundle of dirty clothes which is the board-comber and begins beating him with a broom. The board-comber yells, climbs to his feet. Heavy in his rags and tatters, and with his bag of soapstone carvings, he runs. The mannequin chases him, whacking him with the broom, raising clouds of dust from his clothes.

Each *thwack* with the weapon brings a yell of anguish from the board-comber, who does not so much feel pain as indignation at the treatment.

*Stop, stop*, it cries.

But the mannequin seems to be enjoying the chase. It doesn't relent until they are almost out of sight of the village. Then suddenly it freezes for five seconds, allowing the board-comber to get out of reach. On coming back to life the dummy swivels its head back-to-front. There's a sense of apprehension about it now. It realises it is far out on its own. The board-comber recognises its indecision. He whirls back and lashes out with his hat, striking the dummy's bare chest. He then wrenches the broom out of his foe's stiff hands.

Weaponless, the mannequin begins running awkwardly backwards towards its home. Its body still faces the board-comber, but its head is turned the other way. Halfway home it freezes in motion again, almost toppling on its back. When it comes to, it spins round in order to run properly, at the same time as its head does a half-revolution. Once more everything is the right way round and in the right place.

Deciding not to follow, the board-comber remains where he is, gathering breath.

'You could have chased it back,' says the bat. 'You could have belted it one when it froze the second time.'

*I don't really like violence.*

'Well, that's admirable. But the hunted could have become the hunter – the pursued the pursuer – the chased the chaser . . .'

*I think I get the idea.*

'They think they own the attic, those dummies, that's for sure.'

*The attic has free right of roaming.*

'Yet they capture people and degrade them.'

*We must set the boy loose. If we don't they'll cut off his hair. You know what they're like.*

'Good for you. How?'

*I know where there are lures.*

'Lures? What, you mean like trout-fishing flies?'

*Yes. Mannequins can't resist them.*

'Why would they want trout flies?'

*Not flies. Something else.*

'What? What could a mannequin possibly want?'

*You'll see.*

Chloe felt like falling down and weeping. To her credit she didn't. She stayed on her feet and kept searching. Being a castaway in Attica, a strange land with strange creatures in it, was not so terrible when she had company. However, she discovered that it was quite a different place when she was alone. With no one to talk to, no one to comfort and exchange ideas with, the attic became a place of horror. Every little creak made her whirl in panic. All her thoughts turned in cycles, haunting her every moment with doubts and concerns. The solitude was unbearable and all those experiences she had read about, of lonely shipwrecked mariners in the days of sailing ships, meant more to her now that she was going through the same thing.

'I must keep my head,' she kept telling herself. 'I mustn't let things get out of perspective.'

But even the sound of her own voice, now that she was alone, frightened her.

When night came it was even worse. She found a cardboard box and curled up inside it, hoping that by blocking out the attic she would be safe from anything out there. She slept fitfully, waking at every tiny noise. In the night even ordinary things seem threatening. By the time morning came she was ragged with grey thoughts and lack of rest.

Nevertheless, she continued to do her ever-widening search. At one point she found Nelson trailing along behind her. Never a lean cat in the past, Nelson now looked sleek and dangerous. She picked him up and stroked him until he struggled to be let down. He stayed with her for a while, accompanying her on her search, then drifted off into some shadows. Chloe did not mind him deserting her. Cats were like that. She knew he'd find her again, when he was ready for company.

He lays his lures on the boards not far from the village and waits.

'You think that'll bring 'em out?'

*Just you watch.*

A mannequin is tired of taunting the human and leaves to wander just outside the village. Once outside, however, the shop-window dummy halts in its tracks. It lifts its head and arches itself towards an area which looks like a patch of coloured grasses. What is that out there? Could it be . . . ? Yes, it could very well be. Well then, should it go and fetch them in itself, or should it rouse the other mannequins to accompany it?

The patch is quite a way out from the village.

The mannequin decides it needs company to venture so

far from safety in numbers. It goes back and brings the attention of the other dummies to that peculiar patch out on the boards. Soon the mannequins are streaming out of the village, all eager to claim one of the treasures.

*I knew the wigs would bring them.*

'Well, you were right: here they come.'

*They can't resist wigs. You should see them primping and parading themselves in front of a mirror, once they have a wig on their head. Hair. They crave a hairpiece to make themselves look more attractive. I've never met a mannequin yet that didn't want to cover its baldness.*

'Let's get to the boy before they realise the village is empty.'

But the board-comber does not need to worry. The mannequins are delighted with the wigs. They have forgotten about their captive. They put on the hairpieces and dance around in that jerky fashion, swinging long golden curls, black straight locks, blue tight curls, even green plaits with blue ribbons. They point to each other and rock from side to side, as if passing approval on their companions. What a delightful thing, to find these wigs scattered just outside their village. Everyone is happy.

When they return to the village, however, they become enraged.

Their human captive has gone. A pile of clothes attests to the fact that he has either melted or run away. Since there is no pool of liquid the mannequins conclude that he has indeed absconded. Still, they have the wigs. They have become beautiful. They are now wonderful.

They begin to dance again, freezing every so often for that peculiar five seconds, then springing back into motion once more.

Alex wanted someone to thank, for setting him free, but there was nothing in sight but a pile of stinking old clothes.

Perhaps the owner had shed them in flight? Had there been anyone at all? Who knew what strangenesses this Attica would produce next? After a while he convinced himself that he alone had been responsible for his liberty. Something had drawn the mannequins out of their village, but he – Alex – had managed to escape while they had been thus preoccupied. That's all there was to it.

He felt relieved to be shot of the mannequins of course, but he also felt rather light-headed and triumphant. It was frightening to be a prisoner, but it was exhilarating to escape and put one over on your enemies. It was exciting to be travelling through an unknown, unexplored land. Out there in the real world everywhere had been discovered and seen by someone. In here there were surprises to be had, new discoveries.

Alex sat down and took off his backpack.

Someone joined him, sliding up to his side.

'Hello, Nelson! What have you got there?'

His three-cornered cat had arrived with a dead bird. A pigeon. It must have been roosting in the eaves. Even with three legs Nelson was good at killing things: lightning-fast once he had crept up to his victims. There was nothing wrong with his back legs, which launched him into his leap. Now that the pigeon was a dead weight, he was having trouble dragging it along. He deposited it at Alex's feet and looked up, obviously pleased with himself.

'Oh dear, Nelson. Mum wouldn't like it.'

But the bird was quite plump. Alex studied the carcass with new eyes. The eyes of Alex the explorer and adventurer. It had a good layer of meat on it. He suddenly remembered his cooking stove. Hunger clawed at his belly. He'd never plucked a pigeon before, but he did so now, under the approving eye of a lopsided ginger tom. It took

him a while but he managed to get rid of most of the
feathers. He decided the last few bits of fluff would burn
off.

'Got to do something with the innards, I think.'

With his newly found penknife he cut the bird open
and scraped out all the messy bits. Then he lit the camping stove and roasted the pigeon over the flames on a spit
fashioned from a metal tent peg. The cooked item was
not what you would call cuisine, but it was edible, despite
the burnt bits. Alex was very pleased with himself. He
gave some to the waiting Nelson, then ate the rest himself, only later feeling guilty for not saving some for the
others.

'Chloe wouldn't like it anyway,' he told Nelson. 'She'd
go ape if she knew.'

He decided not to tell her.

Alex stroked his cat's head and fondled his ears. Nelson
purred like the engine of a very expensive car. At last one
of his gifts had been accepted. 'You're a three-legged ginger
wonder. The king of cats. The lion of Attica.' His purring
increased.

Alex felt like a conqueror of the elements and the landscape. He was Doctor Livingstone, he was Sherpa Tensing,
he was Gautama Buddha. In his small frame was the ability
to traverse the unknown and even perhaps become rich in
the process, for there was treasure here. If not diamonds or
gold, then postage stamps and old coins.

He moved on, back towards the place where he had left
Chloe and, miracle of miracles, found the treasure he was
seeking. It was wrapped in an oily rag and left just where he
would come across it. Surely someone had put it there for
him? Not the shop dummies, that was certain. Someone
else. Someone wishing to make friends, perhaps? Somehow
he knew before he peeled away the oily rag, that there was

an object of great beauty and desire beneath. He sensed it. He *smelled* it.

It was not coins or stamps, but a model steam engine. He had always dreamed of owning one – a Mamod or a Wilesco – and here it was, green, red and black, with a brass wheel that gleamed as if it had just been polished. But these were very expensive toys. He'd been promised one at some time, but what with the expense of moving house Dipa and Ben had been honest with him in saying they didn't know when they could deliver.

'Next birthday – or maybe the one after . . .'

And this one was no ordinary traction engine. This was a *showman's* engine. They were the best, the most expensive of all the steam engines.

'A showman's traction engine!' He breathed the words. 'If only I had some methylated spirit for fuel. I've got the matches. I can get the water from one of the tanks. A bit of rag or maybe even some cotton wool somewhere. I bet I could get it up to pressure in no time . . .'

'There you are! *There* you are. Oh, thank goodness you're safe!'

Alex quickly stuffed the engine into his backpack and stood up to greet his sister.

Chloe had found him. She came stumbling out of one of the dark corners of the attic and grabbed him for a hug. Her face was moist with tears. Alex struggled, uncomfortable with this show of affection.

'Steady on, sis,' he said quietly. 'Someone will see you.'

'I don't care. I missed you.'

'Well, I do. I've – I've got my reputation to think of.'

Chloe laughed, despite her tears. 'Oh, what? Your reputation as a hard man? Now, where have you been?' She looked at him and suspicion came into her eyes. 'You didn't hide on purpose, did you?'

'I was captured by shop dummies,' he answered indignantly. 'I was in danger of my life.'

'Shop dummies?' Chloe laughed. 'You're kidding, right?'

'No.' And she could see he was deadly serious. '*Anything* can happen here. We have to watch our backs.' He looked behind him, but all that was there was that old pile of clothes. 'You never know who's sneaking up on you – or rather, *what*.'

'Stop it Alex, you're frightening me.'

'Don't worry, I'll look after you. I know this place now. You just have to keep alert.'

She looked exasperated. 'I didn't mean you're frightening me with the place, I mean *you*. You're going bonkers.'

Alex was hurt and defensive. 'No I'm not.'

'Well, stop talking funny then.'

Alex realised he had to keep his new self hidden a little while longer. All right, he had been a scientist and engineer in his last life. In this one he was an explorer and he was going to enjoy being one. Chloe hadn't yet made the leap from her old world into this one. He damn well had and it felt good. In his last life he had been the quiet one, the thinker, the *slow* one. Jordy had been the quick, flash, sporty one. Chloe had been the clever one, the book reader – and the pretty one. They got more attention than him, there. But things can change.

'Alex, are you dreaming again?'

'Me? No, course not.' He hefted his pack onto his back.

'And what's in there?'

'Stuff I found. Compasses. Binoculars.'

'You found that? Oh, well done, Alex,' cried Chloe, her tone changing instantly. 'Where did you get it?'

'Oh, over there.' He waved vaguely. 'You can get all sorts of stuff here, if you look out for it. Now, are we going to climb that old hill, or what? We need to find the map, don't we?'

Chloe looked towards the Jagged Mountain. 'We need to find Jordy,' she said quietly.

'Oh yes,' said Alex. 'And him.'

They began to walk towards the mountain.

Chloe said, 'So tell me what happened with the shop dummies.'

Alex explained how he had wandered out and been captured by the mannequins, recounting the humiliation he'd been put through, but how he kept his chin up and had escaped when the chance came.

'You did that all by yourself?'

A tinge of guilt went through Alex.

'Well, I thought . . .' he looked back at a pile of old clothes, receding into the back of the attic now. 'Yeah – yeah, all by myself. Oh my . . .' Alex suddenly pointed to something. 'Oh Lord, look at that.'

'What, that toy?'

'Toy? It's a *model*,' cried Alex. 'A Mamod. Look.' He picked up the model traction steam engine painted green and red, with shiny wheels and lots of parts. It was truly a marvellous piece of engineering. 'A traction engine,' he said reverently. 'You've no idea what these cost back in the real world. And here's another one.'

'*Another* one,' echoed Chloe a little impatiently.

'It's mine,' said Alex, as if she were going to take it from him.

Chloe said quietly, 'You sound about two years old, Alex. We can't carry things like that. It's too heavy.'

'Oh yes we can,' said the feverish Alex.

'Alex?'

'I'm keeping it,' he said, putting it in his backpack. 'It's mine and I'm keeping it.'

Chloe did not have the energy to argue.

They reached the bottom of the Jagged Mountain at

noon and began climbing, up along rusty rifle ridge and skirting the chasm of bayonets. It was tough going, especially over the boulders of helmet slope, which had them slipping and sliding. They learned not to grasp on to things suddenly, for there were sharp swords and daggers everywhere. The snouts of howitzers and field guns were waiting to trap an unwary foot and the fins of rockets could slice open a knee just as effectively as a razor. They climbed well, keeping to hanging valleys and chimneys, which offered good handholds and gentler slopes, keeping clear of sheer drops down on to sharp shells. Deep dips full of bullets were waiting to suck under any climber who tried to cross them, for they were as unstable as quickmire.

The higher they climbed the colder it became, until they had to be careful that their hands did not stick to freezing metal. Colder, and more gloomy. Here the air was as still as death. There was the sense – they both felt it – of something watching and waiting. Something ugly and malicious, holding back for the right moment in which to attack.

'Are you all right?' asked Chloe, shivering with the cold and perhaps for some other reason too. 'Can you give me your hand?'

Alex reached out and grasped his sister's wrist, pulling her up on to the shelf of small black bomb cases.

'Yep, I'm OK,' he replied, his breath coming out as steam. 'Flippin' cold, sis. I'll be glad when we start to go down.'

There were snow patches on some piles of weapons.

'Nearly at the top, I think. Every time we go over a ridge, there seems to be another one waiting, but the peak can't be far now.'

'I hope you're right . . .'

At that moment Katerfelto launched its attack. It came sweeping down from above as a dark flapping sheet with ragged edges. There were holes for its mouth and eyes, and its claws were stretched out before it. It screamed as the wind screams, high and shrill. The suddenness of his coming, the speed at which he swept upon them, terrified the children. They turned to run as this giant shapeless fiend rushed down at them. Chloe fell and went skidding down a slope of bombs, her jeans snagging on the fins. Alex kept his feet but his eyes were wide with terror as he jumped from tank barrel to turret, from submarine conning tower to aircraft wing. Katerfelto chased him, herded him back to where his sister was nursing a bruised arm.

'Look out, Alex,' she screamed. 'It's just behind you.'

Katerfelto whirled around them. Now it was in its favourite form, that of a charlatan dressed in a long black gown with a black square cap. It swirled in ever-decreasing circles. The cap flew off and away somewhere and its hair became a spreading net. It flew wild about its head and they saw they would soon be caught in the folds of this flailing trap. Alex dropped down beside his sister, wanting to comfort her, but having to battle with a heart that raced in his chest. What was he to do? Where was all his ingenuity now that deadly danger stared them in the face?

Alex whipped off his pack and looked inside. A torch. Would that do? A penknife. Absolutely not. There were weapons all around them they could use if they wanted to. But Alex sensed that to pick up a sword or a gun would be giving in to the mountain. Perhaps that's what it wanted, for them to acknowledge they could not do without weapons of war? And it would be futile – just as war was futile – because the creature was not substantial.

He continued to scrabble around in the bag. The compasses were absolutely useless of course.

'It's coming closer,' said Chloe, her fingers gripping her

palms so hard they were white and bloodless. 'Closer and closer.'

And indeed Katerfelto was tightening its circle. Soon the black hem of its cloak was flicking over the faces of the children. They could not feel it, but they could sense its coldness. It was like being whipped across the eyes by a freezing wind. Horror built in the minds and hearts of the two children. They wanted to jump up and run. They wanted to flee from this terrible force that moved upon them with such vicious certainty.

'Close your eyes,' ordered Chloe. 'Maybe if we don't look at it?'

Both of them closed their eyes tightly, and Alex tried to imagine that Katerfelto was not there. But even so the coldness of Katerfelto's breath swept through Alex's mind. There was no escaping this fiend simply by closing one's eyes and imagining it gone. Its presence was far stronger than the mere thoughts and imaginings of a young boy. It had crushed powerful men in its time and reduced them to whimpering madness. It had driven women on to the spikes of bayonets, as they strove to escape it. None could withstand naked fear when it rushed in as an evil wind.

Alex opened his eyes and took one last look in the back-pack.

What? These? Why yes, of course.

The matches.

As the darkness continued to thicken he took out the box of long-stemmed matches and struck one, lighting it.

Katerfelto recoiled with a moan.

'Here, hold this, Clo,' said Alex, handing her the burning match. 'I'll do another one.'

He struck a second match.

The dark tail of the monster god retracted sharply.

Fire. It hated fire.

Light. It hated light.

'We've got it on the run,' yelled Alex excitedly. 'See, it's going.'

Katerfelto was withdrawing like a swift tide going out, pulling in its edges, retreating before the fire and light. It was making strange sounds as it left. It was a creature in pain. It seemed to separate now into small rivulets of darkness, which drained into holes in the piles of weapons. Down the barrels of rifles, through the tracks of tanks, under the tubes of mortars, it seeped into the side of the mountain. As it went, so did the terror, and the children felt the fright drain from their hearts and minds. This creature was fashioned of nothing; nothing at all, except fear.

'I hope it doesn't come back,' said Chloe, blowing out the flame before it burned her fingers. 'Have you got any more matches?'

'A whole box full,' confirmed Alex, putting them in his chinos pocket. 'But we'd better be careful with them. After all, fire in an attic and all that . . .'

'Yes, of course. The place is made of tinder.'

'Exactly. But so long as we're careful.'

Somewhere in the attic one of the Removal Firm stiffened and a sudden chill went through him. What was that? Had he smelled burning sulphur again? What dreadful irresponsibility! He took his hands from his khaki dustcoat pockets and formed a cup around his nose with them. Then he breathed in deeply, sniffing the air. Sulphur, definitely. Someone, somewhere had struck another match. This was the second or third time in as many days. Yes, there it was again, another match. Fire, the forbidden wonder of nature. Forbidden to all in the attic. Those who used fire were summarily ejected from the attic, sent out into Chaos, that nowhere place down below the boards. The creation of fire was the deepest, darkest sin, the worst of crimes, in the attic. The Removal Firm might fuss over woodworm, death-watch beetles, dry rot, nibbling mice, canker and other dangers to the attic, but fire was dealt with very harshly. He and his colleagues would continue to seek out the criminals and when they found them, they would remove them.

# CHAPTER 8

# Scissor-birds that Blood
# Your Head

They descended from the mountain to the plains below.

There were broad open spaces, bare wooden boards which stretched lengthways in the direction in which they were heading. They camped for a short while at a spot under one of those mighty timbers that supported the roof. It had some rusty nails protruding from it and Alex hung his backpack and other equipment on it. As he did so he became interested in the pillar itself, which soared upwards, thick as a mature oak, to split and spread itself high above, in order to support the roof.

He slapped the pillar with his hand, feeling strength in its solidity.

'You know, sis,' he said, looking round at other such pillars which stood four-square every hundred metres in each direction, 'without these fellows, the roof would collapse on us.'

Chloe lay back, her head on a rolled-up coat, and stared into the dimness above.

'I've been studying stresses and pressures on the arches of bridges and I'm sure these do a similar job. You don't seem to realise how important they are. If I was to chop this one down there would be too much pressure on the next one, and the one behind, and those to the sides. They'd give way too and that would mean more and more pillars cracking and splitting and collapsing – you know, the domino effect – and finally the whole roof would fall down on the heads of everyone in here. It would be an end to this place for good.' He paused. 'Just one of these pillars down, that's all it would take, to crush this world.'

'Cheerful Charlie, aren't you?'

'I'm just saying how fragile this place is. It looks sturdy enough, it's true, but it ain't.'

'A delicate balance?'

'Well, I don't know about *delicate*, but a balance, sure. You interfere with that balance, and WHAM, the whole lot comes crashing down. Everything underneath would be flattened, squashed to pulp. A few cockroaches might live, but not much else.'

Chloe was happy when they moved on and he stopped talking. She preferred her thoughts to dwell on lighter things than the end of the world.

Mostly the apex of the roof was high, out of sight, but they reached an area where the roof was lower and a tangle of rafters above their heads formed a canopy similar to that in a rainforest or jungle. The children sensed movement occasionally in the rafters and believed there were bats up there. Neither Chloe nor Alex were scared of bats, or really any kind of wildlife. Chloe couldn't stand girls who squealed at anything unusual. Alex didn't like creepy-crawlies but he was all right with bigger creatures.

They were always seeing movements out of the corner of their eyes, though. The attic was that kind of place. It was a patchwork of shadows and half-light and dazzling sun-shine. One drifted from dimly lit corners where the dust was centimetres thick, into brilliant spaces where the sunlight was blinding. Twilight to bright light in a moment. It was no wonder, they told each other, that the light played tricks with their eyes. Shadowy creatures danced with quick movements here, there and everywhere, but you could never catch them in full sight. Maddeningly, they were always fleeting.

However, looking up into the woven network of rafters at one point, Alex was given a start. This was real! No figment of the mind. There, looking down at him, was a doll's painted face. The blue eyes of the doll, set in pale-pink china, stared at him unblinkingly. She had red cupid's-bow lips and bulging cheeks of rosy hue. The doll was clinging to one rafter with chubby little ceramic hands, her tiny feet in black strapover shiny shoes on the rafter below. She was wearing a filthy white dress, torn in places. Suddenly, inexplicably, she smiled with a row of neat even teeth. Then she climbed up, as fast as a monkey, into the upper canopy and out of sight.

Alex was so frightened he could hardly breathe.

'There's something up there,' he croaked.

'I know: bats,' replied his sister. 'Come on.'

Alex said no more. There wasn't any point in worrying Chloe. In any case, they were emerging from the canopy into a more spacious area. There were man-sized figures standing like scarecrows as far as the eye could see. All had definite faces: some hideous, others not so. Alex shuddered, but his sister had been prepared for this.

'A Land of Masks,' she murmured.

'Shouldn't we arm ourselves?' asked Alex, taking out his penknife. 'Any golf clubs around?'

'If you walk about with weapons, you only antagonise people.'

'People?'

'Well, whatever.'

'We could pretend we were playing golf.'

Chloe said, 'It's best we approach pure of heart.'

'Is it?' Alex was unconvinced.

The 'figures' had been fashioned from odds and ends and hardly resembled people at all. Most of them had no arms or legs, being merely cones made of old clothes, washing line poles, waste bins, that sort of junk. But they were topped by the most beautiful – and ugly – masks. Some were traditional carnival masks which Chloe recognised as being from the Venice carnival. Others were more exotic, from Africa, Polynesia, China and Borneo. Some of the African masks were quite scary: they were meant to be, having once been used in tribal rituals to drive out demons. Others from the same continent were obviously meant to represent animals – lion masks, elephant masks, hippo masks – and were not frightening at all. There were grinning devil masks from China and mournful demi-god masks from the islands of the Pacific Ocean. Very unnerving. Most with hollow eyes. There were huge giant masks at the back, on the edges of the attic, and smaller ones near to the path which the children were using.

'Don't look at them,' said Chloe, walking among the forest of figures. 'Try not to answer them.'

'What?' cried a nervous Alex.

'Over heres,' said a mask with a mouth formed in a perfect wooden O. 'Sir, sir, over heres. Thine eyes must perceive my terrible plight.'

'Don't look at him,' warned Chloe, gripping her brother's sleeve. 'Don't listen to him.'

'Oh, please master, mistress, helping me. I am a real and bona fide person in thrall to these creatures,' cried another mask, one of straw and raffia with wild hair and whiskers. 'If you could just assist me to get out, my liberty would be your just afters.'

'Maybe there is someone in there,' Alex said. 'What if there's another kid like us?'

'He has long gone, our Gatherer. Gone, gone away.'

'When have you heard a kid talk like that? Don't listen to it. You mustn't take any notice. They want you to take them out of here and they'll hypnotise you to do it. The bat told me that once they get hold of you, they won't let you go.'

'What – what will they do?'

'Just keep walking.'

'Lord of walking things, borrow me.'

'Happy child, taking please an unhappy face?'

At certain points they had to move quite close to the masked figures, but Chloe kept her eyes determinedly on the far side of the Land of Masks. She gripped her younger brother's hand almost fiercely, pulling him along with her. Alex wasn't always the strongest person in such a situation. He was impressionable and easily persuaded, like the time he gave all his pocket money to a beggar on the London Underground. The important thing was to ignore the pleas of the masks. Oh indeed, it was difficult to ignore the imploring voices around them. Chloe was surprised how hard it was not to turn and look, but she knew how dangerous it was to fall for Attica's tricks. She was learning fast that if they were to meet Jordy again, find the map and get out of this nightmare, they had to keep their wits about them.

'We're out!' she said in a relieved voice, still holding on to Alex. 'We made it.'

'Free,' said Alex in a peculiar voice. 'Brothers and sisters, goodbye.'

Chloe turned, alarmed.

Alex was wearing a mask.

'Oh, Alex,' she said in despair.

The mask he had on was made of raffia and clay. It had a tall conical top to it, like a witch's hat, painted black with white sticks attached to it. The face was painted black with white spots. There were holes for the eyes and a slit for the mouth. Here and there, on the forehead and running up the strange hat, were white zig-zag lines. The final touch was the beard of thick brown raffia. The mouth and eyes were lined with white paint.

'How did that happen?' cried Chloe. 'You must have grabbed it with your other hand.'

Trust Alex to get himself in trouble, even after warnings. Now Chloe felt she had to be firm with him.

'Take it off!' ordered Chloe, gripping the mask. 'Throw it back in there.'

'Leave me be, woman,' it said. 'Desist. I am Makishi. You cannot throw me away like a piece of trash.'

Alex sided with the mask. 'Leave it alone, Clo. I like it.'

'You can't like it − it's hideous,' said Chloe. She was afraid the mask had somehow bewitched Alex into putting it on his face. It might eventually do her young brother harm.

'It lets me see things,' replied Alex mysteriously.

'What things?'

Alex was cagey. 'I'm not telling you. You'll want a go with it. I might let you later, when I'm fed up with it.'

'I wouldn't put that thing on if you paid me. It smells for a start. They must have glued it together with buffalo dung.'

'You're not going to get the chance. It's *my* mask. I found it and I get to keep it.'

'And I get to keep Alex.'

'See?' said Chloe. 'That's the kind of remark that worries me. Now, what do you want?'

'I don't want anything,' replied a peeved Alex. 'I just want to keep the mask on.'

'I'm talking to the mask. Mask, now you've escaped, why do you need my brother?'

'To walk, to move, to be carrying me.'

Of course, the mask was nothing without a wearer. It had no powers at all if it were not worn by someone. Chloe had to believe that Alex was still all right behind the mask. She asked him how he was.

'I'm fine,' he replied. 'I like the mask.'

Chloe said, 'Well, you can keep it on for now. We'll think about getting it off you later.'

For the moment Chloe decided they just had to keep going. The day was fading from the skylights and she wanted to be well away from the other masks before she camped for the night. Still holding Alex's hand – she was afraid the mask might run away with her brother if she let go – she continued on her way. A while later she stopped and stood still for a moment.

'Why do we do a pause?' asked the mask.

'We have to rest. We're only children. We can't walk for ever.'

'Do not be tricking me.'

'I'm not. Look, if I let go my brother's hand, will you stay? I don't want you running away with him.'

'Where would I go? I go where you go.'

The answer sounded genuine. Good. She hoped she was right in thinking that the mask had only limited knowledge. Chloe was weary and couldn't hold on to Alex's hand for ever. Although she was strong in spirit she was tired physically. There would come a time, she was sure, when all this would be over, but for now she had to tough it out. She let go of Alex's hand. He did not run. Good. Now she had to question the mask. Knowledge was the key to many things. If she found out where it came from, who made it, she might be able to discover weaknesses in its power over her brother.

'Where are you from?' she asked, sitting Alex down and removing his backpack. 'You're not from around here.'

'I am from a hot place.'

'Borneo? South America? Madagascar?'

'Many flies. Many rivers.'

Many rivers?

'What sort of animals do you have? Any elephants?'

'Yes, elephants.'

'Big ears?'

'Of course big ears.'

'Well Asian elephants have smaller ears. Do you have any lions?'

'Lions, yes.'

'Ah, Africa – somewhere. How did you get from Africa to here?' she asked casually. 'Were you brought here?'

'I come in brown paper twined-about with strings.'

It seemed that was all she was going to get.

'What did you say your name was?'

'Makishi. I am the One Who Circumcises Boys.'

A startled Alex interrupted with, 'Does what?'

'Never mind,' said Chloe, 'but you might want to get rid of that mask as soon as possible.'

She left the mask alone now and took some food from her bag. Their supply was getting very low. They would need to find another source soon. She wondered how she was going to feed Alex. Through the hole in the mask? She tried it, handing some to her brother, who said, 'Thanks, sis,' in that faraway voice and popped it through the opening. 'Not as good as pigeon.'

What was he talking about? Chloe had far more to worry about than pigeons. Africa. What did she know about Africa? Her heart sank. Not very much.

'Mask, what kind of grass are you made from?'

'Strong grass. Elephant grass.'

'So you're very durable. You'll last a long time?'

'For ever.'

Nelson was having the best of times in the attic. It was one vast hunting ground, better than any garden he had ever owned. The place was teeming with mice, there were birds to be had in the dark corners of the eaves, and there were rats too. He'd already had a run in with a rat and of course had come off best, despite being handicapped. He didn't consider himself at a disadvantage, having only three legs. It actually gave him an edge, since his adversaries took his invalidity for granted. They reckoned ill who did so, for he taught them a great lesson about three-cornered cats.

Now he was going through a strange place full of strange wooden faces, following two of his human family. Suddenly a creature popped out of the mouth of one of the masks and stood before him. The creature was human shaped, but about the size of a large rat. It showed its teeth to Nelson, who had never liked this gesture, even in his own family of humans.

'Gaaaah!' cried the creature before him. 'Eeech!'

Nelson had no comprehension of these sounds and actually was now quite irritated by this strange thing which smelled of candles.

'Urchhg. Aaaaach.'

It did a little dance before him, then took out some sharp needles and pricked Nelson's nose with one of them. The sound that came from the small figure's mouth sounded like triumph to Nelson. Nelson hated birds that crowed over him: and any other creature for that matter.

Another little dance and a stab with the needles.

Nelson had taken enough. He bit its head off.

The body ran away.

The head tasted just like candle. Nelson chewed it into a

shapeless wad then spat it out in disgust. He loped on in as dignified a fashion as his missing leg would allow, thoroughly disgusted at the delay.

Jordy had not climbed Jagged Mountain, but had taken the long way round, skirting the foothills, never going higher than necessary. It was a long and tedious journey but once he had reached the other side he felt briefly invigorated and elated. Here he was, on his own, trekking where no man had been before. Or if they had, there was no sign of him in the dust, for Jordy's were the only footprints. When he looked back there was a long line of them, stretching as far as he could see.

The only drawback was that he felt very, very lonely. Jordy liked company. He liked encouragement when things were going bad and he liked praise when things were going good. He did not like having to fall on his own resources the whole time, with no one to share in the glory or the defeat. The problem was Jordy was more lost than ever and had no hope of returning to the other two as he had promised.

'Well,' he said, divesting himself of the pack he now carried, 'here I am on the other side of Attica.'

He sat down, took out some dried vegetables and crunched on them, studying what lay around him. Jordy too had been visited by a talkative bat in the middle of the night and told of a golden bureau if he would just keep his eyes skinned for soapstone carvings. But there were no hostile ink imps to be seen, nor any other kind of supernatural creature. An area covered with scattered tea chests lay ahead. Jordy stared hard at the nearest chest. He got up and went to inspect it. Tapping the plywood case he found it was hollow. The box was not only empty, it was upside-down. Looking around him he could see that *all* the tea chests were the wrong way up. Not only that, they were not placed at random. There was a roughly equal gap between each of them, as if they had been placed for a purpose.

Jordy looked up at the tangle of rafters overhead. No clues up there. Nothing but cobwebs and darkness.

Why would anyone place wooden boxes in a definite pattern?

Maybe, he thought, this is the work of an artist?

He wished Chloe were there so that she could argue with him.

Jordy sighed. It was no fun being brilliant on your own.

'Time to get on,' he told himself. 'See if I can find that watch by myself.'

If Jordy had not believed in 'ink imps' before, he did now. Unlike the other two, he had extremely sharp eyes and had already caught full glimpses of ephemeral beings. Since they did him no harm he took little notice of them. These little figures formed out of the dust, travelled swiftly for a short distance, then disintegrated into a dust cloud again. Like small whirlwinds, or dust devils, but with definite human shape. Spirits of the attic, he decided, which should be ignored since they were unnatural beings. Jordy wanted no truck with things he couldn't control or fully understand. He let them get on with their short lives and he would get on with his.

He hefted on the backpack and continued out on to the plain of tea chests. Under the chests the yellow boards stretched far away, becoming old gold in the distance. He could see something happening out there. Birds, surely? Like a flock of rooks rising and falling gently on a field of corn stubble. Were they birds? They looked just like rooks.

A short time later he stopped again, puzzled. There was a strange sound in the air. A sort of *snicking* noise. It seemed sinister and Jordy was worried by it, especially when it multiplied and rose in volume.

'What's going on?' he mused.

He stared about. He could see nothing ahead or behind, nor even to the sides. Then he realised the noise was indeed coming from the front, but high up, in the apex of the roof. What was that? Glinting things. Little flashes of light: the sun's rays caught on glass? No, not glass, he decided, *metal*. Metal objects flying through the air. What the hell were they? *Snick, snick, snick, snick, snick*. Hundreds of them. These were his *rooks*, clacking, clicking, snicking, snacking. There were some very large dark ones, some a little smaller but red and green like parrots, the smallest of them pure silver with the sun flashing from their wings. Incredible. Just like birds . . .

'Bloody hell!' he cried, throwing off his pack as a giant swarm of scissors, garden shears, secateurs and clippers descended from the rafters. They swooped down towards him, snicking furiously at the air a dozen times a second. Their intent was obvious: to snip pieces from the intruder. Their blades flashed back and forth, forming the double purpose of wings for flying and beaks for biting. The finger-holes of the scissors were like baleful eyes, leading the rest of the raptors in their descent on the foe.

Jordy went for the nearest hiding place, under a tea chest. Several sets of nail scissors, those fastest in flight, managed to snip locks of precious hair from his head and bits out of his clothes before he was safely under. Then the rest of the flock attacked the tea chest, going at it in a most alarming manner, like a thousand woodpeckers. The noise inside the chest was loud and terrifying. Jordy was curled up inside, his feet on the rim to keep the box from tipping over, wondering how he was going to get out of this terrible situation without injury.

When the metal birds had ceased their hammering on

the box, Jordy quickly leapt out from underneath and ran back to the area where he'd stood before venturing out into tea chest country.

Of course, he thought, once he'd reached it and was looking back at the tattered remains of his rucksack, that's what the tea chests were *for*. Whoever had placed them out there had done so in order that people – Atticans probably – could use them to cross the wasteland. They were to protect travellers from the savage scissor-birds.

'If I'm going to get across,' he told himself, 'I'll have to nip from one to the other – or maybe just use them when I hear the flocks coming in?'

He needed a weapon though, in case he got caught out in the middle. Something to whack them with. Jordy back-tracked a little to where there were piles of attic junk and found himself a job lot of cricket gear lying in a heap. The bat was old and the willow was dented in places, but it would do. He made a few practice swipes with it, through the air.

'A six or a four, or even a single, I don't mind,' he muttered at the rafters. 'You're the balls, not me.'

He also discovered a batsman's helmet which he put on to protect his head from the scissor-beaks. On his arms and legs he put batsman's pads. Several jumpers were worn to protect his chest and a good thick pair of wicketkeeper's gloves went on his hands. There were still vulnerable spots, still chinks in his armour, but for the most part he was covered. He took a cricket bag to replace the rucksack the scissor-birds had ruined.

Thus armed and attired he set out again, thinking: The deeper we go into Attica, the more hostile it becomes.

He dashed from box to box at first, but this became tiresome and eventually he strolled along, though ever watchful.

Indeed, he did get caught between boxes once. They came in as a swarm and Jordy stood ready at the crease as the first pair of scissors swooped on him. He swiped at the pair and caught them full on the blade. The scissors flew off the bat and hit a beam, one of its points sticking into the wood. They struggled, snicking and snacking back and forth, trying to release themselves, eventually breaking off the point and gaining freedom.

In the meantime, Jordy was fighting for his life, slashing other metal birds as they swooped on him. They went flying everywhere. Jordy did not escape completely. They attacked his armpads like demented hawks, ripping and tearing, until the stuffing came out. There was a hammering on his helmet and they tried to peck into his wicketkeeper's gloves to get at flesh. But all the while he fought valiantly, making steady progress to the next tea chest, until he was safely underneath again and protected.

'Bugger off!' he yelled at them, as they rat-a-tat-tatted with fierceness on the outside of the chest. 'Go and find a needlework box!'

Thus Jordy made slow progress across that part of Attica terrorised by scissors, secateurs, shears and clippers. They continued to harass him the whole way across, but Jordy had their measure now. He was not going to get caught out between boxes again. His progress between each tea chest was swift and calculated. The distances could not have been covered better had he been playing for England against the Aussies: one of his long-term dreams, after playing Premier League football and rugby against the Springboks.

Finally he reached a valley draped with the flags of nations and saw that they were intact. If those same flags had been in scissor country they would have been shredded, so he knew he was out of danger. He divested himself of his cricket gear, keeping only the bag. There was a forest ahead and he walked towards it.

★

*They got by Katerfelto. It was the boy who did it.*

'Yes,' replies the bat, 'but with *matches*.'

*A dangerous way to do it, I agree. But he hasn't yet learned to use a mirror like us.*

The board-comber always carries a woman's powder compact on his person. Alex had used matches to provide the light to drive away Katerfelto, but board-combers and other attic-dwellers used mirrors. They redirected the sunlight, reflecting it on to Katerfelto's form, thus obliterating him. Katerfelto, after all, was but a bundle of shadows. And shadows are easily made to vanish in the blinding light of mirror-directed sunbeams.

*I still think it was very clever of him.*

'You won't think it so clever of him when he burns down the attic.'

*We're coming up to the Land of Masks. Is she still around? The mask collector?*

'No, you know she's not. *That* board-comber has gone.'

*Where do board-combers go when they go?*

'Oh my,' murmured the bat, folding and unfolding its wings, 'here we go. A long philosophical debate that goes absolutely nowhere . . .'

# CHAPTER 9

# The Boy in the Wooden Mask

*The voodoo dolls are gathering – see!*

'They seem pretty mad, don't they? I'm glad I'm not in your shoes.'

*I'm not my shoes – they belong to someone else.*

'That cat who bit the head off their chieftain belongs to the visitors. Now the voodoo dolls want revenge.'

*They're after the humans, not me.*

'They're after all of you.'

The board-comber is scurrying across the attic in the wake of Chloe and Alex with the bat hanging from his ear-lobe, his Cocalino mask slightly askew. His collection of soapstone carvings bounce painfully on his back. It's hot and stuffy inside the layers of clothing. He raises dust clouds as he runs, looking for hiding places, knowing that just falling down and pretending to be a pile of rags won't work with the voodoo dolls. The whole nest of wax effigies has been roused by the lingering smell of humans and they have swarmed out of the mouths of the giant masks. The board-comber is almost surrounded, but he manages to outrun the voodoo dolls.

'They know a live pile of old clothes when they see it.

And we can't go back. The mannequins are waiting for you. They know you got the boy away from them.'

*You're a great help.*

The voodoo dolls have knife-long needles stuck in their soft little wax forms. Each doll has about twenty of these weapons, which it pulls from its own body and plunges into the bodies of its enemies. The board-comber knows that these dolls bear so much hatred for humans they won't hesitate to drive their needles into flesh. In the attic they call it 'the death of a thousand points' and the victim bleeds to death slowly. The board-comber, who was once human and is still flesh and blood, is terrified. He has seen victims of the voodoo dolls staggering around, covered in needles. Living pin-cushions, helpless, blind and bleeding from a thousand tiny piercings.

*Are they still coming?*

'As relentless as a disturbed nest of hornets.'

*Their legs are short.*

'But they move faster than yours.'

The voodoo dolls of the attic might well be likened to a nest of furious wild hornets, carrying multiple stings in their vicious little fingers. They bear a horrible but often only passing likeness to members of the human race: some very pale, some very dark, some the shades between. They have been made by voodoo priests out of raggle-taggle materials and the resemblance to the humans they represent is purely superficial. They are loose-limbed and mostly ugly, though one or two have features which make them appear benign. The mild-looking ones are the worst: they carry the dreadful curse of not being quite what they ought to be.

*How did voodoo dolls get up here? Did the one who collected the masks collect voodoo dolls?*

'Who knows? He's gone now. Dead or back to the world

he came from. How's a bat supposed to know? Like will find like up here, won't it? Now they're on our tail and won't give up. We have to find some way of slowing them down.'

*Think of something then, I'm losing my breath. My legs are going all shaky. I don't think I can run much further.*

'Oh, that's right, leave the thinking up to me.'

*You're a passenger. That's what you do.*

'I suppose.'

Over the boxes and old furniture to the rear of them the voodoo dolls come scuttling like crabs over seashore rocks. The needles in their small hands flash ominously as they cross areas of sharp light. The expressions on their tiny faces are intent. They were made purely to carry pain and pass it to another. Their hatred for humans surpasses even that of the mannequins.

'They're gaining on us.'

*You're supposed to be thinking of something – I'll keep tabs on where they are.*

'No need to get upset.'

*Yes, yes, there is a need. A great need.*

'There, up ahead! Low rafters.'

Indeed, there is a canopy of low rafters ahead, one of those areas where the roof needs extra support and the timbers criss-cross in a network of beams. The board-comber runs for this area, his oversized boots slopping on its feet, his Venetian carnival mask bouncing up and down on his face. He leaps upwards, a supreme effort fuelled by terror, and grasps the lowest rafter. His broad-brimmed floppy hat is askew and his musty old clothes hang from his body like curtains from a rail. Splinters in his fingers are the least of his worries. He hauls itself up and climbs. One boot falls, dropping to the ground like a bomb from an aeroplane, to bounce on the boards below. However, his precious bag of Inuit carvings is safely strapped to his back. Nothing must happen to that or the board-comber would have no reason to save himself. The bat dangles outwards, his sensors tuned to the oncoming hordes. He is aware of hundreds of voodoo effigies swarming over the boards, looking up at the figure of the board-comber as he lodges himself in the sharp-angled crook of two rafters.

'They're trying to think of a way of getting up to us.'

*I can see that. No step-ladders around, are there? I hope not. I wish I had fire. I'd melt them voodoos to a puddle of wax.*

'Well, you haven't and a good job too. You'd burn the place down, you would. Uh-oh, they're going to make a totem pole – they're standing on each other's shoulders.'

After looking about for something to use as a ladder and finding nothing, the voodoo dolls are indeed hopping on each other's shoulders. Poles of dolls begin forming and growing upwards. The voodoo dolls do not have enough knowledge of shapes to know to form a pyramid or some other more stable figure. They simply go one on top of the other until they are several figures high, swaying precariously, some of the towers falling and sending the voodoo dolls shooting across the boards.

*Serve you right*, says the board-comber. *Hope you break your nasty little backs.*

One or two of the fallers lie stuck to the floor by their own needles and thrash furiously until they release themselves. Once back on their feet they gather themselves and try again. Those towers which have not fallen come within range of the board-comber's boot. He kicks out, toppling them, sending them flying. The towers hit the floor and explode into their separate parts, the voodoo dolls scattering everywhere. One or two dolls jump for the rafter, scramble up and manage to keep their footing. The board-comber kicks out at these, catches one and sends it hurtling

downwards. The second doll stabs him viciously several
times in the foot with no boot on it.

*Ow! Ow! Ow!*

'I'll get him.'

The bat flies into the face of the voodoo effigy, unbal-
ancing it. The doll drops backwards off the rafter. Its
snarling face is visible all the way down. It hits the boards
and breaks into several bits, an arm going one way, its head
going another, a foot flying into the face of a fellow doll.
The other dolls kick the bits away into a dark area. The
victim was only a warrior: no one of any importance. They
now stand at the bottom staring up. Their faces are twisted
in fury but they do not seem to be able to reason how to
get up there. One or two of them try to launch their needles like spears, but the needles fall short and drop down
among them again.

*That hurts.*

The board-comber pulls two needles out of its foot, left
there by the last doll to attack him.

'Don't I get any thanks?'

*What for? Oh, that last doll. All right, thanks.*

'I should think so. Hey, they're going away.'

The voodoo dolls are indeed leaving. The whole swarm
of them, some in tattered little dresses or smocks, others
with nothing on at all, move in a wave across the attic
floor. They're going in the same direction taken by the
human children. Several of the waxy figures are now
hunched: those who hit the floor with force and dislo-
cated themselves. They look even more sinister than they
did when they were straight-backed. Many needles are
bent. The board-comber feels he has come off best in the
attack, but he knows if he ever runs into the voodoo dolls
again it will be his last encounter. He adjusts his mask with
its jolly puffed cheeks and bulbous nose.

'We must warn the visitors.'

*Why? They should look out for themselves.*

'You know they can't. They've got no idea how to survive up here.'

*They've survived so far.*

'By luck only.'

*Well, they tricked me with that list thing – they told me it was a map. I don't owe them anything. I don't want any more to do with them.*

'Then why leave the traction engine for the boy to find? Why send me out with messages for the older boy? You still think they might lead you to some carvings, don't you? Newcomers often discover old hoards, don't they? Why? Because they're not looking as hard as you old timers do. They stumble across 'em without realising it. You want them on your side if they come across a trove, don't you? A box full of stuff you've never noticed before – maybe with a carving among the junk?'

The board-comber acknowledges this fact. But climbing down from his safe perch is not an easy thing to do. As he attempts it he hears a sniggering from above. Alarmed, he looks up to see a pair of bright blue eyes with long eyelashes. One of the eyes winks at him. It belongs to a pink-faced china doll moving like a monkey through the canopy, her chubby little arms swinging her from spar to spar. Blonde-haired, baby-faced china dolls in rose-and-violet dresses with frilly lace hems are almost as vicious as voodoo dolls. Some of them are wearing mob caps with colourful ribbons. Others are bare-headed, with painted curls. All wear terrible smiles.

The bat says, 'This just isn't your day.'

The board-comber gives a yell and leaps through space to the floor. Fortunately he lands square on his feet. Above him the china doll calls to her clan and a whole nurseryful of even-toothed dolls with chubby-cheeked smiles come chattering through the canopy of rafters in their pretty dresses, white socks and button-strapped shoes. These are roof dwellers and never come down to the attic floor, so the board-comber knows he is safe.

*You bugger off*, he says, shaking his fist at them.

'Hurry, hurry, hurry,' says the bat.

*I'm going as fast as I can. Is that my boot? Oh no, that broken voodoo doll's head is hanging from it — it's buried its teeth in the tongue. How am I going to get that off, without losing a finger? I'll have to prise the mouth open with a knife or something.*

'Leave it there. A ghastly head decoration. You'll start a new fashion among board-combers.'

*You really think so?*

'No.'

'It's all green and tangled,' said Alex. 'Lots of vines and ferns. Oh, look at that tall tree! Soaring like a cathedral spire. Over there's a pool with reddish water in — iron oxide in the soil does that. I learned that in science. Oh, and here's a cave, all mossy and covered in plants and stuff . . .'

'Don't go in!' ordered Chloe. 'You don't know what's in there.'

The pair were on a bare-boards plain. There was an Attican village not far away, similar to those they had already encountered. This one had sewing-machine cars and wardrobes, so they were probably kin to the first village they had stayed at. The people were much the same: short in stature, lumpy, with plaster dust on their heads and shoulders. They seemed a busy lot, collecting clothes which they kept in a warehouse made of book-bricks. That is, they used books like bricks to build it. It was quite a sight and full of old clothes, folded neatly, kept in rows. There were also shoes in there, those too in neat rows. These villagers were obviously traders.

This time the children didn't stay in the village or try to steal any food. They had learned their lesson. Instead they camped well away from it, behind one of those thickets of fishing rods with dozens of vicious hooks like thorns, and tangled nets of lines. Once or twice a villager in a sewing-machine car had surprised them, but they had skilfully avoided being caught. Chloe could tell by the expression on the faces of those Atticans that she and Alex scared as well as angered them.

Above the children – high, high above – was a small skylight which sent down a sunbeam shaft to illuminate them. They both sat cross-legged in the ray, enjoying its brightness. Chloe was stroking Nelson's tummy and he was purring. Nelson had joined them a short time ago, bringing with him a large freshly dead rat which to the amazement and horror of his sister Alex skinned and cooked. He ate the meat, feeding himself through the hole in the mask. Chloe refused to touch it and was most damning in her criticism of her younger brother, who said he couldn't care less.

'If you could see this jungle, you'd be excited too,' Alex told her. 'Have a go now, if you want,' he added generously, removing the mask. 'You simply have to put it on and look hard. You have to *think* about jungles though. If you just sit there and don't try, you end up seeing only the attic.'

Chloe recoiled from the offer, shuddering. 'You don't know *who's* had that thing on,' she said.

The mask said: 'Who are you calling a *thing*?'

'You,' said Chloe emphatically. 'I bet there've been all sorts of people slobbering inside you.'

The mask declined to argue further, having made its point.

Alex returned the mask to his face. He was having great
fun, having crossed the world through the mask's eyes. All
around him was lush jungle with tall buttress-rooted trees
covered in parasitic creepers and ferns. Below the level of
the first canopy there was a second canopy composed of
smaller trees, though in Alex's eyes these too were quite tall.
Then came the undergrowth, steamy, with moist, slick or
hairy leaves, some of them large and thick enough to make
a sunbed. There was wildlife there too, in the form of
monkeys and birds and lots of insects. The smell, through
the mask's nostrils, was of damp vegetation and animal
droppings.

A beautiful swallowtail butterfly flew past Alex's head.

'Clo, you don't know what you're missing.'

'I'll do without it, thank you,' she replied primly. 'Just
don't go inside that cave, you don't know what's in there.'

Alex of course ignored her and went inside. It was dark
so he delved into his pack for the matches. He struck one
and held it up, right in front of his sister's face. She tightened her mouth.

'You're in there, aren't you?' accused Chloe. 'Don't you
ever listen to anything I say?'

'Pictures,' murmured Alex in a disappointed tone. 'In
charcoal I think. A little rhino. And a fish. And some birds.
Just Stone Age people's drawings on the walls. I could do
better than them.'

'I should think so. Art has developed since they were
drawn.'

'Oh, Clo – there's a snake. White one.'

'Drawing or real?'

'Real.'

Chloe said, 'Cave racer. They're blind. They catch bats
and eat them.'

'Yup – I just saw it get one. Talk about fast. Bats look

nice and crunchy. Oh, it's not a bat, it's a bird. There are *thousands* of them in here, Clo. There are nests on the ceiling and all up the walls. Yuk, what am I treading in?'

'I can guess. Alex, come out of that cave. How do you know there's not something dangerous in the back? Caves are full of scorpions, you know.'

'I'm only *looking*, sis.'

Alex took off the mask. His face was sweaty and he wiped it on his sleeve. 'I don't know why you're so awkward, Clo.'

'I just am, that's all.'

Nelson had had enough of being stroked. He went up on his three legs and trotted away with that peculiar gait of his.

'Good old Nelson,' said Alex, picking up a cold drumstick of rat's leg. 'He's a great hunter, isn't he?'

Chloe stared at her brother. 'You don't have to eat that, you know. I found some boxes of apples, and some bottled plums. The people below must have stored them up here. Would you like some?'

'Nope,' replied Alex, tossing away the bone. 'I like rat meat. I was going to keep it from you, 'cause I knew you'd be upset. I like pigeons too. I like them better than rats.'

'Pigeons?'

'Nelson brought me a pigeon. It was delicious.'

'Oh, Alex.'

At that moment there was a sound, out on the fringes of the attic. Both children peered into the gloom, but could see nothing. What was it, an Attican villager? Something else? There were always small noises present: the attic woodwork creaking its joints like a galleon under sail; the birds in the eaves, especially the pigeons cooing in their boring fashion; mice and rats scuttling around, looking for water and food, and each other; the draughts lifting the edges of plastic bags; the steady drip of water in water tanks. Noises of all kinds, some identifiable, others more puzzling. This noise came under the puzzling heading. Soon it stopped, however, and the two children were able to relax again. If there was anything out there, it had halted.

'I'll get some water,' said Alex, standing up. 'We passed a tank a little way back.'

'No – no, don't, Alex.'

'We need water, Clo. I'll be all right.'

'You always disappear.'

Alex said, 'I won't this time. I promise.'

He took some bottles and marched back to the water tank he'd seen earlier. When he inspected the surface of the tank it was much as he'd expected, a bit insecty and with a film of scum. But he dunked the bottles deep under the water and allowed them to fill, watching the bubbles come up to pop on the surface. Once both bottles had been filled, he turned to go back.

'Oh, good grief!' he cried. 'Another one.'

It was a single treasure. It stood there as if patiently waiting to be seized. A model steam car. Not quite as magical and entrancing as his showman's engine, but at one time Alex would have sold his soul for such an engine. And here it was, for the taking. How many more were there in the attic? It was a land of treasures.

He rolled it around for a while with his hand, again wishing he had some methylated spirit handy, but eventually put it carefully under his shirt. For some reason he didn't want Chloe to see it. He didn't know why, because there was no reason why she should disapprove of him gathering steam engines to his bosom. But he decided to hide it. On the way back he came across an old army over-coat, man-sized, and put it on. He found it hid the bump under his shirt very well in its many folds.

Chloe was waiting anxiously for his return.

Predictably she cried, 'What are you wearing that thing for?'

'I just feel like it.'

'Take it off, Alex, it's dirty.'

'No.'

'But look at it. It's *filthy*. And it doesn't fit anyway. Get something that fits if you feel cold. You look lost in that musty old coat.'

'I like it,' he replied stubbornly. 'I'm keeping this one.'

'Honestly, you make me so mad.'

'I don't care, Clo. I like it. I like the coat, I like the mask and I'm keeping them both, whatever you say. They're *me*.'

She looked weary and gave up on him.

'Oh, have it your own way. Who cares? Let's stay here for a while,' suggested Chloe. 'I'm tired. There's nothing to hurry for. We don't know where Jordy is and we might be heading in completely the wrong direction. We might be going in circles for all I know.'

Alex looked at his compass. They were heading directly west.

'Nope – we're still going in a straight line,' he said. 'I've been checking my compass every so often.'

Chloe was impressed. 'That's clever of you. At least we're going *somewhere* then, and not just where we've been.'

'Exactly.' Alex put down the compass and went to pick up his mask, but Chloe said, 'Would you mind not putting that on?'

'Why?'

'Because he scares me.' She whispered, 'I think he wants to take you over.'

'I heard that.'

'What, you mean like aliens invading the earth?' said Alex. 'Nah, he's not going to harm me.'

'How do you know?'

'I can feel it when I put him on.'

Chloe said, 'How do you know that's not him *making* you feel safe and secure, so that it's all the easier to control you?'

'I wouldn't do that. I am Makishi, Most Sacred, Most Feared, but those who tremble before me are my enemies, not my friends. Alex is my wearer and he I would never hurt. Do you not understand the laws of *becoming*? When Alex puts me on he *becomes* me. Therefore he is me and I would never hurt myself. That would be foolish.'

Chloe didn't know what to say to this, but she still couldn't trust the mask.

'I'd still rather you didn't put it on, Alex.'

Alex, bundled up in his thick overcoat, looked at the object in his hand.

The object looked back at him.

'I guess you're right. But I'm not giving him up. We're brothers of the jungle, him and me.'

Alex slung the mask over his shoulder on a piece of cord and Makishi didn't argue with the decision. He knew he had conquered Alex and that he would be carried wherever the boy went now.

'What do you look like?' she asked her brother, sighing, sounding very like Dipa. 'Have you seen yourself?'

Alex ignored the criticism.

'Time we were moving on, sis,' he said, taking out his binoculars. 'Heck, look at those villagers, scurrying around. You'd think that in a place like this there'd be nothing to do, wouldn't you . . . Hello, hello!'

Chloe, who'd been packing her bag, stopped and looked at her brother.

'What is it?'

'Looks like a – I dunno – a swarm of ants or something – no, wait – they're bigger than ants. They're dolls of some kind. Heading towards the village by the look. They've got— you should see their faces. Talk about— hey,' he removed the binoculars from his eyes, 'I bet they're coming to attack this village. Yeah, that'll be it. We've got to warn them.'

Alex pulled on his pack quickly and began running towards the village of wardrobes.

'Wait, Alex. You know we scare them.'

'We've still got to warn them, Clo.'

Alex raced all the way, then ran through the village.

'Alarm! Alarm!' he yelled, not knowing what else to say. 'Enemy on the horizon. Enemy approaching.'

Atticans came running out of their wardrobes and out of the book-built warehouse. One or two of them shrieked and hid their faces in their hands. Others came forward and waved Alex away with both hands, as if he were an escaped animal.

Alex pointed to the oncoming dolls. 'Enemy on the way!' he cried. 'Arm yourselves.'

Chloe caught up to him now and added her own entreaties to those of her younger brother.

Now the Atticans saw the danger and indeed became alarmed. They ran back into their clothes storehouse. Chloe and Alex thought they had gone to hide, but they came running out again with shields and clubs. The shields were old fireguards made of bronze or iron mesh: perfect for protecting the bearers against a small oncoming enemy. The clubs were broom handles which they tested by swishing them through the air.

Alex and Chloe decided to leave the villagers to their battle and make their way on, deeper into the attic.

When Alex looked back, the villagers were doing extremely well. Their skill with the broom handles was almost the stuff of legend. That great Ancient Greek Achilles could have been among them, or the Trojan Hector, such was their talent for this type of fighting. Horrible, ugly dolls ran at them in dozens but the Atticans warded them off with their shields and swatted them, this way and that, with their staves. The villagers had formed a kind of fireguard tortoiseshell, which looked unbreachable. On a single command they took the initiative, moving forward. They forced the waves of barbarian dolls backwards, out on to the plain of boards. The villagers were obviously used to these raids and knew exactly how to cope with them.

Alex and Chloe hurried on, happy to leave the fight in capable hands.

## CHAPTER 10

# Punch and Judy, I Presume?

Having left the villagers to fight their battle, Alex and Chloe continued their safari across the boards of Attica in their search for the region where the ink imps lived among their writing bureaux. With their packs on their backs and the coat-muffled Alex continually consulting his compass, they managed to march in a straight line no matter in what direction the boards lay. They trusted to the compass and set their eyes on the far horizon.

For the moment though, they seemed to be in a wide long corridor, hemmed in with a roof that fell sharply from a high apex. Above and around them the timbers of the attic formed pillars and angled arches and Chloe had the distinct feeling of being inside a magnificent cathedral or temple. Certainly there were benches and chairs of all kinds, lining their route. Whether it was in her mind or in actuality, Chloe had a sense of walking through hallowed rooms and would not have been surprised if priests had appeared to admonish her and her brother for trespassing.

However, they came out of this corridor into a wider, more open landscape covered with fake Christmas trees.

The trees were decorated with lights which were not lit. They were also draped with tinsel and covered in baubles. In piles, here and there, were red-and-white robes: Father Christmas costumes, complete with fake hoary beards.

'How do I look?'

Alex was trying one of the costumes on.

'You look ridiculous in that mask, especially with the white beard decorating it,' replied Chloe. 'Anyway, you can't wear a Santa Claus robe on top of that greatcoat. It looks awful.'

'Ho! Ho! Ho!'

His voice had deepened and he held out his arms as if ready to embrace the children of the world.

Chloe giggled. 'I'd like a red sports car, if you don't mind, Santa.'

Alex growled, 'You'll get what you're given, young lady. Have you been good? I should say not. You've been yomping over attics, haven't you? I can tell by your dusty demeanour, your smutty mush. No red sports car for you. A box of Smarties and an orange, that's what you'll get.'

The game suddenly struck at the heart of Chloe's feelings. A great pang of homesickness went through her and she almost burst into tears. Alex saw the expression on her face and said, 'Sorry, Clo.'

'No, no,' she said, a single tear trickling down her cheek, 'it's not you, I – I was just missing Mum and Dad.'

'Our old dad, or our new one?'

'Both of them, I suppose, but I meant Ben. Funny,' she managed a smile, 'that's the first time I've thought of Ben as *Dad*. I knew it would happen one day. I just didn't think it would be so soon.' She paused before asking, 'Don't you miss home, Alex? Don't you miss Dipa and Ben?'

Alex took off Makishi, who let out an audible sigh.

He thought about it hard, his face wrinkling with the effort, before he replied, 'No, and I'm sure it's because I still think of them as being near. I'm not like you, Clo. I see this place differently. To me Ben and Dipa are just under the floorboards. I *like* this place. I'm having this adventure up here, above their heads, and they're down below, content to wait for me to come back. Maybe they are, Clo? You can't say they're not.'

'But that's not the same as being *with* them.'

He shrugged. 'I guess not. Nelson's here though. He makes it seem like home.'

She smiled again. 'Yes, he does, doesn't he?'

They were quiet for a little while, before Chloe spoke again.

'I feel I've changed while we've been up here. I'm growing too fast.'

'Haven't got a tape measure.'

'No, I don't mean physically – I mean inside. I was a little girl when I came in here, now I'm not.'

'I didn't think of you as a little girl, Clo.'

She laughed. 'Your voice goes all funny when you dress up.'

He took off the Father Christmas robe and beard.

Chloe was pleased when Alex removed the Santa Claus outfit. She was a little troubled by the fact that recently her brother always wanted to be someone else. Whenever the opportunity arose, like with the mask, or with the army greatcoat, he would put them on – and change. The change was not subtle either. One moment he was a shy young boy, the next a great adventurer, and the next someone far more sinister. It was as if he had transformed into some weird personality she alone had to deal with. She wanted to talk to her *brother* not some creep in a mask and costume.

He had never been interested in dressing up when they had been down below. In fact, there had been times in their childhood when she had *wanted* him to dress up. That time she wrote a play and asked him to act in it. Alex had categorically refused, saying he wasn't interested in such things. In those days it would have been quite out of character for him to dress in strange clothes.

'And leave the mask off,' she ordered. 'I want to see your face.'

For once Alex didn't argue. He did as he was told.

'It was getting hot inside Makishi,' he said. 'Hey, we're coming to the end of the Christmas tree forest. What's that out there, more junk?'

'What else would you find in Attica?'

This area turned out to be Chloe's worst nightmare. Along with what appeared to be stage sets there were piles of costumes, fake weapons and jewellery everywhere. Most of the sets were cardboard cut-outs, painted backgrounds, tapestries and cloth hangings. Of course it was the costumes that worried Chloe. No doubt if it was her nightmare, it was Alex's dream. If Alex wanted to be a pirate, he could be one in seconds. Or Henry IV. Or Peter Pan, Sinbad the Sailor, Ali Baba. He could be anything he wanted to be. All the costumes were here along with their trappings.

She glanced at her brother. Indeed, his eyes had lit up as he reached for a plastic Roman helmet.

'We haven't got time for plays, Alex,' she said quickly. 'Come on. We must catch up with Jordy.'

'Plays?'

'You know, messing about with costumes and things . . .'

'Ah,' said a voice from behind them; 'do I detect that we have a Thespian among us? How gratifying.'

Chloe whirled round. At first she could not see the

speaker. Then she realised he was standing in the shadows of a stage set. Was he ugly? He certainly wasn't pretty. With his hooked nose and pointed chin she recognised him instantly. Punch. Of Punch and Judy. He was wearing his traditional brightly coloured costume, including a hat with points and bells. Punch came forward, gliding forward on a skirt, the hem of which brushed the dust on the floor.

'Ah,' said Punch, following her eyes and looking down at himself, 'you're wondering how I walk, aren't you, madam? Being a hand-puppet, I should have no legs, eh? I decline to reveal my secret. It's a puppet thing. I hope you won't consider it poor manners on my behalf to keep it close.' He reached them and held out a small mittened hand. 'How do you do? Punch is the name. But – oh bliss, oh gratification – you know me, don't you? You know this old ham. I can see by your expressions. Many children don't, these days,' he sighed, 'there being so many other distractions for the young. Computers, video games, TV, mobile phones. Still, the seaside remains the seaside, even if most of them go to Spain in these affluent times.'

To her irritation, Chloe found herself shaking the tiny wooden paw.

'How do you do?'

Alex said generously, 'You're not an old ham – I thought you were a pretty good actor when I saw you at my seventh birthday party.'

'A fan! My boy, you've a voice for sore ears. Thank you from the bottom of my little wooden heart,' replied Punch. He sighed again. 'Of course, I always wished to play *Hamlet*. We all did. I know I would have made a magnificent Hamlet. Not to be.' He smiled wistfully. 'There's a little joke in there, if you care to look for it. Very weak, but subtle.' He brightened again. 'Come on home and meet the missus. She'd be tickled to see real people again. Ah! Aha!

Young lady, I can see what you're thinking, but our domestic scene is one of bliss, off-stage. We get on very well, Judy and I, in our way. Of course the violence on stage is pretty bad, but it's traditional you know, and the croc sorts me out at the end. I mean, where would television soaps be without the domestic violence? But I know what you mean, I truly do. It's a bad influence on the kids. That's another reason why we've been discarded, thrown up into the attic. Times change, attitudes change, and if you can't change with them, then you're made redundant. Come on, I'll take you back to the village . . .'

Alex looked at Chloe and shrugged, grinning broadly.

'What can we lose, sis?' He trotted up beside Punch, who was stepping out a bit. 'Have you got anything to eat there?'

'We can certainly rustle you up something. Do you like birds' eggs? Of course you do, a chicken is a bird, isn't it? Well, we can find lots of eggs in the eaves. Not as big as those produced by chickens, who unfortunately don't fly up to gutters and get in through holes, but they lay eggs just the same. I'm sure you could put away a dozen or so, couldn't you?'

'Definitely,' replied Alex. 'Thanks a lot.'

'Don't mention it. Ah.' Punch's voice had lowered as they approached the puppet village. 'There's that fellow Krishna. Thinks a lot of himself because he represents a holy figure – a *Wayang Kulit* he calls himself – but he's not so bad.' He raised his voice again. 'Hi there, Krishna. Look who I've found. People like us, from down below.'

*People like us?* thought Chloe.

There, standing beneath a colourful paper arch which led into the open square, was a puppet Alex recognised from the time they had been on holiday in the Far East. It was a leather shadow-puppet dyed blue for the skin and red-and-green for the clothes he wore. He stood on one leg, leaning against the arch, but hopped forward as they approached.

'Well, well, people from my own land, by the look. How very welcome. What news from Bali?'

'Actually we're not from Bali,' explained Alex. 'We're from Winchester, but our granddad came from India. Our right-hand granddad that is – our left-hand granddad came from Portsmouth. That's what we call them. Right and left granddads. It's a family thing.'

'India?' The puppet brightened. 'What are your names?'

'Alexander and Chloe,' said Alex.

Krishna looked a little disappointed.

Chloe explained, 'Our dad thought western names would be less trouble for us at school. I don't know why. Other kids with Asian ancestry get on all right with eastern names.'

'So, that's the explanation then. Good. Punch treating you all right?'

'Of course I am,' muttered Punch a little testily. 'Why wouldn't I be?'

'Oh, I don't know. I thought you might feel the need to bash them with your truncheon. No? Ha, ha. Well, I certainly wouldn't want to fill them full of arrows or go sticking them with my sword, so there's no reason why you'd want to thump them, I suppose. Well, see you around.'

Krishna hopped away, towards one of the stripy Punch and Judy tents which stood about the place, and disappeared inside.

Chloe asked, 'Why hasn't he got his own tent – a Bali tent?'

'They don't have them, you know,' explained Punch. 'Shadow-puppets are worked behind these white screens. I don't think there are many puppets who have their own tents, like Judy and I. We Punch-and-Judy sets have to share with other puppets. The big fellows – the ventriloquists' dummies – they have a hard job fitting inside one of our tall tents, but what can they do? Live in a suitcase? I think not. Space inside luggage is even more limited. Ah, here we are, home sweet home.'

Punch threw back the flap and called for Judy, telling her to 'bring some eggs for visitors'. After calling to his wife he said to the children, 'I'd invite you in, but there's not room for the two of you.'

'That's all right,' said Chloe, who had been having misgivings about Punch ever since she had met him. 'We're quite happy to wait outside.'

Chloe felt that Punch was being too nice. The attic had made her a very suspicious person. What, she asked herself, if this was an elaborate trap? Most of the creatures in the attic had proved to be antagonistic, if not downright hostile to them. Why should puppets be any different? Surely they had been abused too at times, and held resentment towards the humans that had mistreated them? Chloe was determined to remain on her guard, just in case.

A policeman puppet came out of the tent, trailing his skirts.

'Hello, children, eh? Jolly good. Jolly good. Judy's coming out in a bit. She's dusting herself off at the moment. So, where are you from?'

'Winchester at the moment,' replied Alex. 'We've just moved there.'

'Winchester, eh? Have we done Winchester, Punch? I'm sure we have at some time. I remember a statue of King Alfred.'

'That's right,' cried Alex eagerly. 'In the square.'

'Yes. Yes, we've done Winchester all right.' He tipped his

helmet back on his head with his truncheon. 'Was it a good audience though?'

Here it comes, thought Chloe. Now we get the blame for all the bad audiences they've ever had.

'I do believe it was,' interrupted Punch. 'A *very* good audience. But when did we not get a good reception from our own kind? Small children are easily pleased. We don't have to try very hard, now, do we? Oh, I should like to think of us as brilliant actors, but in truth it's just a bit of slapstick.'

'Slapstick's not *that* easy,' replied the policeman. 'You have to be able to convince them.'

'Well, that's true also.'

Chloe relaxed a little.

Alex said, 'You said earlier, *people like us . . .*'

The policeman looked at Punch, who frowned.

The policeman said, 'Puppets are people too.'

Chloe saw that the situation was about to deteriorate and she jumped in with, 'Oh, he didn't mean *you*. He meant *us*. I mean, my brother has always felt inferior around puppets. I mean, you're so lively and animated. You're so famous. We don't often meet great celebrities like you. We're certainly not in your class.' She laughed. 'We're very ordinary.'

Punch's expression cleared immediately.

'Oh, *that*. You don't want to worry about that. We like mixing with the general public, don't we, policeman? They're our bread and butter – or were. Where's my darling Judy? I must go and chivvy her up. Won't be a sec.' He disappeared into the tent.

Chloe said to the policeman, 'He's a very kind Punch – are they all like that?'

'Oh yes. Up here we can be ourselves,' he replied, 'but to tell you the truth, this Punch is rather special. He believes in acting the Good Samaritan whenever he gets the chance.' He leaned forward in a conspiratorial manner and murmured, 'This one's very *pious*, very religious. It's said that one of his hands is made from a piece of the True Cross.'

The wooden Good Samaritan eventually emerged again.

A buxom red-cheeked Judy in a mob cap and wearing an apron came out of the striped tent with Punch. She beamed at the children, holding the apron out in front of her by its two bottom corners. In the hollow were about thirty birds' eggs: probably pigeons' eggs by the size of them.

'Well, how nice,' she said, clearly very pleased. 'Alex and Chloe. What nice names. Punch said you would like some eggs? I've got some here . . .'

She sat down on the floor. The others joined her. Judy handed one egg to Alex and one to Chloe. Alex went to peel his straight away and was dismayed when it came apart in his fingers. Yolk and white dribbled to the floor. The egg was raw. 'Oh dear,' he said. 'Not cooked.'

Disappointment showed on the faces of the puppets.

'But we can soon cook them, Alex, on your little stove,' said Chloe.

The puppets looked at each other in alarm.

'Not with fire, I hope,' said the policeman. 'Fire in an attic, you know, is not a good thing.'

'Oh, of course,' replied Alex. 'You're right, I wasn't thinking.'

He then took a handkerchief out of his pocket, took the eggs from Judy and placed them in it, tying the corners carefully.

'We'll eat them later,' he said for the benefit of the puppets. 'Raw, naturally.'

'Now that we've met some – some *real* people,' Chloe said earnestly to the puppets, 'perhaps you can help us?'

'Certainly, of course we can,' replied Judy. She turned to Punch. 'Can't we, dear?'

'Naturally, my love, we always try to assist our own kind.'

Chloe had to be very careful in the way she phrased her questions.

'Why is it,' she said, 'that in the attic, things talk that normally *don't*? Like, er – like masks, for instance – can talk. Alex has a mask – the one hanging on his back – which talks all the time. Yet there are other objects that stay as they are, and don't walk or talk.'

'Perfectly reasonable question,' answered Punch, with the policeman and Judy nodding at each other. 'You see, my dear, the attic is like – how shall I put it – like a continent. It is vast. And not only that, it's an invisible vortex – do you know that word? Good! Very bright children,' he said in an aside to Judy and the policeman. 'Without being able to help yourselves you are drawn into the middle, into the very centre of the maelstrom – that's a foreign word for whirlpool which clever children like you need to know.

'As you leave the edges and are pulled further into the middle of the attic, things get more peculiar. Anyway, the long and short of it is all sorts of inanimate objects come to life, can move and talk, even think in a way. Just as we do,' he added quickly. 'Others, as you say, remain *in*animate, unmoving. The attic's not consistent you know. That's what makes it so interesting. One day you might approach a statue and nothing happens, the next day it leaves its pedestal and runs after you. I *love* that side of the attic, the quirky, unpredictable side. Anything can happen. One thing is certain: you should stay out of the middle and away from the eaves.'

Middle? Eaves? What was left? The in-between areas?

Alex said, 'Why, only yesterday we were right up against the eaves. It's hard not to be near the eaves.'

'Ah,' interrupted Judy, 'that's because the roof isn't just an up and down triangular roof. It's *lots* of rooftops, all fitted together. If you were to go up there, outside – God forbid,' she crossed herself, her wooden hand making hollow wooden sounds on her breast, 'you'd be in something like a desert with sharp dunes, if you know what I mean. It goes up and down like wild waves on a stormy ocean, if that isn't mixing my metaphors.'

'I think it is, my dear,' admonished her husband gently, his hooked nose bobbing up and down, 'but you're entitled. It's not easy to describe our roof with just a single simile or metaphor.'

'So keep away from the centre of the attic and the edges?'

'Precisely,' replied the policeman to Alex. 'You'd make a good witness, you know. You catch on quickly.'

'But why are some of the creatures we've met so strange?' asked Chloe. 'I mean, like the villagers.'

'Ah,' explained Punch, 'that's because there are insiders and outsiders. The villagers are insiders, they're *of* the attic, so to speak. They belong here. They are indigenous – I can tell by your expression you know what that means – while we are not. Of course, many of the creatures in the attic are immigrants, like us. Some of us came here by accident or design – like yourselves – others were banished here, exiled. Like us. You are people and as such will come up against a lot of hostility from things that used to be inanimate and now have life of a sort. Objects which were mistreated in the real world – or simply *felt* they were mistreated.'

'The villagers acted very peculiarly,' said Chloe, involuntarily copying Punch's manner of speech. 'Very peculiarly.'

'That's because they see you as phantoms. In their eyes you have a certain translucency. They can't see *right* through you – as through something transparent, like a window –

but you have – now what's a good simile? – yes – you're like a jellyfish to them. They think you want pictures of your ancestors. Did they give you any photo albums? Yes? There you are then. They think that's what you're after.'

'Oh. That's why they sort of jumped back in fright when they came across us? That explains it. But I've got another question. A very important one. You can't tell us where we can find any watches, can you? We're looking for a special pocket-watch that belongs to a neighbour of ours.'

'No, I can't, I'm afraid. You need a map for that. There's a map not far from here. Watches? That sounds like something a board-comber would look for. It's my guess most of the watches in the attic have been collected at some time. You need to find the whole collection.'

'Where?'

Punch shrugged. 'I've no idea, have you?' he asked his wife and the policeman. They shook their wooden heads. 'Maybe beyond the Great Water Tank, which is close to the centre of the attic. None of us have been over the Great Water Tank. None of us ever wanted to go there.'

Alex said, 'What about trapdoors? We don't seem to see any of those any more.'

Punch said, 'There *are* trapdoors, though where they lead is anyone's guess. You'll find them if you look, mostly in the dark corners. But be careful if you go down them. You might find yourself in an even stranger place than the one you're in now. Chinese boxes within boxes, so to speak. If you have to come back up again, it might not even be here, but somewhere else. And the further away you get from your original entry point, the more difficult it's going to be to find your way back. Do you understand?'

'I think so,' replied Alex. 'Yes. Don't go down.'

'It's probably best not to,' Judy confirmed. 'You could find yourselves in all sorts of trouble.'

'By the way,' asked Punch, 'did you go round or come over the mountain of weapons?'

Alex said, 'Over.'

'So you met our monster?'

'You mean Katerfelto,' said Alex. 'I sorted him out all right, with – well, I sorted him.'

'How very brave,' murmured Judy. 'He's terrifying, isn't he? It's all those weapons collected in one place. They've seen death, you know.'

'Dispensed death, my dear,' said Punch, patting his wife's wooden hand with a *clunking* sound. 'Dispensed death in anger. One weapon on its own has very little power, but so many gathered in one place . . . The dark spirits of gun, sword and shell seep out, mingle like gases, and become Katerfelto. An evil cocktail of terrible spirits. You can't experience such horrors as they have seen and made – yes, they have made horror – and come away without absorbing something very dark.'

Chloe said, 'You mentioned *board-combers* a little while ago. What are they?'

'Oh,' Punch laughed, wooden head dipping in mirth, 'yes, of course, you probably haven't seen anything of them, though they're bound to have been around. They're masters at camouflage, the board-combers. They melt into the environment. It's more than a disguise – they're chameleons, those board-combers. And they often follow newcomers around, hoping they'll lead them to whatever it is they're collecting. Board-combers are collectors, you see. They collect the thing that interests them most.'

'Why board-combers?'

Judy explained. 'Rather like beach-combers, only they search the attic strand. It's like a fever, an obsession. Collecting sometimes can be. With some of them it's mirrors, with others it's masks, or toy cars, or watches. Once they've got too many to carry, they gather them in one place and go out on forays, searching for more. The melancholic board-comber who collected the weapons, God rest his morbid soul' – the puppets crossed themselves, producing that drumming noise again – 'succumbed in the end to his very own collection. I believe he was frightened to death by Katerfelto. Very tragic, but I wonder what he expected?'

'How dreadful,' agreed Chloe. 'And are these board-combers native to the attic?'

'No,' replied Punch gravely, 'they're from down below. They often carry a friend with them. An attic creature of some kind. A mouse. A bird. A very large hairy spider with long front legs.' He shuddered a little, before continuing with, 'You know the way pirates always have a parrot on their shoulder? Board-combers carry live creatures much in the same way, for company.'

Chloe suddenly felt overwhelmed by it all.

'If you don't mind,' she said, 'I'd like to get a little rest now. I'm exhausted. What about you, Alex?'

Alex shrugged inside his greatcoat. 'Yeah – if you like.' He got to his feet.

'Where are you staying?' asked Punch.

Chloe was still unsure about the situation and remained a little suspicious of the puppets' intentions, so she waved vaguely at the gloaming beyond.

'Oh – out there.' She got to her feet. 'Thank you for your kindness, and your explanations. We hope to see you again.'

'We hope so too, don't we my dear?' said Punch, nodding at Judy.

'Yes we do, and you'd be most welcome any time,' said Judy, making Chloe feel guilty for harbouring doubt about them. 'Don't stand on ceremony.'

Alex and Chloe gathered up their backpacks and went on their way.

Once the children had disappeared into the twilight zone, Punch turned to his two companions and said, 'That boy is turning.'

'You noticed then?' replied the policeman. 'I did too.'

'I hope he doesn't,' sighed Judy, 'for his sister's sake. She'll miss him, she surely will. You can see she's fond of him.'

'Well,' finished Punch, 'maybe something will happen to stop him. You never know. Miracles do occur, occasionally. Now, my dear, what shall we do with the rest of the afternoon? There's still a lot of light left in those high windows. Let's have a game of cards. I miss my cards. Who's got that pack of Happy Families we found the other day?'

CHAPTER 11

# Dancing Rats in the Moonlight

Having fought his way across the region of the scissor-birds Jordy had settled for a while in a forest of tall clocks. It wasn't that he didn't want to leave it. He did. For one thing, the grandfather clocks were all set to different times, which meant there wasn't an hour in the day when all of them were silent. At least one of them was chiming. And the ticking drove him crazy. He wondered who it was who wound them up.

And of course, the hands were all going backwards, which meant that an hour after a clock had chimed six times, it chimed five.

'Have to clear myself an area,' he said. 'Otherwise I'll never get any sleep.'

And this he did, by opening the fronts to the grandfather and other clocks and stopping the pendulums. Those with weights and chains, he unhooked and let fall to the bottom of their cases. With others he simply jammed pieces of paper in the works to stop the wheels from moving. Thus he managed, after a day, to make himself a silent vale in the forest of tall clocks, where he could wait for his step-siblings. He had seen them coming over the plain behind him: vague misty shapes warped by the moted sunbeam shafts that criss-crossed the space between.

Chloe he had recognised by her posture: Jordy had always admired the straightness of her back when she walked. Alex had been more difficult to identify, for he seemed quite lumpy now. Then Jordy realised his step-brother was bundled up for some reason, with coats and other clothes, a hat, and was wearing some kind of mask. But it had definitely been Alex: you could tell by the way he dragged his feet and walked in that dreamy kind of way which told you he was lost in his head somewhere.

'I expect they're missing me,' he told Nelson, who paid him a visit once the clocks had stopped. 'I can't see them getting on very well without me. They're not practical like me. I'm a survivor.'

Nelson agreed with Jordy, of course: he always did.

But after that initial sighting, Alex and Chloe vanished. They must have taken another turning, or direction. Jordy was disappointed. He longed to have someone real to talk to now. Loneliness was not a pleasant thing, especially in a strange place. It dragged you down. He found himself waking in the middle of the night with a start, wondering if he'd heard voices or had simply been caught in a dream. He would stare out into the darkness, hoping that Alex and Chloe were nearby, and that morning would reveal them. Once or twice he even called out their names, but received so many mocking replies from attic creatures, he never did it again.

At night the attic was like a jungle. Even with the clocks stopped Jordy was plagued with sounds. There were twit-terings, squealing, screeches, scratchings and scrapings and the like. These were noises he could more or less identify and put down to live creatures. But there were other more sinister sounds: whirrings, rattlings, mechanical buzzings, high whining noises, raspings. Some of them were quite loud and near to him, others were softer and further away.

In the night it seemed as if the whole of Attica was swarming with mechanical beasts, roaming the boards, looking for prey. When morning came around, however, it became relatively quiet again. He would stand on the edge of the plain and stare out, thinking to see herds of clockwork elephants, or robot monkeys, or automated leopards out there. But once the darkness had lifted, the boards were bare of such creatures. There was just him, alone, without a single companion of any kind.

The nights gave him the feeling of being besieged, threatened and menaced by hordes of unseen creatures. The days left him convinced that he had been abandoned, acutely aware of his solitude, like a castaway sailor on a desert island. Neither sensation was very pleasant. Yet he was swiftly falling in love with the attic. He guessed it was the same sort of feeling his grandfather had spoken of, when talking of Africa. In his grandfather's youth Africa had been a dangerous place, with wild animals which roamed everywhere. Snakes, crocodiles, lions and other beasts. There had also been the extremes in climate, deadly diseases and mosquitoes. Yet Jordy's grandfather had loved Africa with a great passion. This is how Jordy felt about Attica: it was a dangerous place, but it captured your heart.

When Nelson was around Jordy felt better, but Nelson was not one to stay long and once he'd gone again the bitter taste of loneliness returned to haunt him. He found he needed to talk to himself to avoid going crazy. One's own company is better than nothing. Otherwise he was afraid he might come to believe he was not there at all: a figment of an imagination. How terrible that would be, to discover he did not exist except in the mind of a spider or a fly. To go swiftly from a point where he believed he was the only real living thing in the world, to the sure knowledge that he was nothing but a stirring of the dust, a draught of air, a splash of light.

'I must try to stop these weird thoughts coming into my head,' he told himself. 'Otherwise I *will* go crazy.'

He tried making noises to prove to himself he was there: clashing old saucepan lids together and kicking hollow drums. But somehow the noises made things worse. He found himself listening very hard in the silence that followed, for sounds that he might have missed during the racket. What if there had been a search party out there, calling his name, and he had blotted those calls out with his stupid noises? Every solution turned out to be a problem and every problem grew to enormity.

But he stayed in the forest of tall clocks, and waited. There came a time when he ran out of food and had to go looking for more. Sick as he was of the vegetables grown by Atticans, he knew he had to find some or starve. And true to his determined nature he *did* find some. Two hours' walk from the forest there lay a triangle of three Attican villages. He visited this place twice in two days, gathering crops and filling his larder.

On his third trip he found the villages in the middle of a festival.

'Oh, hey!' cried Jordy, delighted with what he saw. 'A game of hockey – I think.'

It appeared that they celebrated this festival by playing sport with old-fashioned T-squares – such as those used by draughtsmen and architects – wielding them as their sticks. With these sticks they batted an object around in teams of thirteen, attacking three goals placed one outside each village. Jordy watched as the lumpy little Atticans charged back and forth, whacking a ball made of rags. There seemed to be few rules in this game apart from the obvious one: you were not allowed to pick up the ball.

There were no goalkeepers and the goals themselves were sea chests on their sides with the lids thrown back, like open mouths waiting to be fed.

'Oh, wow,' Jordy murmured to himself from behind a cardboard box. 'I'd love a game . . .'

He sat watching for quite a time from his hiding place. Gradually, one by two or three, players began dropping out. Jordy wasn't sure why this was happening, but he guessed that when they got too exhausted to play any more they simply gave up. Once they came off the pitch, it seemed they couldn't or wouldn't return. Before long the teams were down to about three on each side and Jordy realised that the drop-out rate had been the same from each team at any one time. So if a player from village A had had enough, and left the field, village B and C players would follow shortly. Thus the teams were reduced equally and with no advantage to any of them.

One trick with the T-square seemed to be a favourite. A player would slip the T-square between an opponent's legs, so that the top bar of the instrument was behind the ankles, then yank him off his feet. A great cheer would go up from the crowd when one of them did this to another. Jordy could see no referee or umpire on the field and assumed this kind of play was not a foul, even though the aggrieved player would leap back onto his feet and remonstrate loudly with the attacking player.

Finally, when there were only three players, one from each village, left on the pitch, Jordy could stand it no longer. He jumped out and grabbed a T-square which had been left leaning against a box. Shouting wildly, he threw himself into the fray, swinging his T-square with expert hands.

'Go for the ball!' he yelled at himself. 'Keep your eyes on the ball!'

Indeed, one would have expected the villagers to have been shocked into immobility by the sudden appearance of a ghost. Not so. The players still on the pitch fought furiously with him for possession of the ball. Did he think he could be a star T-square-wielder overnight? Not so. These villagers had been playing the game since they could walk. Within two seconds Jordy was on his backside and nursing a bump on the back of his head.

He didn't stop to complain: he was up on his feet in a flash and had downed the Attican who had flattened him. The other two came at him in a rush, but he sold them a dummy and sidestepped them, managing to take the ball with him. Two whirled and chased, the one on the ground followed swiftly. Jordy drew back his T-square to shoot at the nearest goal: what did he care which village it belonged to? But an Attican flung his T-square from five metres, striking the ball and sending it shooting across the field of play, out of his reach.

'Is that allowed?' cried Jordy. 'Is that in the rules?'

He didn't wait for an answer. Jordy chased the bat and ball. Reaching them he kicked the other player's T-square out of reach, sending it skidding over the boards. Then with the other two bearing down on him he did a marvellous turn and struck the ball well. It lifted about six centimetres off the floor and passed between the two oncoming players. Onward it flew, surely and truly, and ended in the corner of a goal on the far side.

The crowd went into an uproar. They surged on to the pitch.

'Yay!' Jordy yelled, elated. 'Goal!'

But the mood was ugly.

They were not coming to congratulate him, to raise him

up on their shoulders and carry him triumphantly through the attic. They were coming to get him. Many had picked up T-squares and were holding them in a threatening manner. Jordy was left in no doubt they were angry with him and meant to do him harm. He decided it was time to leave. He dashed off into the dim regions of the attic. Happily they did not follow, probably feeling that having chased him away was a victory in itself, ghosts in the attic often being quite stubborn creatures.

Jordy went disconsolately back to his camp site among the grandfather clocks and brooded for a while. That game with the T-squares had reminded him of how much he was missing his old life. He moped around for the rest of the day, thinking that he wasn't going to move again until Alex and Chloe caught up with him. At least they never minded indulging him when it came to a game of cricket or hockey or something, even if they didn't feel the same way about it themselves. They could be a pain in the neck at times, but they had their good points.

Jordy went for a walk in the evening, avoiding the three villages. He was on his way back when he saw the villagers gathered in a large group around something hanging from the rafters. He hid behind a pile of junk and observed them from a distance.

At first he thought it was another game, but then the scene seemed too solemn for it to be sport of any kind. Something more serious was going on. He studied the object hanging like a huge plumb bob from the rafters by a long rope. Covered in butcher's muslin it looked like a giant cocoon, a chrysalis. About the size of a large side of mutton, it spun slowly on the end of a rope.

What the heck is that? thought Jordy.

He noticed that the villagers were all dressed in white and some of them, the ones with hats on, had wooden bowls in their hands which they offered to the masses. These containers seemed to be full of grey powder which the Atticans took in the fingers and sprinkled on each other's heads, until their lumpy bald pates were as grey as rain clouds.

Suddenly four villagers appeared with an enormous brass bed, carrying it up on their shoulders, one person to each leg. The brass was polished to a brilliance and sparkled in the evening light from the roof windows above. There was no mattress on the bed, only a white blanket.

The cocoon was cut ceremoniously from the rope and placed on the bed. The four carriers moved off with the crowd following and throwing the grey powder on to the cocoon. Jordy went along with them, ducking and weaving between piles of junk to remain hidden. Eventually the party came to a spot where two villagers stood with tools in their hands. They had removed three boards from the floor. The cocoon was then lifted from the bed and placed in the hole and the floorboards hammered back in place. At this point the creaking voices were raised to a high pitch and Jordy had to put his hands over his ears: the discordant sounds hurt his hearing.

Finally the group dispersed and Jordy was alone once more.

'Wow,' he said to himself, 'that was weird. I wonder what that is under those boards. Something valuable, I'll bet.'

He resisted the inclination to go and prise the boards up to see what it was. Even if it was a treasure hoard he was in dangerous territory. If he was seen it was a long run back to safety and he didn't want to risk being caught stealing valuables as well as food. He returned to his den in the clock forest to think about what he had witnessed.

When the sun had disappeared from the skylight windows,

he lay on his back and mused. Suppose Alex and Chloe *never* came? He'd lost sight of them out on the boards now. They had vanished. What if they'd turned round and gone home? Perhaps they'd fallen down some hole in the boards and were hurt – or even dead? Maybe it had not been a good idea to go on ahead by himself after all? Why was he always trying to be the big brother to them, instead of letting them share the responsibility?

At that moment Jordy sat bolt upright and listened hard.

What was that?

Music?

Definitely music. He could hear the distant strains of a fiddle being played somewhere just outside the forest of clocks. The sound was mournful and melancholy at first, but then the pace picked up and the tune became what sounded like an Irish jig. Jordy jumped to his feet and went in search of the musician, who was no great violinist.

Jordy reminded himself that he ought to be careful. If the musician was an Attican he could expect a cold reception at the very least. It was best to remain concealed until the situation became clearer.

Creeping up to the pale of the forest of dead clocks, Jordy peered into the dense blackness. Anything could be out there: a different people; a herd of strange beasts; even monsters.

But there were no monsters. What there were, were rats.

From a high skylight a shaft of moonlight, very bright, very intense, full of flecks of dust, fell upon the attic floor.

In this spotlight two rats were up on their back legs, dancing. They were gently twirling and spinning, hopping and jumping, both moving to the music from a hidden minstrel. Their tails swished in time to the cadence, their ears twitched and their forelimbs waved. They were lost in the melody, caught up in their own rhythmic steps, as they pranced and leapt, swayed in an elegant manner, and even quivered with the longer humming notes. Two willowy rafter rats with intent expressions, dancing to the magic of a fiddler's tune.

'How can they do that?' murmured Jordy to himself.

But they did. And they did it magnificently.

Then the speed of the music picked up pace and the dance became faster and faster, until Jordy felt giddy for the two rodents. They spun, they somersaulted, they flew through the air. It was a dance of demented red-eyed rats with whirling-dervish suppleness in their bones. What demons possessed their souls to dance with such frantic energy, such frenetic movements? Surely at any moment their limbs would fly off, their heads would shoot from their bodies? Jordy had never witnessed such a scene.

He became aware of an audience out there, beyond the dancing rats, who were just as entranced as he. When his eyes grew used to the darkness he could see they were villagers: Atticans, probably the same ones who had chased him earlier, now lured by a fiddler's tune. The villagers stood and watched the pair, absolutely absorbed by them. None appeared to look for the music maker. They simply enjoyed the dancing rodent duo and ignored the presence of the one-man orchestra.

It was sheer poetry in the moonlight. Jordy was not normally one to appreciate such delights, but this time he knew he had witnessed something quite extraordinary.

Once the music stopped the rats slipped away up into the darkness beneath the rafters.

The villagers had brought gifts with them, of food and drink, which they left standing in the shaft of moonlight. When the Atticans had gone, Jordy waited to see who would take the gifts. No one did. Eventually he decided to take some of them himself. His stores could always do with a boost. So he crept out and reached for one of the bottles of drink. Unscrewing the top he took a long swig. It tasted a little like weak ginger beer and after a diet of plain water it was delicious. Jordy then reached out for a parcel of food: squares of something which looked like confectionery.

A hand of strong thick fingers clamped around his wrist.

'Aahg!' Jordy almost died of fright.

'Leave them where they be,' snarled a rough, coarse voice, 'or I'll snap your arm like a matchstick.'

Still all Jordy could see was this thick wrist in the spotlight provided by the moon, with a bunch of hairy fingers attached.

'Leave me alone,' he cried. 'I haven't done anything.'

'Nothin' but steal the food out of my mouth.'

'I haven't touched the food yet.'

'Nothin' but snatch the drink from my lips.'

Jordy's fear ebbed a little as no threat was carried out.

'It's not your food – the villagers left it.'

'Didn't I earn it?' growled the hoarse-voiced speaker. 'Didn't I busk the life out of two talented and willin' rodents, who danced their socks off to my beautiful music? Who do you think trained the rhythms into 'em? Old Nick? Who put the skill in their little feet? Who gave 'em the music to make 'em dance? This food is payment. Mine. You can bugger off, if you like, and leave my wages where they be, thank you.'

Jordy felt the grip relax and he wrenched his hand free, so that he could run back into the forest of clocks.

Once he'd got away he stood there panting and sweating.

Who the heck was that? Was it human?

Jordy gathered his courage and went back, to stare out at his erstwhile captor.

It was indeed a person. It was a tall powerful-looking boy

in a thick ankle-length raincoat with many folds. On his feet were knee-length leather boots with heavy heels. On his head was a broad-brimmed felt hat with a wide floppy brim. You could imagine rain pouring off that brim as the rugged face beneath stared out over unexplored regions.

'Hey!' cried Jordy. 'Are you a local or are you like me?'

The boy looked up from his task of chewing a sweet-meat. There was a tough air about him. He had a jutting jaw that made granite look like soft sandstone.

'Human? Was once, I s'pose.'

'I'm human too.'

'You be a bloody nuisance, that's what you be.'

It had been a long time since Jordy had talked to another member of his own species.

'Can we talk?' he asked. 'Can I come out there and talk with you?'

'If you do I'll break your neck.'

'No you won't.'

The squatting youth looked up from his eating again and seemed to sigh.

'Come on out then, but mind, I live up here 'cause I don't like my own kind. I prefer the company of rats to people. But you look lost, boy. Come on out and tell me the tale of woe.'

Jordy set his jaw. 'It's not a tale of woe,' he argued, stepping out of the clock forest. 'There's no woe in it. I'm simply missing a bit of company. My brother and sister are around somewhere, and when I find them I couldn't care less what you do – whether you hate people or not – but until I find them I haven't got anyone else to talk to.'

'I'm not sure if I care for that or no – I think I don't. But come anyway, if you must.'

Jordy squatted down near his new companion.

'Was that an Irish jig you were playing?'

'It was a jig all right, but not all jigs have to be Irish. It were a sailor's tune, learned from sailors. I might have been one once. Hard to remember now.'

'What are you doing up here – in the attic? Are you lost?'

Jordy had been about to add 'like me' but pride held back the words in the end.

'Nope. I like it here.' The youth was eating what looked like the roasted leg of a bird. 'It's peaceful and unbothersome.'

'Can I have some of that?' Jordy pointed to the meat. 'I'll swop you for some apples I found.'

The boy gave Jordy three cold drumsticks.

'Here – but keep your shrivelled old apples.'

'How do they cook it?' asked Jordy. 'I haven't seen any fires.'

'And you won't,' replied the boy. 'They use lenses - from telescopes, binoculars, magnifying glasses. With lenses you can cook something under direct sunlight without producing a naked flame.'

Jordy ate the bird with relish wondering why a naked flame was so much of a problem. 'You better watch out for those rats,' he told his companion, 'or Nelson will have them for breakfast.'

'Nelson bein' . . . ?'

'Our cat. He's got three legs.'

'Kind of guessed that, by his name. If he kills my boys though, I'll skin him alive and eat him too. What's a damn cat doing up here in the attic? Who let him up here?'

Jordy felt a little shame. 'I guess we did.'

'Huh! Well, you've been warned.'

'So have you. Nelson won't listen to me. He doesn't listen to anyone. All I'm saying is, watch your rats. If they dance in front of Nelson he'll think it's Christmas.'

Suddenly the youth grinned at Jordy over a legbone.

'I'm beginnin' to like you, boy,' he said. 'You've got some grit about you. Most of the lost ones up here cry for their mummies. This is a good, generous land up here, if you know how to live. I do and I like it.'

'How did you come to be up here?' asked Jordy, taking a swig of ginger beer without asking. 'Did you get lost?'

'Oh, we all get lost at first. I went up into my attic to look for somethin' – can't remember what now, it's so long ago. I was a reader then. Found some books, started readin' one of 'em. Then another. Loved reading in them days. Once I'd read all them I'd found in a cardboard box, I moved out a bit, outside my own attic space. Once you do that, you're a goner. I became a browser. Would be one today, if I hadn't found that book on navigation. Inspired me to become a bortrekker.'

'What's a bortrekker?'

'Someone who treks the boards – a wanderer – an attic explorer of sorts, I guess you'd say.'

Jordy liked the sound of that.

'And a browser?'

'Someone that wanders the attic, lookin' for books. Picks 'em up, reads a bit. Puts 'em down. Moves on. Finds another book. Reads a bit. And so on. Browsing. Just browsing.' The voice became dreamy as he said this, then the bortrekker waved his arm at the darkness around them. 'Lots of 'em out there. Bortrekkers, board-combers, browsers, others. You won't come across many of 'em, 'cause this is a big, big place. And only a few of us roaming over it. How long have you been here?'

Jordy told him.

'Well, you're only just startin', but you'll find out. The boards,' he waved a bird-bone again, this time in one direction, 'they seem to go on for ever . . .'

At that moment though, there were squealing sounds behind Jordy and he turned to see the two rats were descending from the rafters. The bortrekker threw them the bones of the cooked bird he and Jordy had been eating. The rats fell on this fare with great enthusiasm, cracking them in their rodent jaws. They nibbled away at what was left of the flesh on the bones, staring at Jordy as they did so, their small red eyes unblinking.

'That performance tonight,' said Jordy. 'It was good.'

'The audience was expectin' it. They'd been to a funeral. They needed cheerin' up.'

'A funeral?' Jordy suddenly thought about what he had seen at the village. 'Do they – do they bury their dead under the boards?'

The bortrekker gnawed on another bone. 'Yep. First they gut 'em and hang 'em high up in the rafters, though. Way, way up, in the high draughts of the loftiest regions. Dry 'em like Parma hams, so there's no moisture left in 'em. That way there's no smell of rotting flesh, if you know what I mean.'

Jordy's stomach felt queasy all of a sudden. He felt stupid for thinking that what he had seen stashed away was buried treasure. Of course he did not mention this to the youth sitting with him.

'I saw them,' he said. 'They threw powder over each other.'

'Dust,' explained the bortrekker. 'Old grey dust.'

## CHAPTER 12

# Bortrekkers and Electric Dust Storms

'You want to become a bortrekker?' asked the youth. 'Is that it?' He looked up and waved an arm and sighed. 'This here place, the attic, is a wonderful land when you get to know it. I love it. It's in my blood now, every plank, every splinter. When it knows you like it, the attic looks after you, in its timbery way. I can understand why you want to stay here. I felt the same after I'd been here a bit. I never want to leave.'

'No,' replied Jordy honestly, 'I don't want to stay here. This is a great place, I'll give you that. I *like* it here. It's exciting. Things happen to you. But I don't want to stay for ever. I just need to know how you find your way around. I have to find a pocket-watch, you see. Not just any watch, a special one. Could you teach me how to navigate? You say you don't have a compass or a map. How do you do it? I need to know because I also have to find my brother and sister, and then the way out.'

The bortrekker settled back into his raincoat, tipping his big hat over his eyes.

'Compasses are no good up here. The needle always points to the middle of the attic. You see, the natural or the unnatural way of this place is to draw you into the centre. So a compass will take you in that direction. Charts? There is a map . . .'

'. . . in a golden bureau where the ink imps live.'

'Ah, someone told you. Yep, that's where it is, down by the Great Water Tank. Never been that way myself, but I'm told it's there. I'll get there one day, before I die. Other places to go first. Bortrekking ain't so much a living as a pastime. I guess I'm like a tramp or a hobo, wandering the world. There's no great purpose in it. It's just somethin' to do. I could be readin' books – read most of them I wanted to – but I can do that anyway, while I'm roamin' here, there and everywhere.'

Jordy leaned his back against one of the great pillars.

'My sister likes books – my step-sister. Chloe. She carries a list of her top favourites in her pocket always.'

'Used to do that. Till I read all my favourites and started on those I'd never heard of.'

'I've got a step-brother too: Alexander.'

'Magnificent name,' said the bortrekker. 'Alexander the Great. Warrior king, conqueror of empires, horseman, traveller, undoer of difficult knots – he was a bortrekker, you know – reached the mighty river Indus.'

'Well, Alex's ancestors came from India, but he's no Alexander the Great. He's a bit into himself. Likes engines and inventions and things. I'm more into sport myself.'

'Is that so?'

'Yes. I tried to join in with a game the Atticans were playing with T-squares, but they chased me away when I got a goal.'

The bortrekker shook his head.

'You want to stay away from them locals. They're not like us humans. May *look* a bit like us, but they're from here and we're not. You must've noticed I stayed hidden in the dark when I played my violin. That's 'cause they think we're spectres. How would you like ghouls roamin' over your cricket pitch, eh? Not much. That's the way they feel, I guess. They leave me gifts when I get Arthur and Harold dancin' for 'em, but they don't know it's me. I don't know who they *think* it is – maybe some god? – but so long as I don't show myself I can get away with it.'

'Arthur and Harold?'

'My rats.'

The bortrekker pointed to the two creatures who were washing themselves with their paws. One of them now wandered off and found the crook of a rafter in which to curl up and go to sleep. The other kept looking at Jordy with a rather disconcerting stare. Jordy supposed Arthur and Harold were not used to seeing their musician talking with another human.

Jordy said, 'And you call it a violin, not a fiddle?'

'Same difference. I'm told a fiddle is a violin played with the base tucked into the elbow joint, and a violin is a fiddle played with the base tucked under the chin.'

Jordy laughed. 'That's a bit like how you can tell a crow and a rook apart.'

'What's the answer?'

'A rook is a crow if it's on its own and a crow is a rook if it's in a flock.'

The bortrekker laughed. 'God, I haven't laughed in a long time. That feels good. You're all right, boy. Teachin' me to laugh again. Tell you what I'm goin' to do for you in return. I'm goin' to teach you to navigate this world. It ain't easy, but I'll teach you the basics. You're not tired, are you?'

'I'm wide awake,' said Jordy. 'I can sleep tomorrow.'

'Good. All right then, this is how it's done. Short trek navigation. This is the easy bit. If you want to go in a straight line, 'stead of getting drawn into the middle of the attic, you need to look ahead for two sunshafts, comin' down from skylights. Line up two more or less one behind the other. Don't matter if they're a bit out, the line don't have to be *dead* straight. So, then you start off from a particular point and head towards the first sunshaft, still keeping the one behind it in view, keeping them lined up, like the sights on a gun. When you reach that first one, take another sighting on the second and a *third* sunshaft, and do the same again. Simple. All you got to remember is you have to do the sightings at the same time every day – noon if possible – so the shafts are always striking the deck at the same angle. You see what I mean?'

'I think so,' replied Jordy, wondering how this helped someone get from one particular geographical spot to another. 'I've done orienteering and that makes sense insofar as going in a straight line. It won't help me find, say, the Great Water Tank, though, will it?'

'I guess not, but it'll keep you heading in one direction. You see, up here it's a bit like before sailors had longitude to help with navigating. Up here we only have latitude: the cracks between the floorboards. They only go in one direction. So you can tell how far you are along, say, an east to west line, but you can't tell where you are north to south.'

'That *seems* to make sense too, but I don't think it helps me much,' said Jordy. 'Thanks for trying, anyway.'

'You're welcome. Now *long* trek navigation. The stars.'

'Stars?' repeated Jordy, looking mystified. 'What stars?'

'Two kinds. Glass and timber. The first kind is the skylights. The second kind is timber. In the outside world they can only see stars at night. We can usually only see ours during the day, though sometimes a bright moon will illuminate them. Now, over there,' he pointed, 'a bunch of skylights will appear in the morning. They're my *Ursa Major*. Beyond them is a big bright skylight, my *Sirius*, which lines me up neatly for the constellation of Capricorn, a series of glass tiles which dot the heavens of the Far Corner of the attic. Orion's Belt, *Capella*, I've got 'em all in my head. They speak to me, as the night stars speak to explorers in your world.'

'Wow!' cried Jordy, fascinated.

'Now the timbers – the rafters – are different. I guess they're not so much like stars as like mountain ranges. You look up, you recognise angles, shapes, formations. There's the Cat's Cradle Matrix formation just a short day's trek from here, and Johnson's Totems beyond that. That leads to the Mechano group. Anywhere I am I just look up at the rafters and there's a pattern I know – or if I don't know 'em I log 'em in my head for future reference, notin' just where they are in relation to other timber formations.'

'That's ab-so-lutely brilliant,' murmured Jordy, impressed. 'You think I could learn?'

'If you're a lifer, sure.'

'Oh.' That didn't sound so good to Jordy, who certainly didn't want to spend the rest of his life in an attic.

They seemed to have run out of conversation for now and Jordy sensed the bortrekker wanted to be quiet for a while. He found the pillar beneath which the rats were now both sleeping and leaned against it, staring out into the darkness of the Attican night. The moon out there in the outside world seemed to have gone behind a cloud, for there were no lunar shafts striking through from the skylights. Jordy's former loneliness had now drained from him and he was feeling refreshed. He still missed his brother and sister, of course, but that awful empty feeling of forced solitude had gone.

Jordy liked the bortrekker. He knew Chloe wouldn't approve of him: she was a bit funny about purposeless souls, but Jordy found him fascinating. No school. No real work. Nothing but this day and the next, one after the other.

There was a flash in the sky, like sheet lightning.

'What was that?' cried Jordy, sitting bolt upright. 'Did you see that?'

'Happen I was asleep,' grumbled the bortrekker. 'What're you gabbing about?'

'There,' said Jordy excitedly. 'There's another one. Out there. Did you see it? A flash of light.'

'Oh, *that*.' Jordy could hear the rustling of the coat of many capes, as the bortrekker settled back again. 'That's a storm. Probably over the Great Water Tank. Electric dust storm.'

'Electric dust storm?'

'Yep. You know this place is full of dust. Dust on the rafters, on the beams, on the boards of the floor. It's lain here since the attic was created. Some places it's knee deep. There's even areas where it's so thick and wide you can drown in the stuff. Quickdust we call it. You want to stay away from quickdust, or you'll go under and choke, a horrible dry death. Yep, half this world is dust. You can see it in the moonshafts, you can see it in the sunbeams. Dust, dust and more dust. Dead insects, cobwebs, dried rodent droppings and dusty old dust. That's why I wear a kerchief over my mouth an' nose most of the time. Here's not bad, but there's places you can't even breathe when the South Draught blows. In a blistering high summer there's a mistral draught comes in from the fractured roof of the East Wing – hot and weary – and dries you to a piece of leather . . .'

'What's that got to do with the storm?' Jordy demanded to know. 'Apart from them both being dust storms.'

'Well, like I say, dust motes have been here since the dawn of time, since prehistoric attic time. In all that time they've got charged with static electricity. It's in the air, you know, everywhere, even up here. Some particles of dust are negative charged, others are positive charged. When a cloud of positively charged dust motes meets a negative cloud, there's a discharge of electricity. Lightning, you might say. That's what you can see out there. Can you hear the crackle? No, it's a long ways off then. If you count the seconds 'tween the crackle and the flash, that's how many miles away the storm is.'

Jordy was amazed. 'This really is an ancient place then?'

'Ancient? This place must have been built by a powerful creator, you'll give me that. An attic of these dimensions, these complexities? And who had a son who was a carpenter? Maybe the son followed in the father's footsteps, made a trade out of his pappy's favourite hobby?'

'Really?'

'Well, your guess is good as mine, but I reckon it must have been. Maybe he built it as a tree house when he was a kid, supposing he ever was a kid. Being who he was, of course, it was a miracle tree house, bigger than anything of its kind made before. Maybe he built it to play in, when he wanted to get away from the heavy duties put on his shoulders. Then again,' the bortrekker shrugged inside his coat, making it rustle again, 'maybe it was someone else, someone we've never heard of or could comprehend?'

Jordy watched the electrical dust storm. In itself it was a miracle of dazzling light. True, it did look a long way away, but being high in the Attican sky he could see the individual sparks building up, cracking from dust particle to dust particle, jumping motes, until there was one big rush when a million dust specks discharged their static electricity. This terminated in an almighty blanket flash illuminating the whole roof space. What a wonder of nature! The wild elements in their savage glory! He wished he were closer to it so he could get more of a sense of the power being released. He also wondered if Chloe and Alex could see the same storm. There was no reason why not. The idea seemed to bring them closer to him.

Jordy could hear the bortrekker snoring through the whole wonderful experience and thought to himself that he could never get so blasé about such a thing. There was a point when he could see tiny streaks leaving the dust cloud, lit up like fireflies or sparks, which curved out and down towards the boards.

'Falling stars,' he murmured.

What a fantastic sight: nimbus magic, a spangled show just for Jordy's eyes. He did not think he would ever forget this moment, when the pyrotechnics of the attic had been let loose, and had filled his heart with the marvels of navigation and weather.

Chloe woke to see pulsing lights in the attic heavens far in the distance. Every so often there would be a crackle and a lightning fork would flash down to the boards below. Alex was still fast asleep so she left him there while she watched this phenomenon taking place in the faraway regions of this world of boards and timbers. She sat up and wrapped her arms around her knees and enjoyed the spectacle as one might from the cosiness and security of a bedroom window in the middle of the night at home.

'How strange,' she murmured. 'How very strange.'

As with bedroom window storms, the sight was not alarming; in fact, it was somehow comforting. She had called it strange but in fact it felt familiar: an experience which reached down into her racial memory. Humankind has witnessed magnificent storms since they first got up on to their back legs and started calling their fellow mammals 'beasts'. She could have been viewing it from the window of a modern office building or from the entrance to a cave. It was an ancient sport, watching the distant storm.

Finally, Chloe had had enough of the wonders of the attic and once again curled up and went to sleep, a little easier in her own mind.

When she woke again a bleary-eyed Alex was speaking to her from the depths of the folds in his greatcoat. 'Any tea going?'

She was surprised to see his stomach move under the coat.

What was happening to him? Something *was* coming out.

Whether it was a monster which finally emerged depended upon your point of view. Certainly Chloe didn't regard him as such, but a mouse or a sparrow might. Nelson's gingery face appeared in the gap between the second and third button on the coat. He stared, gave an enormous yawn which not only showed his teeth but also the back of his throat, then he squeezed out, popping one of the buttons as he did so.

'What's Nelson doing in there?' asked Chloe indignantly. 'Has he been sleeping inside your coat all night?'

'Yep.'

'And I suppose he's brought you another rat?'

'Nope.'

'In that case, it's a veggy breakfast.'

Alex groaned. He stood up and went for a wash in the nearest water tank, which was about fifty metres away. When he got back he found Chloe had boiled the eggs given them by the puppets. Alex sat down and, full of gratitude for Punch and Judy, ate his fill.

'Not *too* many of those,' warned Chloe. 'You'll block up. Eggs do that to you.'

'You sound like a mum.'

Chloe acknowledged this. She felt a bit like a mum sometimes. Boys needed to be told to wash, eat properly and to change their socks. Why they didn't respect cleanliness or treat the food they threw down into their stomachs with caution she couldn't imagine, but they started out life with a mum and most seemed to need one for ever.

Nelson didn't appear to need anything to eat. He limped over to a spotlight thrown down from the roof, and stretched out again. There he lay in the warmth of the sun, gathering the energy necessary to go out and kill things by the dozen. It was he, however, who rolled over and was suddenly alert when a distant noise was heard.

'What's that?' asked Chloe, a hard-boiled egg halfway to her mouth. 'Did you hear that, Alex?'

Nelson was gone, slipping away into the shadows.

Alex took out his binoculars, looking through them.

'Those doll things with the straggly hair and pins. Them that went for the villagers at that last collection of Attican wardrobes huts. They're coming,' he said. 'D'you think they'll attack us?'

Chloe was alarmed. 'You're sure they're heading this way?'

'Positive. They keep stopping and sniffing the ground before pointing at us. I think they're tracking us.' The glasses came down. 'We're being hunted.'

Chloe jumped to her feet, quickly followed by Alex. They gathered up their things, put them into packs, and began jogging away from the scene. Makishi, on Alex's back, complained that he was being 'bounced'. Alex said he couldn't do anything about it. Things were looking desperate for the two children, who prior to this had no idea they had upset some of the attic's most savage creatures.

As they ran Chloe kept looking at the ubiquitous piles of junk that they passed lying on the boards. Finally she saw something.

'Clogs,' she yelled. 'Quick. Put a pair on over your shoes.'

'But they'll slow us up,' complained Alex.

'Yes, maybe – but they'll destroy the trail. Be careful how you put them on. Don't touch the bottoms. Then our smell won't be on the trail we leave behind. It'll just be old clogs against wooden boards. Wood on wood. The dolls won't be able to follow us then.'

Alex saw the sense in this and found a large pair of clogs that would go over his shoes. Soon the pair of them were clumping along, making the most fearful racket, but hopeful that their trick would work.

However, when they stopped to rest and Alex used the binoculars again, he informed his sister that the dolls were still coming.

'They're gaining on us,' he said. 'What about doubling back and hiding somewhere?'

'I don't like that idea. If they can sniff our trail while we're wearing clogs, they can certainly find hiding places.'

The wooden clogs were abandoned. The pair raced for their lives over the boards, hoping to come across some sort of habitation full of creatures who might help them. Nothing appeared on the horizon though and now the voodoo dolls were visible without the glasses. A dust cloud told of their coming. There were swarms of them, some dark, some pale, scurrying over piles of junk: a horde of warriors. The children tried to throw things in the dolls' path, like old chairs and boxes, but nothing seemed to deter their pursuers. The glitter of long needles was visible now, as the small hunters ran through shafts of sunlight, their beady eyes intent upon their prey.

'We're not going to get away,' gasped Alex. 'They're going to catch us, Clo.'

'You go on,' said his sister. 'I'll stay here and see if I can stop them.'

'Not a chance.'

'I'm the eldest. You should do as I say.' Her tone was desperate. 'You *have* to do what I say.'

'No way. We stick together.'

Chloe said, 'If we split up, one of us might make it.'

'Don't care. Don't want to split up. Nelson could arrive. He'd make mincemeat of those dolls.'

'No he wouldn't. They'd get him too. Look, there are hundreds of them. He wouldn't have a chance.'

There was a pile of hockey sticks in the next junk heap. Alex stopped and grabbed one, turning to face the enemy.

'I've had it, Clo. I'm going down fighting.'

'Don't be silly,' she cried. 'Come on. We can still run.'

'Nope.'

Alex stood there, waiting, swinging the hockey stick.

Chloe knew they had run themselves out. She grabbed one of the old hockey sticks and stood by her brother. The dolls were triumphant, now having their quarry in their sight. They streamed towards the two children, jabbing the air with their nasty steel weapons.

Alex realised at the last minute that he could protect his face from those needles. He put Makishi on. Then he turned towards the dolls, swinging his club. The little fiends were almost on them now, only metres away. This was it, this was where the children's journey through Attica ended. They had been hunted down and trapped by these awful effigies of man, and were about to die.

'Stop. I command you to stop. You will obey.'

Makishi had spoken in a powerful voice.

The voodoo dolls skidded to a halt.

Makishi's expression was severe.

'Why do you attack us?'

Just metres from the children, the voodoo dolls fell on their little knees and bowed in reverence to Makishi. There were rows and rows of them, some still coming, who halted and bowed down low. Finally, all was so quiet you could almost hear the dust settling on the boards. Alex and Chloe waited breathlessly, wondering what would come next.

A shimmering went through the dolls as they stuck their needles back into their wax bodies. They knew there would be no sacrifice here. Makishi was one of their lords. They could do nothing more than sheath their weapons and wait for Makishi's reprimand.

'These are my friends,' Makishi said at last in deep tones. 'You will respect the carriers of Makishi or shame will fall on your heads. The masks have provided homes for the voodoo dolls since our Collector went the way of all Collectors. You are our tenants, our subjects.'

'Yes, lord,' incanted the voodoo dolls. 'We are your subjects.'

'Leave us alone then, with our friends, our carriers.'

One voodoo doll looked up, with the sharp words, 'But, master, we have hunted long and hard—'

A strong baleful stare from Makishi was enough to silence this audacious creature. The dolls gradually got to their feet, looking sheepish. They ambled away, in ones, twos, groups of three or four, heading back in the direction they had come. The audacious one was pricked in the buttocks by those who walked behind him in an attempt to curry favour with Makishi. One of their landlords had spoken and the humans were under his protection.

They could do no more than return to their homeland.

When the voodoo dolls had gone, Alex took off his mask and looked into its hollow eyes.

'Thanks Makishi,' he said. 'You saved our lives.'

'My pleasures!' replied the mask.

# CHAPTER 13

# The Collector of Souls

After the incident with the dolls Chloe and Alex continued on their journey. Chloe was despairing of ever finding Jordy. She wondered if her step-brother were still in the attic. Was he even still alive? She and Alex had come very close to death. Who was to say that Jordy had not encountered some terrible dangers and had not been so lucky?

When she spoke to Alex, he seemed astonishingly careless of Jordy's fate. 'Oh, he's all right,' Alex replied.

Chloe asked him how he could be so sure and Alex just shrugged and said, 'I get feelings now, Clo. He's not far away. Honestly, I can feel it.'

'You're beginning to frighten me, Alex.'

Alex said, 'Sorry.'

'No, you don't have to say sorry. It's not your fault, but you seem to have changed lately. I don't know what to make of you.'

'Sorry, Clo.'

She let this one pass. Indeed, walking behind her brother now she felt she hardly knew him. He appeared quite unconcerned by their plight. Here they were, lost in an unknown world, their parents completely ignorant of

where they were or what they were doing, with the possibility of never finding home again, and Alex seemed
carefree and content. It wasn't that he was *happy* exactly, but
he certainly wasn't worried in any way. Chloe couldn't pin
it down exactly, but Alex apparently had a connection with
the attic that she did not. He appeared to be at *home* here.

Passing through a dim area, where the light clustered
around a few peepholes in the roof, something happened.

'Did you see that?' cried Alex.

Chloe's heart was beating fast. She had indeed seen it.

The dust was still settling from the sudden disturbance. It
was difficult to believe. For many days now they had been
wandering Attica without seeing another human being.
Now one had popped up, just like that. A woman had
unexpectedly opened a trapdoor from below.

The woman had lifted a box and pushed it along the
boards as far as her arms could reach. Then she had vanished again, closing a trapdoor behind her. Another box of
junk for the attic. To the woman's eyes, unused to the dimness, the darkness had been impenetrable. Somewhat
harassed, with fly-away hair, she had disappeared as quickly
as she had appeared. Obviously to her this was not a vast
continent whose guttered eaves were long journeys away,
but simply her own small attic space.

'Look, you can see the cracks now.'

Chloe looked down. There were faint lines in the dust
forming a square. She stirred the dust with her toe, pushing
it aside, and found underneath the unmistakable shape of a
trapdoor. It was the first they had seen since leaving their
own part of the attic. Perhaps there had been more which
had gone unnoticed.

'Oh, Alex,' she said. 'I wish this was our house.'

'Well – well, it's not.'

'But it might be next door?'

Alex raised his hands. 'Is this our part of the attic? No. There's none of our stuff here. That means we're in another part. If you go down that trapdoor, Clo, you might never come back up again. Who's to say where you'll end up? Not just another house in another street in another town. Could even be in another part of the world. You wouldn't want to go down and find yourself in Holloway Prison, would you? Or stuck in a hut in Alaska? I know I wouldn't.'

'Of course I wouldn't,' she snapped, 'but that's just guessing. This is the first trapdoor we've come across . . .'

'No it's not,' replied her brother calmly, staring at her from beneath the brim of his big floppy hat, 'there have been lots more. You just haven't seen them. *I* have.'

'Stop being so know-it-all.'

'Oh, I don't know everything, but I know enough. I can't help it, Clo, I *have* seen other trapdoors. I thought you had too. You mustn't take any notice of them. We'll know if ever we come across our own.'

If ever? Chloe's heart pounded. He really didn't care. You could hear it in his voice. It didn't matter to Alex if he never went home again. She stared back into his deep brown eyes. There was no troubled look in them. They were calm and accepting. If she felt she had grown a lot in spirit since she'd been in the attic, Alex's spirit had somehow been transformed. Chloe didn't know him. He had turned away from her. It was not necessarily a *bad* change; Alex had not become some evil monster. He was simply very different. At least, part of him was.

'Don't keep looking at me like that, Clo. You're scary.' He nodded at her head and grinned. 'You're beginning to look like a witch. You need to wash your hair.'

Now this was more like the old Alex. She reached up and touched her hair. She had always been very proud of it.

It was long, black and silky, like her mother's. Very full, very thick. It had always shone with natural oils, but now it felt like straw. Horrible matted straw. She reached out, lifted Alex's hat, and ruffled his straggly hair. 'You too. You look like a tramp.'

'Do you think we could find some shampoo somewhere?' He scratched. 'I think I'm getting fleas.'

'You can't be *getting* them. You either have them or you don't. Anyway, I'm not surprised. Anything could be in those old clothes you've taken to wearing. A colony of termites. In any case I don't think you've got lice.' Chloe always insisted on calling things by their proper names. 'I think you've just got a head full of scurf. We'll have to be on the look-out for some shampoo. Come on, let's get on now. If Jordy's not far away, as you think, we need to find him.'

'They escaped from the voodoo dolls.'

*Lucky for them.*

''Twasn't luck, master, 'twas Makishi.'

*I think we're wasting our time with this bunch.*

'Then let's not bother with them.'

The board-comber is tempted to let the children go. He takes his bag of Inuit carvings out and feels the soapstone figures through the cloth. How he would love another one for his collection. Perhaps a wolf? Or an arctic fox? Or even another human: a shaman of the clan? What a delight that would be. New eyes. That was what the children represented. New eyes had always been better at spotting things than tired old ones. Old eyes that had travelled over the same piles of junk a thousand times. Maybe he'd better stick with them just a little while longer.

*I've got nothing better to do.*

'That's the spirit.'

*Where are they heading at the moment?*

'Oh dear. Look.'
*We may have to get them out of there.*

By the time evening came Chloe and Alex were in a part of the attic which seemed darker and more eerie than anywhere they had been before. There was an atmosphere of unnatural calm about the place. Chloe sensed that no one had visited this region for a very long time. Nothing seemed to have been disturbed in this corner of thick dust and dead air. On the one hand this was good, for it meant there were no Atticans here or strange beings like the voodoo dolls, but on the other hand there might be a good reason for the lack of life.

'Alex, what do you think?' asked Chloe, shivering and hugging herself. 'Should we stay here?'

'I dunno,' replied her brother, putting down his pack and sending up a grey cloud of dust. 'Don't feel right, does it?'

'No.'

They stared about them, their eyes getting used to the dimness. This was an area of the attic where the roof was lower than usual. In fact there were places here where the children had to duck to prevent their heads banging against rafters. Crouching, they explored a little, finding not the usual piles of old clothes, but clusters of dulled brass crosses and chalices, with heaps of shabby hassocks between. Neither child was particularly religious. Their father had been a Hindu and while he was alive Dipa had followed that path, but neither parent had been particularly zealous. The children had been mildly interested, but they had also had influences of Christianity and Islam on their doorstep by way of school friends. Here, clearly, were the trappings of Christianity, but they had little idea what they meant and why they were here.

The children moved forward.

'It's creepy, isn't it?' said Alex. 'Spooky. Yuk, there's a *huge* spider's web here, blocking the way.'

Alex swept his hand through thick silken threads, breaking the snare of the absent spider.

'You know I'm not scared of spiders,' said Chloe. She tilted her chin in that typical pose of defiance she adopted when she was prepared to do battle against her fears. 'And I'm not scared of spooks. People talk about ghosts being in graveyards, but if ghosts haunt old houses how can they be where their bodies are buried as well? This is just stuff from old churches. You'd expect an attic in England to have this sort of thing.'

'I guess.'

Suddenly they came across a broken sign, held by a rusty nail to a low rafter. It read: DORM, but part of the sign was missing. Beyond this sign was a very low-roofed area – so low they would have to crawl to get in there – with mounds covered by dirty white sheets. At the head of each mound was an oil painting, leaning against the humped sheet. They were all portraits of smiling and unsmiling people, looking stiff and awkward in their poses. Some of the subjects in the paintings were dressed in historical costumes – dark old oil paintings with brown varnished surfaces – others were in more modern clothes, the colours a bit brighter and more vibrant.

Chloe sniffed at the horrible musty odour of the place and shuddered.

She asked, 'Do you think that sign once said DORMITORY?'

'Dunno,' replied Alex in that infuriating couldn't-care-less voice. 'I'm tired. Let's just rest here the night and see what happens in the morning.'

'Well, a dormitory is the right place to sleep,' agreed Chloe, 'if that's what it is.'

'I can hardly keep my eyes open,' complained Alex.

Chloe too found the urge to sleep irresistible. Alex lay down first while she fought against her feeling of deep fatigue.

Gradually though she slid to the floor, sending up a puff of grey dust. There she lay half-awake, half-asleep for a few minutes, caught in that twilight world when the mind flutters in a pleasant state of tranquillity before fully dropping off. How pleasant it was to finally let go and fall, fall, fall, as if into a deep forest pool of warm feelings. Let the world carry on without her.

Just before she dropped off completely she felt her mother pulling up the bedclothes and tucking her in. Her mother seemed to have black hairy claws instead of hands. And her breath smelled of something foul, like rotting cabbages or old drains. But Chloe was too far gone into sleep to worry about things like that.

Once, during the night, she woke up to see a dark figure sitting on a stool. The figure was all in black and difficult to see in the very dim light, but he appeared to be painting. There was a canvas on an easel before the figure and, though very drowsy, almost to the point of unconsciousness, Chloe could see the arm wielding the brush. This brush was dipped in a palette of paints then brought to the surface of the canvas with a sweeping motion. When he saw that his subject's eyes were slightly open, the figure in black smiled, and shook his head as if to say, 'Back to sleep, Chloe.'

Is he painting me? thought Chloe. I wonder why?

Then she dropped off again, into a deep, deep slumber.

*Don't they know anything?*

A dust sprite formed, and then ran like an upright lizard on its back legs for about twenty paces, then seemed to silently explode into a cloud of settling specks.

*You'd think the number of dust sprites around would be warning enough. The place is full of them. They're running around like cockroaches.*

'They don't see dust sprites. Their eyes aren't good enough.'

*Do you think they want to sleep for ever? Some do. I know a board-comber who came here and gave himself up.*

'These are outsiders – they want to live.'

*You'd think they'd recognise the signs then: the mouldering mounds, the tombstones at the heads of the graves. You think they'd smell what it was. They must have sawdust for brains.*

'Don't be so hard on them. You remember what it was like when you first came to the attic. You didn't know a thing. It was a long time before you found out there were malevolent board-combers like this one. How are the children supposed to know he collects souls?'

*Eternal rest. Up here it means what it actually says. To sleep for ever under a dust sheet. There's something a little tempting in that, when you feel as world-weary as I do. But how could they not realise? Look, it even says* DORMIRE *on that sign. Don't they teach them Latin these days? I was taught Latin at school. I've got the scars to prove it.*

'It doesn't say DORMIRE,' the bat points out. 'It says DORM.'

*Well, it's meant to say* DORMIRE. *There's winding sheets all over the place. Who could miss such signs?*

'You did once – and you called them *shrouds* in your day. Are you going to get them out of there before it's too late, or what?'

*I'd have to touch them,* says the board-comber, shuddering with disgust, his breath hot against the inside of his mask. *I'd have to lay hands on them.*

'Well, I certainly can't do it. I'm a bat.'

*I've a good mind to let them stay there.*

But the board-comber knows he will not do that. He still has enough humanity to motivate himself into helping his own kind when they are in trouble. He berates the children for being ignorant, but knows it was the same when he first arrived. There are many traps in the attic, many pitfalls and hazards. If one manages to avoid the first few, one becomes wise to them. One becomes attuned to the rhythms of the attic, so that when unknown dangers appear, warning sounds go off in one's head. It wasn't necessary to know how all the traps worked, just to know what *might* be a trap and avoid it. It got so he could smell snares from a safe distance.

The board-comber sprays one of his kerchiefs with cheap scent found in a little blue bottle labelled *Evening in Paris*. This will protect him from the odour of the sleep gases left by the bad board-comber. Tying this around his nose he then enters the Garden of Eternal Rest and grips the boy by the heels. He does not like doing it, but knows the children will remain here always if he doesn't do something about it. He then drags the boy out in the open, away from the sleep gases exuded by the board-comber.

This board-comber is like all collectors in the attic: it gathers its treasures in one place. This one collects souls. It is one of those creatures like Katerfelto, which has appeared all by itself. It has the shape and form of a human, but the heart and mind of a spider. It waits for the tug on its web and then descends from the rafters to wrap its victims in shrouds. It hangs its souls collection in a secret place, nailing them to rafters where they flap in the four draughts from the four corners of the attic.

Once the boy is out in the open, the good board-comber goes in and drags out the girl. He then wipes his hands on his coat, as if the children had left a sticky substance on them. Somewhere above, the vile collector of souls is watching, grinding his teeth.

Chloe woke to a feeling of intense coldness.

There was a dirty sheet over the lower half of her body and she kicked it off in disgust. She looked round to see a long streak in the dust where she had been dragged while slumbering. In panic she looked around quickly for Alex. He was lying not far away, still asleep. Then she sat up and noticed an oil painting, half-finished, lying face up in the dust. Reaching out to touch it she found the paint was still not quite dry.

She recognised herself as the subject of the portrait.

'Oh, what is *that*?' she murmured, shuddering. It was a ghastly painting. Her features were pale and lifeless, her eyes were closed, her lips were a translucent blue. Her head was resting on a pillow of pure-white lilies. There was a very faint but frozen smile on her face.

It was the portrait of a dead girl.

'How horrible!'

She tore her eyes away from her own terrible image and saw that her brother remained asleep.

'Alex, wake up,' she called.

'Whaa—' Alex rolled over and opened his eyes. 'What's this thing wrapped round me?'

'I don't know. I had one too.'

'It stinks,' he said, kicking it off.

Alex stood up and stretched.

'My head aches. I think there's gas about. Can you smell gas?'

'I don't know. I think we ought to get away from here. This is an evil place.'

They gathered up their packs and as they did so Chloe noticed footprints in the dust. Yes, someone had definitely dragged them out from under that low roof. Jordy? Surely not, or he would have stayed. Perhaps it had been one of the Atticans? The soles of the shoes the person had been wearing were very large though: bigger than an Attican would wear. She sighed. It was just another mystery attached to this weird world of boards and rafters. Whoever was their saviour obviously did not want to be known. An anonymous person: a guardian angel of some kind.

As Chloe caught up with her brother, she saw something which made her pause and think. It was a ball of string, lying on its own, gathering the dust of ages. Picking it up, she had a wonderful idea. It was a scary idea, but it seemed it might be the answer to a very big question.

'Alex,' she said, reaching him, 'I'm going down that trapdoor.'

Alex's expression became serious.

'You *can't*, Clo. You don't know what's down there.'

She showed him the ball of string.

'I'm going to tie the end around my waist and you can reel me down into the house below. That'll keep physical contact between the two of us. If anything goes wrong I'll just come up and join you again. As long as we both hold on to the string we can't be parted. This way I can sort of get our bearings in the real world. Find out where we are.'

'I don't like it, Clo.'

'Well, I don't like it either, but it's got to be done,' she said firmly. 'That woman didn't look like a monster. Maybe she'll help us? We can only ask. Look, I'll tie the string to my jeans belt like this . . . now help me get this trapdoor up. Is there any handle? No, well, use that penknife thing you keep flashing every five minutes. At last we can use it for *something*.'

They struggled with the trapdoor and finally eased it up. Dust clouds went everywhere, making them both cough.

Then Chloe took her torch and shone it down the square black hole.

'What's down there?' asked Alex, peering. 'I can't see much, can you?'

'Only a landing and some stairs, I think,' replied Chloe. 'It's just an ordinary house.' She felt excited. 'Maybe we've found a way out, Alex.'

'But what about Jordy?'

Jordy indeed was a problem.

'If this is a way home, we'll look for Jordy when I come up again, all right? We've still got to find the watch, so we can't go back down again for ever. All I want to do is see where we are, in relation to our own house.'

'OK, Clo. If you're sure.'

'I'm going down,' she said, lowering herself through the trapdoor. 'I'll keep calling up, once I'm down there, so you'll know I'm all right.'

Alex played out the string as his sister climbed down through the hatch and dropped to the floor beneath.

'Are you down there yet?'

Her voice was quite faint. 'Yes, I'm fine. More string, please.'

Alex unwound some more from the ball, playing it out as his sister moved cautiously around the landing below.

At that moment a thought occurred to Alex and this scared him as much as he knew it would scare Chloe and Jordy – he actually *wanted* to stay up here in Attica. He wasn't ready to go home. This was an exciting place, full of adventures, full of strange creatures and the prospect of treasures. You can't win treasures without going through risk. The treasures didn't mean anything otherwise. And the risk could be enjoyed if you knew what you were doing. Alex was beginning to feel he knew what he was doing. It was actually too early for him to go down. The attic was willing to have him. And he was ready for the attic. It was a *great* place to spend time in.

A jerk on the string. He played out some more.

'Clo? Are you all right?'

Nothing.

'Clo?'

A faint whisper on a cold draught of air coming up through the hatchway. Was that her voice? Or was it just the rustling of something down below? This was a bad idea, going down there. Alex could feel it in his bones.

'Chloe!' he yelled, tugging lightly on the string. 'Come on back up.'

No answer. Nothing. Just that cold draught.

Alex could do no more than just sit there, waiting and hoping. At least the string was still moving, so he knew she was still there.

'Fishing?' asked a deep voice.

Alex almost jumped out of his skin.

# CHAPTER 14

# Visit to the Underworld

Looking up, Alex could see a tall young stranger in long capes and hat, with thick leather boots. The stranger had two rats, one in each side pocket of his coat, their little heads poking out. On his back was a huge rucksack, home-made by the look of it, with a wooden frame built to fit his broad shoulders. His face was as creased as a well-used map.

'N-n-no,' stuttered Alex. 'M-my sister's on the end of this line – she's down there in a house.'

'Bad move,' growled the youth, taking off his rucksack. The two rats leapt out of his pockets and came to peer down the hatchway at the landing below. 'You ought to get her out of there, Alex.'

'Y-you know my name?'

'I met your brother last night. You won't know what I am, but they call me a bortrekker. I know the ways of this world, Alex. I know where to go and that's not one of them. Trapdoors – if they're not to your *own* house – lead only to even stranger places than here. Get her out, now. Get her up or you may never see your sister again.'

Frightened by these words, Alex yanked on the string.

To his utter horror, it went completely loose. He reeled it in, finding a frayed break on the other end. The string had snapped. Chloe was down there alone.

There was a light on the landing of the house. It seemed it was evening. Chloe could see a faint pinkness to the sky through the landing window. For a while she simply stood there studying her surroundings. It seemed a very ordinary house. Very ordinary. A sort of mushroom colour emulsion on the walls of the landing and going down the stairs. A carpet of similar hue. At the bottom of the stairs sat a tortoiseshell cat, washing itself. It looked up at her when she moved and *meow*ed softly, before continuing with its ablutions. It looked a gentler cat than Nelson. Along the landing itself were several doors: bedrooms and the bathroom no doubt. Everything was nicely painted or varnished.

'All right,' muttered Chloe to herself. 'Let's see who or what's downstairs.'

She prepared herself for a confrontation. Those who owned this house, who lived here, would not take kindly to an intruder. At least she was a young girl and not a large threatening man. However, if confronted she didn't want to launch into a story about Attica. No one would believe her. She decided she would make an excuse for being in the house and play it by ear. Once she knew where she was in relation to her own home, she would go back up to Alex. They could mark the trapdoor, look for Jordy, find the watch, and all three of them return down through the house to freedom.

It was as simple as that.

'If that woman comes I shall say I just found myself here,' she reasoned, 'and have lost my memory.'

She didn't like telling lies, but there was no other option.

If the police were called at least she would get home and she could convince her mother of the truth: she would eventually believe her daughter. Ben would be a tougher nut to crack, but Dipa would win him over.

Alex's voice floated down to her as if from many miles away.

Chloe began to descend the stairs. The cat stopped washing and regarded her with interest. One of the stairs suddenly creaked rather loudly. A woman somewhere in her forties – the same that had put the box in the attic – came out of a room and looked at Chloe. There was a frown on the woman's face, but it looked like one of those frowns some people wear permanently. She stared up at Chloe with penetrating eyes.

The cat very sensibly wandered off into another room, leaving the humans to their rituals.

Chloe steeled herself for an angry or shocked attack, but none came; instead, the woman's voice had an exasperated tone to it.

'Oh, *there* you are. Where have you been, child? The dinner's getting cold.' The woman peered up at the landing. 'And what have I told you about leaving on the landing light? Electricity costs money.'

Despite being stunned by her reception, Chloe's natural instinct was to defend herself.

'I didn't switch it on.'

'Please, Sarah, do give me *some* credit for intelligence. No one's been up there but you.'

'You were. You went to the attic.'

A befuddled expression came over the woman's face, then she simply said, 'Oh. Well, *do* hurry up. We're all waiting for you. What *have* you been doing in your bedroom? On that silly computer, I expect. I told your father when he bought it we'd never get you away from it. Why can't you be more like your brother? He gets out in the fresh air.'

The woman was quite thin and anxious-looking, wearing a black dress, pearls and high-heeled shoes. Her hair was tight around her head, almost like a black swimming cap. She was dressed as if she were going out for the evening. Suddenly she reached out and pulled one of the ends of Chloe's string which had been tied in a bow. 'What on *earth* are you doing?' The woman stared upwards at the length of string, which led to the open trapdoor of the attic. 'Have you been up there?'

'No, you left it open.'

The woman was clearly very irritated by the puzzle.

'Why have you tied yourself to that string?'

'I – I just wanted to.'

'You really are a most peculiar child.' She stared hard at Chloe, before adding in a low voice, 'I'm glad you're not mine. I'm glad *none* of you are mine. If I had my way . . .' There was a call from inside the room: a deep male voice.

'Are we going to eat, or what?'

The woman put on an attempt at a smile, pushing Chloe into the room before her.

'Here she is. Playing computer games again, George. We should really limit the children, shouldn't we? I try to be reasonable about this matter, but it's become an obsession with them.'

Chloe said flatly, 'I was *not* playing computer games.'

The man, balding, a little overweight, wearing a suit, white shirt and tie, pointed to the chair next to him with his dinner fork.

'Never mind all that now. We'll be late for the theatre. Sit down, Sarah, and eat your dinner.'

Chloe sat, absolutely bewildered by all this. She had been willing so far to put everything down to mental illness on the part of the middle-aged woman. But clearly every-one else in the room accepted her as one of the family. One of their own. Were they *all* mad? It seemed unlikely. Perhaps she'd wandered into a television programme, one of those reality shows? Yet there was no evidence of cam-eras or cables or any of the trappings of such.

And who really was Sarah? Would she come wandering into the room at any moment, a mirror image of Chloe? Or was there no Sarah, just a family waiting to trap one, to draw a Sarah into itself like a fish into a net, with lures of commonplace gatherings and home comforts?

The whole thing was mystifying.

It frightened her more than a confrontation would have done. Something surely lurked around the corner: some terrible truth that would swallow her up with its awful ordinariness.

'Sarah, eat your vegetables,' said the woman, over-sweetly. 'They're good for you.'

There were two other children there.

A boy about half Chloe's age and a girl not more than three. The girl looked impish, with golden curls and a grim smile. She gripped her spoon as if it were a club and she was about to beat the overcooked cabbage to death. The young boy had a snub nose, freckles and a dirty collar. A football boy. A woodsy, ditchy, scouty, catapulty boy. He seemed wholly taken up with his dinner, shovelling the food down his throat with gusto. The father, George, looked a bit pompous, rather flabby and soft about the gills, but nice enough. He smiled at Chloe.

'You should listen to Jane,' he said. 'Not watch too much TV.'

'Not television,' Jane said, '*video* games.'

'Oh, yes,' replied George, wiping his mouth on his napkin. 'Video games. Never understood the interest.'

'That's because you're no good at 'em,' interrupted the boy with his mouth full of food. 'You're *hopeless*.'

'That's enough,' ordered Jane. 'George, why do you encourage them to be so insubordinate?'

'In-sordy-nut,' said the little girl and banged her spoon on the table. 'INSORDYNUT.'

'That's enough, Chantelle,' said George mildly. 'Get on with your dinner. Don't you like it? Jane cooked it specially.'

'She means I'm cheeky, don't she, sis?' the boy said, grinning at Sarah. 'She always uses them long words.'

'Who's *she*, the cat's mother?' asked Chloe, repeating an old family saying then, realising she really was speaking out of turn, said, 'I'm sorry.'

'I should think so,' Jane said, pursing her mouth. 'Really, George.'

'We ought to be going,' said George, putting down his napkin and looking at his wrist-watch. 'We'll be late. Can you put the children to bed, Sarah? Don't wait up for us, we won't be in 'till one or two. You'll be all right, won't you? You've got my mobile number. I can't switch it on during the performance, but I will at the interval, and after, of course. Leave a message if there are any problems.'

'She's not putting me to bed,' growled the boy. 'I can put myself to bed.'

George said, 'You're to go up when Sarah tells you.'

He left the room. Jane swept the faces of the children with an icy stare. 'One of these days . . .' she muttered.

'We were here first,' growled the boy. 'You came after.'

Jane glared at him but left the battlefield.

George came back into the room wearing his own coat and carrying another for Jane.

'It's snowing,' he said. 'I knew it would. Do you think we should cancel?'

Chloe said quickly, 'No – it'll be all right – Dad. You go.' She glanced out of the window. 'It's not coming down too hard. It won't settle. Look, I think it's clearing already.'

He patted her head with chubby fingers. 'You're a good girl, Sarah.' Then in a whisper as Jane went to find her gloves, 'I know it's hard at the moment, but she'll come round.' He nodded at the doorway through which Jane had disappeared. 'We'll win her over, you'll see.' He smiled at what he clearly believed was his daughter. 'You're grow-ing up fast. You'll soon be a woman yourself and then you can be friends. I don't think Jane has any objections to friends at all. Look after the other two. Sorry to leave you with them, but you know we don't get out often, and Jane does love her theatre.'

'I don't mind,' said Chloe. 'Honestly I don't.'

'You're a good girl. I always said so. Now, would you mind going and hurrying Jane up. We'll be late. She's lost her gloves.'

Chloe felt daunted at this small task. Hurry Jane up? Why, the woman disliked Sarah intensely. Chloe was a very bright girl and she quickly decided there was jealousy there. Jane was jealous of the children, probably because they had a past history with George – their father – and she was new on the scene. Chloe didn't think Jane was naturally aggres-sive. She was terrified of having to fight for her place in an established household. Realising this she went into the bed-room where Jane was still searching for her gloves.

'Can I help?' she said. 'Where did you last see them?'

Jane looked up quickly, a suspicious expression on her face.

'What are you smiling at? Have you hidden them?'

'No,' replied Chloe, 'I wouldn't do such a thing. I don't dislike you, you know. Look,' she faced Jane full on, 'this is difficult for all of us. We – us children – are worried about you, whether you'll like us or not. That's why we've been a bit awkward with you, I suppose. I'm sorry for that. We could start again. We could easily be friends. It would be nicer for – for Dad – for George – if we were. Would you be my friend, please, Jane?'

Jane stared at her for a long time.

'I can be nice,' she said at last. 'If people are nice to me.'

'Well,' Chloe laughed, 'you know what my baby brother is like – he's a rotten little ruffian and we won't get much niceness out of him, but he'd be the same in any family. As for Chantelle, well, she's been spoiled by Dad a bit, but if we're firm with her, she'll be all right once she goes to school. It's you and me who have to make the running in this.'

Chloe paused, wondering how far to take this, but finally put out her hand.

'Would you shake on it?'

Jane looked down, seemingly uncertain. 'This is very silly.'

'I know, but I want to *try* to help us all get on better together. A handshake – well, it's symbolic, isn't it?'

Again Jane looked at her for a long while, before saying, 'If you're playing a game with me . . .'

'I'm not, I promise,' replied Chloe, hoping that the real Sarah would prove to be as receptive to tenderness as she would be. 'I'm just fed up with all this sniping. I get enough of that at school with other girls and I'm sick and tired of it.'

Jane's eyes went a little moist. 'So am I,' she said. 'Weary to the bone with it.'

Suddenly, they were shaking hands and Chloe was flushed with triumph. Oh, please don't let me down, Sarah, she thought. This will be so much better for you.

George came into the room, saying, 'What the heck is

happening up here? I said we would be late—' He stopped in the middle of the room and stared.

'What are you two up to?' he said, looking puzzled. 'Making a pact?'

'You could say that,' murmured Jane.

She went forward and straightened his tie possessively, then realised how this looked and turned back nervously towards Chloe.

But Chloe knew the move had been instinctive. Jane had been using these tricks for some time now and they were hard to throw off. Both females knew what had happened and Chloe was determined it would not interfere with this new relationship she had set up.

'You two have a good time tonight,' she said, smiling broadly. 'Off you go. Don't worry about the kids.'

Jane looked relieved and smiled.

'Didn't I tell you she was a good girl?' George cried.

'You did,' agreed Jane, a smile almost reaching her eyes.

'My two best girls,' he said with genuine affection. Then a look at his watch and, 'Come on, Jane. We *must* go.'

They all bounded down the stairs together and George opened the front door. It had a frosted stained-glass panel depicting a robin on a bough. He took one more look at the snow, then stepped outside.

Once the door had slammed, Chloe turned to the boy.

He said aggressively, 'I ain't going to bed yet.'

'No one's asked you to.'

Chantelle, still at the table, was hammering her cabbage with her spoon, sending green bits flying all over the table-cloth. Chloe was at a loss for a moment, then went in and gathered her up in her arms. Chantelle kicked and struggled until she was put down, saying, 'I can do it. I can do it.'

'Upstairs, young lady,' ordered Chloe.

Amazingly the youngster did as she was told. The cat had appeared again and got its fur pulled by Chantelle on her way past. Chloe followed, calling up to Alex as she went beneath the open trapdoor, 'I'll be a while yet.'

She bathed the little girl, found a nightdress and put her into it, and then told her to get into bed while she let the bathwater go. Chantelle obediently trooped off to one of the rooms and was sitting up in bed sucking her thumb when Chloe joined her.

'Story!' said Chantelle, taking her thumb out for a second. 'Big Red Boots!'

When Chloe simply stood there and looked helplessly around, Chantelle got out of bed, found the book she wanted and handed it to her. Chloe sat on the side of her bed and read the battered, dog-eared pages. It was a tale of an elf who had been given big red boots for his birthday. Even before Chloe had finished the story, Chantelle was asleep, her golden curls decorating the pillow.

Chloe went downstairs again and found the boy watching television. She still did not know his name.

'You're next,' she said.

'I don't have to go up yet.'

'You'll go when I tell you to.'

'Bossy boots.'

Still, she left him there for a while and studied the programme herself. It was a quiz show. Chloe didn't recognise it, but then she never watched quiz shows. They just bored her.

'What's this called?' she asked.

'You know.'

'No I don't, or I wouldn't ask.'

He was lying on the floor, his head propped up on his elbows. He turned to look at her. 'It's called *You Know*. That's what it's called. You daft, or what?'

'Don't be cheeky.'

'Bugger off.'

'And don't swear. I'll – I'll tell Dad.'

'Don't care.'

Chloe knew this was going nowhere. She had a younger brother who could be just like this one at times. She tried to focus on why she was down here, in this house. What she had to do was find out where the house was located. It was no good asking this boy. He would look at her as if she was stupid. Instead, she got up and went to look in the drawers of a bureau that stood in the corner. If she could find a letter, she could study the address.

'Those're *her* drawers, they are,' said the boy, without taking his eyes from the screen. 'You'll get it if she catches you.'

Chloe paid him no attention, but continued to root around in the bureau, without success. She went off and had a look in the kitchen, knowing that people often open their mail at the breakfast table. There were no letters there either. Finally she had an idea. She went back to the boy and said, 'Have you seen that letter I got the other day?'

'Never took no letter.'

'I didn't say you'd taken it. I only asked if you'd seen it.'

'That one I give you from Jimmy Caghill?'

'Yes. That one.'

'You stuck it under your mattress. You daft, or what?'

Chloe dashed upstairs and found the room which obviously belonged to Sarah, then after a long search, found the letter. She was disappointed. It had no envelope. When she opened it she read: 'Sarah. I reckon your really something. You want to go to the pictures sometime? I could meet you tomorrow if you wanted. James (Caghill).' There was no address at the top and Chloe thought James Caghill was a dud. As if she would sell her pride so cheaply as to ever go out with someone who didn't know how to use apostrophes and wrote *your* instead of *you're*.

When she left her room the boy was coming up the stairs.

He seemed very reasonable now. 'I'm goin' to bed. You have locked the door, haven't you, Sarah?'

'Doesn't it lock on the latch?'

'You're s'posed to deadlock it too.'

After making sure the boy really had gone to bed she went downstairs quickly and found the key in the lock.

Chloe deadlocked the front door and when she went around to the back door found it had been securely bolted.

Then she began a serious search of the house. After an hour it was obvious that there were no letters in the house. There were no bills or bank statements either. This house was quite devoid of printed paper. There was nothing on the phone to say where they were. She did find a name and a date on the first blank page of a book of Burns' poems which read 'Isabel Sutherland, 1932, Dunfermline', but it was a very old book and had probably been bought second-hand with the name already in place.

'This doesn't feel like Dunfermline,' said Chloe to herself.

As she was replacing the book on its shelf the front door rattled.

Chloe picked up the nearest heavy object, a stone carving. She held it like a club, ready to use.

Her heart was beating fast. She was beginning to realise that she was going to get nowhere in this house. It was far too ordinary yet at the same time, very very strange. It could be a house anywhere in England, Scotland or Wales. And the fact that they thought she belonged here frightened her more than anything else.

Who had tried the door? Had it been the wind, or was

there someone out there, trying to get in? It could have been anything from flesh-eating monsters to unexpected relatives. Both seemed equally scary at that moment. Or it might even be someone like the TV licensing authority, for this family was too average not to be wholly innocent of all crimes and misdemeanours. Chloe did not want to get any further involved in this family's affairs.

She put the heavy carving in her jeans pocket and went upstairs to check on the children. They were fast asleep, both of them. The temptation now was to go, to leave them all to it, but something kept her there until she heard the parents' car returning. Then she ran down the stairs, opened the deadlock, and rushed back up again. She heard them come in, talking softly. Chloe had already put a chair under the hole to stand on, so that she could climb up and pull herself back up into the attic. This she was doing as the woman came up the stairs. She and Jane exchanged quizzical glances, then Chloe was up and through the hole.

Once up in the attic she slammed the trapdoor shut.

'You were quick,' said Alex. 'Did you come up because the string came off?'

'That came off *hours* ago.'

'No – just now. Wasn't it just now?' Alex's question was addressed to a tall boy in a long raincoat with many capes, a big floppy hat and big boots. 'Less than a minute ago.'

The youth said, 'But she's been down *there*.'

'Anyway,' Chloe said, 'it didn't work. I did spend hours down there, but I couldn't find out what town it was. And they were expecting me, Alex. They called me Sarah and said I was one of the family.'

'You can't just go down anywhere you please,' said the youth in the capes. In each side pocket he had a rat both of whom kept looking up at him when he talked. 'It's just throwing a spanner in the works. You don't *fit*. It's a wonder you got back without causing all kinds of damage. Going down through a wrong hole creates a turbulence. It's to do with matter and space. See,' he explained, using his hands to describe the contours of creatures in the world below, 'there's a perfect empty shape for everything that moves and breathes down there, from an elephant to a mouse. Each elephant fills an elephant space. There be only so many elephant spaces. If there was one more elephant than spaces it would mess up the entire universe. Same if it was a mouse, or a bee – or, like you, another human.'

'Oh – oh,' said Chloe, upset. 'They kept calling me Sarah. Do you think I displaced a girl called Sarah? Will she find her – her space again?'

'Who knows?'

Chloe was quite distressed about this. On the one hand she felt that Sarah was well enough out of such a family, wherever she was. But then again, who was she – Chloe – to judge for another girl? Perhaps there were good reasons why Jane was such a harridan. You couldn't just walk in on a family and start making judgements as to what was right and wrong. In many ways they were a nice enough family.

'Well,' said Chloe, 'I've done it now and there's nothing much I can do to repair the damage. I'm certainly not going down again . . .'

'That would be disastrous,' agreed the boy in capes.

'And just who are you?' asked Chloe, now that she'd regained her composure.

'He's a bortrekker,' explained Alex excitedly. 'He treks the boards. And,' his voice rose triumphantly, 'he knows where Jordy is!'

'You do?' cried Chloe. 'Oh, where is he?'

'Yonder,' replied the bortrekker, pointing. 'In a forest of tall clocks. He's safe enough, for the time being, though I have to warn you, the cold Northern Draught is coming. I do believe he be waiting for the pair of you. Saw you coming days ago, but you must have wandered off the straight and narrow. Easy thing to do, up here.'

'Then we'd better be on our way,' Chloe announced. 'Come on Alex, we must find Mr Grantham's watch.' Chloe bent over to pick up her pack and felt a heavy lump in her pocket. It was the little statuette from the house below. The one she had kept in case she needed a weapon. She hoped to goodness that removing it was not going to cause all sorts of chaos and confusion in the world below: altering the tides, the climate and weather, the phases of the moon, the hours of daylight. But she wasn't going to ask the bortrekker. He seemed to like being the voice of doom. She would rather not know.

Chloe quickly transferred the stone figure to her back-pack.

Later, after the bortrekker had left them to continue his odyssey across Attica and they were en route to the forest of tall clocks, she took the carving out again and studied it. She saw now that it was of a beautiful green walrus. Chloe admired the carving, then stuffed it back into her pack again

A little later they came across a bees' nest in an old suit-case.

'I know how to do this,' she told Alex, taking off her pack. 'We need some cardboard from an old cardboard box. We could do with some women's tights or stockings.'

Alex easily found her some cardboard. It wasn't difficult: Attica had cardboard boxes all over the place. He didn't find any tights, but he did discover a box with some old lace curtains in. These, Chloe said, would be absolutely perfect for the job. She put on a hat and threw one of the curtains over her own head and shoulders and bid Alex do the same. Chloe looked like a Spanish bride in her curtain, with Alex the bridesmaid. Their faces were protected against stings, as were their hands when they put on gloves.

Chloe rolled up a piece of the cardboard, then asked Alex to light one end with a match. Once it was burning she blew it out, but continued to blow on the end, making it glow like charcoal embers. She then ordered Alex to lift the suitcase lid. When he did so, the bees began to come out. Chloe lifted her veil enough to blow through the cool end of the cardboard roll and made the smouldering end glow again. Smoke came out and was wafted into the nest. This had a calming effect on the bees and Chloe and Alex were able to steal some of the honey without getting stung. They later ate it by sucking it out of the honeycomb. It was the most delicious meal they'd had in their lives.

'Oh, that was good,' said Alex, patting his stomach afterwards. 'That was really good.'

'I agree,' replied Chloe, licking her fingers. '*Very* good.'

Alex had had a long chat with Makishi about jungles and wildlife in the tropics. He was feeling content and quite fulfilled. He lay back and looked up at the sky, a heaven made of timber. He liked the russet colour of some of the higher rafters way, way up in the ether. Then the dark ones to the edges: the pale softwood lower ones. Vast. Immense. A massive vault which soared to measureless dizzying altitudes. How peaceful it was up there. What was that? A bird? Something very like a bird: a black shape winging its way through the network of spars and beams. Too high really to recognise *exactly* what it was. Did it matter? Not really.

It was as he was lying there that a scent came to him on a draught. It was the kind of smell which might have a bushman murmuring, 'The rain is coming!' The old Alex didn't know what the smell was, of course, but deep within him a new Alex was emerging. Fledgling though it was, it gave voice to its feelings and cried out, 'There's a storm coming!'

Alex huddled against one of the strong oaken pillars which supported the roof, knowing he and Makishi were safe in the protection of its lee.

# CHAPTER 15

# Cold Draught
# Then a Warm Reunion

'You remember the bortrekker told us about that wind,' explained Alex, 'but he called it a *draught*. The North Draught. A cold one. I think that's what's coming our way – the North Draught – so batten down the hatches, there's dirty weather coming, Clo.'

He didn't really know what the last couple of phrases actually meant, but he'd heard them in films and they sounded dramatic enough for him.

'But what I want to know is *how* you know?'

'I just feel it,' replied Alex vaguely. 'It's sort of in the air. Can you see any snowflakes?'

'No. There aren't any. You can't get snow inside an attic. There's not enough moisture.'

'I hope you're right, sis.'

The draught was increasing in strength now, blowing straight down the middle of the attic. It began to get colder too, as the strength of the draught grew. The chill factor increased and increased until Chloe realised she would have to follow Alex's example and put on some more clothes. Luckily there were plenty to be had. They were hardly the height of teenage fashion, but she was prepared to give way on that score. It was better to miss out on being the best dressed girl in Winchester, than to freeze to death. Thus with two scarves wrapped around her neck and head, a thick old-lady's overcoat, sheep's-wool mittens and another pair of slacks over her jeans, Chloe felt half ready to deal with the blizzard which came hurtling at them.

And blizzard it was.

There was no snow, as she had predicted, but the wind was so cold it froze all the surface moisture on the boards and over the junk, leaving a white hoar-frost in its wake. After struggling against it, heads down, the force of the draught was too much for them. Seeking shelter they found two or three tables and turned them on their sides to make a windbreak. There they huddled while the draught screamed around them, cutting through cracks and whistling through holes. No arctic wind was as cold as that North Draught. The bortrekker had tried telling Alex just how fierce it was, but no description whatever could have prepared them for this freezing blow.

Chloe hunched there, her back against the bottom of an upturned table.

'Are you all right?' yelled Alex. 'Try to keep covered or you'll get frostbite.'

She nodded, thoroughly miserable. If there was one thing Chloe hated, it was being cold. Alex didn't seem to mind, however. He peered out from between the layers he was wearing with bright brown eyes, not at all put out by this wild onslaught.

Indeed, the frost turned to ice crystals, which twinkled with a million glints in the poor light. Ice crystals make everything look colder than it actually is. It turns a frosty spring morning into a harsh winter's day. Chloe thought about unpacking their stove, but realised it was no good trying to light the little cooker. Such a fierce draught would not allow it. They simply had to sit and wait it out. Objects picked up by the high draught clattered against the tops of the tables: some were thrown against them with real force. Clothes and other light materials flew through the air like giant birds, flapping helplessly. At one point Chloe thought there were wolves out there, but it was in the end only the North Draught, telling everyone it was king of all Attica.

'Seventy miles an hour, I'll bet,' said Alex. 'Gale force ten.'

For once Chloe remained unimpressed by her brother's knowledge.

When it had decreased in strength a little, Alex emerged to find he was able to keep his feet once more. He encouraged a reluctant Chloe to stand and follow him. Off he marched, into the teeth of the gale, holding his head low, while Chloe trudged on behind. They passed white mounds which were probably junk, and white frozen-over water tanks. The whole aspect of the attic had changed in the frost and ice covering. It was as if the attic were trying to disguise itself with a mask of linen and lace.

Somewhere along their trek that sturdy ginger tom Nelson joined them, his shoulders hunched, his fur fluffed against the cold. He three-leg-limped alongside Alex, his head straight into the blast of the blizzard, as if he was determined to prove that man's best friend is not *always* the dog.

Not long after Chloe had climbed back up into the attic, the bortrekker had looked back to see that some creatures were following the children's trail. The bortrekker, a veteran pioneer of the attic, shuddered at the sight of these creatures. Though they looked like pleasant old men in dustcoats with brown buttons they were of course the Removal Firm.

Young people who stayed in the attic, like the bortrekker and the board-comber, were especially fearful of the Removal Firm. They called them the Removal Firm because that was what they were. They didn't move furniture. They removed anything that was a threat to the attic. Humans who were new needed to checked for spores, insect eggs and seeds in their clothing, which might result in a wood disease. Spores or eggs that might lead to dry rot, or woodworm, or any of those terrible wood-ravaging, wood-destroying blights. Humans were potentially corrosive. Humans were unwittingly destructive. So it was believed by the Removal Firm.

The rumour among the human intruders in the attic was that the Removal Firm imprisoned such criminals in old steel lockers discarded from public changing rooms in the real world. These were never to be opened again. The prisoners would never again see the light of day, or the dark of night. They shared the fate of the boy in the story, who climbed into a trunk during a game of hide-and-seek. They became ghastly secrets.

The bortrekker hid himself in a pile of dried and artificial flowers. He was a tall youth, reasonably strong, but he knew he was no match for the Removal Firm. Those creatures were incredibly powerful and could crush him in their arms if they so wished. He had seen one of them lift a heavy metal safe and place it aside as if it were cardboard. He had witnessed another cracking a thick beam as if it were a twig. The bortrekker was not one to underestimate the strength of his foes. He had not done anything wrong, so far as he could recall, but it was best not to be 'inspected'.

'May you rot yourselves,' he muttered, cursing the Removal Firm. 'May your noses drop off and your toes turn grey. May your livers turn to mush and your tongues shrivel to boot laces. May you—' but there he stopped, for they were coming his way.

The bortrekker held his breath as they passed, the dried flowers covering his human scent. Soon they were gone and he laughed to himself, having beaten them once again. In the opinion of the bortrekker it was fear that had given rise to the Removal Firm, and fear that kept them going. Fear, he was often heard to tell his two dancing rats, is a corrosive thing in itself when it leads to prejudice and irrational action.

The bortrekker went on his way. When he was certain the Removal Firm were out of earshot he took his fiddle out of its case and began to play a jaunty jig. The two rats Arthur and Harold leapt out of his pockets in glee and began dancing on their hind legs around his feet. Arthur's choreography was nothing short of genius, he being the light-footed one with inventive steps, while Harold's rhythm was vastly superior, as he swayed in time to the music. 'O what jolly boys are we,' sang the bortrekker, 'rattling the boards of a wooden sea . . .'

Once the storm had abated Chloe and Alex were able to forge ahead. Nelson stayed with them, hopping tirelessly alongside. Without realising it they were approaching the forest of tall clocks from the most difficult side. The weather here was always inclement and the boards showed it. Instead of the landscape being flat it was violently undulating where the boards had become warped. Extreme cold and heat had shrunk and expanded the planks in rapid motion, causing them to twist out of shape. Humps and dips made walking difficult and both children tripped several times when catching their feet on a board that had come loose or had twisted like a rope. There were gaps out there, large enough to fall through, though Nelson skipped between and around them as agile as any tri-cornered cat.

'Watch out for splinters if you fall over,' Alex warned. 'Some of the planks are split and broken.'

Indeed, there were ragged plank ends in places and shards lay here and there. Bare nails protruded like fangs, some by as much as three or four centimetres.

The rough going got worse before it got better. They crossed an area where a water tank had overflowed, flooding the boards. Some of the planks had actually curled back on themselves here and were like sleigh runners. However, once over this patch they returned to normal undulations caused simply by dampness and swift drying. The reason for the bad weather appeared to be a series of skylights that had been left open. Now they let in the elements: the wind and the rain, the heat of the summer sun, and any birds who cared to venture in from the outside world.

'Hey, guys – how do you like my skateboard park?'

Chloe looked up and her face broke into a smile. It was Jordy. Somehow he'd found a skateboard and was using the undulations to practise his moves. Even Alex, who often found the sporty side of Jordy a bit hard to take, had to grin at his step-brother's antics.

The three of them hugged and slapped each other on the back, then Jordy suggested they go to his camp in the forest of tall clocks. When they got there they found he had made himself very comfortable, using a dust cover over four of the clocks to make himself a tent. He couldn't stop talking at first, running over all that had happened to him since he'd been alone. The other two gave him their accounts and he seemed a little disappointed to find that Chloe and Alex's adventures matched his own, if not surpassed them.

'So, you got a camping stove?' marvelled Jordy, giving Alex due praise. 'Can we get a cup of tea?'

'We could if we had some tea,' Alex replied.

'Never mind. Perhaps we can send Nelson out looking for some, eh, Nelson?' Jordy fondled the cat's nape. 'Good old Nelson. Kept me company, he did.'

'He did us too!' cried Alex. 'He must have been going back and forth between the three of us.' He went on, 'Nelson brought me a pigeon, and a rat. I stripped and gutted them and cooked them up. They tasted good.'

'You ate a *rat*?' said Jordy, studying Alex now as if for the first time since they had been reunited. 'What's all that gear for?'

'What gear?'

'The kit. The big coat. The boots. The hat. The *mask*.'

'Oh, these.' Alex laughed carelessly. 'I just took a fancy to them.'

Chloe caught Jordy's eye and the older brother stopped asking questions about the way Alex dressed.

'So, my little brother's becoming self-sufficient in his old age,' said Jordy after a while. 'How did all this come about?'

'I just woke up one morning – and there I was.'

Jordy for some reason felt a little uncomfortable probing his step-brother like this. He was afraid he was going to find out something he didn't particularly like, though there was no real evidence that he would. But for one thing he was a little disturbed to find such a change in Alex in so short a time. It wasn't that there was anything wrong with the way Alex was behaving. It was just that it was wrong for Alex. Indeed, his step-brother seemed just as shy and quiet as he always had been: still the reserved young man. But now there was a strong quiet confidence in him that shook Jordy a little. A determination about him that seemed to have come from nowhere. And the clothes he wore *were* a little eccentric, even for the attic. Chloe had immediately shed her layers once out of the stormy section of the attic, but Alex continued to keep his on, as if they were now part of his make-up, part of him.

'I learned to navigate the attic,' he told the other two brightly, 'from the bortrekker. The guy you met by the trapdoor.'

'He was some character, wasn't he?' Alex said, agreeing with Jordy. 'I really liked him.'

Jordy was even more put out now. Alex was encroaching on *his* territory. Jordy was the adventurer, the orienteering expert. Alex was supposed to be interested in engines and science and all that sort of nerdy stuff. It was a bit annoying to find his little brother copying him. Unfortunately he said as much, and had to witness another new side to Alex, as his young step-brother gave him a withering look. He muttered something about Alex copying him.

'*Copying?* I'm not copying you. You don't own the rights to map-reading, do you? What did you ever invent that anyone would want to copy?'

'Now you listen here—' began Jordy angrily, but Chloe interrupted.

'Please, boys – we've only just met up again.'

Jordy's eyes were still smarting, but he managed to blink, and soon had his feelings under control. He admitted to himself in the next minute or two that he had lost his cool a little. Thinking about it again, he decided 'So what?' – so Alex was becoming more like him. Did that matter? In one way he ought to feel flattered that his brother was beginning to follow in his footsteps. A good leader makes good leaders of others, he told himself, and Alex was simply learning from him. Good on Alex. Good on him.

'Sorry, Alex.' Jordy put out a hand to shake. 'Just lost it for a moment – this place, you know.'

Alex grinned and shook Jordy's hand. 'Yeah, I know. Me and Clo have fallen out once or twice too. It's the attic.'

'Hey,' cried Jordy, changing the subject, 'what do you think of the dust sprites? They're weird, aren't they? Look, there's one now. Oh, he's gone. Really weird.'

It was clear from their faces they didn't know what he was talking about. Their heads swung back and forth and finally brother and sister looked at each other and shrugged.

'Dust sprites,' explained Jordy, amazed that they were so slow at seeing the obvious. 'I'd seen them but it was the bortrekker who told me exactly what they are. They're the spirits of the attic. They're everywhere – in the rafters, on the boards, in all the nooks and crannies. Sometimes they form themselves into little figures of dust, run along for a bit, then they sort of go *puff* and settle back as dust on the boards again. Don't tell me you haven't seen them?' He stared at their faces, before adding, 'You haven't, have you?'

'No,' admitted Chloe, biting her lip. 'We've seen movements, out of the corner of our eyes, but I thought that was just an overactive imagination – along with the funny light up here.' She was a little upset to realise that an Ariel might be here in the attic and it was Jordy and not her who was aware of him. The attic could be a little spiteful in that way: revealing things to those who had no interest in them, while others yearned to see such sights. How contrary was this land of boards and rafters. It played with its visitors like toys.

While they had been sitting there talking, clocks had been striking at odd times in the distance. Jordy had systematically disabled all the clocks within an hour's walk, so that the constant ticking and chiming would not drive him crazy. Now the more distant chimes were like owl hoots to a camper: for most of the time his brain didn't register them. Once he concentrated, of course, they were there, but he could soon switch them off again.

'We saved you some honey,' Chloe told Jordy. 'We found a bees' nest in an old suitcase.'

'Oh, wow – thanks.' He really was grateful. 'I've been eating veg until I look like a cabbage.'

Chloe said, 'You don't look like a cabbage. You look very – very swashbuckling.'

'Thanks.'

At that moment Nelson slunk away. Jordy watched him go and said, 'What's the matter with him?'

Alex answered, 'He's heard something. Listen!'

They all tuned their ears.

'All I can hear,' said Chloe, 'are the clocks.'

'More and more of them,' said Alex. 'The number of strikes has increased and I can hear the ticking now.'

Jordy cried, 'Alex is right. Someone's repairing the clocks as they come this way. We've got to move.'

They were all experienced enough now in the ways of Attica to know that every new encounter was dangerous. On the one hand they had met some helpful characters, like the puppets and the bortrekker. But for the most part the creatures they'd met had proved to be hostile. Here was a new encounter coming their way. It was best to avoid it. If this thing repaired clocks, it might very well prove a menace to those who had disabled them. There was something a little crazy about a being who took the time to make sure all clocks had been wound up, even though they were telling the wrong time and striking falsely.

Jordy put his arm through the leather loop of his skateboard carrier and slung it over his shoulder. Then he followed Alex and their sister, hastily packing things. They hoisted their packs on their backs, and set off in the opposite direction to the clock-menders. This woodland of theirs could be likened to a forest of dwarf oaks. There was no height to it, but the squared trunks were solid enough to impede rapid progress. Here and there a grandfather clock had fallen over, just as real trees topple in the forests of the earth. If it was on its face there was glass everywhere, sometimes a pathetic hand or two, and in extreme cases, cogs, wheels, ratchets, a large shiny pendulum, chains and weights and other internal works. These were clocks with pretty faces too: pastoral pictures of goosegirls leading their flocks, or ploughboys at the plough. Chloe thought that if she ever owned such a clock she would *never* banish it to an attic.

When they emerged from the forest they came across two massive armies of toy soldiers. A great battle was taking place. Although the generals and their troops were not interested in the human children their numbers were so great they formed a sea of uniforms – many different kinds – spread across the attic's boards. The noise, for such tiny creatures, was astonishing. There were no guns going off, nor rifles which worked, but there was a clatter of tiny swords, bayonets and other metal objects against metal chests. So far as Chloe could see, none of the soldiers could hurt each other, but seemed intent on doing so. Generals of course were having a fine time, ordering battalions here, divisions there, and corps everywhere else.

'Stupid creatures,' she muttered, trying to step between them. 'If they get squashed, it's their fault.'

In the end the three travellers found it easier to sweep a path through the armies, brushing the soldiers into heaps either side. When they first did it they prepared to run, thinking they might anger the troops. But the toys were not interested in revenge. They just wanted to get back into the battle again. The objective appeared to be a line of forts and castles at each end of the boards and Chloe could foresee it

ending in stalemate, with one lot of attacking soldiers occu-
pying their enemy's forts, and the other lot overrunning
their foe's castles. It was all pretty much a waste of time so
far as she could tell. She wondered if Nelson came to this
corner of the attic: he loved little moving things he could
chase and bat about with his paw.

Jordy and Alex had started to take their newly learned
navigational skills quite seriously. They lined up sunshafts
sent down by skylights at a set hour of the day in order to
keep to a straight line. This was much like using a sextant to
navigate a ship. And another aide which had been
employed by early sailors: celestial bodies. The square stars
embedded above lofty networks of beams and rafters were
excellent direction-finders. Jordy had learned about the
clusters of skylights and the star patterns they created.

The bortrekker had given them a route to follow and
Jordy and Alex found their way across the boards with
unerring accuracy now. Of course they made one or two
mistakes but these were corrected by going back to a
known point and beginning that section again. They were
beginning to familiarise themselves with the constellations
of the attic, with its changing landscapes.

Fortunately the weather remained mild. There was a
heavy mist one morning, rising from a group of water
tanks, but though this hid any likely dangers from the voy-
agers, they encountered no trouble. For the most part it was
simply a long slog which had Chloe wondering if they
would ever see home again. To make such a journey back
again, across that vast and troubled land, would take an
enormous amount of fortitude.

Still, she remained outwardly optimistic, being a girl
with a naturally cheerful disposition.

'Come on, you two, step it out,' she cried, her shoes
echoing on the hollow floor. 'Let's get to our destination.'

'I'll tell you what,' said Jordy, going to the side pockets of his huge backpack, 'I just remembered. I've got skateboards for you two as well. Here,' he produced them, 'I found them in a bunch of sports equipment. I always said skateboarding was a sport, didn't I? Well, that sort of proves it.'

Alex was not the best skateboarder in the world, but he could still kick and run with the other two. Thus the three travellers were soon speeding on their way, leaving any followers trailing far behind them.

# CHAPTER 16

# Atticans in Khaki Coats

'The Removal Firm is very near.'

*I know, I know. It's those damn kids. They brought them by using fire.*

'It's not the fault of the kids. You know how relentless the Removal Firm is. They'll hunt you all down in the end.'

*Not me,* says the board-comber, *I've been here since the beginning of time.*

'Yes, yes, ancient fossils were real buttons and spoons when you came – but that won't save you, any more than that carnival mask you wear will fool the Removal Firm. You're an outsider and that's that, fake friar or not. That's all the Removal Firm cares about.'

The board-comber knows the bat is right. The Removal Firm aren't interested in how long you've been in residence. You're an outsider and therefore you have to be watched closely and ejected at the slightest suspicion of any wrongdoing.

'If you had a board with wheels on, like those newcomers, you'd be able to out-distance the Removal Firm every time.'

*Well, I don't and I wouldn't know how to use one if I did.*

'Don't they just whizz along?'

*Too fast, if you ask me.*

'All I'm saying is, if you had one, you'd be a flying board-comber.'

They let the subject drop. The board-comber is a little aggrieved by the boards with wheels. Although they assist the human children in racing ahead of the Removal Firm, they also put a lot of kilometres between the board-comber and his charges. How can he look to their welfare if they are so far ahead of him? How can he watch over them if he can't see them? It is all so frustrating. And to what end? What will *he* get out of it? Probably nothing.

'They're going in the right direction at last.'

*For what?*

'For the Great Water Tank.'

*And remind me what is it that they want there?*

'The map, of course. But in any case humans always head towards the shores of great waters, wherever they are.'

*Is that true? I don't.*

'You're hardly human any more, but all the others do. They seem to need the sights and smells of wide open waters. It's because they were once fish, I suppose, before they crawled out and used their legs.'

*Look, the visitors have stopped. They're camping for the night. Oh! Oh my, look what the girl creature is taking from her pack. Look. Look! A carving. A wonderful Inuit carving. I knew these young people would come up with something. New ones always do. Look what it is! It's a walrus. I haven't got a walrus. I want it.*

'Where do you think she got it?'

*Down below, of course. When she went through the trapdoor and dropped into the house underneath. She must have stolen it.*

'Stolen goods,' says the bat, sucking in its breath. 'She

could get arrested for that. And you. You could get arrested for coveting stolen goods. That's against the law.'

*No, it isn't. You can't be arrested for wanting things. Anyway, I have to have that carving. How do I get it?*

'Trade with the boy – you know what he wants.'

The board-comber is overjoyed at this suggestion.

*Of course, bat – you're a genius.*

'Oh, please,' demurs the bat, fluttering its wings, 'just highly intelligent, nothing more.'

*There's one near here. I remember hiding it for just such a trade as this.*

'There you go then!'

*Look, the children are resting for the night.*

'Ah, the night, the night. The children of the night.'

They could hear the howling of a thousand wolves above the shimmering metallic sound that seemed to run in waves. It was both frightening and fascinating. It didn't sound menacing, exactly, but until he knew what it was, it was certainly worrying.

'Listen,' said Jordy.

'I know, I can hear it,' replied Chloe. 'Weird, isn't it?'

'But what is it?'

'Bottles,' answered Alex. 'Millions of bottles, all standing shoulder to shoulder. Trembling bottles, rattling against each other.'

Chloe asked, 'But what about the howling?'

'The attic draughts blowing over the necks.'

Indeed, now that the other two knew what that peculiar sound was, his words made sense. Jordy took off his backpack and went up a dome like aberration in the boards and stared towards the sound. From that vantage point he could see them: an ocean of bottles of all different coloured glass. Wine bottles, milk bottles, beer bottles, lemonade bottles, medicine bottles, and so on, and so forth. What a sight they made in all their hues, glinting in the fading light from the high windows. For some reason Jordy felt an urge to walk upon them, on that vast expanse of bottlenecks, just because they looked so inviting.

And Alex had been right again. It was the strong draughts making them tremble, chinking their shoulders. And the draught causing that howling from their necks. This truly was a sight one might travel miles to see, like a glacier in the real world, or a strange rock formation.

'Look at that,' said Chloe, coming up alongside him.

'I know. And in the sunset too. The best time.'

The sun leapt as dancing fire from bottleneck to bottle shoulder, sending glints and flashes back to the two watchers. Here it streaked over a hundred clear-glass stalwarts, there it jumped from green to red to blue. And all the while that tinkling sound which outdid waves on a stormy beach, or the rustling of reeds on a windy creek for volume. Quivering bottles, bottles, bottles, sweeping out and away, with nothing else in sight. They could have been alive out there, that gathered multitude of glass: a million empty vessels making the loudest noise you had ever heard in your life.

Jordy looked back at Alex, who was busy getting the camping stove going.

'Clo . . . ?'

'You're going to ask how he knew what was here before any of us even saw them.'

'Yep, I was.'

She shrugged. 'He's different now. He seems instinctively to know things about Attica. If you ask him *how* he knows, he can't tell you. I'm worried about Alex, Jordy. I'm worried he won't want to go home when the time comes. He's altered a lot.'

Jordy became the elder brother. 'He'll still do as he's told.'

'You can't force him to obey you, Jordy. He'll just run off. We can't tie him up or anything.'

'No – but he'll surely listen to reason?'

'Will he? I'm not so sure.'

Jordy walked back down the slope of the boards, to where Alex was quietly humming to himself. He looked like a rag-bag, Jordy thought, in that rotten old hat and now he was wearing yet *another* old coat on top of the first two. And all those scarves and things! Those sloppy over-sized shoes! He was beginning to smell too, despite the fact that Jordy grumbled at him. Why didn't he wash himself and his clothes? Did he want his shirt and socks to stink to high heaven?

And there was another thing, too.

'What's that bat doing?' asked Jordy, pointing to a creature hanging from a rafter not far from their camp. 'It's been following us.'

Alex looked innocent. 'Why ask me?'

'Because I think it's following you, not me or Chloe.'

'Why do you think that?'

'When you go down to drink at the water tanks, it follows you. It doesn't do that with us.'

Alex shrugged and put on Makishi. 'Well?' To Jordy he seemed to be hiding behind that weird African mask.

'Well what?' said Jordy in more of an accusing tone than he actually intended. 'Well I'm right?'

'You could be. I don't know.'

Jordy said, 'I think I'll kill that bat.'

Alex immediately flared up, leaping in front of Jordy and pushing his Makishi face close to his step-brother's.

'You leave it alone,' he shouted with venom. 'Who do you think you are?'

Jordy was shocked. Alex had never spoken to him in that way before. He had never been so threatening in his tone. Jordy backed away, saying, 'All right, all right, it was a joke . . .'

Chloe came down from the slope. Normally she would have sided with her younger brother, but there was something dangerous about Alex now. Instead she told him, 'There's no need for that, Alex. Jordy is just trying to find out what's happening to you.'

'Nothing's happening to me. I'm just me, that's all.'

'You've changed,' accused Chloe. 'You're not like the Alex who came up here with us. You're different.'

'I'm just the me I always wanted to be,' explained Alex. 'That's all. You just leave me be. You just leave me to what I am and who I am. Find another brother. You've got Jordy now. Isn't one brother enough for you?'

It was Chloe's turn to be shocked.

She stood there, stunned and hurt. *Find another brother.* What was Alex saying?

'Alex, are you jealous of Jordy? Is that it?'

Alex sighed and shook his head vigorously.

'No, of course not. I just don't want you fussing over me any more. I'm not worried that Jordy's part of our family. It's just that *I* don't want to be part of the family. I want to be on my own. I don't want a sister. I don't want parents. I don't want anybody. I've got me and Makishi and that's all I need. We don't need anyone else, do we, Makishi?'

'No one but ourselves, Alex,' replied the mask.

It was the first time Jordy had heard Makishi speak and he paled and took a step backwards. Wisely he decided not to make a big thing of this mask of Alex's, even though it appeared to be alive. Clearly Chloe was used to the fact.

Instead he spoke to Chloe. 'There's a bat that keeps stalking us,' he said to his step-sister. 'Clo, Alex has gone loopy.'

Chloe ignored Jordy for the moment.

'Alex, you can't just opt out of a family. I'm your sister. Jordy's your step-brother. You can't change that, whatever you do. You might not want our company any more, but you'll still be our brother. Please, try to understand how we feel. We're concerned for you.'

'That's what I mean,' said Alex simply. 'I don't want you to be. I'm all right. Nothing's wrong with me. I just don't want fussing.'

'OK, we won't fuss. But don't do anything silly, will you? Promise? Don't run away or hide or anything.'

This speech, short and simple as it was, seemed to touch something of the old Alex deep inside. He stared at his sister with big, brown, untroubled eyes through the holes in the mask. It was true, there was no turbulence in Alex, only calmness and tranquillity. He was all right. It was them who weren't.

'Fine,' he said. 'I promise, sis.'

'Thank you.'

She turned away and began busying herself with something, anything, to stop the tears from welling up and flowing. She was losing her brother. Of course they couldn't remain as children all their lives. She would leave for university or a job somewhere, or perhaps to get married. He would remain behind for a time, but then leave himself, perhaps finding work that would take him halfway around the world. Who knew how the separation might come about, but it was a natural process, which would leave no scars and no regrets. They would always think fondly of one another, wherever they were, however distant from each other.

This? This was too soon. And he seemed not to care that he was hurting her. All he seemed to care about was his freedom and solitude.

Well, I won't let him, she told herself mentally. He might not care, but I do, and I can be just as determined and self-ish about what I want.

And that was true too.

'Is that it?' asked Jordy quietly, later. 'Are we just going to let him do what he wants? I like having the little beggar around. I don't want him to become a bloody hermit.'

Chloe could have hugged Jordy for that, but she didn't, of course.

'We'll have to work on him, without him knowing it,' she said. 'We're older, wiser and more cunning than he is, though he thinks he's the bees' knees at the moment. We'll get the old Alex back, don't you worry, Jordy. I'll see to that.'

'What are you two whispering about?' called Alex. 'You hatching something?'

'Listen to Mr Suspicious,' called back Jordy. 'Come on over and we'll tell you.'

'No chance.'

In fact, Alex was feeling a little crowded, being with the other two for so long.

It didn't take him long to forget what he'd just promised Chloe about not running away and hiding. He wandered away from the camp. He made sure the other two weren't looking and went off to see what he could find.

There was something terribly wrong. Every member of the Removal Firm sensed it in the atmosphere. Something very, very bad was in the dust. The whole attic was in danger. A disaster was imminent. Their world as they knew it was about fall down around their ears. The dust sprites sensed it. When they appeared now their brief journeys were frantic affairs. There was panic in them and they knew not the source. Every beetle, every mouse, was waiting in trembling anticipation for something to happen – they knew not what, but they felt disaster coming – and they were full of dread. Hearts beat a thousand times faster. Eyes were everywhere. Today? Perhaps. Tomorrow? Maybe. Soon? Almost certainly.

But who? Who was planning this destruction? The Removal Firm could only think the latest incomers were responsible. Were they not playing with fire, those recent intruders? Had they not caused havoc among the villages? Had not one of them disrupted the underworld by entering the *wrong* trapdoor and disturbed the currents of time and place? No real harm had been done *yet*, but surely these were they who planned something awful, something so heinous it was hard to believe. The Removal Firm decided to step up their efforts to capture the incomers before this horrible crime was committed and the whole attic was destroyed.

There wasn't a great deal of junk in that area. Nothing of any significance for Alex, anyway. He found some old vinyl jazz records, but nothing to play them on, and he wasn't sure he liked jazz anyway. And some golf clubs in a rotting leather bag. And a Chinese screen. He wiped the dust away from the lacquered surface to find some beautiful pictures cut into the wood beneath. But even these did not do a great deal for him.

What he really wanted, what he was really looking for, were model steam engines. Engines like the showman's traction engine and the others he had in his pack. He wanted more of them. A steam car, for example. He'd like one of those. Or a steam roller. Or even a static traction engine. He told himself there must be more of them in Attica – many more. If he searched long and hard enough, he'd surely find as many as he wanted. He didn't know how many he wanted, but at the moment there was just a yearning for model steam engines of steel and brass.

Alex continued to search, oblivious of the time it was taking, quite unconcerned that his brother and sister might be looking for him.

'I know where you can find one.'

Alex was in an area where several shafts of light were coming down from the roof and striking the floor in splashes of golden dust. He stared into the gloomy spaces behind the pillars of light, but could see nothing. There were the ubiquitous piles of clothes everywhere, but nothing that looked as if it could speak. Then one of the piles began moving. Eventually it stood up and, like a walking haystack, shuffled over to where Alex was standing. Its face looked hideously ugly at first, until Alex realised it was just a painted mask, a clownish face. Unlike his own mask, it was unthreatening.

Alex was not terrified, exactly, but he was afraid.

'Are you some sort of cloth creature?' he asked in a shaky voice. 'Some kind of walking basket of washing?'

'No,' said the clothes, 'I'm flesh and blood. Just like you.'

Alex looked down at himself and then stared at the thing before him, realising they were of the same ilk. Then he saw, deep within the many folds of cloth, behind the ceramic mask, two human eyes. He had to look down a long tunnel of fabric to find those human features. Even then, they didn't look *that* human. They were small and wizened, shrunken, like walnuts left too long in their shells. It was difficult to tell where this creature began and ended, there were so many ends of cloth: trailing empty sleeves, trouser legs, bits of scarves, shirt tails and socks flopping from pockets.

'You dress like me,' Alex cried excitedly.

'No,' replied the board-comber, 'you will be like *me*.

But not yet. You're not quite there. You've just started going that way.'

'Is that a bat hanging from your ear? Will I get one of those?'

'I'm sure some creature has got you marked out already.'

'I've seen it following me. Are they pets?'

The board-comber shrugged inside its many layers.

'I suppose you could call them that. Me and my bat, we talk to each other. I think. But,' the board-comber sighed, 'now I've spoken to you, it'll be a longish time before my bat speaks to me again. You have to get in the right frame of mind, you see, to converse with bats. You have to be alone a very long while. You have to be alone so long you start seeing forms that aren't really there. Figures made of dark shadow that dance in the moonlight. Horses made of sunlight rearing on their hind legs and prancing silently across the attic. These things come after a long time of not speaking with another human, of being alone. Do you understand?'

'I think so,' replied Alex, 'but it doesn't matter.'

'No,' agreed the board-comber, 'none of this really matters.'

Alex peered hard down that fabric tunnel.

'Are you a girl or a boy?'

'I can't remember, but I think *he* and *him*.'

Alex then said, 'You called to me.'

'Ah.' The board-comber rubbed its many woollen mittens together. 'Business. Your female companion . . .'

'My sister.'

'Yes, she. She has a carving. A green carving. It's – it's a walrus. I collect carvings like that. I want it.'

'Then you'll have to ask her.'

'No – no, you get it for me.'

'I can't . . . wait a minute. You said "I know where you can find one". What did you mean?'

The board-comber knew he had the boy hooked.

'I know where there's another model steam engine.'

'Where?' cried Alex. His heart suddenly started beating fast and his blood pulsed rapidly through his veins. 'I must have it.'

'It's a swop. Do you know what a swop is?'

Alex was scornful. 'Of course I know what a swop is.'

'That's what we'll do. You get the soapstone walrus for me. I'll get the car for you. Then we'll swop.'

Alex was cagey. 'How do I know you're telling the truth? Maybe you're saying you've got a steam engine, just to get the carving. Show it to me.'

'I can't. I haven't got it at the moment. But I'll get it.'

Alex was still not sure. This creature could be lying to him. Or it could be telling the truth. One thing was sure, the urge to get yet another steam engine to go with those in his pack was very great. Alex had never felt anything like it. He would have sold his own grandmother – *both* grandmothers – to get a steam car. It was as if there was a shape inside him which had to be filled. The shape of a model steam engine. He *craved* it. Could not live without it. It was an irrepressible yearning.

'I'll get the carving for you,' he heard himself saying. 'She doesn't really want it, I'm sure.'

'Good. Good.' A filthy mitten full of holes suddenly projected from one of the many dangling sleeves. 'Shake on it.'

Alex eyed the mitten with disgust.

'I'll take your word for it,' he said, revolted by the dirt. 'We don't need to shake.'

Just at that moment Alex heard a rattling of the boards. Some large Atticans were coming, swiftly and seemingly with some definite purpose. They wore khaki dustcoats with brown buttons. Alarm and confusion rushed through him as the board-comber instantly collapsed into a heap of rags on the floor. Alex copied him, crumpling himself from within, falling and folding down to the planks. There they lay, two piles of old clothes, as the trackers advanced.

The board-comber knew it was the Removal Firm.

The board-comber was cursing his carelessness, hoping for a miracle. His dealings with the visitor should have been short and swift, for the board-comber had known there was danger in the air. Instead they had stood there chatting like two old men sat on a bench. It was not that the Removal Firm would be suspicious of one heap of rags. But two? Why, they were so close together the board-comber could smell the feathers of the human's boa.

One of the Removal Firm stopped and stood between the two heaps, glancing quickly right and left. Clothes. Piles of them. It sniffed hard. Then it sniffed again. All it could smell was attic. These clothes had been up here a long time. They were steeped, saturated, in attic smells. Layers of dirty lambswool and cotton hid the inner scents. The creature might have picked through the pile, but it didn't. It sniffed again, hard.

It must have drawn in dust through its nose, for it sneezed right on to the board-comber, showering the rags with spittle. Then, after a terrible few seconds the tracker moved on, scuttling forward to examine a box. For quite a while afterwards their boots could be heard clattering over the boards. Alex kept very still, very quiet, and thought about something else. He made up a shopping list, for Dipa. In his mind he argued with Ben about football: which was the best team and which the worst, as if he cared.

Finally, he felt a tap on his head.

'They've gone,' said the board-comber. 'Hey, you did well for a beginner.'

'Thanks,' replied Alex, extremely pleased with himself. 'I'm learning. Who were they?'

'Hunters,' replied the board-comber, not wishing to go into time-consuming explanations. 'Beware of them.'

'I shall.'

'By the way,' said the board-comber, 'I love the mask.'

'Thank you,' murmured Makishi. 'Yours isn't bad, either.'

Coming from outside the Mask Country though, Cocalino did not have the power of speech and therefore did not make comment.


'How long has he been gone?' asked Chloe.

Jordy looked at his watch. 'The last time I saw him, it was six o'clock – it's now nearly five. About an hour.' He held up a finger.

Chloe stared at her step-brother for a moment, then said, 'Oh yes, I forgot – time goes backwards here.'

The finger came down. 'One hour precisely – *now*.'

# CHAPTER 17

# Swarming of the Ink Imps

'The thing is, when he comes back, don't make a fuss.'

Jordy was anxious not to upset Alex. He didn't want to give his step-brother an excuse to run off permanently. If they all started arguing, Alex would definitely go away and hide. He did that when he was upset with anyone at home. He just took himself off somewhere. Jordy called it 'sulking' but he didn't really know what caused Alex's moods. Jordy admitted to himself, deep down, that the reason Alex annoyed him was because Jordy didn't understand him. No one really did.

'No, I agree,' said Chloe. 'We'll play it down, yes?'

So when Alex wandered back into camp, expecting to be shouted at for leaving without telling them, they virtually ignored him. He took Makishi off his face and slung him on the cord over his shoulder.

'I'm back,' Alex said.

Chloe looked up from the meal she was making.

'Oh – are you? Didn't know you'd gone. I thought that was you over there.'

She pointed to a heap of rags in a dark corner.

Alex pouted. 'I don't wear stuff like that.'

'Yes you do,' replied Chloe. 'Worse stuff.'

Alex didn't take the bait, but eventually asked, 'Are we moving on today?'

Jordy came over with his backpack already clipped shut.

'Yep. I reckon from what the bortrekker told me that we're very close to the Great Water Tank he talked about. The bureaux are on the edge of the lake, guarded by the ink imps. We'll get the map—'

'What about the ink imps?' interrupted Alex. 'Won't they try to stop us?'

Jordy laughed. 'What can a few imps do to us? Nah, we'll just walk through them and find the map. We need to find Mr Grantham's watch. *Frère Jacques*. Then we can start back home again. Now I know how to navigate up here I think I can get us back.'

'Easy, just like that,' murmured Alex. 'Wonder why we didn't do it before?'

'Because we haven't got the watch yet,' replied Jordy, through gritted teeth.

Nelson loped into camp with a mouse in his jaws.

'Poor fare that,' cried Alex. 'You can do better than that, ginger. Bring us an Attican wild boar.'

Nelson gave Alex a hard stare. He was not a cat who enjoyed being mocked.

'Yuk,' Chloe said, 'I'm glad there are vegetables.'

Nevertheless she stroked her cat until he purred in delight. He flopped over at her feet and began playing with the dead mouse, batting it backwards and forwards. Finally Chloe picked it up by the tail and tossed it away. Nelson stared after it, but decided it wasn't worth moving for. He was in a nice shaft of sunlight that warmed his fur and it felt very good. The boards were cosy beneath his fur and like all cats he loved a laze.

At that moment six Atticans in dustcoats arrived: the

same set that had sniffed around the board-comber and
Alex earlier. They were fusty-looking, much taller and
broader than the normal villagers that the children had met
until now. Their features were stern below their shining
bald pates. They also looked stronger than any villager the
children had come across. They would not have looked out
of place in a hardware store. They had the appearance of
harassed counter clerks.

'Eeerk!' cried the one who pointed.

'Eeerk yourself,' said Jordy, hands on hips. 'And your
name is . . . ?'

Chloe and Jordy did not know who these characters
were. They seemed very hostile. Another of them beck-
oned, indicating that the children should step forward.
Jordy was inclined to tell him to take a running jump.

'These are the ones the board-comber called *hunters*,'
Alex said. 'They look a bit aggressive, Jordy.'

'I'll give them aggro all right,' muttered Jordy. 'Just let
'em step over here.'

Chloe said, 'They're getting angry.'

'Let 'em,' said Jordy. He was actually not feeling as con-
fident as he sounded. 'There are only – six of 'em.'

Seeing that the humans were not going to obey the cur-
sory summons indicated by the crooked finger, the
creatures moved in to arrest them.

Until this point Nelson had been vaguely aware of
intruders. He still lay on his side in the warm sunlight,
stretching his head to look at what all the fuss was about.
He sniffed and on smelling the strange odour of the intruders his hackles rose. Nelson, like many cats, was very
sensitive to unusual odours. When the creatures actually
advanced, Nelson went up on his three paws in an instant.
All his fur was on end now, his remaining twelve claws
were protruding like curved daggers from his paws and he

was hissing and spitting through bared fangs. There was a low growling whine coming from his mouth.

In short Nelson, a large cat, was upset and with his formidable arsenal of weapons he looked a terrifying, spiky, fierce ginger beast.

The Atticans paused in their advance. Nelson spat and yowled loudly. They backed off. Nelson advanced, his eyes slits, his claws scratching the boards as he slunk towards the intruders, alternately growling and giving off low menacing yowls, as if to say, Don't make me come and get you.

They turned and retreated quickly.

'See, they were even scared of a little cat,' cried Jordy. 'Just think how frightened they would be of *me*.'

'More likely they've never seen a cat before,' Chloe remarked, coming closer to the truth. 'I think they looked quite formidable – I think we're lucky, Jordy, that they were wary of Nelson.'

'He's better than a wolfhound,' Alex said, stroking his pet. 'Come on, I think we'd better go, in case there's more of them somewhere around.'

They packed up quickly and were soon on the march.

They came across a huge bowl-shaped valley where the boards had sunk. Jordy gave a whoop of delight, threw down his skateboard, jumped on and went whizzing down into the bowl, then up the other side. He enjoyed this so much he did it several more times. Chloe then had a go and managed to stay on. Alex watched his brother and sister, then finally he too tried the run and was also successful in staying upright. It was exhilarating, this exercise, and their shouts and yells of excitement brought watchers.

It seemed there was an Attican village nearby and the inhabitants, having heard the cries, came to the edge of the bowl to see what was going on. They were amazed to see blurred ghosts with humped backs shooting down into the bowl and then up again, only to fly around the edge. One of the ghosts kept leaping and somersaulting, always landing neatly on its feet. In the eyes of the Atticans, who had never seen anyone or anything go more than ten miles an hour, this was the ultimate in speed and made them feel quite sick. It was something outside their experience and their brains couldn't cope.

'Come and join us!' yelled Jordy, calling to the attic people. 'I'll teach you how to do it.'

One of the Atticans watching their skateboarding was suddenly overcome by giddiness and fell forward to slide down into the bowl. His friends and relations let out a unified cry of dismay. When the terrified villager, his bald head sweating, tried to climb out of the bowl he kept slipping back in again. His movements became frantic, until finally Jordy felt he ought to help him. Jordy went sweeping down from the far side, grabbed the hapless villager, and lifted him up to carry him to the lip of the bowl. Friends and relatives reached out and grasped him. Jordy let go and swept down again, to swoop up the far side of the bowl.

The villager let out a cry of relief at finding himself safe.

White plaster dust rose when his kin punched him hard on the back and shoulders. This was a way of showing both affection and their own relief that he was not hurt and had escaped. The villager, grateful for so many punches, hit back at his beloved. For a while the clouds of white dust flew from the jackets and coats of the Atticans, then it all settled down again and they turned to stare once more at the ghosts. There was some discussion about how unorthodox it all was: they had never before had ghosts who zoomed back and forth too swiftly to follow. Then they congratulated the giddy villager for surviving in the hands of such creatures, and finally, as the sun began to set, they wended their weary way home, back to their wardrobes and washing baskets, to ponder on the vagaries of the unnatural world.

The following morning Jordy, Chloe and Alex came to an enormous water tank: a tank so large there were ladders up the sides to reach the lip. And when you climbed those ladders and looked out over the surface of the water, you could not see to the other side. All you could see was miles and miles of gentle waves, which eventually disappeared into a shimmering haze. On those wavelets, in the far distance, objects were floating. The Atticans, it seemed, were seafarers as well as land creatures.

'Wow!' cried Jordy. 'Look at this. A whole lake. Maybe even an ocean. Who knows what's on the other side of this lot?'

The water in the tank smelled fresh and clean. It *was* like being on the shore of a vast lake where sparkling mountain stream water came cascading into a natural basin and filled it. Instead of mountain streams, however, there were lagged water pipes which led from gutters up on the roof. When it rained in the outside world, as it seemed to be doing now, clean water gushed from the gutters, down the pipes and directly into the tank. In turn other pipes carried the excess away, to tanks all over Attica, where it was used in the inhabitants' strange world. Thus there was a balance which maintained a safe surface level of the Attican lake.

'Isn't that something?' whispered an awed Alex. 'What a marvel of nature.'

This remark caused his sister to look at him sharply.

'What do you mean, *nature*?' she said. 'This isn't natural, Alex. This is an attic, built by someone.'

'Yes,' replied her younger brother, giving her a significant look, 'but by *who*?'

'Whom,' she corrected automatically, then could have

bitten her tongue as Alex gave her a withering stare. 'I mean, Alex . . .'

But he had turned his back to her.

Chloe's heart sank once more. How could she tell him? How could she say it worried her that he thought the attic world was natural? Of course it worried her. It meant that Alex was becoming part of that world: another sign that he was beginning to fit in here, grow into this place. She shuddered when she thought of it. Her brother was changing into someone else. It wasn't natural at all: it was entirely unnatural. She and Jordy had to get Alex out of here quickly, before he became that someone else completely.

'Come on,' Jordy cried, unaware of the tension and the negative atmosphere which had suddenly sprung up between Chloe and Alex like a chill breeze, 'let's find those bureaus.'

Chloe bit her tongue again. Bureaus. It should be *bureaux*.

The three of them traversed the edge of the great lake, which seemed to be square, for they reached a corner and on turning it, found what they were looking for: a vast forest of writing bureaux. They might have been dismayed by the sight, knowing that they had to find one particular bureau in this multitude, but they could see one brilliant bureau. On it were beautiful pictures of long-tailed birds and cliff crags with single trees gripping their ledges and one lovely snow-tipped mountain. But that wasn't the reason they thought it *brilliant*. It was brilliant because it was painted with a crazed gold lacquer and – caught as it was in a shaft of sunlight – it dazzled as if it were made of real gold. In that huge and seemingly endless forest of writing bureaux this one called to them with its astounding beauty.

It had no branches, of course, but it had leaves. These leaves were quills sweeping from inkpots clustered on its shelves. Feathers of fresh-snow white. Other bureaux also had goose feathers sprouting from their inkpots, but not like these. Those on the golden bureau were of a purity which stopped your heart. These must surely have come from the wings of angels for they sang to you with their faultlessness. Not a drop of ink soiled them, not a speck of dust marred them. They were perfect in their whiteness, in their elegance, in their surety that they were hallowed feathers.

'The map couldn't be anywhere else,' said Jordy, 'could it?'

He hadn't said where and they didn't answer him. The other two knew what he meant and Jordy's question was purely rhetorical.

Jordy then cried, 'Well, come on – let's go and get it.'

He ran into the forest before the others could stop him. They themselves hesitated to rush in with him. Both Chloe and Alex were mindful of the warnings they had received regarding the ink imps. They couldn't actually see any of these creatures at that moment, but such warnings always had to be taken seriously in the attic.

And they were right not to follow him. Out of inkwells and inkpots standing on many of the bureaux came the ink imps. They were small liquid creatures only centimetres high but in the shape of men. Coloured they were: green, red, blue and black, according to the ink in the pots from which they had emerged. They left no marks where they skipped and danced over the floorboards. In their tiny hands they carried pens like spears, the brass nibs gleaming wickedly in the gilded attic light. On they came, in their tens, their hundreds, their thousands. These coloured demons swarmed over Jordy, who let out one cry of despair before being overwhelmed. Their weapons stabbed at his bare skin and exposed flesh relentlessly. He cried out in anger and pain.

'We must help him,' cried Chloe, looking round for a weapon. 'Alex, we've got to help him.'

But there was nothing to hand. Alex too started forward, but then stopped again, fearful for his own life. There seemed to be millions of the horrible creatures, bearing down on Jordy, attempting to force him to the floor.

True to his determined nature, Jordy fought back at the vicious ink imps, who were now pinching his flesh with niblike claws. He flailed and raged at them, sending them flying in all directions. Struggling, with them hanging many-hued from his limbs and body, he fought to cover the distance between himself and the golden bureau. To the watchers it seemed a miracle that he was still on his feet with the sheer weight of numbers trying to topple him. But Jordy had a sportsman's competitive nature. He was damned if he was going to go down: not without a terrible fight. Even as he staggered forward he picked handfuls of the ink imps from his body, flinging them away with force.

Some of them were thrown so hard they splattered against the bureaux from which they had emerged. Under such force their skins no longer held and contained them. They smacked into woodwork and metal and burst like ink-filled balloons. Red, green, blue and black ink dribbled down the sides, fronts and backs of the bureaux in a gory show of colour. This seemed to enrage even more those who remained. They crawled over Jordy's body *en masse*, absolutely incensed with his actions. Some tried to reach his eyes, to attack them, to attempt to blind him. Jordy was quite aware of this change of tactics, for he covered his eyes with one hand, peering through the cracks between his fingers. With great effort he finally reached the golden bureau and fumbled around with the catch to open the front.

'He's doing it!' cried Alex. 'Go, Jordy, go.'

'Oh, I do hope he doesn't get hurt,' whispered Chloe. 'Look what they're doing to him. He'll be bruised all over.'

Nelson, who had been watching curiously, now dashed forward on his three legs and began attacking those funny little creatures which were scuttling over the boards. However, after the first two or three ink imps had burst in his claws, he loped slowly back to Chloe. Nelson was not fond of being showered with liquid of any kind, be it water or ink.

The bureau door dropped open, held up like a desktop by two side catches. Jordy's free hand scrabbled around inside the opening. There were paperweights in there, and stamps for franking letters, and all sorts of paraphernalia. His searching hand worked like a spider among them, searching for that elusive chart of the attic. Finally his hands came upon a roll of parchment. He took it out, flipped it open, unrolling it. 'A diploma,' he yelled in frustration. 'A bloody teaching diploma for some bloke called Potterswaite.' Again his free hand went inside and all the while the ink imps nipped and tugged away at him, trying to get him to submit.

He found another roll of parchment. He clutched it. This time he could not unroll it with one hand because it was tightly bound with a red ribbon. They could see he dare not take his protective hand from his eyes and so he had to hope that this time he had the map in his hand. Jordy turned from the golden bureau and thrashed his way back towards the two who were waiting for him. Chloe rushed forward and began picking imps from his shoulders and flinging them into the bureaux forest. Alex, seeing her do this, followed suit. Together they snatched red and blue, green and black imps and cast them away.

Finally all three began running away, turning the corner,

putting as much distance as they could between themselves and the imps.

Unfortunately in doing so, Jordy tripped. The roll of parchment threatened to get away from him. In trying to retain it he fell heavily, his right arm underneath the full weight of his body. There was a ghastly crack from one of his bones. Jordy's face went white with shock. He sat up looking dazed and sick. Holding forth his injured limb it seemed his forearm was fractured in the middle. There was a horrible sharp bump in the skin which was a sure sign of a broken bone trying to poke through. Jordy looked as if he were going to pass out, but he rallied, gritting his teeth.

'Does it hurt much?' asked Alex, almost as if he were curious rather than feeling sorry for his step-brother. 'Is there much pain?'

Jordy sucked in his breath, holding up his injured arm with his good hand. 'Not much. Not a lot, I mean. It hurts, but like someone has kicked me. Not as bad as you'd think it would. It's a sort of numbing pain.'

Alex then busied himself with stamping on those last few imp inks that now scuttled away from Jordy. Coloured ink squirted everywhere. Chloe told him to stop, then closely inspected the damage to her step-brother. She had done First Aid with her gymnastics coach.

'We need to put splints on that,' she said, 'to hold it in place. It'll need to be set by a doctor, but if it gets knocked or moved in the meantime, *then* it'll hurt. Tonight it'll ache like anything. I know, I broke my ankle at hockey. It's tonight it'll hurt.'

'Thanks for the warning,' gasped Jordy.

Alex went and found some pieces of an old orange box for the splints while Chloe looked for something to bind them with. She found some ladies' head scarves, which would do admirably, she said. They then boxed in the broken forearm with three pieces of wood. Chloe did a really good job of binding the pieces together, so that though Jordy could move his whole limb, his forearm remained still. Chloe then made a sling which would hold Jordy's splinted arm.

Nelson watched the proceedings with a distinct lack of interest as he licked coloured inks from his fur in distaste.

Standing up and feeling a lot better, Jordy assessed the problems he now caused the three of them.

'Look,' he said, his face still the grey shade of stale bread, 'I've got to get to a doctor, you know, or gangrene might set in. If that happens I'll either lose my arm or at the very worst, I'll die . . .'

'Don't say that,' Chloe snapped.

'I'm sorry Chloe, but I've got to face the truth. Thanks for doing this up for me, but I've got to get home now, somehow. I'm not sure exactly what gangrene is, or how I would know if I'd got it, but from reading books I do know it smells terrible and that it spreads until it reaches some vital organ.'

'We have to get you home,' said Chloe emphatically. 'You need to get to the hospital.'

'That's what I've been saying,' replied Jordy, managing to smile through his own distress at her anxiety. 'It's what I've got to do.'

Chloe said, 'Well, the first thing we've got to do is see whether we've got the map or not.'

With some trepidation she unrolled the huge parchment which Jordy had wrested from the ink imps. At first her heart skipped a beat as she thought they had the wrong piece of paper. She had been expecting wiggly lines in different coloured inks, with contours and lots of numbers for heights above sea level. What she had here looked like a board game. But then she realised a map of an attic would look nothing like a map of the normal world. It would look like this chart did, a floor plan of a room. Gradually, as she studied it, she recognised areas they had been through.

'Look, here's the Jagged Mountain – and there – there's the Forest of Tall Clocks – and over here the place where we met the friendly puppets – oh – oh . . .'

'What is it?' asked Jordy, wincing as the pain grew in his arm. 'What's the matter?'

'Here. Look. Down here. Almost off the bottom of the map,' cried Chloe excitedly. 'This is where we crossed over from our home attic into Attica proper. I know. I recognise those gently curving rafters, like the flying buttresses on a cathedral. You *must* remember, Jordy, the way they swept across the sky high above us, as we were wandering around, wondering where we were and how to get back?'

'I dunno,' replied Jordy doubtfully. 'It doesn't do anything for me.'

'It must do,' she insisted. 'You remember how I said it looked like we were in Winchester cathedral?'

'Nope.'

She began to grow angry. 'Well, I did.'

'You must have thought you did.'

Chloe stamped her foot the way she might have done when she was three years old. 'I certainly did! Anyway, what does it matter? I know where we have to go. We've got to start out now.'

Alex said quietly, 'Jordy'll never make it.'

'Yes he will,' cried Chloe, close to tears. 'Yes he will.'

'Not on foot he won't.'

It wasn't Alex who had spoken. They all turned to find the bortrekker standing there, towering above them, the capes of his coat making his shoulders look massive in the dim light. He had come upon them without them hearing him, big fellow that he was, which showed just how green were these humans in the ways of the great attic. The two rats, Arthur and Harold, peered from his pockets with glittering eyes. They stared down at Nelson, who was looking up at them with equal interest.

The bortrekker said, 'You watch that cat o' yorn. I'll scrag him if he tries to get at my rats.'

'He won't touch them while they're in your pockets,' Alex replied.

The bortrekker nodded. In his right hand he had his fiddle bow, which he used to point with.

'Now, over there,' he said, 'in that dark corner you'll find something that may be of use to you.'

'What is it?' asked Chloe.

'You go and find out. I'm not sure, see, whether you'll be able to use it. I've never seen it used myself. But there's a picture on the package, which shows what it can do. You can use the high warm draughts. They'll take you the length of the attic, back to where you came in, if you guide it properly. Go on, it may be his only hope.'

'My only hope?' cried Jordy, in anguish. 'Oh heck, go and look, Chloe. See what it is.'

Chloe left them, running for the dark corner.

Alex stepped forward now, his eyes shining.

'Thank you, bortrekker. Thanks for saving my brother's life.'

'You're welcome. And have you finally made up your mind?'

Alex nodded. 'I think I have. It was a difficult choice. My heart races when I think about model steam engines, but having met *you* again I realise they're not really important.'

'Good, then you won't need them engines, will you? Now you're not going to be a board-comber, like you thought you was.'

Alex smiled and took off his pack. He opened it and removed the model steam engines he had collected so far. He handed them to the bortrekker.

The bortrekker said, 'I'll hide these for some other board-comber to find.'

'Thanks.'

Chloe's face broke into a broad smile and relief flooded into her expression. 'Alex, you're not staying here in the attic! You're coming home with us. I'm so glad . . .'

Her brother's next remark crushed any hope within her, turning sudden happiness into anguish with the certainty that he was *not* going home.

'Oh yes I *am* staying, sis. I'm just not staying as a collect-or.' He beamed at the bortrekker and high up in one of the rafters a hopeful bat sighed in disappointment, knowing he would not be wanted after all. 'I'm going to be like him. I'm going to be a wanderer, learning the ways of the attic. An explorer. A pioneer. I shall roam the rest of my days, learning the lore of the attic.'

'When you're ready,' said the bortrekker, 'I'll come and find you. You need to know things. You need to know how and where and why. You're lucky,' he continued, 'I never had no one to teach me. You're lucky you've got me for a teacher. But remember what you're giving up. There's no countryside in the attic – only dead furniture and junk. You'll be saying goodbye to the wild rose and hawthorn, and will be left only with clocks and hat stands. No smell of newly mown grass. No scent of green thyme. Only the dust in your nostrils and the boards under your feet. Gone from you the sight of flocks of migrating swallows. Only swarms of bats fluttering their papery wings. No sudden change from green to silver: a poplar's leaves caught by a gust of wind. Only the draught between the cracks in the eaves, stirring dead spiders and lifting cobwebs. Not for you the flash of a stickleback in a stream, only the dull movement of some sluggish mollusc in the bottom of a stagnant water tank.

'D'you think you can live in such a world?'

Alex nodded, hard. 'I have to find the watch first though, for Mr Grantham. I promised. I can't go back on a promise.'

'If you have to.'

'Yes,' said Alex, 'I do – it'll be my last human act.'

'Oh, Alex,' cried the unhappy Chloe.

Seeing that strange shining in her younger brother's eyes, she despaired for him, knowing she was losing him, had probably already lost him. And at such a time, with an emergency on, when she couldn't give him her full attention. Unfortunately, Jordy needed her more at the moment. She went to look for the package which would help save Jordy's life.

# CHAPTER 18

# Rafter Kings and Rafter Queens

Chloe approached the place and saw a long large kit of some kind, wrapped in plastic.

A tent? It looked like a tent.

Dropping to her knees with her torch in her hand she shone it on a label which was visible through the transparent wrapping. Her eyes widened. Not a tent. A kite of some kind. She wiped away the dust from the covering and stared hard at the illustration. Not a kite either. A *hang-glider*. Her heart began beating faster. She picked it up, gathering it in her arms. It was quite light, despite the bulkiness.

When she arrived back at the edge of the lake, Jordy was alone, nursing his injured arm.

'Has he gone?' she asked. 'The bortrekker?'

Jordy was staring angrily into the middle distance.

'And Alex?' she added. 'Where's he gone?'

'Don't ask,' growled Jordy. 'He's a nutter. He's gone off his rocker.'

'I'll find him in a minute,' said Chloe.

Jordy suddenly became interested in what she had in her arms.

She put it on the ground.

'I know what that is,' he cried, gritting his teeth as his excitement exacerbated the pain in his arm. 'It's a hang-glider.'

'Have you done it? Can you do it?'

'Hang-gliding? Natch, I did it with the army cadets, before my dad married your mum.' His voice took on that old swaggering tone. 'I was pretty good at it. I flew like a bird.' He saw her expression, adding lamely, 'You know.'

'Can you do it with a broken arm?'

Despair registered on his face. He looked down at his sling.

'No, of course not,' he said, crestfallen.

A determined look appeared on Chloe's face. Jordy stared at her.

'Oh no,' he said. 'You can't, Chloe.'

'Yes I can. I'll have to. And you must help me. I've seen them on TV. You can do it with two people. The person who's guiding the glider goes in the harness and the passenger's slung underneath. They do it when they're teaching a novice. We're not even adults. We're quite light, considering. Our combined weight is probably that of one adult. A largish one, admittedly.'

'Yes,' protested her step-brother, 'but you're the novice and I'm not exactly an expert. I know what I said before, but I've only done it a few times. We're sure to crash, Chloe, then you'll end up with something broken too.'

Nelson appeared and rubbed up against Chloe's leg.

'And we'll have to take Nelson with us.'

'Oh, my lord,' muttered Jordy. 'The girl's serious.'

'Of course the girl's serious.'

'And what about Alex?'

Chloe said, 'Once I've taken you to our house, I'll come back for him. I'll be good at it then. I'll have had practice.'

This time she didn't sound too sure of herself. 'He can wait here, by the tank.'

'He won't, you know.'

'What do you mean?'

'Here he is now. Look at him.'

Alex was walking towards them. Chloe was surprised to see he had rid himself of all his old clothes, the silly over-sized overcoats, the scarves and all the other excess clothes. If there had been no other change, Chloe would have been delighted by the alteration. It would have meant that her brother had given up his ideas about being one of those collector things that infested the attic. One of those people who had turned from a human into a dust-living creature obsessed with gathering one or another of the attic's treasures.

But now Alex looked even worse. He had on a wide-brimmed hat, a coat with many capes, big boots. He strode like the tall youth they had just come to know. He walked with great confidence in his step. There was in his expression a new look, a look which chilled Chloe to the bone. She did not know this brother, this new Alex. He was a stranger.

'He's dressed like the bortrekker,' she said.

Jordy murmured, 'That's what he thinks he is.'

'That's what I *am*,' corrected Alex, coming up to them. 'I've always had it in me and now it's come out, and here I stand.'

He still had Makishi slung over his shoulder.

Jordy shouted, 'You're not a damn bortrekker, you're an engine nerd. I should be the bortrekker, if anyone. I was in the army cadets, not you.'

Alex sighed and shook his head. 'You haven't the right kind of mind for the attic, Jordy. I belong here. I can feel it.'

Chloe said, 'Don't I get a thought, Alex? What about

me? I'm your sister. What shall I tell Ben and our mother? Don't you think you're being just a bit selfish, deciding this on your own?'

Alex hung his head for a second, then replied quietly, 'I'm sorry, Clo. But it has to be my decision. We'll be grown up soon. Adults. Then you'll get work as a newspaper reporter or something, maybe eventually go off with some bloke you've fallen in love with. And me? I'll have a career somewhere in a town I don't like but have to be there because that's where the job is. Don't you see, we'll have to part company sooner or later. It's just going to be sooner, that's all.'

'It's not the same. That's natural. That's a natural thing to happen. This isn't.' She grew angry. 'And we'll never see each other again. If it was some old town I'd come and see you. But I can't come back here. You know that. I might not be able to. The attic might not let me.' She stared into his face, realising her words were making no difference. 'Oh, go on then. Do it. I can't force you to come back. I'll never speak to you again, you pig. I hate you. I really hate you. Get out of my sight.'

She burst into tears and turned away from him.

'I really am sorry, Clo. I'll help with the hang-glider. And I'll find Mr Grantham's watch. I've looked on the chart. The watches are on the other side of the lake. I'm going to sail over there and get it and I'll bring it to the trapdoor to our – to your house. You can take it to Mr Grantham.'

Her shoulders stopped shuddering. She stood there for a few seconds without replying, then she turned. 'You will?'

'Yes, I will, honest.'

'All right. Perhaps you'll have changed your mind by then. It's a lonely life, being a bortrekker, I'm sure. You *could* change your mind.'

'It's possible,' said Alex, but he had seen the crafty look in his sister's eyes and knew her plan. She was, he was certain, going to try to kidnap him as he handed over the watch. She would be there with Ben and Jordy, and maybe his mother, and they would first try to persuade him to come home, then – if he refused – they would grab him and bundle him down the attic steps and hold him until he promised never to go up into the attic again. Oh, he knew his sister all right, but he played along with her. 'It's quite possible. As you say, it's a lonely existence. I might change my mind.'

'Good. Help with this then.' She bent down and began ripping open the cover to the hang-glider, her sharp nails put to use on plastic instead of her brother. 'Let's see how we put it together.'

Jordy sat back, instructing them.

The hang-glider was not of a type he was thoroughly familiar with, but he had at least seen the design before. It was not one of the new paragliders, but one of the older gliders with an aluminium-tube frame over which was stretched the fabric, forming a sort of triangle shape with points on the trailing edge. They made a few mistakes, but there was an instruction book, and with Alex's engineering skills and Jordy's actual knowledge, they managed to put it all together in two hours. The harness was a little tricky but they worked that out in the end. Finally it was ready. They strapped Chloe in, adjusting the buckles until she looked right.

'You look like Batman,' said Jordy, grinning. 'Very swish.'

'Do you think I should try a solo flight first?' she asked her step-brother. 'Just to get used to it?'

'Not a chance. You heard what the bortrekker said. The warm air draughts go one way. You haven't got the skill to manoeuvre the glider, even if you manage to stay up there. You'll get carried away and crash into rafters or something.

I need to be with you.' He looked up. 'We've got to get on one of those layers of draught up there, follow the high parts of the attic so that we don't hit any beams or projections from the roof. In most places you can't even see the roof, but it does come down low in others. No, Clo, no practice runs. When we take off, we do it for real.'

'Where from?'

'From the top edge of the water tank. I felt the water when we were up there. It was quite warm. There'll be a thermal above it we can use to gain height. We'll have to take off over the water, gain some height, turn when we can, then head back for the boards.'

Chloe looked at him with admiration.

'You know your stuff, mister, don't you?'

Jordy suddenly went uncharacteristically shy. 'Oh, I don't know.'

'Yes you do, doesn't he, Alex?'

'My bruv?' He slapped Jordy on the back. 'He's brute.'

'Hey, watch the arm,' cried Jordy, wincing.

Chloe then turned her attention to Alex.

'What about you? How are you going to cross the tank?'

'I thought I'd make a raft. There are plenty of packing cases – things like that – about.'

'Shall we help you?'

'No, no need, sis. The bortrekker's coming back to give me a hand. Thanks anyway.'

'Oh,' she said, her looks turning dark again, 'the *bortrekker*.'

'I know you don't like him now, but it's not his fault I'm staying, you know. It's mine. I would've done anyway. I might have been a board-comber. That's what they call the collectors up here. Board-combers. You'd have liked me even less then, wouldn't you? All wrapped up in stinky clothes and looking like a walking rag-bag.'

'Like you?' her face crumpled a little, her large dark eyes moistening. 'Alex, I *love* you. You're my little brother. I love you so much it hurts.'

'Oh.' He felt a knife going into his heart. What did she have to say that for? Girls were so soft. 'Well – you know.'

To cap it all, Nelson limped forward on his three legs and looked up into Alex's face. Nelson's expression was one of puzzlement and just a little contempt. Did he understand? Alex was a little aggrieved at his cat's attitude. If anyone should understand about the right to roam at will, Nelson should. After all, cats were the worst. They wandered where they liked, took no heed of relationships that did not provide food, and generally walked alone with not a care for anyone or anything. It wasn't fair of Nelson to judge him, when Nelson himself was a worse offender.

'You can look,' muttered Alex. 'You're just as bad.'

Jordy was by now feeling exhausted. He fell off to sleep without a by-your-leave. Chloe, after all the stress of the day, did the same very soon afterwards. Alex looked down at the sleeping bodies and became very emotional. He was now planning to leave his brother and sister for good. That meant leaving his mother and Ben too. His mother he loved, of course, and he'd grown rather fond of Ben over the last year. Ben didn't try to push the father bit with him, but was still firm when he felt Alex needed it. Alex had a lot of respect for his mother's new husband, though of course he kicked against Ben's authority sometimes.

'Well, Makishi,' he said, 'it's just you and me now.'

'You are keeping me, Alex? A bortrekker has no mask, unlike a board-comber.'

'Oh, I wouldn't abandon you, you ugly old circumciser.'

'Thank you. You are most kind. And thank you for the compliment. I flatter myself I have always been fairly ugly.'

'You're *extremely* ugly.'

'Nice of you to say so.'

Next, Alex patted Nelson on the head. Nelson gave him a different look from the one a short while ago. Alex sighed. Leaving was a difficult thing to do when it came down to it. Alex hadn't thought it would be. He had seen himself walking away without even a slight feeling of regret. However, he was determined to follow his star. If he went home with the other two he would never get back. He knew that. He had to do his own thing.

So he went, without looking back.

When Chloe woke she shook Jordy.

'Come on. We have to get you home.'

Jordy's bleary eyes opened. 'Eh? Oh, yes.'

He sat up and rubbed his face vigorously with his free hand.

'Damn, it does ache a bit, Clo. It's hurting like mad now.'

'Well, it will, until you get it set properly. That splint's only to stop you jolting it. Now, how do we get the hang-glider up to the lip of the water tank? I need both hands to climb the steps.'

'A thick cord. We'll haul it up. Or rather you will. You go up there. Where's Alex? He could help us.'

'Gone,' said Chloe simply, climbing the steps. She had turned from Jordy quickly to hide the tears from him. 'We can't bother with him now. It's important to get you home.'

Once she was on the top edge of the water tank Jordy threw up a partially unravelled baton of cord. She caught the baton on the second throw. Jordy tied the end to the nose of the hang-glider which was pretty clever since he only had that one hand. But he managed it.

Chloe then hauled the hang-glider up the side of the tank, finding it surprisingly heavy as a dead weight. Once she'd grasped it, Jordy came up the ladder himself, agilely letting go of one rung to catch the next one up, without any danger of falling whatsoever. He was indeed a very good gymnast and athlete. What was more, he had the three-legged Nelson on one shoulder. The ginger cat was looking rather apprehensively at the drop below them, gripping Jordy with his sharp claws.

'Ow, Nelson! Pack it in.'

However, when Nelson saw the water, he gripped even harder and Jordy had to peel his claws off, one by one. Then Jordy made a kind of hammock out of his jacket, tucking the bottom into the top of his trousers, and put the ginger tom in there. Nelson obviously felt warm and much safer inside his cloth cave and promptly went to sleep.

Now Jordy was up and alongside Chloe, he sat on the twelve-centimetre-wide board which rimmed the lip of the tank. He gripped the hang-glider and told Chloe to stand up and then take it from him.

It took quite a time before they were ready. Jordy had shown her how to strap herself into the harness. Then she fitted his harness to him. Finally, they stood one behind the other on the narrow ledge with the hang-glider on Chloe's back. Jordy was in front facing away from the water. Chloe was behind him, also facing away from the tank. When they took off, she would be attached to the glider, face down, and Jordy would be below her, also face down. Everything was set. It just needed a little bolstering of courage, which was not an easy thing to do with such a drop.

'There's about ten metres to play with,' said Jordy, looking down at the boards below, 'so it's got to be a good launch.'

At that moment there appeared a group of those who had attacked them earlier but who had been routed by Nelson.

They swarmed over a pile of boxes and headed for the ladder up the side of the tank. The Removal Firm had arrived dressed in thick protective clothing: overcoats, gardening gloves, shin pads. No savage cat was going to stop them now, no matter how many teeth and claws it had. They were set on capturing the incomers before the disaster occurred. Their grey wrinkled faces were intent. They moved with great purpose in their steps.

'Take no notice of them,' ordered Jordy, sucking in his breath as he looked down on the dust-coated Atticans. 'In a few moments we'll leave them behind. Are you ready? Steady yourself. We've got plenty of time. They've only just started climbing the ladder.'

'I'm ready,' cried Chloe, her knees shaking. 'I really am.'

'Let's do it then!' cried Jordy.

But Chloe still made no move to push off.

The first of the Removal Firm arrived at the top of the ladder and gripped Jordy's ankle with strong fingers. Jordy calmly kicked away the creature's forearm, knocking it off balance. It fell from the top of the ladder with curses on its horrible lips. On its way down it crashed into others climbing up behind it and took them with it down to the boards. There was a terrible commotion among the Removal Firm as they were knocked and scattered over the boards. A screeching went up which would have penetrated Chloe's head, had she not been desperately trying to screw up enough courage to take off from the tank.

'All right,' she whispered in Jordy's ear. 'I'm really ready this time.'

Finally the pair kicked off almost in unison and swooped out into the space above the boards. The jolt on take-off caused Jordy to yell in pain, but he quickly assured Chloe he was all right. Chloe, in fact, was too terrified to take much notice of Jordy's discomfort.

'What do I do?' she cried, as she saw those below her craning their necks, their eyes wide.

'First of all, don't panic. Don't make any sudden moves. If you get into trouble, just straighten the glider out. There's nothing to hit around here. No electric pylon wires or branches of trees.'

And he was right. Above and around them was just the broad expanse of dusty air between the boards and the roofing felt. The several square suns of the attic shone down on this strange new giant bat, whose dark shadow flowed over the boards and objects below. 'Do everything calmly, easily, gently. Now turn back towards the tank.'

'How? How?'

'Just as we talked about. You're still panicking. Calm down. That's it. Now dip your left wing – no, gently, gently – that's it – turn back over the water – turn, gradually, don't dip too steeply, up, up a fraction more, pretty good, Clo, pretty good – you're a natural . . .'

The grim faces of the Removal Firm were staring up at them as the shadow of the glider rippled over their ranks.

Whether Jordy had meant that last statement or not it gave her the courage she needed. Once she was above the water the hang-glider began to lift on the warmer air. She kept it straight for a while, climbing every minute, until Jordy reminded her that she needed to spiral, because they were going the wrong way. He told her how to manipulate the glider, talking her through it gently all the while. Soon she was doing what was necessary, turning in circles, like an eagle climbing up the face of the sky. It felt good. It felt exhilarating. The fresh draught rippled the fabric of the hang-glider, cooled her face. She knew she was doing well.

Then suddenly she looked down and saw a vessel voyaging out on the surface of the lake. There was one occupant aboard and he looked up, startled when the shadow crossed his craft. It was Alex, sailing swiftly towards the far horizons of the water tank. He seemed to hesitate for a moment, then he lifted his arm and waved to the flying couple.

Chloe almost lost it there and then. She pulled down too hard and nearly took the glider into the water. It swept so close to the surface a wave clipped Jordy's face and spray covered his jacket. Nelson looked out, alarmed, made a mewing sound, and retreated down into the depths of the jacket again. Somehow Chloe managed to pull up at the last minute, saving the three of them from a cold wet fate. When she looked again, Alex had sailed into the heaving swell, his raft no longer visible.

'Oh my God!'

'No, I'm not your god, I'm just your hang-gliding instructor, which is pretty much like a miracle, however, since I've only flown a few times myself – but there you go. Or rather here *we* go. Now, turn out over the attic floor. Easy, easy. Brilliant turn! We're on our way home. I've got the map here . . .' He reached inside his jacket and found the map, folded to a manageable size, so that he could follow the route he had chosen. It was warm from having Nelson's furry body next to it. 'We obviously need to steer clear of low rafters,' he called up to her.

They shot over the amazed Removal Firm, every one of them standing looking up helplessly at their escaping quarry.

Jordy yelled down, 'Never seen anyone fly before?'

Obviously, they hadn't.

Jordy then cried, 'Hey, look – we're over an Attican village. The bortrekker figured the whole journey would take us about four hours, to cover the distance to home.'

The draught riffled through their clothes. They were in fact riding on the back of one of the swiftest draughts in the attic: a high level layer of fast-moving air that travelled parallel to the apex of the roof. It was not one of those draughts which brought good or bad weather, but was a constant stream flowing from an inlet at one end, to an outlet at the other.

'Go higher here,' said Jordy, when they eventually came to a plain with tea chests dotting it. 'Go much higher. I know it's difficult, with the air so thin up there, but this is where the— Uh-oh, there they are!'

Below them flashed a thousand glints and sparkles.

'Oh, how pretty!' exclaimed Chloe, ignorant of the danger. 'What a lovely show!'

Jordy knew better.

A huge swarm of scissors had taken off from their perches and were rising on sharpened evil wings. These Siamese-twin knives came snipping through the dusty shafts of sunlight, soaring upwards towards the pair on their hang-glider. Should they reach it, their blades would make short work of the glider's fabric. Fortunately the nasty metal birds proved too heavy once the air became more rarefied and, try as they might, they kept falling back, unable to climb to such heights. One or two pairs of nail scissors, being lighter than the kitchen or barber's scissors, actually made it to within a metre or two, but even they did not have the strength to reach the glider.

'You don't know how close we were to disaster,' said Jordy, relieved. 'Those pretties would cut us to shreds.'

'I can see that now,' replied Chloe in alarm. 'I thought they were Attican fairies.'

'Attican demons, more like.'

The pair fairly flashed along, sometimes so fast it made Chloe feel giddy. Down below, familiar landmarks swept under them. After more than two hours they came to Jagged Mountain, that monstrous pile of weapons upon which sat the shadow-beast Katerfelto, feared throughout the attic.

The flight was a fantastic experience for Chloe. She was conscious of a wonderful feeling of freedom, a lightness of form, a sense of release from the tensions of being locked to the earth. It was as if a leaden anchor in her had suddenly changed to feather-down and the world had to let her go. She had wings. She was flying through the air. How privileged she felt, to be born among the fortunate in a world of modern devices. This was a miracle of science, to be able to fly using just a rag and a few aluminium struts. There was a gentle power in her which filled her with joy.

'Birds must feel like this,' she cried, wholly aware of the rhythms of the draught, its strong surges and uplifts, its minor eddies and currents. 'And angels.'

'Angels, is it?' called Jordy, back up to her. 'Well, there's a little devil here, who's waking up.'

Nelson poked his head out of the neck of the jacket and looked down. His feline eyes widened in disbelief. The next moment he had turned completely round and had his nose pressed to Jordy's stomach, his heart beating fast.

'Didn't like that, is my guess,' laughed Jordy. 'I don't think we'll see his face again during the flight.'

At that moment Chloe lost concentration, along with meeting a side-draught which came out the blackness of the eaves. The hang-glider lurched to starboard, the right wing-tip dropping sharply. For a moment it appeared they were going to turn over and spiral downwards towards the solid boards far below. Then to make matters worse a low area of criss-crossing rafters appeared in front of them. Chloe actually went through the first triangle of timbers, almost sustaining a fatal rip in the wing. As it was, one of the thin aluminium poles which kept the framework rigid caught an upright beam and bent at right-angles. They rapidly started to lose height.

'Pull up!' said Jordy in a calmish voice laced with urgency. 'Not too sharply now – easy, easy. Steady. Get the glider level. Don't worry about those rafters: we're going to miss them.'

They did miss the timbers, but only by centimetres. Jordy was suddenly shocked to see a girl scrambling around in the network of rafters. The girl looked lithe and strong, and had very long hair. She was dressed in a ragged shirt. Grabbing for a rope, she swung from one rafter to another to avoid being hit by the hang-glider. Jordy locked eyes with her for a second, then he and Chloe were gone, leaving the roof's canopy and its occupant behind them.

In that awful second Jordy had fallen in love and he felt a terrible pain, an unbearable ache. He knew he would be looking for this girl of the attic jungle in all the other girls he met, and none would ever compare with her athletic beauty or the character he had seen in those eyes.

Jordy wanted to tell Chloe that he at last understood.

'What the heck are you doing?' cried a fraught Chloe. 'We're about to crash, you oaf! What do I do?'

Jordy snapped himself back to the task in hand. He issued some orders, which Chloe followed to the letter.

'Now straighten her out properly. That's right, bear down on that side. Excellent. WATCH THAT RAFTER! Phew, that was a close one, missy.'

'Don't call me *missy*!'

'Sorry, OK, here comes another one. Ease by to the right, that's it, now swing in a bit steeper than normal – not *too* steeply – OK, OK, that's it, we're nearly out of 'em. God, *that* was close. Last one – under it – bank to port. Port! *Turn left*. That's it. Super cool, babe . . . sorry, sorry, Chloe. Super cool. Now level off again and just keep your sights on that dark patch at the end there. That's it.' Jordy consulted his map again, then stared at the topography below. 'Yep, head directly for that spot.'

Once they had reached this 'spot' they found a sort of twilight area which led into almost total blackness.

'I think we're nearly home,' he said with relief. 'Are you tired, Clo?'

'Exhausted,' confessed Chloe, who had now been guiding the hang-glider for nearly four hours. 'My arms are dropping off.'

'Well, we've got the most dangerous bit of all coming up, but don't tell Nelson.'

Chloe said, 'Landing?'

'Correct. Now this is what I want you to do . . .'

He gave her clear and unequivocal instructions. They would not be easy to follow in themselves but she could not fault him for clarity. It was now up to her not only to land the hang-glider, but hopefully for the pair of them to come out of it with only one broken arm between them.

Jordy then proceeded to go through the landing instructions again, talking her down as they did it, until they were almost on the ground. Then Chloe, misjudging it, for it is easy to have the illusion that the floor is reachable with one's feet when in fact it's still quite a drop below, she relaxed. The glider dipped suddenly and sharply and the pair of them hit the floor with an unexpected thump.

Fortunately Chloe managed to keep her feet. She ran along the boards at a stumbling pace, her legs getting mixed with those of Jordy. Finally both of them fell over and went sliding along, the wing of the glider on top of them. They ended up in a heap against an old sofa, which if it had not been there would have seen them smash into a solid pillar of oak. Tangled string, torn fabric and twisted aluminium

spars kept them prisoners for a short while, until they managed to unravel themselves. Neither was hurt. Not even
Nelson had been banged, since Jordy had slid along on his
back. Nelson extracted himself from his hammock and
made a dignified three-legged exit into the darkness where
they were all eventually going.

'Wow,' said Jordy, undoing the final knot to a cord
around his neck, 'that was really something! You did good,
girl. You did good.'

Chloe was staring at him.

'Oh, what?' he cried. 'What have I said wrong now?'

'Nothing. Show me your arm. Your *broken* arm.'

Jordy looked down at himself and saw that he'd taken his
bad arm out of its sling and was using it just like the healthy
one. In fact, both arms were all right. The injury had disappeared without leaving any mark that he could see.
Somehow, now that they were in their own attic space all
was well.

'My watch! The hands are going the right way round
again!'

He showed Chloe the watch. It was indeed back to
normal.

'Let's go down now,' he said, taking out his torch and
stepping into the blackness of their own attic. 'Let's get
out of here.'

Chloe hung back.

'What is it?' asked Jordy. 'Is it Alex?'

'We may never see him again,' replied Chloe, sorrow
filling every artery and bone in her body. 'Will we ever see
him again, Jordy?'

Jordy replied in a flat voice, 'I don't know.' Then he lifted
his tone. 'But what I do know is, he'll be all right. He's a
dark horse, isn't he, your brother? He's got some guts, I'll
give him that. Follow your dream. Well, he's following his

all right. I never thought he had it in him. Oh, I know – we *both* want him back, but it's got to be his decision. I bet he'll get bored of being a bortrekker and we'll see him back again soon.'

'I'm not so sure,' Chloe said. 'He's very stubborn.'

'Are you up there? What are you doing in the attic?'

Dipa's voice floated up to them through the open trap-door.

'We're coming down!' cried Chloe, eager to see her mother. 'Won't be long.'

They heard Dipa say something to Ben. She sounded annoyed.

'Oh well,' said Chloe to Jordy, 'we might as well go down and face the music sooner rather than later.'

Jordy went first.

Just before Chloe followed him she took one last look into the dimness. Lo and behold, out of the half-light came her first and last dust sprite. It dashed out of the darkness of Attica, into their personal attic space, and right up to her. A grey, featureless being the size of a squirrel. Then before her eyes it went *puff* and fell to the boards as a cloud of motes.

The attic taunted, and teased, then it finally showed you what you wanted to see.

'Goodbye, spirits of the attic,' said Chloe grimly. 'I don't think I shall be back again.'

They descended the ladder and turned to face their parents, expecting to be chastised or overwhelmed with emotional greetings after so long an absence. Instead, Ben looked at his watch and said, 'I don't know, we go out for the afternoon and you all disappear. What are you messing around up there for? Aren't you supposed to be doing some homework today, Jordy? And where's Alex? Is he with you?'

'Ah, Alex,' began Jordy in a faltering voice, 'yes, well,' and though Jordy had intended to be entirely honest with his parents, at the last minute he chickened out. 'He's – he's up there. He won't . . .'

# CHAPTER 19

# Voyage over the Great Water Tank

The bortrekker and the board-comber helped Alex build the raft out of plastic bottles, wood and cord. When it was finished it looked like a jumble of junk, but it was serviceable. It floated well, bore his weight easily and sported a mast with a square sail made out of a bed sheet. All three boat builders were pretty pleased with themselves. They held a celebratory dinner before Alex set sail. The two young Attican pioneers gave the sailor some provisions before he set out, for which he was most grateful.

'Stay clear of the Removal Firm,' said the bortrekker, shaking his hand for the last time. 'They're ugly brutes, they are.'

'And if you *do* happen to see . . .' began the board-comber.

'. . . any Inuit soapstone carvings,' finished Alex with a smile, 'yes, I'll gather them up and leave them here, on this spot for you. Oh, that reminds me, of course, this is for you. I pinched it from my sister's backpack. I doubt she even remembers she had it.'

Alex reached into his pocket and pulled out the soapstone walrus, handing it to the board-comber. The board-comber's eyes widened under his mask. He took the carving reverently and stroked it. Then it disappeared into the folds of his many-coloured, many-layered clothes.

'Thank you,' replied the bundle of rags before him, 'and the bat says thank you, too.'

The last thing the two attic-dwellers did was give Alex a bag full of beautiful paperweights, to trade with any creature he might come across.

Alex set sail at about the same time as Chloe and Jordy were climbing up the ladder of the tank, hauling their hang-glider behind them. He too managed to miss the Removal Firm by a very short time. They stood on the shore and shook their fists at him. Alex replied with a rather crude gesture which he knew would have shocked his mother. However, any shame he felt was crowded out by a feeling of triumph. He had beaten the Removal Firm and what was more had drawn them away from the bortrekker and board-comber, to allow those worthies to escape back into untrammelled regions, where they would be safe from these human ejectors.

Then there was the final shock of seeing Chloe and Jordy, flying high above him. He thought at first it was an attempt to get him back, but then Alex realised they were not after him. They were simply using the warm air above the water to carry them high up into the attic's atmosphere. He watched them sweep through dusty shafts of light, waved when he realised that Chloe had seen him, then adjusted his sail and sped on. There was a heavy swell on the surface of the tank and very soon he had sailed down into a trough of water and the hang-glider was lost to his sight.

'Bye, sis!' he called, wondering if she could hear him. 'Bye, Jordy!'

Then his craft called for all his attention, as he started to climb up out of the trough and on to the heights of the swell. He soon dispensed with his heavy coat and hat, and took off his boots. It was much more comfortable to sail in his shorts and bare feet only. He piled his clothes in the little cabin they had built in the middle of the raft, which kept his food dry. There was a bed in there, a canvas camping cot they had found, and several other home comforts. From the map Jordy had shown him it appeared to be several days' sailing to the far side of the tank. Comforts would be needed.

Though the bortrekker had never made the voyage he had spoken with others who had, and had given Alex instructions.

'You follow this star pattern, as the skylights appear over the horizon one by one, bearing in mind that this constellation here must always remain on your right shoulder, and this one here on your left. If you sail between those two groups of skylights, you can't go wrong. Then there's the swell, which always comes from the near left corner of the tank. It will carry you naturally to your destination, but beware of a maelstrom . . .'

'Maelstrom?' Alex had repeated.

'Um – a whirlpool. A huge whirlpool, somewhere in the centre of the tank. It's a drain hole that serves the pipes which lead to all the smaller tanks of the attic. It's about a mile wide and if you get sucked in, you've had it, so keep a sharp look-out. Watch out, too, for obstructions – hidden underwater reefs and shoals you can't see when you're level with the surface. The way to spot them is to study the dust clouds above the lake. They'll reflect what's below them, to a degree. So you'll expect to see dark shadows on the dust clouds, in among the golden specks.'

'What are these reefs and shoals?'

'Oh, clusters of pipes, mostly, and there'll be moving

stuff – flotsam and jetsam – junk thrown in by irresponsible vandals. Just keep your eyes open and you should be all right.'

Alex said, 'Thanks,' and, feeling slightly facetious asked, 'No giant squids or submarines?'

'Ah, as to those, if you run into one, pray like mad.'

Alex's face fell.

The bortrekker's own face creased as if someone had screwed it up like a piece of paper. 'Got you,' he said. 'No, no squids or submarines but – but there is a monster of a kind in there, now that you mention it.'

'Ah, you won't get me a second time!' said Alex, wagging his finger.

'No, this is serious. There's a sort of blanket creature – huge, bigger than a football pitch, it's the only way I can describe it – which rises up with large waves and falls on to unsuspecting craft, enveloping them. I don't know how to tell you to avoid it. Again just keep your eyes open. It enfolds ships whole and sinks with them to the bottom of the tank.'

'Oh heck – what is it then? A live thing?'

'It looks like green blanket-weed but it's not a vegetable. It's wholly animal. It's developed an instinct, a killer's mind. With a sharklike predator's intellect, but a thinking mind nonetheless. It floats, imitating the water's surface, and strikes along with the rearing waves which crash over the sailing vessels. The good news is there's only one of them. Any new blanket-weed creatures which come about are quickly swallowed by this monster and become part of it. That's why it's so big.'

A lump formed in Alex's throat.

'Where's it come from? I mean, how did it come about?'

'It's an ancient prehistoric beast, which has grown from live organisms in the tank. Minute one-celled creatures which have sought each other out and locked together for defence against larger eaters and have themselves become a feared predator. That's all any of us are, after all – a mass of single cells – tiger, cobra, man, whatever. Any live being. This amorphous mass, which we in the attic call the Loving Flounder, will enfold you in its winglike form and drag you down, there to digest you whole.'

Alex had swallowed hard after this warning.

'Loving Flounder – that's a strange thing to call a horrible beast.'

'It loves you to death.'

So, there was much to think about while he steered his makeshift craft over the surface of the tank's water. Navigation, monsters, gales. On the first night he witnessed one of those electrical dust storms they had seen when on dry Attican boards. Entrancing, but also dangerous. Lightning flashed down around Alex and the waves were roused to turmoil by the atmospheric disturbances. If the Loving Flounder came now, he thought, I could do little to save myself, for the waves were rearing high and crashing down on the deck, draining away through the gaps in the bottles and planks.

The storm lasted all night. A howling draught accompanied it, which blew as if it had come from the pursed lips of gargantuan demons, almost stripping the raft of its sail. Alex managed to reef in the bed sheet before it was ripped to shreds in the terrible draught which whipped up the waters. The raft held up well under such a battering. The reason was it was very flexible, having been built in a loose fashion, the pliable ropes tied with firm knots. Had it been of a more rigid construction, the vessel would surely have perished in the blast, for it was a night of white blinding spray, of deep, seemingly bottomless, watery hollows, and terrible sudden squalls which spun the raft like a top while Alex clung on to the decks with all four limbs.

In the morning he was drenched, fatigued, but whole. Lightning had zig-zagged about his head, lighting up the attic sky for brief brilliant moments, but had not burned him to a crisp. Mountainous seas had all but engulfed him but had fortunately passed over, leaving him battered and breathless. Screaming draughts from the mouths of heaven and hell had nearly wrenched him from his handholds and flung him into the maw of monstrous waves, but had not managed to prise him from his grip.

There had been the thought that the Loving Flounder – such a pretty name for such an ugly monster – might enfold him, but it hadn't. Here he was still, now sailing gently on a freshwater ocean which looked for all the world as if it were dressed in its Sunday best and off to church. It was calm. It was peaceful. It was a day for drying out in the pillars of the sun, among the warm motes of dust, while contemplating the vagaries of nature.

A white-painted sign with black lettering floated past the raft at about noon. Written on it were the words:

NOTICE
No Dreaming.
No Wishing.
No Swimming.

'Weird,' muttered Alex. 'Totally weird.'

Next he saw two other craft, sailing together, passing him within hailing distance. One was an upturned table, the legs used as masts, the other was a bookcase on its back, the mariners aboard using shovels as oars. They waved to him and smiled. They were obviously sea-Atticans, small brown people with quick, light, graceful movements, not at all like land-Atticans. The latter were lumpy awkward creatures, used to manual labour in a heavy environment. These people were like the fresh draughts, nimble creatures with bright eyes and ready grins which flashed greetings even to strangers. Alex waved back and cried, 'What are you doing out here?'

One of the sailors held up a battered fishing rod and a child's seaside crabbing net as if they understood.

'Fishing?' questioned Alex.

That was plain enough. But on board the sea-Atticans also had goods, presumably to trade with. There were feather boas and other such items on the decks. Alex hove alongside one of the vessels and indicated he would like to trade one or two of his exotic paperweights. He had onyx pyramids, glass hemispheres with rainbows locked inside, mythical brass animals. The sea-going Atticans seemed delighted. They gave him a thick quilt coat in exchange for two of his treasures, happy with the bounty.

Alex had not really wanted the coat, but he had enjoyed meeting with other beings. He realised at this point that he actually needed company sometimes. That was all right, he thought, because there was company to be had. He didn't have to deteriorate into a complete hermit in his quest to become a bortrekker.

After waving goodbye to the Attican water tank farers he set sail again on a day when the sky was reasonably clear of dust clouds and the many skylights lit up his seapath like searchlights. The mariners had given him a fishing line, which he now proceeded to employ, using bits of weed as bait. However, either the bait was no good, or the fisherman was no good, for he caught nothing. Fishing in the deep sea, Alex decided, was a difficult occupation.

He suddenly remembered he *did* have a companion and spent an hour or two chatting with Makishi, who was willing enough to talk, but because of his limited experience of life did not have a great deal to say. He knew about jungles, rainforests and tropical storms, but he'd already talked a lot with Alex about these and tended to get repetitive. After a while the conversation petered out and a silence fell between the pair once more.

In the afternoon Alex slept. He lashed his tiller to the mast so that the raft kept a straight course, checked his bearings with all those visual aids he had been given by the bortrekker, then dropped off into a deep and dreamless sleep. The long night of the storms had kept him awake and he was always a boy who liked his bed.

It was the tiller banging against his knee which woke him. He sat up abruptly, startled to find his tiller had worked itself free and his rudder was finding its own course. All too late it seemed he was caught on the edge of a great swirling body of water which was, at the moment, spinning the craft gently round in wide circles.

'The maelstrom!' he yelled, grabbing the tiller.

It was indeed the central whirlpool. Somewhere deep below him was a drain hole which was sucking water down by the thousand-gallon. If he did not free himself of its power he would taken down too and used as a plug. Not only would he drown and rot in the weeds below, but with his corpse stopping up the exit hole the tank would over-flow and flood the attic, perhaps drowning many others in the process. Naturally, at the moment, he was more con-cerned with his own life than those of others, but if he failed to save himself he would leave behind a terrible legacy, of death and destruction.

'Oh heck.'

He grabbed the tiller in a panic and tried to steer the raft out of the current. It was of no use. The raft simply spun in the current and continued to follow the ever-decreasing circles it was drawing.

Next he fixed the tiller again then tried to paddle out, using one of the light shovels which served as his oars. He made a little progress this time, but not enough. The raft neither moved out of the current nor went further in. Stalemate. But soon his arms began to ache and tire, he weakened, and he knew he could not keep it up.

'Help me!' he yelled, thoroughly frightened now. 'Somebody, please? Anyone around? Help me.'

The waters around were bare of boats or any sign of life.

'I'm going to drown if no one helps me,' called Alex to the attic in general. 'Is that what you want? Eh? Get rid of the unwanted newcomers. Well, you've got your wish.'

He slumped back on the floor of the raft, staring up at the roof-sky, a bitterness filling his heart with black bile.

'I hate you. I hate everyone!'

He was going to die. It didn't seem possible. It wasn't fair. He was only doing this to help Mr Grantham. The raft was going faster and faster now, spinning, turning, heading towards a slope of water that went down into a hole. In the centre of the mighty whirlpool was a hole where there was nothing but air. He would probably drop all the way without even touching the sides. Without even getting wet. Once his body hit the bottom though, the water would come gushing in around him and suffocate him, filling his lungs to bursting. His brain would explode in bright lights. He knew what it was like to hold his breath – most kids had tried it – and it hurt like hell. It was a horrible death. *Any* death was horrible.

A huge fat crinkled worm flew over the raft.

Red, green and gold.

With whiskers.

It was there and gone in a second.

Alex sat up quickly and stared.

What was that? Was he seeing things?

No, there it was, heading towards the horizon.

It *was* a worm. At least it looked like a worm from where he stood.

'Hi! Don't go,' he yelled in panic. 'Come back here.'

He stood there waving and yelled again, this time angrily.

'Get back here, you rotten bugger!'

This time the worm-thing seemed to take notice. It flew through the air with wavelike movements, flowing up and down like a serpent. When it turned back – and it *did* turn back – Alex could see it was an oriental dragon, the kind that Chinese people used for celebrations. It was long and tubular, with the usual mythical head and huge eyes. It flowed through the air like a kite and returned to the raft, its eyes blinking. There were long tapes dangling from its body and as it flew over Alex grabbed the end of one of these ribbons, expecting to pull the creature to a halt. However, it didn't jerk to a halt, but almost pulled Alex off his feet. Alex quickly tied the end of the ribbon to his mast and stepped back, hoping for the best.

The flying dragon, roaring to bolster its strength, pulled hard. Gradually the raft began to leave the swirling waters of the vortex into which it was being dragged. With Alex encouraging his saviour, the raft was eventually pulled clear of the whirlpool's clutches and out of danger. Until now most of the animated objects of the attic had been hostile. But here was one, like Punch and Judy, which seemed only too glad to help. The attic, like anywhere else, had good and bad about it. Alex was growing fonder of the place all the time.

Once he was clear he released the dragon's tapes and the creature continued on its journey to an unknown destination.

'I must not fall asleep again so soundly,' Alex told himself. 'I was lucky that time. Next time I may not be. I have to remain alert.'

The trouble was, he was alone, and had to sleep *sometimes*.

Over the next day or so, Alex met with more of the brown fisherfolk he had encountered earlier. They were almost always cheerful, waving to him, shouting greetings. Once or twice he traded with them for food, his store of paperweights standing him in good stead. There was one time when a sullen one passed by his craft, rowing a canoe fashioned from half a car roof-rack pod, who refused to acknowledge him, but this was a rare occurrence. For the most part they were a delightful race of people, who seemed only too eager to make contact and help if at all possible.

Alex did of course fall asleep again – he had to rest – but nothing untoward happened to him.

One evening he was enjoying what appeared to be an aurora borealis, the northern lights of the attic. They seemed to have been produced by the moonlight shining through the bevelled edges of skylight windows. The cut glass acted like a prism, splitting the white light into its natural colours, which in turn were sent in ribbons into the atmosphere of the attic. Outside, the wind was blowing, rattling the windows, thus making the bands of colours ripple, twist and wave, producing movement. The northern lights of the attic were almost as wonderful and mystical as the real aurora borealis.

It was as he was watching that he felt a slight movement beneath his feet. He looked down at his raft. It had not been a wave or the swell. Something had touched the craft underneath. He glanced over the side and his eyes widened. There, passing below his vessel, was the largest snake – or eel – he had ever seen. It was a monster, but he was relieved to see that it wasn't the Loving Flounder. This creature was as thick as the belly of a jumbo jet and moving silently and effortlessly through the water. At the front end it had huge jaws, partly open, which revealed a thousand sharp white teeth. At the other end – well, Alex couldn't even *see* the other end – but he could see enough to know it was finned.

It took an age for the serpent to pass under him and when it was gone Alex was still standing there, watching where it had been, long and green like a deep-sea current made manifest. The episode sent a chill through him. There were monsters in these waters he had not been told about, yet perhaps very few knew of them. The bortrekker and board-comber might never have come across them. And even the fisherfolk might have only legendary tales instead of actual experiences to go on. Maybe he was privileged to be one of the only humans to have witnessed such a monster?

'I wonder why I don't *feel* privileged,' he said out loud.

'I would, if I were you,' interrupted Makishi. 'It was an amazing sight.'

Makishi was perched on top of the mast. Alex had put him there after the incident with the maelstrom, to act as a lookout. So far he had seen nothing and could not be blamed for not warning of undersea monsters since his job was to watch for any potential problems on the horizon. His occasional remarks, such as the one he had just uttered, were somehow comforting to Alex, whose yearning for society had increased.

'Thank you, Makishi. In that case, I shall.'

Later they was passing between archipelagos and atolls decorated with bird cages and bamboo umbrella stands. At one lonely island he found a shivering little Attican boy, whom he rescued and took aboard. It seemed from some drawings the child made in the dust that he had been marooned by pirates. Pirates? Why had no one warned him about pirates?

On a later island where the bird cages were draped in feathers he found inhabitants, more of the fisherfolk, who used cricket bats to paddle their island canoes and floating light bulbs to moor them in the bay. The child seemed to know them so Alex passed the boy on to them.

Alex spent the night with them and enjoyed an evening of dancing and creaky singing beneath paper lanterns that glowed with a faint light and were found by him to contain fireflies. It was here the dragon returned and swooped down to swallow a long line of the lanterns. This brought the inhabitants out of their huts. They spent the next hour throwing marbles at the dragon, trying to drive it away. Alex pretended to join them. No one noticed that he wasn't trying very hard to hit the target.

The dragon, on seeing him, gave him a hurt look and Alex, knowing he owed this creature his life and breath, felt a little ashamed.

After the dragon had been chased away the grumbling Atticans unveiled some strange contraptions. It seemed they had forgotten to wheel out their dragon-scarers to guard their lanterns while they enjoyed their festivities. The dragon-scarers were made of bicycle parts, bits of vacuum cleaners, old radios, lawn mowers, kitchen utensils, gardening tools and electric fans. These were fashioned into giant mobiles which moved in the slightest draught. Wheels spun and worked arms and levers and ratchets, which had the giant dragon-scarers swinging their arms and rolling their heads, as if they were live creatures.

On yet another archipelago was a forest of artificial Christmas trees decorated with tinsel and paper chains.

This brought a lump to his throat as it reminded him of his family, now far away. It was on the beach of an island such as this that he was attacked by what he thought were scarecrows, but turned out to be Guy Fawkes dummies. Christmas tree angels saved him by flying in like a swarm of sparrows and hampering the efforts of the guys until Alex had launched his raft and set out to sea again.

One morning he woke to find calmer waters than usual and there on the horizon was a thin black line. He knew then that he was coming to the end of his voyage. That black line was the lip of the other side of the Great Water Tank. In the space beyond were the vague shapes of objects of a far place.

It was on these inland waters, which the bortrekker had called the Farside Roads, that Alex encountered another craft. It was very similar to his own makeshift vessel and was sailing the other way. Those on board were not Atticans, but a boy a little older than himself and a girl about his age. They had obviously entered into the spirit of seafaring, being dressed in naval attire, the boy with a white peaked cap with an anchor badge on it, and the girl in a blue-and-white striped jersey and navy-blue knee-length trousers.

'Ahoy there!' called the boy. 'You a real person?'

'Yes,' cried Alex. 'You?'

'Yes. We're lost.'

'So am I – or I was.'

'Weird place, ain't it?'

The girl called, 'We're looking for our old attic.'

Alex didn't know what to say to that. Naturally he didn't know where their personal trapdoor might lie.

As they passed by one another, Alex said, 'You should find a bortrekker or a board-comber. They'll help you.'

'Thanks,' the boy replied. 'A bortrekker, eh?'

'Yes – like me.'

'We met an attic boy who called himself a rafter king,' called the girl, 'who was climbing up there.' Her eyes swept the roof space. 'He said he was once human, but he wasn't much help in the end. Apparently there's quite a few of them, up in the roof space. He said he'd lived up in the rafters too long and had a little hut up there. He told us he'd become a rafter king to stay out of the way of the Removal Firm. Do you know them?'

'Yep – large Atticans in khaki dustcoats. Stay out of their way if you can.'

The boy leaned forward, hanging on to the mast.

'Atticans?'

'Villagers.'

The girl's expression brightened. 'Hey, you want to come with us?'

Alex shook his head. 'No, sorry.'

They both seemed disappointed.

'OK, good luck.'

'You too. Try and find a map. There must be more than one, I'm sure. You'll get home then.'

'Thanks.'

They watched each other's vessel for a long time until they both became specks in each other's eyes.

'Nice people,' said Makishi, afterwards.

Alex thought the idea of being a rafter king sounded exciting. Board-comber, bortrekker or rafter king? How many others were there, in this wooden world of the attic? Beam-walkers? Roof-rangers? Maybe even tank-voyagers? Nah, he'd made his choice. Bortrekker.

Over the rest of the morning Alex sailed towards the edge of the sea and finally hove in with a slight bump against the side of the tank. He moored his craft, not knowing whether he was going to use it again. Dressing once more in his bortrekker gear, he was ready to go ashore.

He disembarked and began walking along the wooden rim. His legs felt wobbly and it seemed as if the solid ground beneath his feet were moving. That was just an illusion though, after days on a rolling vessel. He was here on dry land once again and close to the end of this quest.

Descending the ladder on the side of the tank he found himself among huge dunes of hearth tools – coal scuttles, tongs, brushes, shovels – which he climbed over with no difficulty. Beyond these dunes was a solid wall of upright pianos. These looked so much like fortifications that Alex wondered if he'd wandered into hostile country. Were these defences here because someone or something lurked behind them? A creature so insecure and unsavoury that it needed walls to keep out its enemies? Or perhaps the piano walls had been built to keep something *in*? Like a giant ape or a people so savage the attic would be devastated by their release?

'Tread softly here, Alex,' he told himself.

He climbed up on one of the pianos, to peer at the land beyond.

# CHAPTER 20

# Attack of the Music Makers!

'I hope you haven't come to steal my watches.'

Alex turned and was surprised to see a short stocky girl, in the rags and tatters of a board-comber. This one was quite different, however, to the board-comber who collected Inuit carvings. For a start, the mask she wore was quite attractive: a gold-dusted carnival mask which hid only the top half of her face. There were three scarlet feathers protruding gaily from the top of the mask. Her dress was even more flamboyant, with outrageous colours and lots of tassels and hanging ribbons. There were reds and purples, greens and blues, yellows and oranges. All these were happily mixed in together, making a spectacle more suited to a fairground. Instead of a bat hanging from one ear, this board-comber had a small owl on her shoulder. The owl regarded Alex steadily with round serious eyes.

'Watches?' asked Alex. 'What watches?'

'Don't think I don't know.'

'Don't know what?'

'Why you're here. No one comes here. You must've come to steal my watches. There's no other reason.'

When the board-comber stepped in closer, Alex could see that in physical age she was not much older than himself. Probably about Jordy's age. However, her eyes contained the promise of more wisdom than was owned by Alex, Jordy and Chloe put together. Her skin was like a smooth parchment, with a whole life history written upon it. Alex would guess she had been up in the attic many years and had learned its seasons, its cycles, its myriad quirky rhythms and tides. No doubt she had witnessed the moon locked in every glass in the roof and had seen the sun roll from one window to the next a hundred times.

This was a veteran of the attic: an ancient of days.

'You're wondering how long I've been here.'

'Yes,' said Alex.

'A hundred years.'

Alex said, 'You just made that up.'

'No,' she replied earnestly, 'I've been here a hundred years. Don't you know *real* time doesn't move for us humans in the attic? It seems our bodies are caught in some kind of time-limbo between the two worlds. Have you seen the clocks and watches here?'

'They go backwards.'

'And in our old world, they go forwards.'

Alex realised he was supposed to see something significant in that and finally the answer came to him.

'Oh, I see,' he cried, 'they oppose each other. They keep real time at a standstill.'

'That's it,' replied the board-comber. 'Just for us intruders. Now, what are you doing here? You'd better tell me, because I'll find out sooner or later. It's to steal watches, isn't it? You want my treasures. Did the Organist send you? He did, didn't he?'

Alex decided to be truthful. 'I – I just want *one* of your watches.'

'One is everything, one is all.'

'You can spare just one. It's for a good cause. Where are they anyway?' He looked around. 'Do you keep them locked up?'

'Wouldn't you like to know, little boy?'

'I'm not a little boy. I'm a bortrekker,' said Alex, drawing himself up in a dignified manner. 'Don't you know a bortrekker when you see one?'

She looked him up and down contemptuously.

'Dressed like a bortrekker, but all shiny and new.'

Alex was huffy. 'Got to start somewhere. Bet you had to start *somewhere*. You can't learn everything in one day.' He paused and pleaded with her. 'See, the reason I want this particular watch is because it would help an old man. He threw it in the attic many years ago, in a temper, but he's – well, he's going to die soon – and he wants to make his peace with his memories. You can understand that, can't you? I've got a letter here,' Alex patted his pocket, 'which will help, but I really came up to get the watch.'

'Then you'll go down again?'

Alex drew a deep breath. 'No, no, I don't think so. I want to pass the letter and the watch on to my brother and sister, so they can deal with it. But I want to stay up here.' He looked around him and waved a hand. 'I like it here. You do too, or you wouldn't stay. And all the other board-combers and bortrekkers. The attic's a great place, isn't it? You can almost feel it liking you back, once it knows you want to be here . . .'

She walked around him, looking him up and down, and studied him from every angle.

'Are you *sure* you want to stay up?'

'I – I think so.'

'Hmmm, think so don't get it done.'

'Will you give me the watch?'

She stepped back from him, shuddering. 'I couldn't. Those watches are the wheels that run my heart. If I lost just one, my heart would stop beating. They're my treasures. I need them *all*. If one went, I'd pine for it, I know I would. The other watches would pine for it. We'd all be *terribly* upset. I don't like being upset. Give it up, this quest. Tell the old man you couldn't find it. Say it's lost for ever.'

'I'll tell you what, let me look at your collection?'

She screwed up her face and seemed about to refuse. Then she must have changed her mind, because she brightened, her face breaking into the most wonderful smile Alex had ever seen, the corners of which almost reached her ears. 'Oh, I love showing it off. I do. I really do. I love showing my collection to those who haven't seen it before. It's a magnificent collection of watches, the best in the attic. Here, let me put this on you.' She tied a scarf over his eyes, then cried, 'Come on, come with me.'

'I can't see you,' he said, feeling the air. 'How can I follow if I can't see?'

He felt a small, slim, warm hand slip into his own and his blood turned to warm olive oil in his arteries.

The board-comber seemed very excited. Of course, thought Alex, she would be. There's nothing a collector likes better than showing off his or her collection to an interested stranger. Someone to go 'oh' and 'ah' at prize possessions and say 'aren't you lucky?' and 'isn't that fabulous?' and 'where on earth did you find it?' – things like that. Someone to whom the collector can explain how difficult certain pieces were to come by and, in this case, someone to point out highly prized movements and tiny hairsprings, escapements, and other delights of the internal workings of watches.

He was taken, he knew not where, and the blindfold removed.

There before him was one of the great supporting pillars, but this one was covered in wrist-watches and pocket-watches. Hanging from nails by their straps or chains, they covered the pillar to a depth of three watches and a height of two metres. They were all ticking away madly, creating a terrible din, all showing the correct time, all going backwards. There were silver ones, gold ones, black ones, white ones, every other colour you could think of. In the burnished light from a distant window they glinted, they flashed, they glimmered, they burned. Snakeskin straps, golden chains, expanding silver bracelets. There were those which proudly announced they had '17 Jewels' on the face. Others were 'Waterproof'. There were watches with Roman numerals and there were watches with Arabic numerals. Some of the makes he knew to be very expensive, others quite cheap, and a thousand he had never heard of before. Some pocket-watches had their face-covers open, others had them closed. One or two had perspex cases and you could see the brass-toothed wheels turning, the flysprings quivering inside.

He thought of something.

'No digital watches?'

The look on her face told him she had the same opinion of digital watches as he did.

'How do you wind them all up? There are at least a thousand here,' he gasped. 'Do you do it all yourself?'

'I spend two hours every day winding those that are running down.'

A thousand second hands sweeping, a thousand minute hands ticking, a thousand hour hands crawling.

'Wonderful,' Alex breathed, stalling for the hour, which was fast coming up. 'Any of them chime?'

'A few,' she said. 'This one, and this one, and others. Do you like chiming watches?'

'I love 'em.'

Finally watch fingers flicked at the hour. Of course the chimes didn't all come at once. Some came and went before others even got started. Some just tinkled tunelessly, a few had a definite melody. But nowhere, nowhere among those several chiming watches could Alex detect *Frère Jacques*. Perhaps Mr Grantham's watch was there but the chiming mechanism had long since given up the ghost? It was a very old watch, it was true. Perhaps the chimes had seized? How rotten, to get so close and not be able to identify it. In any case, even if it could chime out its little French air, finding it among its peers would be the devil's own job. It was like looking for a single ant in a nest of ants.

Alex went for broke. 'Did – did you ever have a watch that chimed the tune of *Frère Jacques*?'

A frown appeared on the board-comber's face.

'*Frère Jacques*. No, never.'

'You're sure?'

'I would know, wouldn't I?' she exclaimed hotly.

'Yes, sorry.' He was morose. 'All this way for nothing.'

At that moment the owl's head swivelled backwards.

'Eeerch!' it screeched. 'Eeerch, eeerch.'

The board-comber began running back towards the wall of pianos, not staying to blindfold Alex again.

'Attack!' she was crying. 'Big assault on the border!'

'Oh, right,' replied Alex, having no idea what was going on, but following her anyway.

'Here's a chance to earn your spurs,' she told him as he caught up to her. 'Help me fight the Organist's Music Makers.'

'Music Makers?'

'The enemy. You'll see. Quick, grab these.'

Alex was handed a sword and shield, the kind knights carry into battle or at tourneys. The girl armed herself likewise. Then she leapt in a very agile manner up on to a piano, urging Alex to do the same. Indeed, he found he had to clamber up, but he joined her nonetheless. The pair of them stood side by side, armed and ready for conflict, staring out into the darkness. Naturally, the owl was with them, staring hard too. It kept making chattering sounds in the back of its throat, as if it were keeping the board-comber appraised of what was happening out there in the beyond.

'Are you *sure* there's an enemy coming?' asked Alex, putting on Makishi to protect his face. 'It's awfully quiet out there in the dark interior. Who are these Music Makers anyway?'

As if in answer to his question an arrow came hurtling out of the inky blackness beyond and struck Alex's shield. Except that once it fell away from him, Alex could see it wasn't an arrow at all. It was a violin bow. Then another, a larger one, swished by his ear: a cello bow.

Now came a horrible sound: the kind of noise cats might make if burned alive. Alex was startled and not a little terrified to see giant spiders coming out of the darkness, racing towards him, with riders on their backs. The riders were mercenaries, village children. And these hostiles, hired by the Organist, weren't riding spiders, but mechanised bagpipes.

The pipes of these long-legged steeds raced the riders towards the border of pianos. The riders on their inflated tartan bags were archers using violins, violas and bass viols to shoot their arrows. Violins had become bows, bows had become arrows. A flute whizzed past Alex's ear, puffed like a blow-pipe dart from the horn of a trombone. Panpipes came humming past, crashing into the pianos. On the edges of the charge were nimble drum-riders on rolling bass drums and snare drums. Trumpets blared in rage, drums rolled out thunder, piccolos piped shrill anger. This really was a serious attack by the so-called Music Makers: the air was full of missiles and the noise level could not be louder if they had elephants and horses.

'Look out!' cried Alex.

A rider on his bagpipes tried to climb one of the pianos to get at the board-comber but the girl reached forward and thrust with the point of her sword. Her weapon pierced the bagpipe bag. It gave out a *flarrpping* sound and immediately deflated. Its rider fell off it, letting out a loud curse. The girl laughed and shook her sword at her enemy. Then another tried to mount the barrier and the colourful board-comber dealt with this attempt in the same way. Soon Alex found he was having to defend himself, piercing bagpipes with his sword and warding off 'arrows' with his shield.

'Watch out for the lurs, serpents and crumhorns!' cried the board-comber. 'They're trying to sneak up on our flanks.'

Alex turned to see snakelike instruments whizzing through the air at him. He swept them aside with his sword-blade, sending them back into the bouncing ranks of hurdy-gurdies. Massive cymbals rolled with knife-blade edges and sliced into the pianos. Ceramic ocarinas, thrown like hand-grenades, exploded on the piano tops, sending deadly shards of pottery flying around Alex's feet. An oboe spear was aimed at his head but he managed to chop it in the air as it flew towards him.

'Look out!' cried the girl.

The enemy had taken an upright piano and sent it rolling

at speed towards Alex. However, its castors must have been loose because it veered off course and slammed into one of the big oak pillars. The pillar juddered violently with the impact and bits of debris fell from the rafters above. Alex looked up, alarmed. However, the support was only shaken loose in its joints and remained fast. It didn't fail in its job of keeping heaven and earth apart, though there had been a moment . . .

'You have to watch those pillars,' Alex yelled at the board-comber. 'If one of them comes down, the whole world will collapse.'

'Don't exaggerate,' she laughed, warding off a flute-arrow.

'I'm not. Don't you believe me? If one comes down, they'll all go, one after the other. The pressure will be too much for them.'

'If you say so,' she called back grudgingly. 'Now watch your flank – there's a sneak attack coming!'

He turned to face the danger.

Finally, Alex and the board-comber routed the attack. They had a good defensive position which was difficult for the enemy to surmount. They also had the owl whose swivelling head and keen eyes helped to warn of any sneaky tactics. Alex and the girl stood back to back. They cut this way and that with their swords, protecting themselves with their shields. In the end the two warriors of the boards sent the enemy running.

While his rival was thus engaged, warding off attacks, the Organist crept forward towards the great pillar. In his hands was an object wrapped in brown greaseproof paper. In his pocket was a crudely printed pamphlet dated 1917, with the title *A Simple Explosive Device*. The grammar and spelling on the pamphlet were poor, it having been written by some anarchist group whose main concern was the destruction of property and not the correct use of the English language.

The Organist was a tall, sly, sallow youth, dressed all in black capes. He had on a long mournful mask which he had worn for so long it had fused with his face. Now he could not remove it. His pale long-fingered hands were the only parts of his body visible in the dimness of the interior. Those hands were engaged in carrying the home-made bomb he had fashioned. Home-made it might be, but it was very powerful, having enough explosive to rip the pillar apart and blow the watches to pieces.

The Organist was aware that the Removal Firm would hear and investigate, but the bomb would go off on her territory, not his, and he was sure that she would get the blame for the explosion.

Once he got to her collection he quickly scooped away watches from the base of the pillar and strapped the bomb to it, covering it again. He was sweating profusely. Those beautiful hands shook violently. He'd never done anything like this before, nothing so heinous, but then he was at the end of his tether. If he did not get rid of the girl he would surely go mad with frustration. She was the bane of his life. He had been before her and she had simply settled here without his permission. He hated her with venom. Why wouldn't she go away? It was *her* fault he was driven to such desperate measures. She had forced him to do it.

It had been different once. When she had first arrived in this part of the attic they had been friends. Good friends. But after a while she turned funny on him, started rejecting his friendship, told him he was not respecting her privacy, her right to solitude. He had argued with her, put his point of view, but she just kept saying she would prefer it if he left her alone. Then no matter what he did, what he said, she would not listen. She would have nothing to do with him. Well, damn her! He would be noticed. He was a genius. Who did she think she was, ignoring such a great musician? Was he *nobody*? Was he *nothing*? He would have the last word!

He set the timing device, a pocket-watch, so that the bomb would explode at noon in several days' time.

It would go off on the very last of its final chimes.

Finally, out of the depths of hinterland Attica came a single, long, deep, resonating note which made every stringed instrument vibrate. A hastily formed charge halted at once in its tracks. Spidery bagpipes turned and limped away. Twice more the bass notes came, without doubt from a great chapel organ. This seemed to be the signal to the musical instruments and their riders to return whence they had come. All those which had not been broken or injured trickled away into the gloom. Some of the mercenaries dismounted and picked up their wounded, turning to shake their fists at the amazon girl standing on the piano wall, her rags and ribbons flapping like victory banners in the draughts from the interior.

She laughed at their creaked curses and waved her sword.

'You'll never get me to go away,' she cried, delighted at her triumph. 'Tell your master I'll be here until dooms-day!'

The owl hooted in derision at the retreating enemy.

Alex climbed down from his piano and removed Makishi. He wiped the sweat away from his forehead with a rag.

'What was all that about?' he asked.

'Oh, it's the Organist. Selfish brat. Just like a boy. He wants the whole of this corner of the attic for himself, for him and his musical instruments. Well, he can't have it, because I'm here now and I'm not leaving. You give some people a little room and they want it all! He won't listen to reason. I choose to live here and no one is going to chase me away, so there. And no, you can't have the watch. I need all my watches.'

Alex let the 'Just like a boy' go without an argument, though he was wrinkled with annoyance.

'You're wondering if you can steal my watches, now that you know where they are, aren't you? It's no good thinking crafty thoughts. I'm on to you. You won't get halfway across the lake. I'll be after you like a shot.'

Alex said haughtily, 'I wouldn't steal from *anyone*.'

'Not even a girl over a hundred years old?'

'Not even you.'

Alex wanted to get back on her good side again, though, and needed to flatter her.

'Your collection is superb,' he said, dredging up a few Chloe words from his memory. 'Those watches are simply exquisite!'

'Yes,' she squealed, jumping up and down and clapping her hands, making the owl sway dangerously, 'that's what they are. Oh, I'm so glad you came. I just *knew* there was a word which would describe them exactly. *Exquisite*. That's what they are, aren't they? Simply exquisite. Superb and exquisite.'

That he had pleased her was beyond doubt. But he still had to try to find Mr Grantham's watch. That's what he'd come for.

'A hundred years old,' he said, looking into her clear blue eyes. 'I still can't believe it.'

'More than,' she replied. 'I came up here when I was at

a Board School. But they used to tease me a lot, because I didn't know who my father was, so I stayed up here. Been here ever since.' She looked over her shoulder. 'I could go back. It would be as if I never came in the first place. But I don't want to be teased again.'

'But a hundred years!'

'I know.' She sighed, adoring him for his sympathy. 'I know you think it's horrid. A hundred years in a dusty attic. But it's my home and I love it here. You wouldn't understand.'

Alex blurted, 'But I do.'

'I *might* go back, one day.'

'You should. Your mother will be missing you.'

'Not really. That's the beauty of it. I'll only have been gone a few seconds. Strange isn't it, this *time stopped*. You think there would be a great hue and cry the length and breadth of the land.' Her voice suddenly changed to a falsetto. 'Where is Amanda? Oh, where has she gone, my darling girl?' Then back to her normal tone, 'But no one calls, no one knows, because no time has passed since I left. Here we are in a place stuck between two minutes, not moving, still as dust in a box.'

'Amanda. That's a very nice name.'

She hugged her knees. 'And what's yours?'

'Alex. Alexander.'

'Alexander, don't you miss your parents? Why do you want to stay up here?'

He shrugged. 'Oh, I don't know. It's exciting, isn't it?'

'Will you stay? Will you?'

He became almost as deflated as one of those bagpipes he had pierced earlier with his sword.

'I really don't know. I think I want to. I thought I did.'

She smiled. 'It's not all magic dust and moonbeams, you know. It's very, very lonely.'

'I'm beginning to learn that.'

'Loneliness can gnaw away at you, or come up on you suddenly and suck all the spirit out of you, so you feel hollow and wasted.'

He shuddered and nodded. 'I guess it can.'

'You should think about it very carefully. If you wait too long to make a decision, it becomes so that you can't go. The attic increases its hold on you. It grips you with soft unseen hands. Firm hands. You're speaking with one who knows, Alexander. It seems to me I've been here almost as long as the dust. If it weren't for my collection . . .' Her voice had grown very dreamy. '. . . I might go home tomorrow.'

The pair of them spent the next few hours together. Amanda said there would be no attack from the Organist's regiments for some time to come, because of the heavy defeat the pair of them had inflicted on them. Thus they had time to enjoy each other's company, which was wonderful for the board-comber and would be remembered forever by the novice bortrekker.

'Can you sail?' she asked him.

'Sailed all the way here,' he answered.

'Yes, but on a raft you said. Can you sail a small boat?'

'Never tried.'

'Come with me.'

She took him out on the waters of the tank in a small sailing boat. Probably in order that Amanda could move about swiftly and without hindrance, the owl left her head for once and perched on the bowsprit. Once on the great lake, however, Amanda became a tyrannical captain, yelling at Alex to pull this sheet or reef that sail. He might have guessed he would become a slave to her commands in such a situation. When he complained that he was being treated like a drudge, she explained that unless he obeyed orders to the letter and very quickly, they might capsize.

'You are the deck hand. You have to learn to react quickly. Now jump to the jib . . .'

He jumped, wondering what the heck a jib was, but Amanda was not a girl to be ignored.

Nevertheless, Alex enjoyed her company, and so far as he could tell, she enjoyed his. But as the days progressed he began to seriously consider whether this attic life was for him. Even though it was a thousand times better than being completely on his own, he grew bored. He was not content within himself. It was no wonder the bortrekker he had met and who had influenced him kept moving. Just as all bortrekkers were restless souls. They had to be in order to interest themselves. New landscapes, new adventures, new horizons were necessary to ward off that corrosive boredom.

'There are those who're born to the attic and those who hope to grow into it,' she told him one day, after looking into his eyes and seeing emptiness there. 'You are the second kind. Oh, I do not doubt you're sincere about wanting to stay, and perhaps if you did you'd come to grow into it. But you're not like me. I can spend a thousand years up here and still not lose interest. I am one of those people happy in my own company. I have my owl of course, and he's enough for me.'

The owl blinked and climbed down from her head, to walk up to Alex and stare him directly in the face. Alex found this very disconcerting and tried to ignore the bird, but it was difficult when you were the sole object of someone's attentions. The owl continued to peer at him with unwavering intensity.

'Look somewhere else,' he muttered at the owl. 'Go on, shoo!'

The three of them were sitting together on the edge of
the water tank, looking out over the wavelets that had
gathered purple light to themselves. Technically the bird
was standing, but it seemed as if he were squatting, since he
was all hunched, with feathers fluffed.

'A hermit,' Alex stated, continuing their conversation. 'Is
that what you want to be?'

She wrinkled her nose. 'I don't like that word. It sounds
old and stuffy. I'm not old and stuffy.'

'No, you're not,' he said bravely, 'you're the most exciting and interesting person I've ever met.'

The owl nodded, as if satisfied, then climbed back on to
his perch on Amanda's head.

Amanda glanced at Alex quickly. 'Oh, dear – Alex.'

'No, no – I'm not saying I want you for a *girlfriend*,' he
added. 'I just think you're – you're really cool.'

This was not the first time he had used phrases or words
which meant very little to her.

'I hope I am your friend, even though a girl.'

'Well, yes, I didn't mean that . . .'

'And I don't mean to be cool towards you, but you must
understand a young woman like myself has to maintain
some distance, some decorum. The Organist didn't understand that.'

'What I meant was,' he said desperately, 'is that I like you
and I think you're great company.'

She gave him an elfish grin. 'Thank you, that's a very
nice compliment.'

A fresh draught suddenly caught Alex unawares. It ran
its invisible fingers over his face. On its back it carried
many scents and fragrances, as well as a few less pleasant
odours, but one in particular made him sit up and take
heed. There. There was a faint whiff of curry. Was it
curry? Yes, surely it was. All of a sudden he missed his

mother's cooking. Dipa could whip up a curry that would have you drooling before a single mouthful was taken. If he stayed in the attic he would never taste his mother's curries again, would he? And with the thought of that loss a thousand others came crowding in, things he missed about home and family, things that would be out of his reach for eternity if he remained a bortrekker. He loved his mother and sister, was growing fond of Ben and Jordy, and he needed Marmite on toast for breakfast like people needed to breathe air.

'Will you ever go home, do you think?' he asked Amanda, as the owl turned a complete circle on her head. 'You might want to one day.'

'No,' she replied. 'I cannot. I have been here too long.'

'Does it hold you then?'

'In a strong grip – of which I approve,' she added hastily. 'This was my choice, to stay up here. You are not yet in its thrall, but the longer you stay, the less likely it is you will be able to go back. You must make your choice soon, you know. To remain, or to return. Ah, I see a new light in your eyes, Alexander the Great, you have made up your mind.'

'Yep.' He stared out over the waters of the tank. 'I can't do it. I thought I could, but I can't. I need to go home. I know you say time has stopped for me and them, but I've got this image in my head, of my mother crying, putting notices in the newspapers, searching for me. I can't get hold of the idea that nothing is moving down there. It's got to, somehow or other, and when it does I won't be there. I can accept that time has stopped for me, but I can't get the idea that it's stopped for them. It just doesn't work in my head, no matter how many times you tell me it's true.'

'It is a difficult concept to grasp,' she admitted. 'It doesn't hold with the science we've learned in the schoolroom, does it? Well, if you have to go, Alexander, you should do so very soon. I know of a way to get you back quickly and easily, without a great deal of danger.'

# CHAPTER 21

# Saviour of the Wooden World

'I can't do hang-gliding,' Alex said, 'if that's what you're thinking.'

Judging from her expression that wasn't what Amanda was thinking.

'I don't know what you're talking about,' she replied. 'What I mean is, I can sail you across the Great Water Tank much swifter than you can travel on your raft. Then I can lead you through the attic on the safest and quickest paths, avoiding horrible mountains and the scissor-birds.'

'You would do that for me?' Alex said, surprised. 'Don't you have to stay here and guard your watches?'

On the mention of the word 'watches' the owl swivelled its head, first 360 degrees one way, then the same the other way. Two complete circles. It seemed disappointed there were no watches on view. It gave Alex a hard stare, as if it believed the boy had been trying to trick it.

'Oh, I have to go sometimes. There are more watches out there to collect. It would be a poor collection, Alex, if I didn't seek to enlarge it, to make it the best collection the attic has ever seen. I usually go after I've beaten back an attack by the Music Makers. That brattish Organist takes time to reorganise and regroup, before attempting another assault.'

'What if he stole some of your watches and hid them?'

'He's tried that. I always find them again. They tick, you see.'

Alex said, 'Why doesn't he just smash them?'

She blinked several times then stared hard at him as if he had just told her he approved of murder.

'That would be such a terrible wanton act of destruction,' she said, 'which no sane person would even contemplate. In any case, a thousand watches? How would he carry them all away? How could he manage to smash them before I got to him and scratched his eyes out?'

'How long has it been going on like this?'

'Oh, years and years.'

'Well maybe this Organist has become so obsessed with the idea of getting rid of you he's not sane any more.'

She said, 'I can't even *think* like that.'

They were quiet for a while, during which Alex thought he heard something, in the far distance, that he recognised.

But she soon interrupted his thoughts.

'Now, Alexander the Great, we have to plan our passage. I'm a very good pathfinder you know, Alex. It's not just the bortrekkers who can find their way across the world. The board-combers are good at it too. Perhaps not quite so good as bortrekkers, but nearly. How soon can you be ready? Shall we set out tomorrow morning?'

'You want to get rid of me that quickly?'

The owl nodded thoughtfully.

'Alex,' said Amanda, looking him in the eyes (it was very difficult to take her seriously with an owl on her head), 'I've told you, if you don't go down quickly, you'll never get down at all. Every day counts. The attic is working on your soul every moment you're here.'

'But I haven't found Mr Grantham's watch yet.'

'It's not over this side of the tank, Alex,' she told him. 'I've covered every inch of this territory, believe me. We'll have to search for it on your way home – and if we don't find it, why, then it's truly lost, for the other side of the Great Water Tank is a vast landscape. No one has ever explored all of it to the eaves. It seems to go on for ever. I'm sorry.'

He sighed. 'That's all right.'

There it was again, that familiar sound. Faint music. A tune from a folk song. Was it in his head? Or was it really out there somewhere? Perhaps he too was becoming obsessed. Obsessed with the idea of finding Mr Grantham's watch. Now it had stopped. Very spooky.

The owl screeched loudly, shattering his reverie.

Amanda dashed forward and leapt on someone sneaking around out in the darkness. She struggled for a moment, then returned into the evening gleam of the skylight. She had a village boy by the ear, one of those mercenaries who had ridden the bagpipe-spiders in the attack. His face was screwed up into a tight wad of indignation.

'A spy,' said Amanda, satisfied with her own detection. 'I thought I heard something out there.'

The boy was about half her size. He had stopped kicking and struggling and now stared at the ground. Amanda began to speak to him. To Alex's ears she sounded like a creaking gate, but he had heard the language before and knew it to be Attican. The boy answered her, defiantly it seemed, glaring at her. He kept pointing back into the darkness, in the direction where the Music Makers had come from. He seemed adamant about something. Finally Amanda let go of his ear. The Attican youth remained for a few more moments, still creaking away, then he ran off.

'Well?' asked Alex. 'What was all that about?'

'Fireworks.'

Alex raised an eyebrow. 'Fireworks? You mean bonfire night fireworks?'

'That brat,' she waved a hand at the departing child, 'said the Organist had made a firework. A very big one. I don't believe him.'

'Why not?'

'Why make a firework? They had a box up here that went off once. The Removal Firm dealt with it, but it was terrible. It started a great fire which spread over a large area of the attic. They managed to put it out but if it hadn't been close to a water tank the whole attic might have been destroyed. You can go to the place now and walk for three days over charred wood with charcoal beams overhead. Now the Removal Firm seek out any boxes of fireworks that are put up here and throw them in a water tank.'

'But one firework – I doubt that would do much harm.'

Amanda shrugged. 'Then what would be the point?'

Alex thought about it for a bit, then said, 'I suppose – I guess it would depend on *how* big it was.'

'The spy said the Organist had put torch batteries on it.'

'That doesn't sound right,' admitted Alex. Then he asked, 'Why did the boy tell you – about the firework?'

'He said he was scared – he said they all are – they don't like sudden loud noises, the village children. He said the Organist is bragging that it'll make the loudest bang the attic has ever heard. That one said the other children had sent him as their messenger, behind the Organist's back.' She sighed. 'I don't believe it. I think it's another one of his tricks.'

'Does he think you'll run, threatened by a firework?'

She shrugged again. 'He'll try anything. We'd better get some sleep now. We've got a long journey in the morning.'

Alex found himself a comfortable spot and curled up, trying to go to sleep. But something was bothering him. He kept thinking about the big firework and the batteries. In the middle of the night he woke up with a start. Something awful had come into his head. Something really bad. He went over to where Amanda lay and shook her.

'Amanda! Did he say anything about a timepiece?'

'Wha— who, what? What timepiece?'

'Did the boy mention a timepiece of any kind?'

She sat up and rubbed her eyes.

The owl, guarding the camp, looked down with contempt on Alex from a rafter above his head.

Sleepily, Amanda said, 'Oh – the firework. Yes, that was the stupidest part. The boy said the Organist had fixed a pocket-watch to the firework.' She thought for a bit. 'I suppose the Organist *might* have stolen one of my collection. Do you think he's going to launch one of my watches into the high rafters on a skyrocket?'

'No.' Alex stared at her. 'I think he's made a *time bomb*.'

'A bomb?' Amanda shook her head in disbelief. 'He wouldn't do that.'

'Why not? He's crazy, isn't he?'

'A bit – well, quite a bit, actually.' Amanda stared at Alex with wide eyes from behind her mask. 'Do you really think he'd make a time bomb? Only anarchists do that, don't they?'

'We call them terrorists.'

Just at that moment Alex felt himself being gripped by strong hands. He tried to break away, but they held him fast. Looking round, he saw he was being held by two large Atticans wearing dustcoats. He recognised them as the same ones Nelson had chased off on the other side of the Great Water Tank. The others were standing close by. Six in all. One of the others tipped out the contents of

Alex's backpack. Among the things that fell out was the small camping stove, along with boxes of matches.

'You let me alone,' Alex cried. 'Who do you think you are?'

'The Removal Firm, that's who they are,' replied Amanda in a low voice. 'Are those your matches, Alex?'

'I only use them to light the stove. I need to cook my food.'

'Oh, Alex,' she said in a voice of despair. 'You're in very grave trouble.'

'But what about the bomb?'

Amanda said something to the Removal Firm. One of them, a male with very dark eyes, answered her. Then he looked at Alex very sternly, and said something to the two who held him. Alex's arms were released. He rubbed the circulation back into them. They had gripped him *very* hard. Amanda continued to speak with the leader of the Removal Firm and there followed a lot of pointing and gesturing in the direction of the region where the Organist had his Music Makers.

'It seems,' said Amanda, turning to Alex at last, 'the Organist has fled. The Removal Firm came here looking for you because they sensed that the attic was in great danger. They believe a disaster is about to occur and of course they blamed you, the newest incomer. But when they got here the Organist saw them. He panicked and ran. Oh, Alex, I'm sorry.' She regarded him through the eyeholes of her mask. 'If I doubted you before, I'm inclined to believe you now. The Organist would never run away and abandon this place if he wasn't guilty of something very bad.'

'Who said he's gone?'

'They did.' Amanda nodded towards the Removal Firm, who stood like a solid wall before Alex. 'They came past his camp. When he saw them approaching he ran like a scared rafter rat. He won't get very far. They'll catch up with him, sooner rather than later. But they're very concerned about the possibility of this bomb. Are you *sure*, Alex? Are you certain?'

'Of course I'm not,' Alex answered. 'It was just a theory. But torch batteries and a watch? It's got to be more than some *firework* banger. We've got to find it, Amanda, before it goes off. You know him best. Where would he be likely to plant it?'

The bits of Amanda's face that weren't covered by the mask went very, very pale.

'I don't know,' she whispered. 'In one of the pianos? Perhaps he's trying to blow up my defences?'

'Well, we'd best start searching. Who knows how powerful he's made that bomb? I bet he doesn't even know himself. If he's good at music, he's probably lousy at science. Tell these twerps they'd be better off helping us than beating me up, if that's what they're going to do.'

Amanda spoke rapidly in that creaking voice. To give them their due the Removal Firm went into action with alacrity. All six ran with Alex and Amanda to the line of pianos and began lifting lids and looking inside. Once they had exhausted the pianos they tried other places, peering in dark corners, looking in odd shoe boxes, tipping out crates, lifting the lids of trunks. There were so many places the Organist could have hidden his bomb.

Bundles of clothes were turned over, the underside of card tables were inspected, rattan chairs were frisked. The Removal Firm went to the village and questioned those who had assisted the Organist in his battles, but the villagers insisted they knew nothing more about the firework than had already been divulged to Amanda by the boy.

Amanda thought about her boat and ran to the quay to go over it, but the bomb was not on board.

'Where? Where? Where?' she cried. 'We must find it.'

Once, while they were all searching, something returned to irritate Alex: that little melody that had been haunting him. He couldn't pin it down though. It was like the faint sound of some insect in the air. It hummed on the edge of his reasoning, but he could never quite decide whether he could actually hear it or not. Then he forgot about it, deciding that seeking the bomb was the most important thing. Other less worrying things could wait for a more tranquil time, when he could think more clearly.

The others were sitting in a circle not a great distance away from Amanda's collection of watches. Alex looked round at them. There were six bald-headed wrestlers in khaki dustcoats and, in stark contrast, a girl festooned with coloured ribbons and feathers. They all looked very tired. Was he leading them on a wild-goose chase? They didn't seem to think so, or they would have scorned his theory and dragged him away to his fate.

The Removal Firm, he had to admit, worked like Trojans. They battled tirelessly with piles of junk and heaps of rubbish, sorting through them with never a creak. Finally they seemed to have exhausted every possibility and even Alex was beginning to think the whole thing was a hoax. Perhaps the Organist had made a fake bomb and had then taken it apart and scattered the pieces over a large area? But then why would he run? That bit didn't make sense. He had fought Amanda for years over this territory. Why would he abandon it just because the Removal Firm were close by?

Yet where was the bomb? They had looked everywhere.

At that moment Amanda's watches began to chime the hour.

It was noon.

Among the tunes that started up came the one that had been haunting him.

He put words to it in his head:

*Frère Jacques, Frère Jacques . . .*

There it was! That was it. The bothersome sound.

*. . . dormez vous? dormez vous? . . .*

'Out of the way!' cried Alex, jumping up and leaping over the heads of the Removal Firm.

He ran to the pillar of watches.

*. . . sonnez les matines, sonnez les matines . . .*

All the chiming watches were in full sound now, spilling out their own tinkling variations.

*. . . ding, dang, dong . . .*

Alex scraped away at the base of the pillar, scattering Amanda's precious collection over the boards.

*. . . ding . . .*

There was the bomb! There Mr Grantham's watch! There the batteries!

*. . . dang . . .*

Alex ripped out the wires, tore away the watch.

*. . . dong.*

Alex fell back, sweating, the watch in his palm. He felt drained. He held up the pocket-watch and looked at its hands. The hour hand had been bent inwards so that when it reached it, it would touch the metal figure 12. Hair-thin wires were connected to both. Vertical noon. It had almost made it. Almost. If it had touched that would have completed the circuit and detonated the bomb. How close it had been! After a while he was aware of a ring of faces above him, looking down on him. Amanda was smiling. He could see the curve of her mouth below her mask. He could see the twinkle in her eyes. There was hero worship in those eyes.

'Alex, you did it. You found the bomb. You are *so* clever.'
She gently took the pocket-watch from his hand.

He explained. 'I heard the tune. I've been hearing it all day, somewhere in the distance. But it didn't connect until now. Frère Jacques. You said you hadn't got a watch that chimed *Frère Jacques.*'

'And I don't. I didn't. The Organist must have found it himself, while he was out looking for musical instruments.'

Alex sat up. 'It nearly did for us, that French monk's song. If the bomb had gone off – well, I think it would have brought the pillar down.' Alex slapped the wooden support. 'And if that one had come down, they would all have started snapping.' He looked up. 'The roof of the world would fallen on our heads.'

Once this had sunk in, Amanda interpreted it for the Removal Firm, who all nodded their heads sagely and patted the pillar.

Amanda turned back to Alex and said, 'They agree with you – they say you saved the whole attic from destruction.' Her eyes showed how proud she was to be associated with him. 'Oh, Alex.'

He shrugged modestly. 'Anyone would have.'

'No, they wouldn't. They wouldn't have the brains. An *engineer's* brains. However . . .' She looked downcast.

Alex said, 'What is it?'

'They – they say you can't stay. You have to go. Go back to where you came from. You're a risk, you see. You play with fire.' She looked into his eyes again. 'But they won't arrest you. You're free to go. In your own time.'

'That's nice,' he remarked sarcastically, then said, 'Oh well, you can't fight the Removal Firm. Will they let you take me?'

'Yes – they trust me.'

'That's all right then.'

Alex turned away. He felt a little flat now. The saviour of the world ought, he felt, to be given a parade or something. But they wanted him to go: said he *had* to go. He'd broken the rules, the law of the attic. All right, he'd take his punishment. He knew he had done one of the best things in his life. Something he would never forget. They couldn't take that away from him. Nobody could. It was his moment and they all knew it too.

'Goodbye,' he said, turning and shaking their hands, one by one. 'May all your removals be as easy as this one.'

They looked surprised. They probably weren't used to shaking hands, he thought. Maybe they didn't do such things? But they looked pleased. These were the guardians of the attic, the preservers of wood and life up here among the beams and timbers. And he, Alex, had shaken their hands. Not many humans would have done that.

They left then, probably in pursuit of the Organist. Would he get the same punishment: banishment from the attic? Or did they indeed imprison criminals in sea chests or changing room lockers? He couldn't think they did. But then again, this was not Alex's world. This was the attic.

Amanda left him to go down to the jetty to prepare the boat for sailing. He noticed she had not given him back Mr Grantham's watch. Was she going to keep it after all? He trailed down to the quay after her.

'Hello,' he called, walking down to the jetty where the little boat bobbed on the waves. 'Are we ready?'

The owl looked at him and nodded slowly.

'I don't like your owl much,' he told Amanda, as he put his backpack into the boat. 'Or rather, he doesn't like me.'

'Oh, he's just jealous. Usually he gets all my attention.'

'Well, he'll have you all to himself soon.'

Once they were all in the boat, the owl left Amanda's head and perched on the prow. Then they were off,

scudding across the waves at a speed which thrilled Alex.
Spray hit his face and ran down his cheeks in rivulets.
They cut through pillars of golden sunlight, and tacked
through avenues of deep shadow. Once or twice Amanda
barked an order and Alex had to jump to some task with
alacrity or earn her displeasure. Still, even though she
treated him with less respect than gentry do their scullery
maids, he found the whole experience exhilarating. He
loved it. It filled him with a white wind that carried his
spirit to the very heights of the attic.

'Free!' he cried, as the little boat shot over the surface of
the water, its spinnaker billowing proudly. 'Free as a bird!'

The owl's head swivelled and the big eyes glared.

'Well, *some* birds,' amended Alex weakly. 'The ones that
actually are free.'

They made excellent progress. Amanda taught him even
more about the skylight suns and stars, filling in his knowledge where there were gaps. She was much more adept at
following the motion of the swell than he was and her
touch was sensitive enough to feel it in the tiller when it
was hardly even there. Certainly when Alex tried it, he
could feel nothing at all. The shape of the dust clouds, the
colour of the waves, the angles of the rafters high up in the
roof, these were her guides. Her navigating skills were, as
she had said, almost as good as those of the bortrekker. She
also had the mystical uncanny knack of missing flotsam and
jetsam which might damage her boat.

Sometimes, privately, Alex took her for a witch.

They made the far side in good time, even when a fog
delayed them in a busy part of the tank known as the
Rust-riven Roads, where she said many an Attican had
fallen from the mast or rigging to end his days. The owl
helped them in the fog, by hooting to warn other vessels
of their intentions. When Amanda was not listening, Alex

whispered to the owl, 'At least you're good for something.'

The owl farted.

Once they made the far side, the trekking began. Days of it. It was sometimes tedious, sometimes exciting. They circled villages full of lumpy, plaster-covered Atticans with their sewing-machine cars. They avoided dangerous places, like mountains made of weapons. They crossed deserts of boards with dunes of old clothes and forded shallow tanks on the edges of dark plains of planks. Forests there were, of many different trees, and valleys of dust, and lanes of boxes. Sometimes there was kindness and food from local people. At other times Amanda avoided contact, knowing the region was hostile to people, both native and not. It was long and arduous yet – yet deep down in some way Alex did not want it to end.

The owl was a constant companion, sometimes on Amanda's head, but now sometimes on one shoulder or the other. Alex was surprised to learn she had conversations with it, always just out of his hearing. Did it reply? It seemed to. He was never quite sure. It reminded him that Amanda was not quite human any more, no longer a real person. She was something else, something part fey, part human, part attic-creature. Even if he were to stay a hundred years with her, he would never really get to know her.

As she had promised, Amanda knew her paths. She took the pair of them through seemingly untrodden ways where the dust had previously gathered, unsullied by boot or claw. They left their mark on the trail. Amanda said that their footprints would remain a thousand years, gathering more dust in the hollows of the heels and in the shallows of the soles.

'Just like the footprints of astronauts on the moon,' he told her, but she was shocked when he explained. 'Have you never heard of Neil Armstrong and Buzz Aldrin? They were the first men on the surface of the moon.'

'Men have desecrated the surface of the moon? Titania and Oberon will *hate* that,' she told him, as if Shakespeare's fairies were real people. 'How could they soil the silver moondust with the mundane feet of men?'

He thought that sounded very poetic and kept the sentence in mind to pass on to his sister, when he next saw her.

One morning there was a hoar frost. A chill draught had blown down from the upper reaches of the attic and turned any moisture to crystals that glittered in the early sunlight from the windows. Young Jack Frost was about, dancing with twinkling toes on box, board and bagatelle. Alex woke thrusting the crackling blanket from him to rub his legs with his hands. It had been a cold night and he had shivered for the last hour. The owl seemed to smile at him, saying, Now the feathers come into their own.

'You'd better watch it,' muttered Alex. 'I've had pigeon pie since I came up here, and I wouldn't say no to owl pudding.'

'What did you say?' asked Amanda, rising and yawning, stretching her arms up in a big Y. 'Did you speak to me?'

'No, I was simply saying good morning to your owl.'

Just then Alex noticed something lying twenty metres away.

'I know that pile of rags,' he said, getting up. 'He's got himself a fox fur for a topknot.'

He walked to a heap of clothes and poked it with his toe.

'Morning, board-comber,' he said. 'Like the hat.'

The Inuit carvings collector stirred himself. He had wrapped a fox fur round his head in the night. He looked up at Alex. The nose of the fox ran down the nose on the mask of the board-comber. Its dark eyes glittered. To Alex it was like addressing a boy with two heads. The board-comber looked about a hundred kilos heavier than he had before, but it was only more padding, several more layers of old clothes.

The black bat dangling from his ear twittered, and the board-comber said, 'I'm just about to ask him.' He turned to Alex. 'Did you find me any you-know-whats on the other side of the lake?'

'No, I'm sorry. I did look.'

The bat twittered and the board-comber sighed.

'Oh, well – never mind – so long as you looked.'

'I did. And now I'm going home. Hey, you should meet another board-comber, my friend over here. She collects pocket-watches.'

But a funny thing happened. The two board-combers refused to look at one another. They didn't speak. They completely ignored each other. There was a kind of shyness there, or rivalry, Alex couldn't decide which. Perhaps a little of both? But it was obviously a professional board-combers' thing. Board-combers didn't acknowledge one another, and that was that. Some code of culture which was unbreakable, even for a mutual friend. The old board-comber wished Alex the best of luck and said goodbye, and the new board-comber yelled that she was ready to leave. Alex told the old one if he ever got his hands on some carvings down below, he'd chuck them up into the attic and know they would end up in good loving hands.

'Come on!' called Amanda in a testy tone, not looking at either of them. 'Time we were on our way.'

'I'm coming.'

Before he ran back to her, the board-comber he was with leaned closer and pressed three small packages into his hand.

'For your sister,' he whispered. 'A gift. For your brother. And for you. For helping me find a new treasure.'

'I know what mine is,' said Alex, grinning, weighing the largest of the parcels in his hand. 'Thanks. Thanks a lot.'

Alex shook a hand that had the texture of crumpled paper.

He put the gifts in his backpack.

When he got back to Amanda, he said, 'An old friend.'

'Huh, can't be that old, you've only been up here five minutes.'

'Well, he helped me, just as you're helping me.'

'Who cares?' she said.

Alex wanted the two board-combers to become friends, but they clearly would have none of it. He thought it a little sad that there were so few nearly-humans in the attic and those there were could not be sociable with one another. Yet, when he thought further he realised that was precisely why they were up here. They wanted as little social contact as possible. Then a chill ran through him, as he realised his own dark side. *He* had contemplated remaining in the attic. *He* was one of them, one of those who wanted to break away from people and become a loner. What had done that to him? Why had he become so disenchanted with other people?

'My dad,' he said to himself grimly, 'that's what did it.'

'What?' asked Amanda. 'What did you say?'

'My dad died. He didn't stand a chance.' Alex's eyes brimmed with tears as he thought of his father, deep-set eyes ringed with dark circles from working late in the evenings, very gentle, very caring. 'It just happened, like that,' Alex snapped his fingers. 'One minute he was standing in a supermarket, the next he was lying on the pavement outside. No one knew what to do. Ben would've,' he said savagely. 'Mum would've. But that crowd, they were useless.'

'Your father died?'

'Of a heart attack, lying on the ground. Absolutely use-less. Oh, they called an ambulance of course, but that came too late to save him. I *hate* that crowd. Someone should've done something. They just stood there. The bloody bug-gers just stood there and did nothing.'

Amanda stopped and looked at him. 'Would you have known what to do?'

'Me? I'm just a kid.'

'Alex, most people know very little about what to do in emergencies like that – they haven't had the training. I wouldn't know what to do and I'm a hundred years old.'

Alex was reluctant to let go of his anger. 'Yes, but you lived in a different time, when people didn't know very much.'

'I know as much as you,' she retorted hotly. 'What's the capital of Ceylon?' she challenged.

'Never heard of it. There's no such place.'

'Yes there is and it's Colombo, Mr Thinks-he-knows-it-all!'

'Ha! Colombo is the capital of Sri Lanka, not this place Ceylon.'

'Sirry Lanker? Never heard of it. You made that up.'

They both glared at one another as they walked along, still moving towards Alex's eventual destination.

Finally, after a while, Amanda softened. 'I'm just saying,' she said, getting rid of her defiant pose, 'that you can't expect ordinary people in a crowd to know what to do with a heart attack.'

Miserably, he had to acknowledge this. He himself lived in a household where medical things were talked about all the time. He guessed others lived in houses where banking or bricklaying was the subject around the dinner table. It was hard though, to lose a dad to something so quick and vicious. Alex found it difficult to live in a world which could snatch a loved one away from a family so quickly and easily. What if his mum were next? Or Chloe? Or Ben and Jordy? It wasn't fair. Someone should do something about it, because it made you want to leave such a world for good, and stay in Attica where you'd never have to face such losses. If you didn't have anybody around, you couldn't lose anyone, could you?

He hung his head. 'I'm sorry, Amanda.'

The owl clucked and ruffled its feathers.

'That's all right,' she replied. 'You should think about your father sometimes. Try to think of the good times, though. He would want you to do that, wouldn't he? His death probably lasted only a few minutes, but he was alive and well for many years, wasn't he?'

'I guess.'

'Then why concentrate on those few minutes, horrible as they probably were, when there's a whole life to look at?'

'I dunno. It's just that every time I think of him, I get this image of him lying on the pavement, his eyes all wide and frightened. I just can't get it out of my head. So I don't think of him very often.'

'I can understand that, but you've got a strong spirit, Alex, you can force yourself to remember him as he was. Did he laugh?'

'Oh yes, quite a lot. But he could get angry too, when my school reports weren't good. He was dead keen on education. I used to get annoyed with him for that. But he was good with jokes too.'

'Did he take you fishing?'

'No – he wasn't that kind of dad. He worked too hard to see us that often. But when he had some time we'd go to the Science Museum in London – somewhere like that. He loved engines, just like me. And books, he liked books too, like Chloe. He used to share things with us.'

Amanda's eyes twinkled. 'Maybe he didn't like either, engines or books? Maybe he was interested because you two were interested? He sounds like a good dad to me. You had a lot of him. I didn't have a father, not one who I knew, so you're lucky you got what you did.'

Alex stared at Amanda, realising why she was a board-comber.

'Yeah, I guess.' He tried to imagine what it would have been like to have no father at all, not even a step-dad like Ben. 'You had a bad time, eh?'

'It wouldn't have been so bad,' she replied, 'if they hadn't beaten me so often . . .'

She shook in anger, stirring her colourful ribbons and rags: little flags of rage fluttering at the past.

Bullies, he thought. Even worse than people who did nothing for a man having a heart attack. There were bullies at his school who could make your life a complete misery. These days there were lots of kids who had no dads at home and no one thought much about it. But the bullying still went on, just the same. If they didn't call you one name, they'd think of another: the colour of your skin, the fact that you had freckles and ginger hair, the fact that you wore glasses – anything, really. And if taunting didn't stir you, they often resorted to threats and violence. Bullies were another reason why you wanted to escape from the world, if you didn't deal with them.

'Well,' said Amanda, bringing him out of his reverie, 'we're here.'

He looked up. 'Where?' he asked, surprised.

'That patch of darkness is where you go.'

Alex blinked hard. 'In there? My house?'

'That's where you came from.'

'Oh.'

The time had come to say goodbye.

Alex unslung the African mask from his shoulder.

'Well, Makishi, I can't take you with me – you'd just become a wall-hanging down there.'

'I do not want to part from you, Alex, but I do not want to adorn a wall.'

Alex handed Makishi to Amanda. 'You'll look after him, won't you?'

She nodded. 'I'll wear him sometimes.'

'Well, he's a boy's mask really, but I'm sure he'll like it better here than down in my world.'

'And we must say goodbye too, Alex.'

Alex said weakly, 'Oh well, here goes – see you, then.'

'No,' she replied seriously, 'we won't see each other again, I'm afraid, but I did like meeting you, Alex. I haven't spoken to a human in – oh, I don't know how long – but I enjoyed our time together. Now you must go back to what you know, and me to what I know.'

'You make sure that old Organist doesn't come back,' he said fiercely. 'You keep those Music Makers on their toes.'

'I will,' she laughed. She touched his cheek with her fingertips. 'Goodbye, Alex.'

And she was gone, a pretty creature of many-coloured rags running across the boards, heading for a forest of standard lamps.

Safe inside the forest, she turns and looks at him standing there, until finally he enters the dark patch behind him.

'What was all that about?' asks the owl.

*Oh, you know. What if you were to meet another owl?*

'I'd scratch her eyes out.'

*No you wouldn't. It's just that he had that* smell, *you know, of down there. That faint odour of* real world *about him. I miss my mother, and my grandmother.*

'You can go down, if you want.'

*And leave you? And my lovely watches? No. But he was a nice young man, wasn't he? Very exotic. I think he had ancestors from the Orient.*

She sighs and thinks about a favourite watch which is covered in stars and moons and comes from that part of the world.

'Well, I didn't like him,' says the owl emphatically. 'I thought he was drippy. Didn't seem to know what he wanted.'

*That's just part of being young. You've been old for so long you can't remember what it's like to be young.*

'I'm just glad he's gone.'

*Didn't you like him at all?*

The owl ponders and a little truth comes out.

'Well, he was quite humorous sometimes. He made you laugh.'

*And you?*

'Just a little.'

'Owls don't laugh.'

# CHAPTER 22

# The End of the Beginning

Once Alex was in the darkness of his own attic, he could see the square of light which was his doorway to the real world. He made his way towards it and paused on the brink, looking down on to the landing of their new house. Hearing low voices he knelt to peer inside and something banged against his thigh: something in his jacket pocket. He reached in with his left hand and pulled out a shiny object that made him gasp in delight.

It was Mr Grantham's pocket-watch.

'Amanda,' he murmured. 'Amanda put it in my pocket.'

He descended the loft ladder to the landing, just in time to hear the end of a sentence from Jordy at the other end of the landing, where he and Chloe were standing with Ben and Dipa.

Jordy was saying, '. . . be very long.'

'Here I am,' said Alex, smiling weakly, realising he had come down from Attica just seconds after his step-brother and sister. 'I was right behind them.'

Alex could not fail to see how the faces of his brother and sister lit up with pleasure and relief on seeing him. It was worth it, to come back to the real world, just to see how much they thought of him. If he ever doubted he was loved, he doubted it no longer. These were his family. They had missed him, even for that short time. Chloe especially. He wanted to go up to her and hug her, but of course he couldn't, not in front of his parents. They had no idea what the three of them had been through. Maybe next week he would want to strangle his sister, but today he thought the world of her.

'What *have* they been doing up there?' asked Dipa, folding her arms and looking at Ben. 'Look at them! Where did you get those smelly old clothes, Alex? And you two,' she turned on Chloe and Jordy, 'you look like rag-bags on legs.'

'We found them in the attic,' Chloe said.

Ben said with a questioning look, 'Aren't you all just a *teeny* bit old for playing dressing-up?'

'It was only for a laugh,' said Jordy. 'We were just amusing ourselves.'

'And the backpacks?' enquired Dipa.

'Oh, these,' Alex said, 'we found them too – and look – I've got Mr Grantham's watch.'

He held it up triumphantly, with both Chloe and Jordy crying things like, 'Well done, bruv.' 'What a star!'

'Mr Grantham's watch?' asked Ben, looking at Dipa. 'What's that all about?'

Dipa's folded arms tightened round her chest. 'Don't look at me. I've got no idea.'

'Mr Grantham lost a watch in the attic when he was a young man,' explained Chloe. 'We said we'd look for it for him. And Alex managed to find it.'

'And a letter,' said Alex, 'from his old girlfriend.'

He pulled the envelope out of his pocket and showed it to them.

'I hope you haven't read it,' Dipa said. 'That wouldn't be right.'

'What?' cried Jordy, who was better at fibs than the other two. 'Up there in the dark?'

'Well, I'm glad you Boy Scouts have been doing good deeds,' Ben said impatiently, 'and I'm very impressed by it all. I'm sure Mr Grantham will be grateful. But now I think you'd all better go to your rooms and get out of those rags. You, young man,' he addressed Alex, 'smell like a sewer. In fact, you all pong. You're a filthy bunch of herberts and I want you showered and changed within the hour. Your mother's going to cook us a curry for supper.'

Nelson suddenly appeared as if by magic from round one of the bedroom doorways. He limped into view and let out a pathetic yowl. Curry. Nelson loved left-overs, and of all the left-overs he liked best, curry was at the top of the list, followed by sardines and beef sausages. Nelson knew only a few words in English and 'curry' was one of them.

'Yes, we know,' said Alex, bending to stroke his erstwhile ginger saviour, 'grub is very important, isn't it?'

Nelson purred.

The children went to their rooms, but as soon as Dipa and Ben descended the stairs, they all met up again in Jordy's room.

'So,' whispered Chloe to Alex, 'you found it?'

'Wasn't easy,' murmured Alex, showing them the silver watch again. He wound it round to the hour so that it played *Frère Jacques* a little before snapping it shut again. 'I had to cross that water tank and . . .' He gave them a brief overview of his adventures since he left them on the edge of the tank. 'Anyway, Amanda gave me the watch in the end – put it in my pocket, so's I couldn't even thank her for it.'

'She probably wanted it that way,' said Chloe.

'Amanda, eh?' chirruped Jordy, nudging his brother and smirking. 'I see – the quiet ones are the worst.'

'No, it wasn't like that. She's older than me, anyway.'

'Only by a hundred years, you said. Hardly significant in a relationship as strong as yours.'

'Oh, shut up, Jordy,' Chloe said.

But Jordy's eyes had suddenly gone misty and distant as he remembered the Tarzan-girl he had seen in the rafters.

Alex then recalled something. 'Hey, I ran into that other board-comber, you know, the one with the bat hanging from his ear? He gave me a present – I think it's another model steam engine.' Alex took off his backpack and reached inside. 'And there's a gift for each of you two. This is for Chloe. And this for you, Jordy, though he said you didn't deserve anything, being as you're a pain in the butt.'

'No he didn't,' replied Jordy, taking the small round parcel. 'Wonder what it is?' He unwrapped it, producing a red leather ball.

'An old cricket ball.' Jordy was disappointed at first until he turned it over in his hands and then he exclaimed in delight, 'Signed by Nasser Hussein! Wow. And that old guy, Ian Botham. And a couple of others. Wait till I show this to everyone at school.'

'Cool,' said Alex, not meaning it. 'A cricket ball. Hey, your arm looks better.'

Jordy flexed it for Alex's benefit. 'Good as new.'

Chloe peeled the brown paper away from her gift. She gasped in delight. It was a small book, a children's story, entitled *The King of the Golden River – or The Black Brothers – A Legend of Stiria*.

'Never heard of it,' muttered Jordy. 'Is it any good, Clo?'

'It's a first edition,' breathed the enchanted Chloe. 'It's a rare antique volume by John Ruskin.' She leafed through it carefully. 'Look at the illustrations. They're beautiful. "Illustrated by Richard Doyle." This is a treasure. It's probably worth thousands of pounds.'

'Let's not go overboard, girl,' said Jordy. 'A few quid, anyway.'

She clasped it to her breast. 'I shall never sell it. We've all come out of the attic with wonderful treasures, haven't we?'

A female voice came floating up the stairs.

'Are you getting washed and changed?'

'Yes,' they chorused, scrambling away in different directions. 'Coming.'

Mr Grantham looked irritable and confused when he answered the door the next day and was confronted by the three children. Clearly he had been sleeping in one of his armchairs and had been woken by the bell.

'Yes?' he said shortly. 'What is it?'

'We've been up there,' replied Chloe.

It took but a minute for his annoyed expression to clear and a new and sparkling light came into his rheumy old eyes.

'Well, what did you think?'

'It nearly did for us,' muttered Jordy darkly.

'Well, it was supposed to. You don't want to live in boxes of cotton wool, do you? You need a bit of danger in your lives at your age.' He looked them up and down. 'Besides, you're up to it. I can see it in you. Him,' he pointed at Alex, 'made it back by the skin of his teeth, didn't he? He's got the look.'

'I found your watch,' said Alex, stepping forward. 'Here.'

He put the silver watch into the open wrinkled hand of the old gentleman and let the chain coil into his palm. Mr Grantham opened the timepiece and stared with glistening pleasure at the face. He turned the hands to the hour. *Frère Jacques* came tinkling out. Then he studied the faded photograph, cut to fit the lid, and his expression turned to one of sadness.

'She hasn't changed a bit,' he said, 'in all those years. But of course, she wouldn't. This is *my* Susan, not the one who lives somewhere else now, this is the one who was fond of *me*.' He lifted his head to face the children again. 'I'm very grateful. I know you've had an adventure. Had one myself once, when I was about your age, but you've guessed that. Anything else up there, while you were rooting around?'

Alex said, 'Oh yes,' and reached into his pocket. 'Here, this letter was there. You'd better read it in private, it's very personal . . .' Then he realised he had given the game away, and added, 'We just glanced at it.'

'That's all right,' murmured Mr Grantham, taking the letter and removing the envelope. 'You can keep this, young man. I expect you collect stamps, don't you?'

Alex didn't argue.

'Thank you, Mr Grantham.'

'You're very welcome.' He looked at the watch again, his pleasure evident in his smile, then he said to Chloe, 'And you've been very kind to an old man. You too' – this was directed at Jordy – 'I'm sure you had a part to play. I'm sure you all worked very hard up there. It's not an easy place to get around. That place changes you, doesn't it? I like to think for the better. I'm sure you'll all thank me for what I've done for you, one day.'

'You could have warned us,' Jordy said a little huffily.

'Oh no,' replied Mr Grantham, 'that would have spoiled it for you, now wouldn't it? Where's the challenge, else?'

Jordy left it at that, though he did not entirely agree with Mr Grantham's reasons. The young people left the old man and returned to their parents feeling rather good about themselves. That evening Ben took them all to a restaurant to celebrate a little rise in his salary.

When Chloe went to the salad bar, she almost bumped into a family of five filling their bowls. She recognised four of them. The cheeky boy was there scowling at the beet-root and grimacing at the spring onions, with George the father standing behind him, and Chantelle the spirited little girl who WOULD BE HEARD – and of course Jane.

The scruffy small boy, jaw jutting out in defiance, was talking with his mouth full of food as he began to eat directly from the salad bar, dipping his fingers into the beetroot and onions. 'I never took no old walrus. What would I want a rotten old walrus for? It must've got lost somewhere or someone else took it. Maybe it exploded? Maybe it swum off somewhere, down the plughole in the sink, swum back to the Eskimos where it come from?' He let out a raucous laugh which no one joined in with. His protests were not over, however, and the grumbling continued. 'Who's to know? All I know is I din't take it. Wun't want it, would I? A rotten old walrus? Huh. You always blame me for everythin'. Why not blame *her* or *her*?' He pointed to his sisters with a fork. 'Maybe,' his eyes lingered on Chantelle, 'maybe she et it. She eats everythin', she does. She'd eat Big Ben an' the Houses of Parlyment if you give 'em to her in a sandwich . . .'

Chantelle, in her father's arms, blew her brother a wet raspberry which sprayed the salad bar and Chloe instinctively covered her plate.

Chloe, remembering the carved walrus now, wondered where it had gone, at the same time as admiring the boy's inventive language. The boy was eventually silenced by his father, who said he did not want to hear another word about the damn walrus, from anyone. The walrus was gone and that was that. He would buy another carving for Jane, just as expensive, just as nice. If they could get another walrus, fine, but if not, Jane would have to make do with a seal or a sea lion or something similar.

While he was talking Chloe studied the older sister of the boy.

She was about Chloe's age but they looked nothing like each other.

'Hello, Sarah,' whispered Chloe, moving closer to the girl at the salad bar. 'How are you?'

Sarah looked up, startled.

'Do I know you?' asked Sarah. 'I don't think . . .'

'Just a little,' replied Chloe, who couldn't help smiling. 'You might say our paths crossed – once upon a time.'

Sarah continued to look puzzled, then finally she shrugged and drifted away, to join the rest of her family. Chloe was later thrilled to notice that Sarah and Jane were smiling and laughing together. Clearly they were enjoying one another's company. There was pleasure written on George's face too, as he contemplated his family.

I wonder if I helped to do that? thought Chloe. I'd like to think so.

In the meantime, Jordy was looking into the eyes of a slim young waitress taking his order. Sadly he found them wanting.

Seven months after the children had left Attica, Mr Grantham died peacefully in his bed. He left the pocket-watch in his will to Alex.

'He got the wartime stamp as well,' Jordy pointed out.

The stamp proved to be very valuable, having been franked by the British Post Office, the Swiss Post (acting as a neutral go-between while the countries were at war) and finally the Deutsche Bundespost. Susan could have sent the letter via the Red Cross but in her distressed state had put it through the normal overseas mail instead. It must have lain in some corner of a foreign sorting office for several years and was only returned to Susan in 1948, a few years after the war had ended. This last was scribbled on the back of the envelope and dated by some postal employee.

Alex got so much for the stamp in an auction the whole family benefited. They purchased the other half of the house from Mr Grantham's relatives so they had more room.

Jordy was the first to congratulate his brother on bringing good fortune to them all. 'Good on yer, kid,' he said, 'you can borrow my cricket pads anytime.' Alex thanked his brother kindly, but politely declined the offer.

Chloe simply hugged him and told him she loved him, which made Alex squirm.

Dipa and Ben were delighted with all their kids, but that they had always been.

A PREVIEW OF ANOTHER FANTASTIC ATOM BOOK ...

The
# EXTRAORDINARY
*and*
# UNUSUAL ADVENTURES
*of*
# HORATIO LYLE

*Catherine Webb*

# Murder

*1864, London*

In the west, the sun is setting.

It is orange and yellow fire, the sky sooty grey and brown smudge. The sky is full of chimneys and asthmatic birds. The fog is rising off the river, all the way from Greenwich to Chiswick, crawling up past Westminster and hiding the ravens sitting on the walls of the Tower, who blink beadily, waiting for something interesting and edible to happen in their lives. The fog is grey-green – grey from the water suspended in it, green from the things floating in the water.

In the west, the sun has set.

A man is running through dark and silent streets. He knows he's going to die, but still feels that if he's got to die, he might as well die running. In the world in which he moves, this is all a man can wish for, and tonight he has already seen his death mirrored in the death of another. The streets he runs through are silent and empty, their inhabitants either behind dark shutters hunched over their work by candlelight, or out, or asleep, or trying to sleep. He keeps running. A black bag bounces against his shoulder as he moves. He wonders how he ended up this way, and tries not to think of emerald eyes burning in his skull, the heavy weight of the body as it fell into his arms, or the blood now seeping through his fingers.

The rigging on the ships creaks as they rock slowly back and forth in the docks. The water that slaps around their long wooden hulls is brownish and just a little too thick for comfort.

And though he's running, he can't hear anyone following him. For a second he wonders if he's made it, if he's escaped, and knows that it's not that far to the Bethnal Green rookery from here, to the maze of shadows and cellars where anything and everything could disappear without a trace, knows that he could get there, knows that he won't. He half-turns to see if he's still being followed, bent almost double over the gaping knife wound across his belly, and stares straight into a pair of bright green eyes, burning emerald eyes, and a thin, slightly satisfied smile. He chokes on blood and steel and slips down into the shadows, clawing at the fine black sleeves of his attacker, of his killer, blackness that smells of dead leaves in a dying forest and burning wood and salty iron and black leaves falling on to a black floor like a black rain from a black sky and . . . and . . . and *don't look at the eyes* . . . He looks. The man holding the knife starts to grin, razor-sharp teeth, like those of a fish, bright green eyes, almost glowing, almost dancing with satisfaction and anticipation. The body slips to the ground. The bag falls off its shoulder and lands on the cobbles with a faint clank of heavy metal shifting inside.

The theatre halls of Shadwell are draining out in crowds of girls and boys cackling and clinging on to each other's arms. The fat man has reached the end of his song about the glory of Empire, Britain's majesty and amorous flirtations in barnyards.

This latter aspect is what appeals most to his yelling, swaying audience. Down at Haymarket, the fat woman is dying to the mild applause of the bourgeoisie, top hats on their laps for the men; opera glasses held daintily in white gloves, and huge dresses spread like a map of the known world for the women.

A carriage rattles down a street, then stops. A door opens. A couple of horses stamp their hooves against the old cobbles, the sound muffled by centuries of rubbish and dirt, softening into a brown, thick sludge, through which the grey stones are rarely perceived. A voice says, very quietly, 'Mr Dew?' It sounds like black leather would, if it could speak. A man with bright green eyes stirs in the shadows and carefully wipes blood off the tip of a very long, slightly curved and highly ornate hunting knife.

'Yes, my lord?'

'He is dead?'

'Yes, my lord. He has joined his brother.'

'Very well. Give me the bag.'

The clang of heavy metal moving inside the bag, as it is passed into a hand gloved in white silk and attached to a body clad in black velvet. The rattle of hands digging through metal. The faint glow of a lamp catches against gold. The rattling stops.

'It's not here?'

'My lord?'

'I said, it's not here!' And now, if the voice sounded like black leather, then that leather had just found itself driven through with nails, and wasn't pleased.

'He . . .' A little breath, steadying against fear of those burning green eyes, above a tight smile that makes sharks seem sympathetic, staring with the hardness of granite on a dark night. 'He said he had it, my lord . . .'

'And you killed him before he'd given it to us, killed them *both*?'

'I wanted to save . . . inconvenience?'

'If we cannot find it, you will pay. They will not tolerate further delay; her ladyship has already been sent here once asking questions!'

'Yes, my lord.'

'Hide the body! *Find it!*'

The thieves are hiding in the shadows under the bridges, waiting for their prey, fingers drumming on their knives. The policemen are trudging through the streets, rattles duly sounding as they whirl them around and announce the hour, long blue coats slapping against their white-clad knees. The horses are bedding down in the mews of Mayfair. The street-walkers are plying their trade in the gutters of St Giles, all false white faces and falser red smiles.

A dark carriage clatters away down a dark street, fading into the thick, choking green-grey fog that rises off the river and from the factories into an itchy soup in the air. It leaves behind nothing, except a dying gas lamp and a small red stain of blood, seeping gently through the cobbles and into the mud below.

The gas man is putting his ladder against the side of another black pillar along Green Park, and wondering whether his career prospects really do his talent justice. The girl has sold her last little bag of nuts and is going home with her few pennies of profit for the night. The master of the cress market below Shoreditch is laying out his trestle tables for the night's trade. The mechanics are wiping dirt from their faces as they walk away from the seething railway yards of King's Cross, with dirty hands rubbed on dirtier hankies.

And in the darkness of the carriage, a still man with a black leather voice carefully inspects his white gloves by the light of a bouncing lantern, observes a tiny speck of red blood on the tip of a finger, pulls the glove off a long, white, elegant hand, and sighs. He drops it on to the floor of the carriage for someone else to worry about. He sits back, and thinks very quietly to himself, *Soon, we will rise.*

As the driver pushes the carriage on into the night, he puts a hand inside his coat and feels for something to eat. He finds nothing but an immaculately intact knobbly peel from a small fruit, and a single round stone. He curses internally. He tells himself that he shouldn't have eaten the lychee, and throws both peel and stone away into the gutter. After murder, littering isn't really a priority. At least, it isn't tonight.